FICTION
O F A N
A S S

WILLIAM JOYCE

WATERMARK
P R E S S

Watermark Press, Inc.
149 N. Broadway
Wichita, Kansas 67202

Printed in the United States of America.

Library of Congress Cataloging-in-Publication Data

Joyce, William, 1945-
  First born of an ass.

  I. Title.
PS 3560.0888F5   1989   *813'.54*   *89-5412*
ISBN 0-922820-04-X

Cover Art: Kirsten Johnson
Design: Kirsten Johnson
Production: Cynthia Mines, John Hiebert

First Edition

For the class of '59
in Swissvale, Pennsylvania,
who cultivated gleeful anarchy,
eccentricity, and adventure,
and are saner because of it.

FIRST BORN
OF AN
A S S

I

Those who are against Religion, must needs be Fools; and therefore we read that, of all Animals, God refus'd the First-born of an Ass.

—Jonathon Swift

Gorm did not like sweets but he relished the idea after years of serving as a punching bag that something delicate persisted in the air. He liked to stand in front of Ma Goolantz's Confectionary and stare dreamily at the smoke which billowed from the ball-bearing plant where his father worked. The smoke was brick-red and reminded him of cotton candy freed from the stick.

Even when Ma Goolantz, herself, offered him—on the house—the dregs from the hot chocolate pot, Gorm refused, opting for black coffee till one of The Boys came along with the news that his mother, whom he hadn't seen since he was three, had just been spotted at the B&O Railroad crossing with a mattress on her back and a sign offering "CURB SERVICE" for twenty-five cents a hump. Mothers were the favorite launching pad for put-downs by the teenage boys who hung out at Ma's. Some days Ma Goolantz would chuckle at their blasphemous inventions as she stirred yesterday's pork fat and beans in a three-gallon pot. This would feed the workers who stomped toward her Formica counter shortly after the three-thirty whistle from the Union Switch & Signal crooned into the perpetual shroud which hung over Hopewell.

Then The Boys would be nudged down the aisle past the rack of Wonder bread and Twinkie cakes out onto the sidewalk. After a few manly hockers into the gutter, some belligerent stares at passing motorists who did not return their scowls, they beat on Gorm. Not hard. There was just enough authority in their fists and forearms to kill time without irreparably damaging their object so he could serve in his accustomed role the next day. Years of extracting lumps from Gorm had wearied them so that after some preliminary blows they had to devise new and more daring stratagems to humiliate the boy.

To proceed within inches of crushing his spirit was their goal, not physical punishment. And when the pride of Gorm had curled in upon itself as he lay in the doorway of Coznowski the barber, the red and white bands of the barber's pole corkscrewing into one another like a giant insect boring into the Hopewell smog, he would find himself snatched up by the lapels of his surplus Navy peacoat and thrust into a circle to fight a boy smaller and more frightened than himself.

"Bite his ear!" his tormentors would cry but it was all Gorm could do to squeeze the enemy's head and make him cry "Uncle!" It was enough to restore Gorm's hope that he might someday be accepted on equal terms by The Boys. For The Boys his victory meant the assurance of his return the next day for some new and exhilarating torture.

Not long before the fierce wind came up that was to change Gorm's life, his cohorts, led by Beanhead Simko and Mickey Wholesale Pike, came up with the idea of letting Lester Day the village idiot get in his licks. Day was a 45-year-old paperboy who, when he'd completed his regular route, would sell the *Evening Herald* at the redlight just before the entrance to the new Parkway. He held the *Herald*'s tabloid against his chest and screamed the latest crime into the windshields of stopped motorists. "READ ALL ABOUT IT . . . EX-COUNCILMAN STRANGLES WIFE WITH NYLON STOCKING . . . HANGS HER BY TOES TO CRYSTAL CHANDELIER ONE-HUNDRED YEARS OLD . . . READ THE GHASTLY DETAILS. . . ."

On bad days when motorists refused to stop and buy, Lester Day broke soda bottles in front of the light, then raced deflating tires to their clunking halt. If broken glass failed, Day simply exposed himself, his giant proboscis leering just below the seamy graphics of the city's latest victim.

He did not hesitate when Beanhead placed a Mars Bar in his hand and told him he was needed to teach someone a lesson.

Four of The Boys held Gorm against Ma Goo's wall in an alleyway while the others coached the demented paper carrier on the most advantageous way to complete the assault. They tried to get Day to punch the victim in the stomach. His hands were so stiff from rheumatism and exposure to cold rains he could not make a fist. Neither would his knees or feet serve as weapons because he wasn't agile enough to zero in on his target nor maintain his balance after he'd struck. He did try a halfhearted rehearsal. One of the holders, Pumperdink the Pukeroo was accidentally kneed in the groin. Day fell to the cinders, slicing his hand open on a piece of glass. In a paroxysm of rage and holding his wounded hand against his stomach, he tossed his battered Homestead Grey baseball cap into Ma Goo's trash barrel. To shouts of encouragement he backed off from Gorm (who did not struggle, as experience had taught him the futility of such effort), counting the ten paces the way gunslingers did, then launched himself forward in urgent duckwaddle strides, all the way screaming "NIGGER," his Wildroot-laced hair streaming behind him and his psoriasis-pocked scalp showing a harmonious pink into the late afternoon gray till it at last found its target.

After he had butted Gorm three times, Day picked his cap out of the trash barrel. The victim sat against the wall spitting blood onto his lapels. Then the paper carrier saddled the straps of his *Herald* newsbag across his chest and walked briskly to his station by the redlight, knowing this was one day when he wouldn't have to expose himself.

The billows of smoke Gorm studied were wafted as gently as real clouds, their linings neither gold nor silver, but light crimson like the blood which ran regularly from his mouth and nose, floating serenely beyond the gray, humpbacked hills which surrounded the city. In time he learned to make shapes out of this smoke before it disintegrated altogether. Mushrooms blossomed after a brief stem-like surge from the lips of industry. These were always a sign of prosperity. Every two years just after a steel strike was settled there would be a prolonged period of mushrooms in his salad and the boy would have the satisfaction of knowing that what he ate and what he saw were the same thing. Other billows blossomed into ferocious hippos which gored the sky with eight or nine horns. Gorm had observed his only hippopotamus in *National Geographic* next to some African ladies with boobies as big as soccer balls. Though he would have liked to have acquired a harem of these ladies if only to up his esteem with The Boys, he settled for the hippo because this was the one animal he knew that wallowed in the mud without complaining about it.

Storm days were the worst days of all. Not only the smoke from his father's plant but the belchings from Bog & Bliss, Armco, Arsenal Sheet & Tube, and thirty other heavy industries along the Monongahela were swallowed into the sullen abyss of nimbostratus clouds. Then Gorm would have to look at what The Boys looked at: Betty Gombroski getting off work from the Silk N' Smooth Beauty Shop across the street, her sweater swaying like a hammock loaded with coconuts; Pa Goolantz on his hands and knees in the middle of the street at the intersection, painting pedestrian lines for the third time that winter; or simply the gutter after a rain or a snowfall had melted when The Boys made bets on how many Popsicle sticks would cruise past Ma Goo's before the light changed to green. On such days, smoke and the elements spun themselves like rayon over the city and it was all shroud.

On clear blue days or cirrus ones, cirrostratus, cumulus or altocumulus days, Gorm could indulge the industrial puffs to the most remote ceiling of his fantasy. Dirty snowballs raced themselves till they grew legs, three-legged horses with the heads of chickens. The eyes of one chicken unraveled like thread from a plastic button. A new puff from Armco maintained itself, yet was buffeted intact like the steel ball in Ma Goolantz's pinball machine. Gorm stared regally skyward working his fingers on the flippers of his peacoat lapel. A tyrannosaur spun from Bog & Bliss with six heads. Someone smacked Gorm on the back of the head.

"Whattaya dreamin' about, Gorm?" "I dunno . . . things." "What things?" asked Wholesale. "I dunno . . . dumb things." "Well don't think about dumb things. Think about smart things like pussy," Jism Jack Sodder advised him.

Jism Jack had quit Hopewell High in his senior year to take a job at Kennywood Amusement Park to operate the Tilt-O-Whirl. In the off-season he collected unemployment and ran a steady monologue on the efficacy of pussy. His great dream was to travel to Disneyland where he planned to operate a similar thrill ride. In the bargain he hoped to nail down a rich California divorcée who in appreciation of his "stamina" would support his vices during the unemployment season.

"Gorm don't know what pussy looks like," said Pumperdink.

Pumperdink the Pukeroo had been born with club feet which had been partly straightened through a series of operations. The previous fall his present nickname had replaced an earlier one, "Crabs," when he'd vomited a half quart of port wine along with his dinner on Ma Goolantz's pinball machine. Wads of pumpernickel bread had spewed over the brilliant glass but The Boys pronounced it "pumperdinkel" and the name stuck in a slightly shortened form.

Gorm said he did too know what pussy looked like.

"What?" asked the Mayor of Noble Street.

The Mayor, alias John Johns, was the smallest of The Boys but his stature was immeasurably increased by the lincolnesque top hat he wore tilted over one eye.

"It's all fuzzy," Gorm replied with dignity. He watched a billow from Bog & Bliss splay into myriad strands. "It's kind of like a Brillo pad."

A round of laughter greeted this remark.

"He means a coon's snatch. With nice girls it's different," said Wholesale.

"The trouble is we're talkin' about the outside when we should be talkin' 'bout the inside," said Jism Jack. "All the action's on the inside."

This struck The Boys as logical. Standing within the glow of Ma Goolantz's neon sign, they imitated Jack's stance, hands plunged in Levi pockets, thumbs dangling over the edge like luck charms. Their backs were slightly hunched in meditation. As if on a given signal, they turned deferentially toward Jism Jack.

"Don't ask me no more. I ain't no baby doctor. But I can tell you this. It's kind of like a long tunnel. It can handle any sort of traffic you give it. There's a funny sort of knob at one end that controls the general flow. After that it's endless. Spend nine months of darkness tryin' to get out. Soon as you get out, spend the rest of your life tryin' ta get back in. Either way, nothin' but darkness. Don't ask me no more. I just do it, I don't think about it."

A sadness embraced the group.

Between them, Gorm stood numb and expectant of his daily harassment. He tried to remember whether he'd actually ever imagined a girl's private parts. He thought he had but he wasn't sure. If he had, he wondered whether he'd conceived of himself as penetrating this magical circle that could so improve his position with The Boys. Certainly he would want them present for his deflowering. They would not believe him otherwise. The trouble with even this fancy was his most fervent machinations were related to Laverne Link, comic heroine of "I Love Laverne."

Gorm watched the show each afternoon when he returned from school. To his sober, pre-orgasmic mind, Laverne came off as a dimwit who could fuck up a hard-boiled egg. The plots of the show made no sense to him. They always began with Laverne railing at her new husband, a Cuban immigrant named Gonzalez Gonzalez, over some imminent household catastrophe like a broken pipe. The show ended with the plumbing problem solved in as mysterious and daffy a way as it had begun and Laverne deliriously planting kisses on the immigrant's cheeks.

Between the beginning and the end, Gorm embraced a knotty-pine pillow to his chest and ejaculated fiercely into his underpants and down his legs. He did not understand why someone as pretty as Laverne Link would marry a man whose only talent was the rumba, who couldn't even speak English correctly.

What fascinated him about Laverne was precisely the same characteristic which made him deflate her in his conscious mind. She was goofy. This goofiness translated itself into a good-humored tolerance of Gorm's own persistent bungling as she traipsed about the house, sticking her finger in the toaster or overheating the oven till smoke filled the kitchen and eventually the living room, a model of the lovable but incompetent housewife, preparing a surprise birthday party for Gonzalez Gonzalez.

To do anything as rash as undressing Laverne Link in his conscious mind would have struck Gorm as treason. In the 20 min-

utes before his father returned home from the Union Switch &
Signal, the queen of late afternoon comedy simply held him in
her arms. Not even Bloom deodorant commercials broke the
spell once Laverne Link started her trance on the ball-bearing
inspector's son. Gorm embraced the knotty-pine pillow and admired the heroine's latest permanent. She in turn brushed back a
stray lock from his forehead. In tones as svelte as the permanent
she told him he was a big boy now. With her on his side The Boys
would not molest him. They would not stuff him in a trash barrel
as they had the week before.

Some of her advice was less practical but all the more endear-
ing because Gorm could not fasten it to any particular locale. She
said she had missed him during the rehearsals. Now that the real
show had started she hoped she would always be able to spot
him . . . out there in the audience . . . even if it was far away . . .
the 70th row in the balcony . . . or in a provincial industrial town
plunked in the Appalachian trough as Hopewell was . . . in front
of his new Motorola . . . surrounded by brick walls thrown up
during the depression. Yes, she could still see him . . . even
behind his knotty-pine pillow.

Struggling on his hands and knees toward the set, Gorm knew
Laverne Link's solace to be true. The Bloom commercial was
breaking and there she was . . . emerging from the bedroom in a
housecoat. She held a box of candles. A door opened. Before
Gorm could discern who the birthday beau was, he reached for
goofy Laverne and the vertical-control knob at the same instant.
The picture was breaking up and he did not want to lose it . . .
ever. The Union Switch & Signal mooned its prolonged mourn-
ing whoosle like a bloated cow's mooing, releasing his father
from its latticed mouth. A braceleted arm reached out of the
Motorola box to hold Gorm. He rolled from its grasp, knowing he
was not worthy of that uppity bitch, and coming, he went on his
side like a wounded infantry man. A few seconds later he arose
and went to the hall closet to wipe himself with his father's
shoeshine rag.

"If I ever found the right woman, I'd make her Queen for a
Day. I'd buy her anything she wanted," Pumperdink was saying.

A milk truck rattled past, its bottles clanking with the driver's
effort to free his machine from trolley tracks.

"That's just the trouble," said Stash Conroy, "You'd last *one*
day with her. She'd get a look at the scars on your feet and hide

under the bed."

Stash had just been released from the Hopewell pokey for stealing cases of beer from back porches during the Christmas season. His habit was to stash them in the weeds behind Armco Steel and drink the heist at his convenience.

Pumperdink had been his accomplice on one foray and it was inturned footprints in the snow which had led to their capture. Pumperdink's father paid his son's fine. Stash had originally been sentenced to one day at painting his cell aquamarine blue but when he extended this service to the rear of Lieutenant Choppy Doyle's custom tailored blues, his talents were confined for two more days.

Pumperdink said, "Not if I made enough money and set up my lady in real style. If I had a million bucks I could stick my feet in front of her nose and she would just smile and pretend it were roses."

"How you going to get a million bucks, Pumperdink? You don't even know how to work the flippers on the pinball machine."

There was a brief applause for this put-down. Then Albert Goolantz came out of Ma's carrying a paint bucket and admonishing "youze bums" to make way for a working man. They gave Albert a Bronx cheer on behalf of his efforts. Ever since he had passed out bumper stickers for Fritz Conover the tax collector, he'd been the reigning Maintenance Engineer in Charge of Pedestrian Crosswalks and Fireplugs. This would be the second time since the advent of the new year Albert Goolantz had painted that emergency water source. Even Gorm joined the celebratory mood. The fire hydrant was the brightest object at the intersection where Frick and Mellon avenues crossed.

Late one Sunday afternoon while Gorm was alone studying billows in the shadow of Ma Goo's, waiting for someone to come along and torment him (Sunday was an off day), a fierce wind came up. Immediately the billows were staggered into curlicues, frail wisps. Tatters of the *Evening Herald* were lifted from the gutter, hovered, flapped in midair. The wind snatched leaves and soot from Ma's rain spout above Gorm's head and flung it in all directions. A tiny piece of cardboard, an empty matchbook floated down toward the boy. In his childhood he had been a trash collector. Instinctively, he reached out and grabbed it.

"Everybody kicking sand in your face?" the back cover que-

ried. It advised Gorm to look inside. Here a man named Charles
Atlas said he, too, had once been a weakling. He'd gotten the
worst of it on beaches, school playgrounds, dance halls, gymna-
siums, crowded supermarkets. Twice his violin had been stolen,
the strings reappearing the next day in school as suspender
straps on bullies. As he got older, girls standing in groups blew
smoke rings in his direction and laughed like hyenas.

After six months of rigid training with barbells, dumbbells,
handgrips, wrist rollers, chin-up bars, headstraps, inclined
boards, exercise stretchers, and 50 different protein supple-
ments, the brutes had backed off. Why? What had lifted a 90-
pound weakling into a state of semiexaltation by the masses?
Power, that's what. Power in his triceps. Bicepses. Lats and
delts. Rectus abdominis. Power in his throat, heart, knuckles.
Nothing remained untouched. Power oozing out his vastus internus, sternomastoid, his once concave chest. Gorm was as
impressed by the mystery of Latin terminology as much as by all
the fine print a match cover could hold. Charles said he was now
the envy of everyone who knew him. The first month he had
gained seven pounds. As the wind died down, Gorm reached for
his biceps and felt the loser's stingy pinch, the exposed surface of
his humerus for the first time. "Want to be a sandkicker?" the
match cover asked.

That night Gorm sent away for the free brochure.

Gorm's father was a frugal man. At first he balked at spending
$149.72 plus shipping charges for the weight equipment and Mr.
America training manual to make a bohunk of a he-man out of
his only son. Let him lift ingots. Besides, his long eyelashes and
cute dimples made childless aunts sigh. At Xmas their checks to
the boy covered Mr. Gorm's yearly car insurance. Would they
still sigh and sign when his body was as hard as an ironing
board? His bicepses as big as apples, his neck as fat as a hippo's?

One morning at work, Mr. Gorm rolled a faulty ball bearing
along the grooved ridges of his desk and thought. When he
thought of all the dough he had forked out for Band-Aids to
patch his son's wounds, he was urged to think some more. Ten
years of Merthiolate, adhesive tape, ice packs for concussions. . .
days lost from work to rescue his son trapped by a gang in a
complete stranger's house . . . he never knew when the phone
would ring. Only the week before he'd been called out, much
like the cavalry in an endless rerun to discover his son, his only
child, curled like a cat under Mrs. McKivitz's Dodge while The
Boys poked at him with broom handles.

The inspector knew self-defense to be the law of every civilized man. Maybe the kid would at least learn to throw a sucker punch and run. Mr. Gorm had taken to stealing Band-Aids from the company first-aid kit but lately he'd been getting sneaky looks from Riley, the vice-president in charge of maintenance. Except for his genitals, he could not think of a single part of his son's body he had not patched. Sooner or later they would get those too. "Where are you going with those Band-Aids, Gorm?" "Oh, hi Riley, how's things?" "Things is fine. The Band-Aids, Gorm." "These . . . oh yes. I was just going to patch one of my son's balls. I think it's the left one." "That's the one part of the body you can't patch, Gorm. Shrink and expand, sideways and longways. It never stays the same. If I were you I'd chalk up that kid as a reject. How long have you been patching him up, five years, 10? Some children are like automobiles, born lemons. Greeks used to put them in caves. They could spot a loser a few hours after birth. Why don't you try again, Inspector Gorm. Kind of like a trade-in. You might get a Rhodes scholar, an MVP in the senior circuit, a filibustering senator, think about it. Whatever you do, leave the Band-Aids in the kit. Sorry, house rules."

The kid reminded Gorm senior of the bicycle inner tube he'd patched and repatched during the depression. Finally it lost all semblance of rubber. Its identity was its patches. Home repair, not the original material, had become the essence. An American ethic, thought the inspector, you are what you make of yourself. A nation of arrogant retreads turning their backs on retreads. Still, he would not steal anymore Band-Aids from the company kit.

Gorm senior threw the faulty ball bearing into the wastebasket and reached for his checkbook in the top drawer. The matchbook offer could be a bargain, a veritable boon from heaven.

At that instant there was a shout from the far end of the plant where individual bearings were tested under realistic conditions. The lubricant nozzle had jammed. The dummy pistons seized and smoked. The air filled with a dry rattle of parts floating in limbo in the main combustion chamber.

Gorm began quietly lifting the tempered steel as if it were delicate pearls he was filching from a jewelry shop.

He did not put weights on the bar. The bar, itself, weighed 20 pounds. It was all he could do to raise that single pipe stem over his head. He lifted in the shadow of a single lightbulb which hung over the laundry tub, unused since that day 14 years ago when his mother had run off with a sporting goods salesman. Gas had replaced coal and the grilled mouth of the coal furnace stared at Gorm from the far end of the cellar like a toothless crone. His only disappointment that first day was that The Boys could not see him holding 20 pounds all by himself high over his head. He held the bar so long in that position, delirious with possibility, he became fearful of ever getting it down.

First Gorm developed one knot, then two knots. The one on his right biceps was the size of a chick pea; the knot on his left biceps grew almost as large as a ball bearing. Every afternoon at the hour he would normally have been growing willowy over Laverne Link he sat on a bench and admired his two knots. They felt like nodules rather than muscles but the manual said nothing about the *stages* through which he would develop, only that he would somehow produce new muscle tissue. Anyway it was a start. The disappointment came when he had to begin his exercises again.

After three weeks he was not able to lift more than the 20-pound bar above his head. One day he pressed it twice. The next day he slipped back to one and even then it got stuck above his head and he had to yell for Laverne Link to come help him. She, however, was busy adopting an orphan through a mail order catalogue for her and Gonzalez Gonzalez. At the last instant Gorm threw the bar to the floor.

He still hung out with The Boys at Ma Goo's but the beatings were not as bad as before since Jism Jack and Wholesale Pike had been recruited to run numbers for Tiny Mancuso and the truckers for the *Evening Herald* had gone on strike.

He did not tell them he was training to become a sandkicker, partly because he badly needed a secret besides Laverne Link, partly because he knew they would not believe him. Any venture outward at nobody's expense but the venturer's was regarded with sarcasm by The Boys. He took his slaps, drank an extra quart of milk, sprinkled Charles Atlas High Protein Powder on his cornflakes, embraced the 20-pound bar, and waited. And nothing happened beyond the two nodules he squeezed at the beginning of each session.

In despair Gorm paced the length of the concrete floor one afternoon. He wore his standard uniform: a pair of white shorts and a Charles Atlas hernia belt. When the gas furnace clicked he'd reached the end of the cellar. He stood at the entrance to the coal room. He could not remember what it was like in there except it was dark and had once been filled with coal. He had no idea what he was looking for but he peeled back the door on its single hinge.

Darkness, the dank pulpish odor of a jungle floor.

He flicked the light switch. The first image that came to life was a compressor which had never compressed under Gorm's care. It had lain there against the breast of the bituminous lumps since the day he had dragged it home from Mrs. McKivitz's trash barrel. It did not matter that gas had replaced coal the year after his mother's disappearance. Soft coal had been outlawed for private use though everyone knew industry mixed it with anthracite, leaving the skies as black as ever. As the coal in the damp and darkness had turned in upon itself to produce the semi-mulch of its first Carboniferous state, the compressor had sagged with coal's fortune till it lay nearly on its back, its gauge's needle showing red under the coal room light.

Gorm's first thought was to turn out the light and run upstairs to renew the caresses of Laverne Link. The disintegrating coal said, "This is your room."

The coal room was filled with the debris Gorm as a child had dragged from trash baskets and would never allow his father to throw out. The husks of three lamp shades sat in the corner. Next to them a waffle iron lay on its side, its cord leaking a ganglion sprouting nerve endings. There were deflated inner tubes patched and repatched, cotter pins, the tinny sheen of curtain rods fashionable before venetian blinds had swept Hopewell like the Asiatic flu, an entire icebox Gorm had once towed from Skeetersville. A Bendix alarm clock sat on top of the pile. One of its hands was gone; springs sagged from its rear. It moved to its own peculiar time with each new fault in the coal pile. It ticked, a miracle in its decrepit state. Gorm slammed the door.

He placed 15 pounds on each side of the bar, tightened the collars, lifted. It was more than double the weight he had attempted before. When he held the barbell above his head, he cried, "Brace firm, trapezius! Don't buckle vastus internus. Grow delts, grow."

"Grow delts, grow," the disintegrating soft coal sang back to him.

This chant fitted perfectly each stage of the press. The reverberations from the coal room coordinated with the three movements of the weight drop compressed into one.

"Grow delts, grow!"

For an encore with 50 pounds, Gorm sang a new chant. It was basically a song of hate but it was couched in the cuteness of fairy tales as told by adults. It was too long and jagged in its

rhythms to fit the press. Gorm held it out like a string of taffy, a reward after he'd raised the bar over his head and his eyes were tilted toward the rafters. It went:
"Nighty-night Jism Jack, nighty-night
The Boys. Nighty-night my silent mummy.
Nighty-night the sky and stars. All
Herald Gorm the Strong."

On his off days, Gorm took to sitting in a red wooden wagon in the complete darkness of the coal room. Charles Atlas had told him the literal contest of man against the inertia of dead weight is a destructive process. Gorm tore his muscles down so they could rebuild themselves during alternate days of absolute quiet. Atlas advised his adherents to sit under a tree and contemplate pretty girls. If that failed he told them to study their navels as the yogis of yore had done. Since there were no trees around his house (and in any case it was the coldest winter anyone in Hopewell could remember), the boy opted for the coal room. In his brochure, "Beginnings of a Sandkicker," Mr. Universe said, "The common hot water faucet runs cold before it produces warm flow even as the panther lies at complete rest before it attacks."

Gorm did not know what to make of these homilies but he liked to sit in the dark and talk with the trash he'd collected as a child and listen to his body bulge. The trash did most of the talking.

The springs of a Sealy Posturepedic mattress dumped into the darkness by father told him his mother had indeed run off with a sporting-goods salesman but not before she left a note under a Heinz ketchup bottle reminding her husband to buy knockwurst for dinner. Gorm could not remember what he'd done after he ate knockwurst. He ran his fingers over the ridges of the wagon's wheel rims.

The wagon told him the wheels had once been encased in rubber, shredding at the time but sufficient to carry trash along the city's alleyways.

The discards of postwar affluence were set out for Black Jack the trash collector each Tuesday but Gorm had got first pick as he poked through the folds of smog and fog which had always hung over Hopewell. Sitting in the darkness, he knew he'd had no interest in making sneak attacks on enemy bunkers, hide-and-seek, nigger-baby-run, or masquerades of Batman or the Lone Ranger, only a desire to make the waffle iron glow red once again, the alarm clock to sing with its tick-tick-ticketing and rickety shrill bell, the lamp shade to find a naked bulb around which to fasten its wire clamps, the comparatively minuscule cotter pin to locate its tiny pivotal groove.

When Gorm spotted a precipitous mountain of junk in the distance, his remote expression sidled into a snigger. His kidneys rollicked for release in some nearby bushes. "Throw Mama from the Train a Kiss," by Patti Page was the hit song of that year. As it wafted its way from breakfast tables into alleys where the wily Gorm was zipping up, he sang the refrain minus the last two words—"Throw Mama from the Train."

With his growing sense of recall, aided by the darkness and decaying bituminous coal, Gorm's bicepses grew a quarter inch that first month. His lats spread slowly like bat wings. The first spread of new pectoral tissue hinted at possible concealment of his concave sternum.

"Make me a poitrine out of a dream," he cried to the rafters. He threw a left jab at his shadow. It did not retreat.

He was no longer satisfied to listen to trash recite his history only on rest days. He wanted to hear all the time about his past before he had become a scapegoat.

Plastic and aluminum whipped the Dow Jones averages into a frenzy the year Gorm became a trash collector and it was a good thing. As the promise of the Promised Land came true the boy had felt his pulse soar to the cold, ungiving touch of each fly-wheel, sprocket, wrought-iron wardrobe caster Hopewell tossed on the heap of the boon of postwar prosperity. He had held a five-pound iron skillet to his cheek and known the dense, impregnable fiber of its tempered pores. On its black moony face he had chalked eyebrows, a nose, a mouth meant to be his own but more like a caricature of the moon itself. It proved to be the one piece of junk his father retrieved. Gorm awoke one morning to see two yellow eyes popping in it. He thought they were his eyes plucked from his skull by a witch during a nightmare. He poked his fingers into his eyeballs searching for the truth and knew then he and his father were going to eat the embryos of chickens for breakfast.

Shoulder shrugs, bent-over rows, continental dead lifts, squats for his gluteus maximus, Gorm did them all. Quietly . . . deftly . . . retreating to the coal room between exercises.

He learned from the body builder's Bible, *Flex*, that proportion was as important as power. He labored with Latin pronunciations of his body's parts, shaping them on his lips, joyous in the jargon of each muscle group, which even as it progressed outward separating him from the old loser's pinch of his humerus, added an entirely new sound, elastic compared to the coarse, metallic strife which tumbled from the mouths of The Boys. Gorm heaved and grunted and his muscles expanded, grew new tissue layer over layer. "Grow latissimus dorsi," he sang to his barbells during bent-over rows.

In the fumes of the decaying coal room, he rejoiced at his newfound usefulness. The darkness no longer yielded cast-iron skillets to his touch but he knew they'd existed. He ran his fingers over his skull. He had the lumps on his head to prove it.

The next Tuesday the child had brought four more skillets home for his father. He tested each skillet softly on his skull, then on his kneecap. The skillets held together and since his relatives shied away from him and his father after their loss, and his father worked overtime providing enough greased bearings to speed the wheels of comfort-hauling freight trains, no one noticed the gathering storm of knots on little Gorm's head. Mr. Gorm graciously accepted the skillets which he hid under his and his former wife's orthopedic mattress stashed in the coal bin.

One night he had read his son a fairy tale. It was "Tom Thumb" after which the boy had embraced a pillow. "Papa," he said, "tomorrow, bring me a ball bearing from the plant."

The postwar boon had had other metallic goodies to offer the scavenger Gorm. Down by the Tassey Hollow Bridge in the shadow of the railroad trestle where ragweed made his sinuses tremble and he could hear the lathes screech at Mesta Machine, he discovered that even the darkies of Skeetersville could now afford refrigerators. He carted one of their iceboxes home on his wooden wagon.

The same day his father brought him a ball bearing. While little Gorm did not understand the mechanics of his father's job—the precision zigzag grooved for oil in the ball that would keep the shaft from freezing—he felt that a ball bearing would be good luck since it had made the trains rumble so far so fast. He longed for escape, though from what and to where he could not say because he could not conceive of another world different from Hopewell. His father told him his mother and the sporting goods salesman had flown the coop on a Flexible Flyer, a night train to the far west. Gorm had visions of joining her someday if only to display the vast collection of junk he'd accumulated. The ball bearing would bring him good luck. This was needed because now that the cellar was filled with Hopewell's junk, Gorm felt only he could revive it and make it function in its original way. Should not the big Bendix tick-tick, its immense hands swing the night into day and himself upward half as high as a smokestack? And lo, on the sixth day there was light so let the waffle iron glow, the brass lamp's limp socket light a bulb so the husk of a shade will have light to shade? He rolled his new luck charm around in his mouth, tasting for the first time the heady aroma of lubricating oil. When Mrs. Vidoni, the kindly babysitter with a large wart like a spike protruding from the center of her forehead, found him that afternoon, he was curled in the icebox (minus its door which Mr. Gorm had removed) asleep, the ball bearing revolving in his mouth like an incubating chick about to hatch.

Persistent as little Gorm was, he could make nothing work. The waffle iron remained cold. The clock rained ticking on his ear when he shook it. It stopped cold as the concrete floor on which he sat when he placed it level.

His lone hope was the brass lamp which knocked him across the cellar when he stuck his finger in the socket to test it but would never make the bulb glow. After he had been jolted twice more he resigned himself to its illusory life. He curled up in the icebox to suck his luck charm. As the bells in the belfry of Saint Humiliata of Our Lady of the Feast ding-dang-donged twelve noon, Gorm swallowed the ball bearing.

From the day of that memory Gorm's body building was never quite the same. In the midst of the most effortless exercise, his forehead would furrow in doubt. His mouth would purse with a strand of Latin anatomy when suddenly his eyes would retreat, dim, then go blank. The pride of weeks of patient and tenacious rehabilitation of his body contracted before a single notion in Gorm's head. He became convinced there was a lubricated ball bearing hiding inside his body.

He wasn't sure where this alloyed ball he had swallowed as a child had chosen to reside. The coal room, pregnant with so many memories, reminded him there might be as many dark corners in his body as there were in his brain. The sad little luck charm could be stuck in his pancreas, festering in the labyrinths of his gallbladder. Perhaps it had taken up residence in his small intestine. At this very second it was being tossed about like a punctured life boat from underwater forests of flailing villus to flailing villus, a hanger-on even during peristalsis.

Gorm had heard of instances where a coin, paper clips, a religious metal, stores of metal flotsam had been found in the stomach of a respectable citizen upon autopsy. Stirred by this vision, the boy stretched himself at a 45 degree angle on the incline board on which he normally did his sit-ups and probed his esophageal tract relentlessly. A vast gurgling answered his fingers. Next he tried to induce the bearing to shift positions by tickling his tummy. This had the effect of reducing him to a prostrate case of the giggles. With the same exasperation which had made him swallow the steel ball, he beat on his abdomen with his fists. It was hard now. It sang to his pummelings with the density of steel itself.

From habit Gorm continued to lift weights.

Yet the smooth coordination of former times disintegrated into spastic jerks, bursts of furious strength followed by creeping lassitude. The old refrain, "Grow delts, grow," mocked his muscles. And the coal room did not sing back. Where once the embrace of his hands on a steel bar had been the most natural activity in the world, it now felt like a greased worm. Every step of the press revealed Gorm's cautiousness. He did not lift, he heaved. Instead of lowering weights, they lowered him, banged off the concrete like discarded bricks. He had begun to think, often thinking upon those thoughts which in turn gave way to thoughts thinking upon the instrument which had tried to assort the original thunk.

This thinking took the form of a detective's bloodhound sniffing up and down the millions of canals in his body for the ball bearing. The dog outran its master. It would not be retrieved with any amount of thinking. Gorm knew he should have put his mind on a leash but there it was, racing into a vast forest of villi, blood cells, phagocytes, lymph glands, with its nose down, hot on the scent. There was little to do but chase after it.

At night the boy woke screaming, "Get back in your kennel!"

All hours of the day he heard vague growlings but he could not be sure whether it was the dog answering him or vague protestations from his guts.

He did not go to the coal room anymore. He saw it now for its literal darkness, its fetid odor of disintegration. If he had never gone there in the first place, he never would have known. If he had never known, the bloodhound would have remained in its doghouse. Then he would have been Gorm the Strong, Gorm the Magnificent, Gorm the Incorrigible. His poitrine would have been the stuff of dreams, his trapezius the hulk and bulk of amnesia. *To forget was his mission* . . . as soon as he tracked down the ball bearing.

In the succeeding days, Gorm advanced his search for the lost metal over his entire body. It had expanded prodigiously in two months. Surely his pectorals, thigh muscles, swelling arms could hide something as small as a steel ball. As with his abdomen, he poked, probed, teased, tickled, and verbally coerced his tissues. In this way, he inadvertently discovered his body.

A landmark on his thighs; a diminutive pimple had the fascination of a volcano about to erupt. He popped it, laughed, moved on to further delights. In the glare of the laundry tub light, one kneecap showed more rounded than its partner. He spent two hours massaging a mole he discovered in his hairline, precisely where the sternomastoid ascended into his medulla oblongata. The hairs on his left shinbone were black, whereas brown was predominant on the right one. One foot sweated more than the other while the drier of the two produced more toe jam. Gorm fingered his umbilical knot, wondering if he untied it, would his innards slide forth onto the cellar floor. Gorm saw himself as an orgy of unexplainable bumps and fissures, a morass of untutored near opposites that would fight symmetry to the death. This logic wasn't dispelled even when Gorm stuck his little finger up his rectum, wiggled, pulled it out with nary a hint of shit, shat, or bona fide stool.

"Where's your porportion now?" he wanted to ask Charles Atlas.

Gorm's greatest perception, though, was not a gradual cognition of the body as a complex and miraculous machine formed through eons of subtle evolution as the textbooks had taught, but a walking tidal fault, formed like the earth of other faults similar to earthquakes, fluctuations in rotation, deceptions by the sun that had once thrown the earth ass over tincup, polar bear to jungle, mountain to sea bottom, civilization's pedestrian temples lofted intact to plateaus where they would be called mystery and miracle.

Gorm, himself, was upside-down when this perception came to him. He was balancing himself on his head and elbows, feet against the wall, probing glands in his neck while rocking gently to fashion a firm sternomastoid, when he farted. Instantly, the truth was his.

The coils were shot.

"Damn if the coils aren't shot," he said to the wall. "The reason your junk won't work is the coils are shot," his father had told him 11 years earlier, shortly after he'd swallowed the ball bearing.

As a scavenger child he had taken his clues from throwaways. His father was a healthy, self-sufficient man who lived in another world, the world of people, of production, authority, quick decisions, and a quicker mouth. Gorm saw his father was responsible for smoke. He made steel balls and the smoke drifted willy-nilly toward the horizon. The boy would not resign himself to a summer of collecting and hoarding doomed to futility. In a fit of despair he had thrown the Bendix clock at Mrs. Vidoni's forehead, mistaking her for the ugly witch in his dreams.

It had missed, clattering instead off the faded rose wallpaper in the living room. From the clock a coil sprang forth like a joke. The black hand scrambled down the face hovering upright at the half-hour mark. Gorm retrieved it, smashed the glass facing, snatched up the hand. "Don't hit me or I'll swallow them," he'd cried at the warty witch. When Mrs. Vidoni spun to find the yardstick, he'd swallowed the hand of the clock anyway.

Gorm's career as a rehabilitator of junk had ended soon after that. The wheels of his wooden wagon gave him away. The shredding rubber exposed a grooved, hollow rumble which made Hopewell's workers and wives run from Patti Page at the radio to confront a skinny, sallow urchin giving off an odor of lubricating oil. They stood in front of their junk piles like sentries, arms crossed, their corneas keen with property rights.

Who was he and where did he live?

Gorm told them he had been born in a ketchup bottle. Recently he had swallowed a ball bearing and the hand of an alarm clock and now no one could touch him.

After he'd swallowed time his voice had grown deeper. He sang them a bar of "Throw Mama from the Train."

The workers of Hopewell were pleased with such a brassy profundo belting out a hit tune. Still, to a man, they said junk was junk. There was only one man in Hopewell who got their junk.

"Black Jack gets our trash," they echoed down Orchard Alley past Donofrio's grocery store while flies buzzed on the watermelons setting outside on bench slats, past the Landers' house where out-of-town truckers stopped and it was said the daughters harvested cooties under their hatpins.

Past Concelli the shoemaker's where a "tap-tap-tap" followed the rumbling, empty wagon from the end of Orchard Alley to the crest of a hillside leading to an offshoot bank of the Monongahela River. There was nowhere else to go. Behind him a wall of voices he could not dissolve with his brassy song rose like dust. Beyond, the smokestacks of Bog & Bliss stood like toy artillery, silent, inconsequential, pale under their own voluminous outpouring. They made the metal that furnished his cellar. He knew that. The smoke rose to form mushrooms, chemical vegetables metamorphosing from metal. Between the voices at his back and the odd transition below him, Gorm cried. Tomorrow he would have to go to school.

Still standing upside-down on his head, flooded with fresh blood, Gorm now understood there were two dogs loose in his system. The first mutt tracked for the missing ball bearing while the newest dog, no doubt an offshoot, perhaps the son of the first dog, barked from his watery orifices, "Heal me." 'One must be reasonable under such circumstances,' he told himself. 'I must think out each step.'

'If a ball bearing entered my body via my mouth,' he thought, thinking, 'There are only two ways it can get out. One: out the way it went in. That is to say, should I vomit, burp, or belch, it might plop out all by itself.' The second escape route, he reasoned correctly, was his rectum.

The latter route presented problems his mouth did not. It was unlikely the ball bearing would pass out his ass unencumbered. It would need a carrier much as Hopewell's trash had once needed his red wagon. And would not this conduit of his lost luck charm have to be solid . . . fecal matter . . . poop?

The trouble was Gorm did not poop. He shat. Shatting as he did, his waste was seldom of one piece. Like his conversation the few times in his life he had chosen to talk about what was really on his mind, it sprayed in all directions. Afflicted with chronic diarrhea, Gorm regularly splattered every visible portion of the commode's white porcelain innards.

It was a condition that had become apparent at an early age not only to his father and Mrs. Vidoni but to the community as a whole. At Xmas Gorm's rich aunts Lydia and Alvena inquired after his condition. At school Gorm's teachers, fierce vanguards of hygiene, upon hearing his polite request to be excused to do a number 2, ran ahead to make sure there was enough toilet paper. Before Little League games, Gorm's coaches pointed out clumps of trees that would conceal him, whose leaves would supply emergency tissue . . . just in case. Doctors and dentists did not show the boy a waiting room or a hydraulic chair when he came for routine appointments. They pointed out the "Men's Room" to him, winking slyly but secretly disgusted with his previous visit.

Had he been a pooper of some excellence, some internal control, the community as a whole would have been more tolerant of Gorm. A flasher of unmitigated chaos in the most private sector of their homes, institutions, businesses was something else. As Gorm grew, gaining with each year further frailty and sallowness like an expensive candle burning at both ends, people asked only one question of him: "Did you flush?"

Teachers asked it in the middle of Bible exercises upon his return to the room. Even before that the janitor and assistant principal looking for gold brickers, had accosted him in the hallway and asked the same question. "Did you flush?" asked Ma Goo after she spotted him lingering near the pinball machine next to the john. Gorm told her he hadn't had to go yet that day. Ma had told him she wasn't taking any chances. The last time he'd used her toilet he'd forgotten to flush and Albert had spent twenty minutes on his hands and knees scouring and scrubbing with Bon Ami to clean the thing. Secretly Gorm felt this act of Pa Goolantz's had supplied him with the proper training to fulfill his duties as Hopewell's maintenance engineer even if Ma's husband was reduced to fire hydrants and pedestrian lines.

Much of the gossip around Hopewell blamed Gorm's spirited salvos on bad toilet training. Its more experienced citizens said, "Not enough roughage." Gorm's shit became something of a joke. Other people would be greeted with timeworn familiarity. "How's the hubby?" "Some weather we're having." "Fancy meeting you here." No matter where Gorm went, the supermarket, shoe shop, athletic diamond, library, a casual stroll for old time's sake down one of Hopewell's back alleys, or who he met, close relative, distant relative, cop on the beat, schoolmate, teacher, appliance repairman, all asked, "Did you flush?" and laughed their way to the Ritz Cracker counter.

Gorm was not proud of his diarrhea. His bowel movements had the velocity of a shotgun without its lethal effect. Raising up from his head, and positioning himself on the bench press bench in the glare of the laundry tub bulb, Gorm reasoned with accuracy that like the waffle iron, the Bendix alarm clock, the compressor with its gauge showing in the red, the defunct lamp, his coils were shot.

He did not know where it had begun or how. Was it a congenital defect inherited from his mother, a broken piece of plumbing passed on to one Gorm after another, shit backing up in watery state and clogging the colon as far back as the first Gorms' and Pfeitzes' arrival in Boston dressed as Hessian soldiers? Or were his defective coils merely a product of his environment—Hopewell—of years of trying to make meaningful shapes of spirals of smoke since that first morning he'd looked down on the Monongahela while other people pursued verifiable shapes—tits and fire hydrants? Whatever the source, Gorm knew he had one job to do. He had to get his shit together to usher the ball bearing into the open air

In the succeeding days, the boy sought with all his earnestness to manufacture fecal matter in copious quantities, to store it, to examine it minutely, all for the purpose of identifying his waste, not his real waste, but his adopted waste which was not really waste at all, only an inexpendable part of train locomotion. Neither could the ball bearing be called real. Gorm had swallowed it, did not know its exact location, or even if it had taken up residence inside his body. His presumption that the steel ball lay within his vital organs was an act of faith. Its reality could be affirmed only when it emerged in the context of his personal waste which he had convinced himself was not waste but a swelter of unidentifiable shat myriad as atoms, a convulsive act without redemption. Gorm saw clearly he owned a bunghole without purpose. He was not used to working out such a laborious logic (his previous life having been one of reaction and further reaction) and such thinking left him more exhausted than weight lifting had. His pursuit, though, of the ball bearing was remorseless.

If it was true, as Jism Jack said, that all the action was on the inside, how could he begin to revive his rotten intestines?

His waste was not identifiable as poop or crap or stools with their status of scientific measurability. Oh, a stool would certainly be respectable but what about shat? Shat hinted at neither sociability nor health. Even mongrels left more convincing evidence of health than he did. Gorm saw little in his bowel movements to join him to the fraternity of his fellow man—the big league of bona fide poopers, citizens who were respected, who relieved themselves regularly after a breakfast of bacon and eggs, quietly, issuing full-bodied stools without gaseous afternoises, who never forgot to flush.

He decided to work from the outside towards the inside with the only means at his disposal—sit-ups.

The first day he did these on an inclined board, plying his stomach muscles (or "abs" as the Sandkicker manual called them) with his fingers on the upsurge. With one ear he listened to his coils, their occasional soft gurgling . . . the wry, silent seepages of gas which fanned gym shorts . . . odd shiftings in his gut. He felt hope. He pressed on, wielding his "abs" with the fastidiousness of a sculptor.

When Gorm wasn't working on his innards, he meditated on the commode waiting for them to reveal themselves. Of course much of this meditation was devoted to anticipating the day his first full-bodied stool would emerge. The second afternoon there were vague barkings and growlings. Gorm could not decide if this was noise from his coils or protests from the dog hounding his ball bearing, or from the second dog, born of memory which had followed him out of the coal room, its tail flapping in his skull.

Hunched over, expectantly clutching a roll of toilet paper, after a peripicacious burst of flatulence, Gorm heard, "When the red red robin . . . comes bob-bob-bobin' along. . . ."

They were standing around the piano in Miss Purefoy's first grade class. Their teacher wore two long braids topped by a pink bow. When she sang she rocked. Her shoulders swayed and she played. She was sweet Miss Purefoy and when all the little boys and girls sang "Ohhh . . . when the red red robin comes bob-bob-bobin along," she swayed.

She quit rocking when little Gorm farted during the third re-frain of "red red robin." No one had noticed Gorm until then. All the children turned their heads and giggled. Miss Purefoy blushed the color of her bow. It was a noxious way for Gorm to begin his first week, his first year of public school. The Purefoy woman snatched him by the collar and put him in the cloakroom.

In the half darkness of the cloakroom, Gorm still amused his newfound friends with bloated pucker sounds out of his mouth. His lips grew tired after three of these so he played with some metronomes next to a stack of textbooks, *Adventures with Jane and Spot*. While the metronomes went tick-tock, first one, then two, tick-tock . . . tick-tock . . . none of them in tandem, he wondered if Jane and Spot had ever played In-and-Out with metal curtain rods. These were the last items he had collected before the wall of voices had followed him down Orchard Alley.

Illustrations showed Jane and her floppy-eared dog racing frol-icsome up and down glades and dales. Gorm did not know what a glade or a dale was. He understood concrete and steel. In Hopewell he could see as far as the next confectionery, smoke-stack, red-brick row house the color of the smoke. He could see as far as the tall buildings like trays of inverted icecubes where powerful men decided the shapes of the smoke. Tick-tock . . . tick-tock . . . tick . . . he had never seen green grass either unless it was the sparse blades which lived for a week or two each year surrounded by stakes and strings at the back of Donofrio's grocery.

In the cloakroom Gorm grew lonely for his ball bearing. He remembered then the bells of Saint Humiliata of Our Lady of the Feast and the heady odor of lubricating oil as the steel-alloyed ball eased down his gullet. He fell asleep on the floor listening to the six metronomes he had set in motion tick-tock in ragged variations while Miss Purefoy was telling the class: "Now kids if you feel a funny feeling way down in your tummy not part of your tummy but near it and you think maybe it's time to do your doodly-doo's down at the ha-ha place, remember one thing. Remember to take the wooden block with our room number marked on it. It's hanging from the wall over there next to the pumpkin. That way we will know where everyone is at and no one will ever get lost."

On the commode, Gorm wiggled and strained and flexed his abs.

Gorm's first full-bodied poop blossomed like a long-awaited hydrangea one morning as his father was dressing for work.

The boy had previously made plans for inspecting his waste.

After the first delicate plop, he raised on his haunches slowly, since the tangle of underpants and pants about his ankles forbade abrupt movements. Waddling duck fashion to the medicine cabinet, he plucked from the bottom shelf a pair of rusted eyebrow tweezers, his mother's, which had lain unused for 14 years. With these he would preen for the nugget after he'd lifted the tender slug from its waters.

He'd just bent with a cupped hand to scoop his first poop when there was a knock at the door.

"Hurry up I gotta go. I'll be late for work."

"Just one second," Gorm called to his father.

He made a deft grab but like a fish the turd squished from his hand.

Again there was a knock at the door.

Gorm started to perspire.

"What are you doing?"

"Lookin' for somethin.' "

The boy knew immediately what his father suspected.

He could hear his shuffling and jing-a-linging his keys and coins.

Grunts of resignation and disgust made their way through the keyhole.

"No wonder you're always dopey."

In one desperate lunge, Gorm grabbed the glory of his poop no longer shat and squeezed. Filaments fired from each end of his fist. None of them were big enough to conceal a ball bearing. Gorm stuck the squashed remains in his pants pocket, buckled his belt, flushed.

With considerable aplomb he opened the door for his father. Dignity fastened itself onto his stolid shoulders. Gorm majestically eyed a far horizon where his bowel movements would be accepted as part of him.

"You forget to wipe or what? You smell!"

His father slammed the door behind him.

Gorm's first full bodied shat, that is to say poop, was anti-climatic. It yielded not a ball bearing, only itself. And that in a stage of solidification which could best be described as axle grease. After he examined it he threw it out of exasperation into the coal furnace. He hid the tweezers behind the laundry tub.

When he returned home from school, he went to work on his pants pocket in the same tub. He performed the rhythmic motions on the corrugated washboard his mother had exercised before she ran off with the sporting goods salesman. He drove the pocket back and forth in the tub of suds. It did little good. No matter which way he turned, his nostrils twitched with the odor of his first compact bowel movement. He hung the dripping pants over the clothesline. Trepidatiously, in his underpants, he tiptoed to the far end of the cellar near the coal room. Still his nostrils twitched.

His father wasn't home yet. He dashed up stairs to the kitchen . . . stood anxiously by the stove where the grease from that morning's bacon had coagulated in the bottom of an aluminum frying pan . . . waited for his nostrils to twitch. They did. They twitched again when he scooted to the dining room. And again when he stood by the venetian blinds in the living room.

"I am not shit!" he cried. The empty house was sympathetic.

The gas furnace clicked on. The blinds rustled softly, in one key, a rusted xylophone.

In despair, Gorm sat down to write Charles Atlas.

Dear Mr. Atlas,
I have profited much from weights plus your advice. My arms are bigger, so are my lats and other parts. I don't know how to explain this. It's just with all this lifting and eating protein I still can't quite get my shit together.
Please advise.

Yet, did not everyone shit? Oh, certainly their waste emissions were more solid and consistent than his. Still they could not escape their own poop. Something of its odor would always cling to them. If this was true, why then had he never noticed it? Why should he be the one to feel guilty about something everyone did?

In the succeeding days while he waited for an answer from Charles Atlas, Gorm lifted barbells and studied his bowel movements with the aid of his mother's rusted tweezers. He pressed nearly his weight now. He drank milk, sprinkled wheat germ on his meals. He was gaining roughly two pounds a week. His bicepses had increased by two inches. The rest of his body had developed proportionately. He was hardly aware of it.

A sullen mechanical quality had sifted into Gorm's workouts, arrested only when he studied his stools between exercises. When Gorm stole a magnifying glass from his father's tool box, these examinations took on a heightened dimension.

It was one of three glasses Mr. Gorm had once used to study for imperfections within the grooves of ball bearings. Precise measuring machines made the magnifying glasses obsolete after the war but the instruments were too expensive to throw out.

The boy Gorm adopted them like a scientist. Shit took on a fascination beyond its usefulness as a conduit for the lost bearing. He adopted the stratagem his biology teacher had taught him when the class sliced open anesthetized frogs. Cautiously dissecting the stool, he probed for its vital parts which to his surprise turned out to be undigested food. He and his father ate mostly precooked frozen dinners, meat and potatoes, fried foods—-the general nourishments of Hopewell's workers.

During his first dissection Gorm discovered an entire noodle stretching the length of his stool. The next day he found a pea, intact, almost as warm as when he'd lifted it to his mouth from the reheated TV dinner foil. Excitement filled his days now. Each schoolday ended in the knifelike chill of anticipation. Not even the sentries The Boys posted along the main routes to his house diminished this glow. The memory of the circuitous alleys of his junk-hauling days enabled him to elude his oppressors and return to the mouth of the furnace where that morning's bowel movement, hardening in a cold oven, waited for him with its contents of undigested food.

"You eat shit, you become shit," was his pronouncement to these examinations.

These were happy days, as happy as Gorm could be.

Gorm began to eat on the run. Raw turnips, carrots, a banana. He stole these from the A&P. He rejoiced at the cold, damp feeling of rutabaga against his chest, leaves of lettuce sliding down to tickle his rippling abs. His father did not mind that his son left the dinner table early, his plate still half-full. The boy was giving off a strange odor these days which made the tired inspector's nostrils twitch. Gorm observed this twitch. Though no one said anything, the nostrils of his schoolmates were starting to twitch too. An amateur scientist specializing in his own stools, Gorm maintained enough perspective to know most people ate the same shit they shat but since the original shit passing as food was odorless, he had to *assume* he still stank.

The next day a strand of his poop confirmed this. It happened just when Gorm believed his waste could not furnish him with any further surprises. He was haphazardly going through the old routine, dissecting lengthwise, then crosswise, plying with the tweezers where the magnifying glass revealed an odd protuberance, a color not consistent with the multifarious shades of brown, when one strand isolated from the rest sang to him.

It sang "Little Tommy Tinker."

Gorm wondered if this had been one of his favorites as a child. Songs of all kinds appealed to him. He did not sing because songs were almost always sung in a crowd and he was afraid his voice would stand out and bring him ridicule. He paid lip service to the words "Little Tommy Tinker."

Six strands of his stool were flailing away like successive dogs' tails in his head. These were the voices of children greeting him from the schoolyard with the most appropriate song they could think of.

Gorm's shyness and precocious farting had deeply attracted the other children. His preschool companions had been skillets and alarm clocks and cotter pins. He missed the remote completeness of his ball bearing. The children in Miss Purefoy's class fell this way and that with an energy they could not control. They ran up to him and said greatfastfunny things. Their eyes rolled wide and their tongues flopped over the syllables. Gorm stared at them with the evenness of metal. He longed for words too. All he could think of was ketchup bottle so he told them he had been born in a ketchup bottle. He threw back his head and sang them a bar of "Throw Mama from the Train."

The other children thought this very funny. They smacked their tummies and rocked back and forth saying, "m' . . . ummm' . . . ket-chup." At lunch time they would suddenly break out with, "Oooom Gormmm, tell us where you were born?" With upright heads they waited. With wide open mouths masticating bread and jelly and peanut butter and cold cuts, saliva stringing from incisor to incisor, the children of Hopewell Elementary waited for Gorm to tell them about his birth.

After Gorm told them for the twentieth time during a two-week period about the ketchup bottle, wee Pat McCurrnan drove the ketchupy heel of his liverwurst sandwich into the flat of the boy's back. The children of Hopewell waited again in the playground, waited for Gorm to mangle McCurrnan, waited and waited. Gorm glared with the remoteness of metal. They hooted and hollered for real action. Gorm glared and sang, "Throw Mama from the Train."

"Where's the kiss?" cried Miss Purefoy advancing on them with her whistle. "The song has a kiss at the end."

"In the ketchup bottle," Gorm told her.

The next morning when it was time for penmanship class, Gorm discovered someone had peed in his inkwell. He held his nose and pointed.

"Where's Gorm's ink?" Miss Purefoy asked the class.

"In a ketchup bottle," they cried, hysterical with their unanimity.

Miss Purefoy sent Gorm to the cloakroom, back to the dark and the metronomes never in sync and the stacks of frolicsome Jane and Spot. Order was restored for penmanship class.

In the game of Cat and Mouse Gorm was invariably tapped by a girl with a massive jaw and Cro-Magnon forehead named Mary Alice Woiczesheski. Her nickname was "The Bulldog." As Gorm sped up and down the aisles, never gaining on the speedy "Bulldog," the first grade children shrieked "Throw Bulldog from the Train." Gorm couldn't catch her. One day as he fell breathlessly into his seat, relieved the game was over, McCurrnan said solemnly from the rear of the room, "Poor Gorm, couldn't even catch 'The Bulldog.' "

That day at recess, McCurrnan and four other boys made Gorm pay homage to "The Bulldog." They twisted his arm behind his back until he knelt on the cinders at the feet of the ugliest girl in the class and recited the lines "Jinks" Callahan had discovered in his mother's *True Confessions*: "I yearn for your caresses, O bride of my dreams."

Mary Alice could not be appeased so easily.

"Say it again louder!"

She eyed freckled Pat to see if she'd got the right effect.

Pat twisted.

"I yearn for your caresses O bride of my dreams."

"That's better. Now go home and eat spinach so you can be strong like Pat McCurrnan."

The next day McCurrnan allowed "The Bulldog" to carry his carton of chocolate milk to the playground. Gorm followed behind, a kind of valet. In one hand he squeezed the rubber band for Mary Alice's ponytail. Now the loose strands of her hair whipped around her cheeks and low forehead. In the other hand he guarded Pat's combination can opener-jackknife used for mumbly-peg in the soft dirt.

He was never tapped again in Cat and Mouse.

And no matter how hard he tried, he could not hold his hand still enough to keep his s's and o's from unraveling across the page despite the new ink Miss Purefoy had brought him for his inkwell.

In the cellar separate strands of his stool wagged like dogs' tails and sang, "Oh poor little innocent guy."

They flailed like nervous S's and O's: "Little Tommy Tinker sat on a clinker. . . ."

The waste of his years floated upward in separate spirals. Barbells clanked for reparation. The mouth of the coal furnace chimed "and he began to cry, 'Ma-ah, ma-ah,' poor little innocent guy."

His child's voice had grown deeper after he swallowed the hand of the clock but he had had no song to sing. Each morning when he entered the schoolyard, the children of Hopewell Elementary serenaded him:

> "Little Tommy Tinker, sat on a clinker
> And he began to cry, 'Ma-ah, ma-ah,'
> Poor little innocent guy."

Everything he sang in those days was converted to ridicule by the children. The more established songs of harmony he, himself, had subverted with his farts. He had looked forward to a time when he would speak openly and often. He did not know what he would talk about. Perhaps the victims of the Cisco Kid.

The tails of the dogs flapping in his head rested only when he remembered the birth of television and the dozens of victims it had acquainted him with. When Gorm was eleven his father took up with a new woman and this gave him the opportunity to study and imitate a new genre of fall guys. He had spent hours on the couch curled in rapt numbness watching hoods, cops, loose women, Indians, cowboys, and Mexicans take precarious pratfalls in an effort to simulate death. Gorm smiled wistfully at the justice the most gaudily decorated of the cowboy heroes meted out to crooks but he openly sided with the victimized crooks. They were the ones who were chased, shot at, and pitched face forward from speeding mustangs. During commercials Gorm rolled recklessly from the couch, the odor of hot metal rising from his gut, hitting the floor with abandon for two months until one night he cracked his seventh rib on the left side.

Fortunately a note from Charles Atlas arrived:

"Can't quite get your shit together? Try mirrors. Brochure enclosed. Ten-day trial. Not happy, your money back. For best effect use Bud Blossom Body Oil."

Two weeks later, lathered from head to foot with the mixture of baby oil and suntan lotion, wearing only his Charles Atlas genital supporter, Gorm strutted like a peacock among three mirrors. These were stationed strategically: one against the coal furnace, a second by the laundry tub, the last positioned against the coalroom door. In this way, no matter where he looked he would never loose sight of himself. Between exercises, he flexed. Some days he was more fatigued from strutting and flexing than from hoisting barbells. He chalked this up to inexperience and flexed every chance he got in order to increase his stamina for flexing.

At school he kept a careful eye for shiny desktops where he could at least admire the heft and bulge of his pronator. A seat near a window proved best for gauging the growth of his bicepses. Even during writing exercises Gorm maintained a rigid left arm, propping it against his chin, peeping between sentences at the reflected biceps. Teachers thought he was daydreaming as usual. They did not notice his biceps.

A certain mixture of suspicion and admiration developed among girls toward Gorm. Although they were ready to acknowledge to themselves the tremor his new definition sent through their tums, the intensity with which he stared at them made them grow fearful. Before the morning bell rang and during class changes, they sensed him peering at them out of the corner of his eye. They, themselves, were developing their own definitions, faint demarcations outlining mammarial nubs, they tried to subvert with gleaming love lockets. They suspected Gorm of yearning for their budding teats. The voraciousness of his glances caused them to raise a hand to their clefts to shield themselves from the pinprick of his narrowing eyes.

Had they ever made their accusations public, Gorm would have been shocked. He had not an iota of interest in anyone's pectorals which were inferior to his own. No, Gorm sought out girls wearing V-neck sweaters and low-cut blouses for the reflection of their lockets. It was himself he searched for in those cheap imitations of love's jewelry, the clean swell of his own neckline, his sternomastoid ripe in a reflection so close to the hearts that had always ignored him.

His glances for a clean miniature of himself met failure. Word of his mammarial eavesdropping spread and when girls couldn't avoid him altogether, they took to clutching a purse or books over their clefts till his footsteps were a dim echo along the hallway.

Away from home, Gorm was forced to search out larger and more original surfaces to gauge his latest progress. He cocked his head this way and that in front of Happy Days Bakery. On sunny days, Hopewell's shoppers could observe a young man positioning himself in profile before the window of the Crest shoe store. When Gorm felt he was attracting too much attention before shop windows, he crossed and recrossed streets, studying the grills of cars. Big cars were better than little cars for observing his sternomastoid. Buicks were his favorite.

Only Charles Atlas's mirrors could grant him the true measure of his progress. Under the stark light from the single bulb above the laundry tub, he observed himself in three mirrors, his proportions made svelte by Bud Blossom Body Oil. He gleamed and stank like a rotting fish but for the first time the name *Gorm* had meaning for him. He took to addressing himself in the third person in front of the mirror.

"Show the folk your pectoralis minor, *Gorm.*"

And Gorm, with his chin tilted upright, eyes righteous with Promethean purpose, would make those strips of muscle just outside his sternum bulge, ripple, relax before he gave the folk a glimpse of his vastus internus.

A name so pregnant with association as *vastus internus* Gorm had once assumed must refer to his heart, stomach, possibly his vast, soggy intestines. No, it was that prominent bulge of muscle just above and to the inside of his kneecap, itself a landfill of scars garnered from crawling under cars to escape The Boys.

When Gorm became bored with a front view of himself he had

only to peek over his shoulder to spy a rear view: the neat meld of his calves with his knee joints, the double V's within a V of squat-thrusting thighs, power packed even in his ass—the twin ripe pears of gluteus maximus held to position by the two elastic straps of his athletic supporter. "Ahhh," said Gorm. "Ahhhhhh," echoed his obliquus group planed as if by a sculptor, the base of the torso V, framing the first major muscle group, the knotty spinalis. It was the Latin sound of "obliquus," however, which captivated the boy. "Obliquus" had the resonance of cast-iron seasoned skillets. Dense, impregnable, it clung to the tongue like slowly hardening glue, "Oooobleek—uus . . . O—bleak-us. . . ." Gorm was disappointed it didn't identify a more prominent set of muscles, a proper advertisement for bunches of power. Instead they sleeked deftly downward, a thin membranal girdle to cover his kidneys, gall bladder, liver.

Nothing was named as it should be. "Heart" was too hard. "Brain" sounded like "rain," like pebbles pinging in a tin pan. What should have had consistency didn't. What was palpable bore the linguistic texture of brick. Whoever had named things had little sensitivity to the body. It was an instrument for ulterior ends, a digestive tract with appendages capable of fortifying embattlements. An English-speaking person was doomed to approach his skin, muscles, organs, nerves, bones with foreboding. Not his latissimus dorsi nor the mammouth molding of his trapezius. His up-curving deltoids had the ring of a vague nasal disease. The straightline edges of his sternomastoid likewise had a medicinal sound like an overheated chancre ripe for surgery.

Rearview, frontal gloss portrait reflected in the mirror leaning against the extinct coal furnace, Gorm was only pleased when he had taken in the whole of his development and recited his own name aloud.

"Gorm.

"Gormmm.

"Gorm has form.

"No harm will come to Gorm. Gormmmm. . . . has weathered a storm. His name is Gormmmm.

"Ahhhhhhhhh . . . Gormmmmmmmmmmmmmmmm. . . ."

That night at dinner, Mr. Gorm asked his son if he were in pain.

"Ahhh . . . Gormmm," the boy answered.

"What kind of an answer is that?" his father said.

It was Friday. The eyes of three fried perch stared from a pool of Crisco in the aluminum skillet.

Gorm turned from the kitchen table, took the skillet from the stove, and bent it in half. The three fish fell on the floor. Gorm, the son, did not pick them up.

For all his obsession with his muscle development as revealed in the Charles Atlas mirrors, Gorm did not neglect his search for the ball bearing. He was not so fastidious as in former days. Still, each morning after his alarm went off, he took his bowel movement, scooped from the shiny porcelain bowl with cupped hands of tribute, and carried it to the cellar to be deposited in the coal furnace to harden to a coprolite by late afternoon. He did all this before his father awoke.

Mr. Gorm was proud of his son's new habit of going to bed early and rising early. With each presunrise gurgle of mock flush, he thought to himself, "Early to bed and early to rise makes a poor man wise." He listened for the clank and rattle of barbell collars but heard only the stealthy grating of the furnace door.

"Maybe he's dismantling the furnace," the father thought. "Never mind. In a year I'll get him a job in the foundry. Then let him test his pretty muscles in real work."

Instead of cutting his shit fine, as he had in more compulsive days, Gorm hastily poked at it with the end of a poker, extinct like so many other things in the old house. The poker hung from a nail in the rafters. If the cleavage wasn't so thorough, the poker at least got the job done in a hurry. Daily, coprolites disintegrated to its touch leaving a fine powder like the residue of moths on the cellar floor. Gorm swept these remains into a dustpan and tossed them back into the furnace as if he expected them to be recycled back into something useful. There was no sign of the ball bearing.

Only on rare occasions did the other dog flap its tail. This happened when Gorm was near the end of a workout, about to embark on his curls, fatigued, the single bulb casting his shadow bigger than his actual self across the cellar floor. Gorm having finished with the coal-room minute examinations of his poop, this dog sang no connecting melody nor flapped its tail to a distinct rhythm. Instead it barked in short bursts as disconnected as the objects schoolkids had once bounced off the back of Gorm's head.

"Gorm stinks," sang the happy revived gradeschool eyes.

Spitballs affirmed their consensus . . . so did erasers, rubber and chalk coated . . . unwanted sandwiches, fried chicken livers on rye with mayo were the favorite . . . on rainy Mondays there was always the chance of an entire textbook, *Our Neighbors North and South*, hitting him in the back of the head, driving his upper torso forward. Eyes six inches from his inkwell, Gorm saw a proud Indian thumping his bare chest on a pinto pony on the dirt-crusted page in the aisle. . . . "Now what is going on here? You again, Gorm? Go to the cloakroom! Do not pass Go! Do not stop at the Reading Railroad! Go directly to the cloakroom!" The children thought Mrs. Dieffenbacher a wit. They applauded her authority to the rhythm of many metronomes, tick-tick-tock, tick-tock, Gorm released in the cloakroom.

Gorm had more imaginative embellishments waiting for him. His junior high friends practiced their penmanship on love notes to the most homely girls in the class. They signed them, "Gorm." "I sigh for you, tragikly, Gorm of the funny smell." "I think of your pretty, pretty, curls during my number 2. Gorm with the runs." "Your sky-blue eyes even behind your Coke-bottle lenses leave me longing. Gorm, the lover."

One day Gorm's intimidators picked on the wrong girl. They sent a love note, on his behalf, to Dorothea Millikan, the fire-chief's daughter. "I want to ask you to the Halloween Sockhop," the note began. "The trouble is you're taller than me and I don't want people to see me taking a girl bigger than me to a dance. Once we're inside, in the dark gymnasium, it will be okay. Then you can stoop, lay your sweet head on my shoulder and no one will know the difference. I'll whisper sweet nothings, blow in your ear till your glasses steam up. To get us there and get us back home, I wonder if you could ask your father, the famous fire chief, to drive us in his big hook and ladder. You could hunch down in the middle. I would sit tall and proud in the shotgun seat. Even better your father could sound the siren and blink the lights. That way everyone would think we were on the way to fight a fire. We'd go fast around corners and I would hold you tight on the way to the untrue fire. At the end of the sockhop, I would like your father, the famous fire chief, waiting outside the gym for us with his engine running. I hope this is not too much to ask of your busy father.

With hope in my hose,
Gorm the Magnificent"

The letter was one of three Gorm had to deliver that day, his seventh that week, and he thought nothing more about it. In the past, girls' reactions to "his" letters had varied immensely. For some reason the chubbier girls took the joke in stride. Sometimes they would turn in their seats and blow kisses and wink at Gorm and the entire study hall would break up in laughter. Other times they would erase her name, write in the name of a classmate about to ascend to the level of "popular," a girl who had something to lose by being associated with Gorm or even connected with a prank from the Hopewell Junior High rowdies. These nearly popular girls invariably became angry. They glared fiercely at Gorm, to the immense delight of the boys at the back of the room. It was the skinny girls who took these bogus letters the hardest. On more than one occasion an exceedingly bony girl, flush with zits, and dismally lonely, praying that someone *would* ask her to the Halloween Sock Hop, had broken into tears and lain with her head buried in her arms till the bell rang and her eyes emerged reddened and hopeless. These displays of emotion excited more hilarity than any other reaction.

Gorm was seated before a bowl of noodles when he heard the clanking, rumbling sound of the fire engine as it rounded Orchard Alley and came to an abrupt stop in front of his house. He paid it no attention. His war with his bowels made him dream a great deal and he was slow to get the connection between sounds and sights. A moment later there was a knock at the door and when Gorm finally looked up he saw the fire chief.

The fire chief was a large, ruddy man, and perhaps to demonstrate the authority of his position he'd worn his complete regalia: knee-length boots, yellow asbestos raincoat, red fire chief's helmet. Fearful of all authority, particularly those who wore uniforms, Gorm hid under the dining-room table. He could see in the doorway the massive boots that tramped through rubble and smoke to rescue the old, the helpless, the overcome.

"What's the meaning of this insult to me and my daughter?" the fire chief yelled and waved the bogus letter in front of Mr. Gorm's nose. Having heard the resonant rumble of the hook and ladder, the neighbors had gathered at the bottom of the steps. The fire chief turned his head while addressing Mr. Gorm so that his remarks wouldn't be lost on the crowd.

Mr. Gorm tried to read the letter. As he did so, the fire chief berated him.

"I've worked all my life to get where I'm at. My position is a responsible one. I will not have it made a joke."

Mr. Gorm had got as far as the part about the steaming glasses and was mumbling the contents aloud.

"Only last year I braved falling plaster when the A&P caught fire. I carried the cash register out the back way through the meat department without the aid of a mask."

" . . . and I would hold you tight on the way to the untrue fire."

At the foot of the steps, the crowd nodded and murmured in consensus. Fires were a serious business. The Firechief's was a responsible position.

Clutching her father's hand, homely Dorothea wept large tears which she wiped on her father's asbestos sleeve.

". . . with his engine running."

"My Dorthea doesn't have a mother," the fire chief announced. "The Big C got her three years ago." After he'd blessed himself, he continued. "If something should happen to me during a fire, who would look after her? She has only 20/100 vision in her eyes."

"Outrageous!" someone in the crowd yelled.

"The poor girl. I knew that Gorm kid would come to no good," said Mrs. Chidester. "Always sneaking up and down alleys getting in people's junk."

"And relieving himself," someone muttered. The crowd laughed.

Dorothea's tears had subsided for the moment.

"He molests me during our lunch break," she cried.

"What!" yelled the fire chief.

The crowd tensed.

"He squeezes up to me and makes me give him the edge around my bologna sandwich," she lied.

The fire chief became very theatrical when he heard this. "Ahh," he cried clutching at his chief's badge which was pinned over his heart.

"Stealing the motherless girl's lunch!" said Mrs. McKivitz. Her lugubrious tone spread throughout the crowd. Someone said Gorm should be sent to a home for juvenile delinquents.

Dorthea broke into convulsive sobs.

"He . . . he . . . he gives . . . gives . . . me . . . me strange looks," and again she lurched at her father's asbestos sleeve.

" 'With hope in my hose, Gorm the magnificent,' " Gorm's father read aloud.

"I'll give him 'hope' in his hose," Mr. Gorm shouted.

"Where are you?" he bellowed.

He stood framed in the doorway, the love note held high over his head. Gorm could not see the veins throbbing in his forehead, only the ominous bulge of the toes of his steel-toed work shoes poised like weapons on the home hearth.

Just then someone reminded the fire chief his engine was still running.

"From my own experience, Mr Gorm, I would say he's hiding under something," said Mrs. McKivitz. "Like I say, it's from my own experience which is a great deal considerin' the way that no-good husband of mine used to sneak out but if youse was to ask me I'd say, 'Look down low.' That's the way them snakes do it."

"Copperheads," someone said.

A number of the neighbors had advanced to the doorway to help with the search.

Years later Gorm would remember the scene like a group portrait: his father down on one knee, hand horizontal across his forehead like a visor; the Millikan girl, whom he'd never spoken to in his life, on her knees in an identical manner, scanning too for the deviant. Behind them, bent at the waist, stood Mrs. McKivitz and Mrs. Chidester peering. Each face wore self-righteous vigilance. The portrait was complete when the fire chief, returning from his engine, thrust his helmeted head between his daughter and Mr. Gorm. It was Cat and Mouse all over again. Gorm prayed to Jesus, Clark Kent, and Buck Rodgers that he could turn into a mouse, a small enough one to hide behind a chair leg or scoot under the china closet.

The picture grew as if no one wanted to be left out of this community portrait. First one neighbor . . . a head . . . then the ubiquitous forefinger . . . another neighbor in bright kerchief, purposeful eyes . . . a third, a fourth neighbor . . . the houses were bunched closely . . . only two blocks away and you had 136 neighbors. The doorway at last filled . . . a dozen fingers aimed like revolver barrels . . . Mr. Gardner's straw hat wiggling for position . . . silence through the large house . . . silence silenced in Gorm's usually gurgling entrails. "HOLD IT!" cries the cameraman. "POP" went the flashbulb. Dorothea Millikan was the first to spot him, curled mouselike, his nose quivering in dusters, behind a leg of the dining room table.

Gorm's punishment was an apology before Dorothea and her father and the assembled neighbors. He promised never again to make fun of the fire chief or the fire chief's daughter. Furthermore, he promised not to give her shifty glances or mooch her lunch. Gorm recited what his father said to say but his recitation wasn't convincing. Years of humiliation had dimmed in him not only the hope of justice but the ability to fake repentance when it would do him the most good. He did not ask his father to question the signature of the letter. The tenor of his apology was remote, mechanical, the same tone he used for all social discourse whether it be a recitation of Tennyson's "Flower in a crannied wall" or a "Phillips screwdriver for my father" from the hardware store.

The crowd booed his apology.

His father shook his head.

"No humiliation at all. Dorothea, what else would you like my son to do for you?"

"Carry my books home from school," she said with glee.

The fire chief nodded in agreement.

The crowd went home disappointed. What kind of retribution was lugging a few books after school? "Sounds like courtship to me," said Mrs. McKivitz and she went to her house to see if her husband had skipped out during all the commotion.

Each day afterward, an oddly aligned couple could be observed climbing Teeterman Hill near the Monongahela River where Gorm had first studied the shapes of smoke so many years before. A tall girl with pigtails and a pronounced stoop took lurching strides. She wore thick glasses and appeared to be studying the ground for lost coins. Behind her, a boy, a head smaller than her, moved like a dutiful pack mule. From each of his shoulders hung a bookbag. One bookbag though must have been heavier than the other because his left shoulder tilted lower than his right one. He took grudging steps behind the girl and some days no steps at all. Even when this happened, the girl lurched up the hill ahead of him in her meaningful myopic stride.

She would arrive near the top before she remembered she had forgotten something. Then, with her hand tilted like a visor, she would spy her helper standing at the bottom. He was studying billows of smoke high over the Monongahela but she did not know that. She charged back down the hill, her mouth working in a furious rehearsal of how she would berate him. By the time she arrived at the bottom she could think of nothing to say. She merely snatched him by the hand, jerking him so hard the bookbag's straps lassoed his neck and nearly strangled him. And up the hill he climbed after her.

And on some days, a large vehicle with a clanking and rumbling in its engine would pass them. This was the Hopewell Hook & Ladder No. 1 engine and the chief wearing his red helmet drove it. He smiled as he passed the oddly aligned couple. He waved too, and blasted the firetruck's oogah-oogah horn which he had installed himself. His daughter waved back but the little fella behind her maintained his eyes dutifully on the heels of the fire chief's daughter.

When they arrived at her house, she would ask him if he would like to come inside to have some milk and cookies and inspect some of the fire chief's equipment which he kept in his top drawer under his nylon stretch socks. Gorm could not imagine what piece of fire fighting equipment her father would keep under his socks. He told the girl he never ate sweets.

This routine went on for one week. One afternoon while he was waiting by the fire escape of Hopewell Junior High to carry out his punishment, Tiny Baumgardner showed up. Tiny was the son of Earl Baumgardner, the undertaker, and Gorm's stand-in for spitballs, erasers, whatever the market was serving up that day, whenever Gorm was absent. He said he'd come to walk the fire chief's daughter home.

Gorm thanked him and went to wait in the brush along the route they would have to take to her house. He had no idea why he wanted to spy on a girl he had no feeling for. It simply seemed natural to lie low, to watch, to listen, to gauge the caliber of other people's intimacies. It was like watching a movie except it was really happening. Gorm was hungry for secrets.

In a short time Dorothea Millikan and her new beau Tiny Baumgardner came along. From his position low in a clump of ragweed, Gorm observed Baumgardner carrying out his, Gorm's, own functions. He carried two bookbags and walked, his left shoulder dipped lower than his right one, behind the fire chief's daughter. Each time he tried to catch up with her, she lurched forward in her myopic style.

Gorm was amazed how interchangeable his and Tiny's roles were. Any boy would have performed in roughly the same way, with Dorothea offering the same responses. Tiny played out Gorm's role on days when the latter boy missed school. When Gorm's father took a day off from the Union Switch & Signal, his replacement would stand before the lathe grinding ball bearings in the same way his father had and make chatter to those around him, in the same way his father had. Gorm was only 12 but already it seemed to him that punishment was meted out to those who couldn't or wouldn't talk and perform pretty much as their predecessors had.

Tiny and the fire chief's daughter had struck up a conversation.

"What's up with you these days, Tiny?"

"Not much," said Tiny, "What's up with you?"

"Not too much. Anyway, I asked you first what's up with you?"

Tiny Baumgardner said his family had eaten a lamb roast the night before. He asked Dorothea what she had had for supper.

"Chops," she said.

They were growing closer together, their steps slowing with each new burst of information. Less than three feet from Gorm, they stopped altogether.

"Darn, this is heavy. What do you have in this bag, bricks?"

"I study a lot," said Dorothea.

"I'll bet."

When Tiny reached for the buckle on the bookbag, Gorm heard the fire chief's daughter shriek.

"Ha! Caught!" cried her wooer.

From his lowly position Gorm could not see what his replacement had discovered. The unadulterated sameness of life was just beginning to oppress him when the evidence, which had weighed him down for an entire week, had made him falter and sweat, arrived in abrupt crashes a few feet from his skull. First one brick, then two. Each elated cry by Tiny Baumgardner brought the lady's bogus cargo closer and closer to his head and Gorm wanted to jump up and yell, "That's mine, all mine. I carried it for a whole week and it belongs to me," but he did not know whether he meant the bricks or the fire chief's homely daughter or both and he would have jumped up if he hadn't ascertained that with his luck he would have got hit in the face with a brick. They were yellow bricks and Gorm recognized them immediately from the stack piled outside the A&P for its new addition.

From his hiding place, he observed Tiny Baumgardner reverse roles with the devious Dorothea. He grabbed the giggling girl, draped both bookbags around her neck and bade her follow him up Teeterman Hill which she took lurching and laughing and pleased with her catch till the Halloween Sock Hop when her father, the famous fire chief, drove them to the dance in the Borough squad car. When the dance ended he was waiting for them with the engine running.

The "Sandkicker Brochure" advised Gorm to lift for both bulk and definition. He did so, neglecting nothing, even improvising exercises for those muscle groups not quite up to snuff. For example, during bent rows where the barbell is raised from ground level to the chest while maintaining a bent position, Gorm swung it in a circular rotation just above the ground to strengthen all the muscles around his spinal column. He called out "Gorm Gor-rrmmm" like a drowning man going under in a whirlpool. Then he ran to a mirror to see if there were any new ripples up his backside.

It was an exhilarating time for the young man partly because everyone else to a smaller degree saw what Gorm saw. His development was spectacularly obvious because he wore the clothes of a skinny 118 pound weakling as depicted on the matchbook cover, receiving a kick of sand in his kisser. All his parts bulged in these old chinos, V-neck sweaters, wash n' wear shirts with neutral brown and cream blocks. His father offered to buy him a new set of clothes but Gorm said he preferred to keep what he had. This was not vanity, a desire to appear in a permanent condition of flex, though this might have appealed to Gorm, but rather an obstinate refusal to give up what he thought of as properly his. So the clothes threatening to burst at the stitches remained on his back and hips much as the coprolites took up permanent residence in the extinct coal furnace, metal junk sank intact with the steadily disintegrating coal pile, and one social downfall after another clamored for room in his memory bank.

He thought of these as investments against a day when he would collect a windfall like a man who buys stock at a reduced rate in a near bankrupt company, waiting for the time when it finally shows on the "preferred" list on the Big Board and he can cash in and take a vacation. Now that he had prominent muscles he did not know what to do with them except display them, but as yet no one had asked him to take off his shirt.

To display himself without his shirt soon became an obsession almost as strong as finding the ball bearing in one of his stools. Flexing between sets now had a purpose. From exuberant doses of Bud Blossom Body Oil his skin had taken on a glow. His new muscle tone had the sheen of a light-colored copper pipe. Beyond his mirrored applause for himself—daily recitations of muscle groups in Latin, his name sounded over and over—somewhere out in Hopewell there was an audience waiting to see him naked, or almost naked . . . waiting to see his separate muscle groups . . . grow . . . pop . . . stagger gravity in brown sugar-coated little lumps . . . "You out there in the third row . . . yes, you . . . the lady with the wooden cherries on top of your hat . . . yes, you . . ." In the meantime, Gorm had to settle for cautious glances at clothed Gorm at Hopewell High. Even in the cafeteria he sat alone, nibbling an apple . . . a peach . . . staring at the outline of his forearm in the polished Formica.

It came as a mild surprise to him that now that he possessed power he had little desire to use it on his former tormentors. It was enough that they saw. The skull slappers, spitball marksmen, love letter scribes, hoaxers par excellence. The bullies, the playground instigators, the blackboard artists, the homely, verbally hamstrung girls waiting for a Gorm to get slapped so they could retrieve their wits. They saw. Ahhh . . . and the teachers saw, too. The teachers—chronically intimidated, the perpetual run-at-the-mouths, the congenial hound dogs after trench and BAR nostalgia; kindly, posey-ridden marms in orthopedic shoes—they saw.

When Gorm said, "I do not wish to take part in a recitation of *Julius Caesar*," Miss Bromfield did not insist.

"You can make it up on the multiple choice? Okay?"

"As you wish."

His language became as formalized as his bicepses.

And they heard.

Since he had never belonged to any group except The Boys with their monosyllabic grunts punctuating vast silences, he had no other language but that of his rippling trapezius, deltoids, pecs, vastus internus, and pronator.

And they saw.

Even while eating an apple, Gorm flexed the biceps of his grasping limb.

Everywhere he went, students and teachers made a wide path for him as if a steel curtain preceded him down the winding institutional hallways. He looked straight ahead, not focusing on anything in front of him. His eyes were aimed inward, toward his esophagus and downward where teeny phagocytes might be bearing his ball bearing along his caecum, ascending colon . . . upward and onward to the final drop . . . his transverse colon, descending colon, sigmoid, rectum. Ah obliging anal rectum, fastidious pucker, all, harvesting bumgut, spewing his luck charm into the open air again. Cocoon of his lost childhood, concealing only more metal.

As Gorm's coils healed, he farted openly and often. But silently . . . vague whispers from another world he knew to be shameful. Some days his chinos bulleted with sharp gusts. If the students of Hopewell steered shy of his methane and its hydrogen disulphides, carbonic gases, thousands of assorted forms of putrefaction and fermentation wafted or shot over clinical desk tops . . . mixtures of ammonia and methane, phenol, cresol, indole, skatole . . . gases as varied as the individual particles of the human race but concealed and categorized under the single word "Fart." Gorm did not know if the waves of classmates parted daily for his muscles or for his farts. In strength as in weakness he had gormed himself into a corner. He was chronically *on* and on display but as isolated as the strongman in a freak show.

He lifted barbells and waited.

One afternoon Gorm's father upon returning home from the Union Switch & Signal descended to the cellar and called the boy aside.

"Your development has been totally unexpected," he said.

"I know," said Gorm.

"You're growing in leaps and bounds."

"That's true."

Both of them felt the artificiality in the air.

Gorm's father stared at his feet, Gorm at his barbell collars.

"I wanted to ask you a favor. It would be for both of us."

"Sure," said Gorm.

"It happened in a funny way," Mr. Gorm began. "I ran into your Aunt Lydia and Aunt Alvena by the meat counter at the A&P yesterday. I was telling them about you."

Gorm sat on the bench-press bench. He could see one of his calves in the laundry-tub mirror.

"Oh I know they're your mother's sisters but what the hell. Water under the dam is water under the dam I always say. Let bygones be bygones. What say?"

"Yeah," said Gorm.

"I mean I told them about your muscles. 'You should see him,' I said. 'Muscles on top of muscles. A body you wouldn't believe. Did it all himself.' I said that. 'No weakling that kid.' I really laid it on."

"You shouldn't have done that, Dad."

"I know. They only come around at Christmas. They don't even take off their coats. I'm sorry. I couldn't help it."

"Is there something I can do?" Gorm asked.

"They want to see for themselves. Don't get me wrong. It's not that they doubt. They just said, 'We'd like to see this powerful son of yours doing his act.' "

"I said, 'Well, I'm sure he'd like to see you but the cellar's his. He hardly wears anything when he lifts. It's very personal down there.' And they said, I mean you know women, they said, 'Does he still have cute dimples?' 'He's got dimples everywhere,' I said and they laughed and now they want an appointment to see your dimples."

In two of the three mirrors Gorm could see both his own calves and his father's Iron City work shoes shuffling and poking at the concrete.

"Maybe if they could just have a peek. They're always good for a check. 'What if he goes to college?' I said to myself by the meat counter."

"I don't wanna go to college."

"Okay! Then think of the house. It's not what it used to be. A couple of hundred bucks would buy us a set of storm windows."

"Okay, pop, I'll do it."

"Gee, thanks . . . and one more thing. . . ."

Gorm turned his head from the mirrors to see his father nodding down at the muscular swell of gluteus maximus which bulged beneath his supporter over the edge of the bench.

"Of course, Pop, I'll wear shorts."

"Thanks, kid.

On the day of Gorm's presentation of his muscle groups to his aunts, he wore boxer shorts over his supporter and a hernia belt. He was willing to snatch and jerk massive weights above his head but he hoped the women would settle for some poses. Gorm could hardly contain his excitement that someone would finally see the development of his near-naked self.

Aunts Lydia and Alvena arrived just before dinner with hearty how-do's. They caroled repeated greetings at his father like a pair of brass bells summoning worshipers to high mass. From his bench-press bench Gorm heard them bestow cheerful admiration on the furniture, the wallpaper, and the living-room rug with its fading Chinese mandarins. They started to compliment the old Stewart-Warner refrigerator but Gorm's father bolted ahead of them down the steps and into the cellar. A vapid trail of Evening in Paris perfume and Cutty Sark followed their descent.

As a boy, Gorm had been embraced by them to the clack of pearls, the flash of diamond earrings dancing to the light of the overhead chandelier, the brief metallic jingle of bracelets as their arms encircled him and their lips planted dry kisses on his dutiful cheek. Today they merely extended a gloved hand which Gorm took gingerly, careful not to overdo his newfound grip.

"Well, here he is," said Gorm's father.

"Yes, here he is," said Aunt Lydia.

"My, doesn't time pass," said Aunt Alvena.

"And how," said Aunt Lydia.

The latter tapped her toe while Aunt Alvena circled the bench. "Yesterday he was skinny as a pencil. Now look at him."

Gorm felt his trapezius tighten. He felt as if he were a refurbished nightstand on sale in the bargain basement of Kresge's. Two women, whose husbands he knew made large profits on

sheet metal, had wandered in by mistake and dared not get too
close to the merchandise. Still, they could not make themselves
leave. A sudden spasm fluttered Gorm's right deltoid.

"Look!" cried Alvena, "One of his muscles is moving all by
itself."

Aunt Lydia chuckled and applauded with gloved hands. She
said she had observed strong men in the circus but their muscles
had never done that.

Gorm's father stood behind them smiling proudly.

"What do you call that muscle that's moving by itself?" asked
Aunt Lydia.

"Dummy, that's his shoulder," answered Alvena.

"Delts!" snapped Gorm.

"Delts," echoed the two aunts.

Gorm's father excused himself to put the oven on preheat for
their TV dinners. Gorm told him he would settle for a vitamin
pill and a tangerine. The spasmodic right deltoid came to rest.

When Mr. Gorm had gone, the two aunts sighed.

"Long time no see," said Alvena.

"That's true," said Gorm.

The two women glanced around the cellar as if they suspected
a fourth party to be hiding thereabouts. Aunt Lydia's nostrils
quivered slightly.

"Can you make any of your other muscles wiggle by itself like
your geld did?" asked Aunt Alvena.

"Delt!" the boy corrected.

"Oh yes, delt."

"Don't ask him that," said Lydia, "He's liable to embarrass
you."

The two women chuckled at the double entendre. Gorm was
puzzled at what they were laughing at.

He crooked his left arm so its biceps displayed all its tension. A
bulge the size of a handball bobbed slightly.

"That's not fair," said Aunt Lydia, "You're working it yourself.
You're making a muscle. Let it jiggle by itself."

Gorm dropped his arm.

And nothing happened. Every muscle came to rest.

The two women resumed circling him as if they were stalking
the value of a young Thoroughbred they might add to their
stable.

"Would you like to see me pose?"

"No, you're fine where you are."

"That way you would see all of me. A body builder's body
can't really be appreciated till you've seen it in one of its poses.

That's when all the muscles work together."

They were at his back though he could observe their bemused expressions in the coal furnace mirror.

"You look fine the way you are," said Lydia.

"Only yesterday he was so skinny."

"Slender," said Lydia.

"That's the word . . . slender."

"And now look at him."

Gorm was longing to perform for his aunts but a curious thing was happening. With each of their circling appraisals, the circumference between him and his aunts widened.

"How did you get into this sort of thing?" asked Aunt Lydia. She leaned against the laundry tub.

"It's hard to explain," said Gorm, "It kind of came up in a wind."

"Life happens like that," vouched Aunt Alvena.

"What I'd like to know," said Lydia, "is what are you going to do with it? I mean . . . what the hell . . . all these months . . . lifting and what not . . . getting your body hard for the big push . . . you're going to be graduating soon. What happens then?"

"The movies," volunteered Alvena, "He could do like Victor Mature did in *Samson and Delilah*. He tore down the temple."

"He'd have to have elocution lessons," snapped Lydia.

Alvena said he should get started with some modeling.

Aunt Lydia said he was too muscular. For that kind of work you had to have an all-purpose look, not too fat, not too thin, not too weak, not too strong. Selling, she said, was the art of offering everybody a little bit of something. Besides, most models were fags.

"Lydia!" cried Aunt Alvena.

Then to Gorm, "Don't mind her; we've been nipping between stores."

"Well it's true. Remember the nice young man we met in 'The Tender Trap' who said he handled the wash 'n wear at Penney's. I saw him the other day when I was walking Daisy in the park. He had his arm around a cute little boy not as old as this one." She pointed toward Gorm. " 'What a waste,' I said to myself, 'What a waste.' Didn't even let on he knew me and I certainly wasn't going to be the one to say something."

"You did right," Aunt Alvena advised her partner.

"I did the only thing I could," the latter woman snapped back.

Aunt Alvena said they still hadn't settled on Gorm's career. Maybe Barnum & Bailey was the answer.

Lydia advised that Bailey was dead. It was just Barnum now. In any case Gorm would need an act. When you got to the big time, she said, lots of men had firm bodies.

"He could work something up at firemen's carnivals," said Alvena. "They always have a strong man. You know, the kind who roam the country during the summer. I remember one as a child."

"That was the old days," Lydia fired back. "Now it's the big time or nothin'. That means TV."

"You hear that young man," Aunt Alvena cautioned her nephew, "You'd better get your act together."

"And he'd better do it quick. I put a roast in the oven at three-thirty and it's quarter to six."

On the bench-press bench Gorm stared down at his shadow, large and sprawling on the concrete floor like the spread of a stingray he'd once seen on "Undersea Adventures." It was divided by the bench.

"Which one of you would like to touch me?" he asked his aunts.

"Listen," said Aunt Lydia, "if you want a future—sheet metal. Of course, your father's in a derivative and ball bearings aren't bad either. But if you want to zero in on the action, take it from me, SHEET METAL."

"Plastics won't last forever," added Aunt Alvena, "Anyway we've got more iron ore than oil. That's what George says."

"You've got a point," said her partner. "Bog & Bliss was up two points on the Big Board last week. All the big boys in petroleum were down at least three-quarters."

"Who'd like to touch me?" Gorm repeated.

Both the women had their butts braced against the laundry tub. They were tall and blocked the light from the single naked bulb which hung over the tub. They appeared to Gorm as silhouettes.

"You go first," Lydia said to Alvena. "Naked men give me the willies."

"I'm not naked," Gorm said.

"After all, he *is* one of the family," said Aunt Alvena.

"That's right. I'm your nephew. Get over here and touch me."

"There's a funny smell in here," said Aunt Lydia.

She worked her nostrils with exaggerated quiffiness.

Aunt Alvena agreed. She said she noticed it when they first came in but she hadn't wanted to say anything.

"Who's going to be first?" Gorm asked them.

Both women worked their nostrils like veteran hound dogs.

"You go first," said Aunt Alvena to Aunt Lydia.

"Bullshit! I paid for your lunch. *You* go first."

As Aunt Alvena started forward, Gorm rose up on the bench so every muscle in his body would display itself prominently. His aunt stopped in midstride.

"What should I touch?"

Aunt Lydia smacked her stomach and cried, "Ha!"

"Anything you want," said Gorm.

"I wouldn't know where to begin. There's so much of you."

Gorm flexed his right biceps.

"You can touch this."

Aunt Alvena resumed her cautious advance.

"Christ, it stinks in here," said Lydia.

Her partner stopped and turned. She was now less than five feet from Gorm.

"I know and I can't imagine where it comes from."

Gorm's older aunt on his mother's side was less than a stride from him when his deltoid, the right one, twitched of its own volition.

"There it is again," cried Aunt Alvena pointing toward his shoulder.

Gorm clapped his left hand over it to arrest the spasm.

Aunt Lydia stepped forward from the laundry tub to get a look for herself,

"Ah haa," she cried, "don't look now but there's another one twitching."

"Where?" cried Aunt Alvena.

"Down by his knee."

Gorm dropped his right hand from its flex position and clapped it on his vastus internus. Spasms rippled his pectoral muscles. He jammed both hands on his chest. A second later the spinalis group got into the act. He threw his arms behind him. For the first time, he struck his aunts as a young man in pain.

"This is quite an act. Young man, you may not have to take elocution lessons afterall," Aunt Lydia said with considerable glee.

She was advancing from the laundry tub toward Gorm, her hand acting as a visor to zero in on this wild and original show.

Each of Gorm's carefully developed muscle groups was dancing a jig of its own accord as if trying to free itself of his bones.

"Look! Another one." Aunt Alvena pointed to his stomach.

"I've never seen anything like this in my life," said Alvena.

"Hell, our men went to flab twenty years ago. Maybe this happens all the time with men who take care of their bodies," said Lydia.

Gorm's entire body had become a series of contradictory waves. He was wrenched first one way, then another. He no longer tried to quiet the separate convulsions but embraced the bench with both hands to keep from falling on the concrete floor. A new wave of spasms broke up his pectorals and he was thrown backward onto the bench. He lay thrashing like a patient undergoing shock therapy in an asylum. His Adam's apple quaked. His own nostrils quivered.

Lydia suggested he might be suffering an epileptic fit so Alvena bent close to check. No, she said. She could see his tongue waggling behind his incisors like the rest of him.

Even Gorm's cock tried to manifest itself.

A semi-hardon, it too began to surge and flail beneath his Atlas gym shorts like the tail of a fish. Perhaps it was this that made the ladies reach for their checkbooks.

They wrote quickly, balancing their checkbooks on the thin ledge of the laundry tub, scribbling their signatures with such haste they were hardly legible. The dots over their i's hadn't dried before an ominous clatter sounded from the coal room at the far end of the cellar. This was where Gorm had stored all the junk he'd collected as a child from Hopewell's alleys on Trash Day. A vast rumbling followed this as if the room itself were being swallowed up. Alvena and Lydia slapped their checks on the washboard lying in the tub and scooted from the cellar. Gorm continued to writhe on the bench.

"What's going on down there?" Gorm's father cried and just then his two sisters-in-laws started up the cellar steps.

"We had quite a treat," they told him. "Your son put on a real show for us."

By the time Gorm's father arrived in the cellar, Gorm was able to sit upright. Some of his muscles still rippled, occasional spasms he was able to control by pulling the fetid air of the cellar into his lungs and holding it there. There were spots on his Charles Atlas gym shorts. In addition, he'd shit himself.

"Well, did they come through?"

Gorm stared down at his rippling pectorals.

"I don't see nothin,' " Mr. Gorm cried at his son reflected in one of the mirrors.

Gorm looked down at his feet. The sudden disintegration of his stools, the damp semicongealed mass at his ass had gotten to him, too. He was repelled by himself.

"Ahhh," cried his father, "Here they are."

Gorm raised his head dismally to see his father gingerly pluck two pieces of rectangular paper from inside the laundry tub. He held the checks by two fingers under the light to ascertain the amount.

"Hmmmm . . . uhh-huhh . . . yes . . . they came through . . . quite remarkable. . . ."

The ball-bearing inspector stood for some time under the light, sputtering and admiring the amount of the checks.

"Enough moola to buy forty storm windows," he advised his son.

"Better buy some toilet paper while you're at it," Gorm told his father.

"Those old bowels of yours acting up again, boy? I'll buy you toilet paper by the ream. After the performance you gave to loosen the fingers of those crows you deserve it. Where there's money there's hope, even for bad plumbing."

Then Gorm's father went upstairs to let the checks, whose edges had caught the drip of the faucet, dry by the heat registers.

With a winding sheath of dusk on the rim of the sky, Gorm baretoed it over the ruts in Mrs. McMivitz's backyard. He mounted her wire fence. Next, the Petrinos', Stevensons', Hartwicks', Casperians'. Each time he straddled a new fence along the series of interconnecting backyards shit scudded down his legs, leaving a perverse trail.

A cold March wind fanned his Charles Atlas gym shorts. Otherwise, Gorm the Weightlifter was naked.

At the final backyard bordering on the alleyway, Gorm paused to admire a boxful of ladies' hats. Along with other boxes, baskets, cans filled with newspapers, dead clocks, a broken canary, cotterpins, defunct doorknobs, burst pillows, stacked the width of the exitway to the alley, and then on top of one another to the height of Gorm's bulging pectorals, they awaited the Trash Man. Only, there was no Trash Man, not in the old sense of a specialty befitting a lone man who made it his craft.

Just as there was no longer a Rag Man nor an Umbrella Man nor a Bottle Man nor a Paper Man nor a Strawberry Man, there was no Trash Man. Gorm lifted a woman's black hat which resembled a beret and sat it on his head. An imitation-pearl hatpin stuck through its crest.

Standing cross armed and regal, as if he were already the strongest man in Hopewell, the sludge-like drippings from his rectum still running down his legs, here, at the end of Hopewell's melting pot, Gorm ascertained that had he been a child again about to embark on a career as a junk collector, he would not have had to compete with Black Jack the Trash Man. The junkman's garrulous cries at midday, "Waydown . . . hoedown . . . traaaassshhh. Trash Man's here." "Traaaassshh," had been replaced by the soft whirrr of an engine idling, then the lightning click of gears, the pistons' faultless charge down this nameless alley. All things expendable had come to be lumped under the single entity of "Refuse." The Hopewell Refuse Company gathered all refuse. Unlike the old days, Gorm seldom saw it. His neighbors set out their trash just before dark. By dawn it was gone. No time for the city's assigned vultures to choose and pick and resurrect it in the shanties of Skeetersville; no time for wandering children to pry and grow accustomed to the death of things. No time for collectors to smell the corpse of their collection's limbo. The sun rose through yesterday's auto fumes and sulfide billows from the mills to shine on the city gathering itself up like a ghost cosmeticized during the night.

Gorm knew the rear-facing mouths of the Refuse Company trucks swallowed everything which could be considered waste. What they couldn't digest, they spewed into an incinerator on the banks of the Monongahela. Bedsprings were carted away with banana peels, newspapers with coffee grounds. Bottles, broken or whole, were fed into the hydraulic mouth to be ground to its quiddity. Only a vague hieroglyph of the days when waste might be resuscitated remained in Gorm's mind. You could build a pyramid to honor a ruler but how could you erect a tribute to the various components of trash?

Gorm had wandered up and down this alley all his life yet suddenly it occurred to him it did not have a name. Names gave life but life never gave names. Or if this alley did have a name, no one had ever revealed it to him. Gorm briefly thought of calling it, "The Alley." If he could paint, he would paint this alley, "The Alley," with its asphalt winding abruptly like a corkscrew among the secrets of the city. The new housing developments did not include alleys. He would call his painting, "The Alley at Twilight." First he would make himself a twilight, then an alley. He would have them meet at the horizon. Naturally, his picture would include a garbage can. With a glee both exultant and fearful, Gorm imagined himself emerging from the garbage can, brawny, muscular, a shy smile on his face as he bored up through the mass of coffee grounds, orange peels, Tom Tucker ginger-ale bottles. "Happy Weightlifter Emerges from Garbage Can in The Alley at Twilight," he retitled his picture. Then he imagined the loneliness of the weightlifter, particularly at such an hour when all the world slid to its haunches and only the cry of a stray cat searching for dinner distinguished The Alley from the rest of Hopewell. On a neighboring garbage can he hung a few strands of a girl's hair to keep himself company. Retitled, the picture went: "Happy Weightlifter Emerges From Garbage Can at Twilight to Study Girl's Locks in The Alley."

At this stage Gorm realized his picture had grown unwieldy. How could anyone see the horizon, get the drift of an average alley in an average town on an average day if so much attention was focused on the happy weightlifter and the neighboring locks peeking out of their respective garbage cans? His perspective shot to hell, Gorm scratched the vision of The Alley.

Besides, he wasn't a painter. He was Gorm. He was naked and cold and had the runs. Also, he was suddenly dissatisfied with the name he had conferred on the nameless alley. "The Alley" sounded too much like "The Man" or "The Refuse Company," vague entities which could swallow everything.

With the giddy resonance, the intoxicating sense Latin lingo had conferred on his muscles, Gorm whispered to the night air, "Gorm's Alley." He smiled like a young man who has just propositioned a banker's daughter. And said it again . . . this time to a black, undulating wave of asphalt . . . "Gorm's Alley." Louder . . . "Gorm's Alley." He said it to the box of dishes next to the box of hats. The box of hats repeated it to some soggy newspapers tied with unfashionable neckties. Up and down the heap of throwaways, a chorus rose. The junk held hands and rocked to have a title conferred on its pathway after years of nameless formation in foundries and assembly lines . . . Gorm's Alley.

And why not! Had not he, Gorm, explored every one of its twists as a child? Then, when he'd found a new career as a scapegoat, had he not discovered every nook, concealed ledge, accessible garage roof, roofed cellarway, to conceal himself as hordes of exhilarated school chums chased after him with beanshooters, sticks, and belt buckles? Nothing exhilarated a mob more than to have someone on the run.

He knew which families tied the lids of their garbage cans, and which homes built slatted wooden foundations for their waste. Some garages housed cars; the ones along the sixth curve served as tinker sheds, their floors strewn with pine shavings. There, asphalt gave up its softening hardening softening bumps to cinders . . . cinders to mud. In the spring, wind stirred the morass of mud into folds which hardened into ruts like the backyards of his neighbors. By simply following the route of this one nameless alley, Gorm had learned the secrets of an entire city.

He had learned bathrooms in America are always concealed at

the rear of a house like the ailimentary canal in the human body.
There Gorm had observed shadowy figures squatting. He would
curl beneath some newspapers in a crack between two garages,
the ragged breathing of his pursuers soaring past, and he would
look and see this silhouette hunched above him in translucent
folds as if in meditation. Ten minutes later it was still there . . .
the only movement a flapping near the top of the window . . .
then stillness. The voices of his pursuers shredding from their
familiar coagulated screeches into broken threads of disappointment . . . "Not there, try behind that garage Hunky Joe, check
inside the garbage can . . . cowards will hide anywhere . . ." and
the shadow above him larger than life did not budge . . . except
to give the phantom sheets a turn.

In late spring, Gorm could hear through partially opened windows flaps and rattles. The phantom newspapers swelled in the
transluscent glass to gray wings. He learned the hulks holding
them, poring over them on the commode, who had previously
resembled manly, guardian presences, or a vast penumbra of
conscience, were assembly-line workers from the Union Switch
& Signal who were hiding from their wives. He knew this when
one day he heard a woman scream, "Jack, get your ass off the pot
and empty this garbage." Had Jack complied, Gorm would have
been discovered hiding as he was under week-old *Evening Herald*. Jack replied, "Little Orphan Annie's trapped in a tunnel.
Stick the garbage up your menopausal ass."

And Gorm sighed between the cracks.

If these grown, brawny men were not hiding from their wives,
then they had constipation. Gorm had observed shadows that
remained on the pot for an hour at a time. Who was in worse
shape, he, Gorm with his perpetual runs or they, the working
world of practical-livers and doers, who, clogged to the gills,
revenged their bloated guts on those closest to them? It was a
difficult choice.

If men used the bathroom to hide, Gorm discovered women
used it to manufacture a mask so they could return to the world
without fear. This process often took a half hour. Eyebrows
plucked, preened, scanned . . . nostril hairs checked . . . lips
freed from the impending menopausal moustache . . . "ahh,
there's a fat hair coming right out of my little birthmark . . . uhh,
got the bugger. . . ." Facial creams, dozens of them . . . layer
after layer . . . a fashion model blossomed . . . in the clear portion of the window where Gorm watched tired faces bob, dip,
screw up their mouths, tilt their chins . . . "not bad . . . a little
mascara here, some more rouge there . . . ho-ho, not bad for a

housewife who's scrubbed, vacuumed, washed, ironed, fed the kids while that no-good Jack drank his lunch . . . maybe I shouldn't be so afraid of that young mailman's leer. . . ."

Below . . . covered in quivering newspaper blankets. . . . Gorm grew pleasantly surprised. All that flapping jowl . . . blackheads . . . facial flesh the consistency of bread dough resurrected to an alert proximity of beauty or at least alertness. Sometimes when the window was open . . . and a woman was putting the final touches to her face, a little song trickled out. Just a refrain . . . like a thread of protozoa called up from the dead. "A Bicycle Built for Two," one woman sang. Gorm wondered if his wagon would be acceptable.

Standing in the twilight, admiring his alley, "Gorm's Alley," Gorm realized the secrets were endless and all the more secret because so few people walked the alleys anymore. No one ever bothered to pull their blinds anyway.

In the old days when he'd wandered this alley, searching for junk to revitalize, Gorm had been able to observe the private moments of men. Through kitchen or dining room windows, he had watched men meet the day in befuddled silence.

The mist rises to meet their nostrils from cups of coffee. Except for a car's engine coughing in the distance . . . whining . . . lurching . . . heaving back into abortive silence, there is quiet. In undershirts which reveal tufts of hair, they sit . . . embracing with both hands the cup of mist . . . as if all existence began and ended there.

These are the men who strike Gorm as unimpeachable at any other time. They have stern brows. They make engines go. They talk in low voices of fan belts and generators. They putter with lawnmowers and the lawnmowers putter back and give their token lawns a crewcut just like Gorm's. Stolid, eyes fixed upon what can be fixed upon, always in control, talking of what can be measured . . . gasoline mileage, batting averages, they represent a cliff Gorm never believes he can scale.

In succeeding years they look at him with amusement . . . for signs of a recent pummeling. Now standing before his, "Gorm's Alley," Gorm remembers them unconscious of the world at dawn, staring down into their mugs of coffee. One . . . two sips, they sigh and scratch. The magical masculine chest tufts first. Such hair reminds him of bedsprings. They finger to the middle, wiggle, lift a wavering finger. The index fingers are reserved for their ears and the kernels of multicolored goo Gorm digs out in private too. Chest and ears relieved of the night, they head straight for the scalp. It's a regular symphony. Dandruff falls like notes on a scale into their mugs. But no one will know. And like the revitalization of a sleepy engine, electricity returns to each part . . . absent mindedly . . . between sips. Their armpits get a thorough scratching next. They cough. . .pound their chests. . . pour caffeine into their tanks . . . burp . . . sigh . . . not yet. Let the engine linger in its half-dream limbo. Anyway, their nostrils haven't been scoured yet.

The fingers treading into the mouth of the nostril's cave is the Grand Finale of Waking Up Each Morning. Gorm observed an orchestra once and this final scouring is the drums and cymbals. It is the ultimate pronouncement to a background of violins and cellos, of sparrows chirping on the telephone wire outside the bathroom window, of French horns and trombones resounding from the distant honking of freight trucks on Monongahela Boulevard, of flutes wafting after the wind from the Ohio Valley playing in the extinct chimney flues, the bassoons snorting from a tugboat on the Monongahela River.

There is no stealth at all. As a child, Gorm watches fingers take the plunge like pneumatic jackhammers into concrete. If he were close he knows he would hear great adenoidal trumpetings. For now he must settle for eyebrows twitching, the eyes spinning in quiet plunder. Coffee has been forgotten. So has the Missus beginning to stir in the floor above. The world is very far away. So are imminent punch clocks, surly foremen, lunches to be packed yet. All that remains for the day to be born is this last remnant of the night to be disgorged.

Upward and onward, they dig like feverish forty-niners. "There's gold in them thar hills." Gorm observed one assembly-line worker of Union Switch & Signal raise his forefinger aloft with pride. Jack Moriarty, the Lathe Grinder, smiles at his booty like the trophy of the buck he brought home on his roof rack last fall. If he had his way, he would frame this prize. Such is the joy of preparing the senses for their daily work. But no one loves a booger debugged . . . inanimate as the toe of a skeleton or a piece of ore in deserted country. "So hide that nugget, Jack!" And Jack the Lathe Grinder heeds Gorm's silent cry from the alley. He hides his ragged clot of snot to dry under the kitchen table.

"More," cries Gorm.

Jack the Lathe Grinder obliges. He drives his forefinger fastidiously up . . . one knuckle disappears . . . two . . . Gorm holds his breath. Jack's nostril . . . the left one, wiggles.

At last he withdraws . . . slowly . . . savoring this moment, this solitude, seldom so forthright. Daintily, Jack proffers his booger to the single naked lightbulb overhead. "There, I'm clean." It is a peace offering to the sun, or what passes for the sun in Hopewell. The last vestiges of the dead inanimate night scoured from his intake orifice, Jack the Lathe Grinder holds the booger aloft for a long time. He smiles at it . . . turns it in three directions . . . all the better to study it . . . and wipes it under the kitchen table.

This is the same place Jack's wife hides her boogers. The kids dig their noses and clot the underside of the kitchen table too. It has been going on for years like this. Each member of the family uses the underside of the kitchen table for their nasal retreat. No one knows about the others. Jack's ma and pa previously owned the house. Unknown to little Jack, they, too, used the table for furtive wipings. It is a family tradition. His mother and father had been sneaky gold diggers too. They had wiped where their parents had wiped, and Jack wiped, and Jack's children wiped. Each in his turn had begot a sneaky wiper.

The upshot of this family tradition is there is no room for Jack the Lathe Grinder's joyous early morning booger. Gorm does not know what is wrong. He can only observe one hand disappear under the table . . . Jack's eyeballs retreat, pivot, grow incensed. A crust has built up from generations of secretly hoarded waste. Jack fumbles and probes for his little spot on the underside of the horizon. He sits upright at the kitchen table and wiggles and wiggles. What he had previously thought rough-hewn wood needing a Sears 660 electric sander, now has a familiar and more disturbing texture to it.

He dives under the table and surfaces a few seconds later. Stuck with his waste, he holds his forefinger in the air like a useless appendage. "Who's been mucking up my table?" Gorm hears Jack scream. The cough and sputter of a starting car answers him. He makes a fist of his free hand, the left one, the one unencumbered with a booger, and brings it down hammer-style on the kitchen table. Salt and pepper shakers, a sugar bowl dance . . . coffee leapes from the mug. Jack the Lathe Grinder curses a world he's sweated in . . . a house he paid for . . . with not enough room to even find a spot for his cherished booger. And still the begrimed forefinger is held out from his side, limp, only vaguely searching now.

Gorm watches the manly, muscular lathe grinder bleating in circles around the kitchen, a man about to begin his day with a crippled wing if he can't find a spot to wipe.

Gorm the child observes the day begin in quiet solitude, then joyful and freewheeling exposure of the night's dry pickings, now turned to frustration and rant. Jack the Lathe Grinder circles and recircles the table like a bottle on a conveyor belt. He curses not only his own misfortunes, which began with a table too crowded with boogers to accommodate his own booger, but lances outward with his orphaned forefinger to indict coons and wops and communists, and probes his neighbors who are too close and too many and do not deserve his own dignity.

As Jack is about to take further revenge on the kitchen table . . . one fist raised . . . his face gone red with bloated rage . . . his wife appears. In a bathrobe . . . curlered . . . moist with sleep . . . she says, "What's wrong, honey?"

How do you explain not enough space for your waste to another human being? Caught . . . with his forefinger still held like a useless talon, Jack could only wipe on his pants, look sheepish, turn his back and sputter at the wall.

Gorm then watches the lathe grinder embrace his wife. He whispers something in her ear which makes her smile and rub her curlers against his head. Jack fumbles under her bathrobe. With his foot, he reaches backward and gives the kitchen door a kick. Curled under his newspaper, Gorm sighs at such strange gropings. Another day begins in Hopewell.

Gorm's runs had run to his bulging calf muscles and hardened. He had learned secrets, forgotten them in his desperation to survive, and now remembered them in his hunger to assume control over an asphalt alley which, in its abrupt turnings, mimicked the anarchy of his own intestines. He was not even sure of the nature of the secrets he had observed in those early voyeuristic accidents born of the chase. At least he knew where his waste was—in a heap in the coal room . . . except for the ball bearing . . . and that was inside him . . . somewhere. He had not sloughed off the bearing in casual wipings . . . given it away to an anonymous refuse truck that might as well have been entitled *God, Incorporated*. He was a collector . . . not a rejector. If it had been up to him, he would have cornered all of existence, loaded it on his wagon, and ushered it to the coal room for safekeeping. But how do you hoard a space? The alley, "Gorm's Alley," was mostly space. It was soot and sulfide air and carbon monoxide between garages and backyards. The Hopewell Refuse Company had corrupted its essential give-and-take nature, relegating the parasites of trash to isolation, the official public dole, or worse, a job and respectability. Gorm shivered. It was the shiver of intoxication with his new sense of power. Had not God said, "Let there be light." Well, Gorm would say, "Let this be my alley" and having said it, it would be so. Never mind that it was almost dark. The coal room was dark. His intestines dark. His mother had fled with the sporting goods salesman into the night.

He saw it now—first a proclamation in the *Evening Herald*:

"Until further notice, there will be no more junk pickups along the alley leading from Orchard Alley to the banks of the Monongahela. This alley has recently been named 'Gorm's Alley' after the muscle builder who is slowly becoming a bigshot for his bulging lats and deltoids. Mr. Gorm named it his alley and it is his alley. He has eaten there, slept there, towed junk there, and hidden from mean boys there. Also, he has observed the citizens of that alley do things to their bodily openings that would make a monkey proud.

"On Tuesday nights Mr. Gorm will help the alley's residents sort their junk. No useables, please. On Wednesday, small boys will tow the durable junk through town on wagons. They will cry, 'For Sale, Used Junk But Good Junk. Trade-ins Accepted.' This is the wish of Gorm, your town muscle builder."

"Gorm's Alley," he said to the box of hats.

"My oh my, yes," the throwaways agreed.

As he gained power over *his* alley, Gorm knew he would have other wishes, further proclamations for the citizenry of Hopewell. It was all a matter of deciding what was yours, then claiming it.

In the distance where his new alley made its first bend before convoluting in spirals and zig-zags, Gorm spotted a small figure moving through the dusk like a specter. He could not tell if it was a man or a woman, only that it advanced in a torturous fashion. For every step forward, it took a sideways step, rotary style like a windup doll. As it got closer, Gorm saw that it carried something which made it list slightly to one side and perhaps accounted for its mechanical movement. It was a bag, a simple shopping bag. Since the alley was now his, Gorm decided to exact tribute from this cripple.

"Halt in the name of *Gorm*," he cried at the figure as it swung past him. It stopped.

"You get some clothes on, smart aleck, or I'll call the police and have you arrested for indecent exposure."

The voice of this admonition was deep-throated, hoarse, but still a woman's. Gorm advanced on her and when he could clearly make out a babushka, a Navy peacoat which hung to her knees, and a slight hump on her stooped frame, he held himself akimbo, flexing his pecs, letting this arrogant transgressor see the magnificent swell of his deltoids.

The old woman reached back over her shoulder with her free hand and patted her hump.

"I got bulges, too," she told Gorm.

The cripple's arrogance infuriated Gorm. He did not like the idea that someone would try to assume power out of a deficiency and contest him for his own alley.

He clenched his fist and offered her a fierce biceps to squeeze. "Feel, woman!"

The woman jabbed a finger at the contracted muscle.

"Tissue paper compared to this here," and she held up her aluminum leg for Gorm to play with while she balanced herself against his shoulder. Gorm caressed the polished metal as if he meant to seduce it.

"Tempered iron's better," he advised her, thinking of the glory of his skillet days.

"Not portable enough," the old woman snapped. "This here baby I can take off and sling back on with one hand. Oiled once a week . . . never makes a noise. Modern science can replace anything in the human body, even the heart."

Gorm told her his heart was irreplaceable. This was why he had decided to take control of this alley. He asked the woman what was in her bag. She said it was her work equipment which reminded her she was late. She wound up with her artificial leg and tried to make an exit around him. Gorm snatched the bag from her hand. It was filled with cleaning rags.

Darkness slammed on the alley like a closet door. The nearest streetlight was a half block away. Still Gorm could make out a faint protrusion on his ex-babysitter's forehead, the stigma that had branded her for life.

"All herald Gorm the Strong, Mrs. Vidoni."

"I knew you'd make trouble when you grew up. Give me back my rags."

"If it had been light I would have known you by your wart, Mrs. Vidoni."

The cleaning woman said hospitalization had paid twice for removal of the wart. Each time it had grown back. She told Gorm a human being could get used to anything. After the second burning and consequent growth, she'd decided to keep the wart in the middle of her forehead. She'd even grown to like it once she'd decided there was no getting rid of it. Every Tuesday morning she powdered it, she said. The wart had returned the favor by not growing any bigger.

Gorm would have liked to counter with a prodigious defect of his own but how could he converse about soggy entrails, his lack of peristalsis, the mysterious ball bearing that might or might not have influenced the former two? Besides, he hadn't converted them to an asset yet. He blocked the cleaning woman's way and told her he would not return her rags until she had paid tribute to the owner of the alley where she now walked.

"Say, 'All Herald Gorm the Strong' and kiss my foot," he advised her.

"You need more than your foot kissed. Why I remember when you were a little tyke. Everything went straight in your mouth. There wasn't nothin' you wouldn't swallow."

"I've changed, Mrs. Vidoni. Get down on your knees And swear allegiance."

"Ha," said the cleaning woman, "I've babysat for half the brats in this town. Once a crybaby, always a crybaby. You'd swallow anything."

Once again the left leg of Mrs. Vidoni swung forth like a door supported by only one hinge. At the same time she reached for the bag of rags in Gorm's hand. In the laborious movement before Mrs. Vidoni could plant the noiseless aluminum, Gorm kicked her good leg out from under her.

Seated in the middle of the alley, she said, "You wouldn't hurt an old crippled woman, would you?"

Gorm stuck one of his bare feet under her nose. "Kiss it," he said.

The cleaning woman said there were things she had been meaning to tell him.

"What things?" Gorm asked.

"About your childhood," she rasped. "I mean I always thought you had loads of promise. You was always different from other kids. I always says to myself, 'There's nothin' that Gorm kid can't become if he just sets his mind to it.' Nothin' mind you."

In a voice as formal as his stance above her, Gorm said he agreed with her.

"Only you should have said it to me then," he told her. "The foot, Mrs. Vidoni."

"I might catch something." She had risen to her knees. "My

health isn't what it used to be."

Gorm kicked out one of her support arms. "Sonofabitch," said the cleaning woman.

Gorm said he couldn't dispute that.

Again, he reminded her of his need to have his foot kissed. A peck would do but frankly, he said he desired a little passion in her tribute. It was true, he said, he needed some of his other parts kissed but since he wasn't the kissing type, never would be, it was unlikely these other parts would ever get kissed.

The cleaning woman rose to her hands and knees.

He told her he would like to present something more respectable than his foot for her to kiss. His foot was not by any means his strongest part. He wasn't sure which of his many parts was strongest but he knew one thing. There wasn't much to develop in the human foot. No sirree. The human foot was what it had been since the day it first tippytoed over God's earth. Except for stretching the Achilles tendon, there just wasn't much to develop.

"Mostly bone," he said.

In the darkness, Mrs. Vidoni crawled on her hands and knees. She tried to grasp Gorm's bare legs but he backed off and continued his speech.

Hard, hard. The feet were like the ball joints in a car's suspension.

Standing over the helpless woman in the alley he'd named after himself, Gorm could not remember when he'd talked so much. He was cognizant that part of his speech took the form of a confession. This thought embarrassed him.

"You should reach out for the Lord," Mrs. Vidoni told him.

"Naw," said Gorm, "That would only be one more person to make a sucker out of me."

"Your father did the best he could."

"Nobody's blaming anybody. First I got my muscles together. Then I named an alley after me. Now I want my foot kissed."

Gorm said anybody he'd ever known or heard about who was anything had had their foot kissed. Sure the pope only got his ring kissed. Sure the queen of England only got her cheek smooched. But those who really believed, the novitiates, kissed the papal foot. Gorm said they never regretted it. He said the same held true for Julius Caesar, Jesus Christ, Attila the Hun, and Mahatma Gandhi. All of them had assumed power after they had had their feet kissed.

"I don't want the whole world . . . or the U.S. of A . . . or Hopewell. It all stinks. I just want this here alley. You got five seconds to say, 'All Herald Gorm the Strong' and kiss my foot," Gorm told his ex-babysitter.

Somewhere in the distance Bog & Bliss clattered . . . always a signal smoke was issuing from its bowels. In the alley, by the shadow of boxes filled with junk, Gorm's ex-babysitter said, "All Herald Gorm the Strong." The mixture of awe and reverence in her voice made Gorm think of troops addressing their general in firelit camps the night before the big battle. He, too, wanted to offer words of inspiration, words that would make his followers throw themselves into lines of enemy bullets but when he looked down he was reminded that his *only* devotee was an old cleaning woman, one with a wart on her forehead, a hump on her back and an aluminum leg. Her conversion was such she chanted the exaltation to Gorm like a run of Hail Marys. On the sixth "Herald . . ." he sighed and made her stop. He was anxious to get on with the kissing part.

It wasn't till the cleaning woman's tongue worked up the side of his big toe and her resilient wart tickled his instep that Gorm became aware of where he was, the source of his rising sensuality, the overall perversity of his situation.

"Enough!" he cried at the humped figure huddled at his feet. Gorm retreived his foot and backed off.

"You've done fine tonight," he said.

The cleaning woman pursued him on her hands and knees.

"All Herald Gorm the Strong, Mrs. Vidoni."

"All Herald Gorm the Strong!" the cleaning woman cried but it did not stop her advance.

"I'm an old woman. Don't leave me like this. I could help you."

The thought of even touching this woman he'd reduced to her knees was repugnant to Gorm.

"Don't leave . . . I know all about weightlifters. I used to mop nights at the Y. Strongmen need their bars chalked. I watched them through the grating in the ventilators. They need progress charts . . . their weights stacked . . . collars tightened . . . I could bring you milk and cookies at the end of your workout."

He told her he did not like sweets. By way of getting rid of her, he told her she could assist him in his daily workouts.

"Thank you . . . thank you," the prostrate woman cried, and launched forward to kiss his feet one last time but they evaded her. They were hurtling in retreat over the same fences they'd climbed with patience on the way to assume power over the nameless alley and anyone in it. Gorm did not look back.

The next day Gorm found his first recruit waiting for him on his back steps. He was surprised to discover that Mrs. Vidoni's wart did not signal the wicked witch of his childhood dreams. When she turned her head to three-quarter profile the splotch of March sun lifted the horny protuberance to brown bloom. Gorm stood staring at it, trying to make up his mind whether to poke it to gauge its sturdiness when Mrs. Vidoni thrust a bag at him and said they had better get started.

In the bag, Gorm discovered not only Bud Blossom Oil—the tonal slick of all musclemen, but Rhubarb Rubdown Lotion, a bar of chalk, carob bars for fast energy, and a cloth measuring tape.

After Gorm had stripped to his Charles Atlas shorts, Mrs. Vidoni cried, "Straighten up, big boy, I want to measure those sweet pecs," and pinning him against the wringer bar of the washing machine, whipped the measuring tape around his massive chest and pulled it so tight, Gorm cried, "Uncle," whence the cleaning woman gave him slack. "Forty-four," she groaned. "Why, the Binghamton Basher had a forty-eight and he was only a wrestler."

All during his workout, Mrs. Vidoni scooted around the cellar like a famished badger. It was during bench presses Gorm found his ex-babysitter most useful. Not only was she strong enough to "spot" him, but her wart centered the lift from his prone position. While completing the concentrated intake of air, arching his spine, and heaving with his upper torso toward the wooden rafters, Gorm saw his position centered by the keratinous growth. In the explosion of his sternum, ribcage, pectorals, forearms, triceps, and facial grimace, Gorm saw nothing but this magnificent wart, polished by the same Bud Blossom Oil he used on his muscles, poised like a ledge from which he swung over the multitudes, making his adjustment with the world.

During such moments it seemed to Gorm he would fly but never walk. If by some miracle he were lowered to earth, he would tiptoe in his former fastidious fear, guarding each limb as if it were the frail appendage of an insect. The barbell with its 180 pounds was poised. His elbows were locked. He saw himself as both the arbitrator of this wart yet growing upside down out of the concrete cellar floor, embraced by metal and swung like a miniature trapeze doll from Mrs. Vidoni's virus growth. He did eight repetitions . . . held the bar aloft for Mrs. Vidoni to ease back into the bench press slots. "The self-made man never quits, one more!" Gorm lowered the weight to his chest and drove it upward one more time. He concentrated on the centering wart as if that were the object he was lowering and raising.

It was time then to study his daily coprolites.

He told Mrs. Vidoni there was one exercise he could not perform in front of a lady. The cleaning woman nodded. She said she understood all parts had to be developed, not just the visible ones. With a cackle she retired into the coal room, where Gorm's childhood collection of junk had collapsed the day before into the mire of water and coal.

With great delicacy, Gorm removed that morning's hardened stools from the extinct coal furnace and placed them on a piece of newspaper for examination. He plied first one, then the other turd with his mother's eyebrow tweezers. On the second tweeze of the second coprolite, Gorm heard voices identical to the ones that had formerly cried, "Grow delts, grow," from the coal room. This time they chorused, "Grow turds, grow!" This struck Gorm as very strange because he was certain that if there was one thing his stools couldn't do, it was grow.

A few seconds later, the voices chanted softly, "Grow turds, grow."

Because a certain logical quietude, owing in part to the discipline of weightlifting, had replaced his former frenetic responses, Gorm tried to think the matter to its logical conclusion. What he concluded was this: His turds, like the rest of him, had indeed grown if he took into account his early diarrhea and the subsequent solidifying of his feces into manageable nuggets. Yet that was inside him. Outside of him turds could only diminish. They dried up. The simple exposure to the elements eventually left them resembling mud pods. A turd was a turd regardless of having been exposed. Why grow? Whence the voice?

He opened the coal room door abruptly.

"Were you singing a song to my bowel movements?" he asked Mrs. Vidoni.

The old woman's eyes and wart gleamed in the darkness.

"What's shit got to do with strength?" she snapped.

Gorm slammed the door.

He bent with the sharp kitchen knife to begin the dissection of the second coprolite. He sliced it longways and sideways. He repeated this maneuver. He now had eight pieces of semihardened dung. The coal furnace acted more as a primitive cloaca than an incubator. Again a chorus of voices welled up, "Grow turds, grow." And the eight turds fashioned as neatly as butcher's sausage became sixteen turds.

Gorm studied them at some length, then decided he could not remember having sliced them into sixteen pieces. They did not wiggle their tails as they had in former days when Gorm deeply relished his shit which was always in a process of becoming something just this side of liquid. Nevertheless, they had subdivided now like the miracle of the fishes. But who would consider them as inspiration, let alone eat them? Where was the multitude who would eat shit? Everywhere! It was only a matter of careful packaging, then a franchise. Gorm ran to the coal room again.

"My shit's growing!" he yelled in panic through the door at Mrs. Vidoni.

"And I'm suffocating," she cried back. "Every time I stretch a hand in this closet I touch something wet and hard. You done?"

Gorm asked for three minutes more.

It was during that brief time that Gorm decided he could no longer suffer his shit. Why should he? If he had once been something of a shiteater, he was a strongman now. How strong? Strong enough to own an alley, confer on it his name, and recruit a convert from its path who recognized his strength. He was grateful to shit for introducing him to his past which in turn had shown him the need for enjoying his own flesh. Anyway, your turds were not something you could share with the world. Mrs. Vidoni would do many chores for him on behalf of his burgeoning body. But she would not pluck at his feces with tweezers in an effort to discover a ball bearing. Gorm was smart enough to know that. He threw the sixteen strips into the lower compartment of the coal furnace that housed ashes. He was a strong man now. He advised his ex-babysitter she could come out of the coal room.

II

What does it mean "to be born again" for man? It means for the first time to be subjected to the terrifying paradox of the human condition, since one must be born not as a god, but as a man, or as a god-worm, or a god who shits.

—Ernest Becker
Escape from Evil

Whether it was only coincidence or mysterious psychic cause and effect, from the day Gorm gave up the collection and study of his feces, he began to gain a following. Milltowns bordering on large cities still have their orderly grapevine down which all news of an unusual nature passes, each additional purveyor subtracting and adding an ingredient to give it spice and substantiate his own authenticity as witness of major events. The news of Gorm's growing muscles began with Albert Goolantz.

It was not that Albert was held in any unusual esteem by Hopewell's people. It was just that he was always at a convenient spot—the corner of Frick and Mellon—to receive news. Since Gorm had left his scapegoat's post in front of Ma Goo's, Albert had painted the fireplug three more times and applied two additional coats to the pedestrian lines. The Allegheny County commuter bus stopped there. All three shifts of Union Switch & Signal passed that corner where they could often find Albert in rapt conversation with the idiot newsman Lester Day.

The weather might change with frightening regularity, and fly ash from the power plants could blow one way one day and over their recently scrubbed windowsills the next. Just as they had settled into a modicum of prosperity—could afford a paint job on the old Buick—a steel strike would scratch a dozen plans. The one thing Hopewell could count on was the frazzled, three-day-old stubble of a smile from Albert Goolantz as he dipped his brush into his bucket, gave it a stir, and looked up to see Mrs. Pendergas lugging an armful of groceries from the new A&P. Pleasantries ensued. Albert inquired after the price of coffee, the local weatherman's prediction. Snow flurries again. Seconds passed while a genuinely saddened Albert dipped his brush a second time (not having disposed of the first dip) and offered condolences for such poor luck in the heavens. Wiping the excess off the brush, Albert said, "Promise you won't spread this, Mrs. Pendergas," and Mrs. Pendergas crossed herself twice in holy secrecy. "It's about Gorm, Mrs. Pendergas." "Not that skinny kid they used to dunk headfirst in the trash barrels?" "That's the one, Mrs. Pendergas." Only they ain't shakin' 'em upside-down no more unless it's to see if he got muscles where his brains used to be. He's got a secret formula for strength . . . named an alley after himself and everything. Mrs. Vidoni's helping him . . . she told me. Says he bends steel bars in half. Says he's as strong as Victor Mature in 'Samson and Delilah.' " "Maybe he needs a haircut." "Say what you want, he was just a pipsqueak four months ago." "Well, like I always said Mr. Goolantz, a person can be what he wants to be. Afterall, FDR got himself paralyzed and still ran the country. Abe Lincoln learned by candlelight in a teeny log cabin and it didn't hurt him none. Start from where us common folk is and you can never go wrong." "You said a mouthful there, Mrs. Pendergas," and Albert Goolantz gave the nozzle end of the hydrant a delicate dab with his brush.

Mrs. Pendergas told her son Alexander who told "Squeeze" Murphy who told cynical Burnside the barber who in turn relayed the information to "Jism" Jack Sodder while he got his monthly trim in preparation for the magical quim he knew lay in wait for him at the Webster Hall Dance, attended primarily by revengeful divorcées looking for a free ride to California, where as everyone knew, all property was common and split 50-50 at divorce time. Since Gorm was quickly becoming a regular item of gossip, Jism Jack was eager to add his particular stamp. Had Gorm not hung out with The Boys, had not Jack himself given the lad training for the ways of life that lay ahead?

"Each night he's attended by three girls wearing nothin' but bathing suits. They rub his back and bring him little snacks to give him energy between sets," Jism testified before The Boys. Still, The Boys should have more detailed information on the development of one of their own, he said. Pumperdink the Puke-roo was assigned reconnaissance: Find out the nature and source of Gorm's strength.

The next day Pumperdink reported back to The Boys assembled in front of Ma Goo's. "He's got muscles," he announced solemnly. Jism smacked him across the back of the head. "We know that asshole. Who's backin' 'em? Were's he got the idea he can just dessert us and go off and be a strongman?" "And what about those pretty girls who give him rubdowns?" cried Stash Conroy.

Pumperdink dutifully reported there were no girls and no one behind Gorm. "What no gurls!" The Boys hemhawed in chorus. Jism Jack said, "Nothun' comes from nothun' and when Gorm left us he was nothin.' So don't tell me, Pumperdink, he made himself muscles out of nothin.' "

"Mrs. Vidoni, that old lady who cleans the schools, helps him."

The Boys guffawed and beat their thighs at this.

They became quiet when Pumperdink said Gorm was bench pressing thirty pounds more than his weight. He said their former punching bag was one continuous strip of rippling muscle from his neck to his ankles. "I didn't believe it myself so I says 'Gorm, let me have a little poke at one of them arms.' It was hard

I tell you." The Boys belligerently stared about them as if the world had reshaped itself over night without their permission. They hunched into themselves, their heads receding into their upturned collars like turtles retracting into their shells.

"During bench presses, Gorm looks right up into Mrs. Vidoni's face," Pumperdink told his cohorts.

"What's so special about that old cleaning woman?" Wholesale Pike wanted to know.

"Maybe he studies her wart," snapped Jizm Jack but no one took this seriously. A wart like any imperfection was something to be joked about. The mystery of Gorm's strength remained mystery. Jism Jack was particularly irritated by this and assigned Lester Day to accompany Pumperdink to the next day's workout.

In the following days, the mystery of Gorm's strength gained monopoly over Hopewell's gossip. Older citizens who had only been associated with the family in a casual way, let their remembrances cling to his fits of diarrhea as a child. To tales of his new strength, they were apt to pass it off with a joke: "Well, I'm glad to hear the lad's getting his shit together." Those who had had some tie with the family—the milkman, mailman, furnace repairman, teachers, tax collector, Dr. "Give 'em an Aspirin" Pound, Grime the coal merchant, all saw Gorm's resurrection in another light. He was the little engine that would never say "die" no matter how many hills it had to climb. In this they echoed Mrs. Pendergas. And Mrs. Pendergas echoed her friend Mrs. McKivitz.

Mrs. McKivitz and Mrs. Pendergss led the charge on the fresh piles of ground chuck at the A&P each Thursday afternoon. They were followed by a dozen other women in love with the neon breeziness of the franchise . . . the incredible space of it all after years of claustrophobia in Donofrio's peanut-shell grocery store. Row after row of color. Even the meat gleamed in neat trays behind glass . . . a jewelry store of fresh carnage.

One afternoon as the ladies discussed Gorm's muscles, Mrs. McKivitz testified that as his neighbor she had been privileged to hear him groan regularly for the past four months. The ladies sighed and stared wistfully at the meat. Mrs. Pendergas asked what this groan sounded like. "Comes from deep in his gut like he's havin' a baby," said Mrs. McKivitz. "Could be bowel trouble," snapped Mrs. Pendergas. "George groaned like that the year his hemorrhoids acted up." "No, this is the groan of a man reaching for his strength. I know. I always hear a clunk afterwards. That's when he sets the weights down." Mrs. McKivitz turned and ordered two pounds of chuck and a bone for her dog.

"Naw," she said after she got her meat, "the Gorms don't have a bathroom in their cellar. I hear it first thing in the morning. One groan, one clunk. Then everything's quiet. In the afternoon it starts up again. Only this time, eight groans . . . nine. My walls shake . . . it's hard to keep track. If you listen close you can hear little clinks. . . ."

Others did not see it in such a sensory vein. For them Gorm was simply the little man perfecting perfection in his tinker shop. In this case it happened to be his body. From this he differed little from Edison or Franklin or Westinghouse. He fashioned life alone out of movable parts which would benefit the masses. Oh, it was hard to say how Gorm's bulging pectorals would benefit an entire town as Westinghouse's air brake had. That was unimportant. It was the principle that counted. For there was not a man in Hopewell who didn't think himself an earnest disciple in the process of becoming the master of his machine. Whether the machine was an automobile, a radio, or simply a model railroad, they could pretend they were part of the system that was rising up all around them in metal and concrete. A clog in the copper flues of the gas range . . . a broken window sash . . . a faulty water heater . . . a short in the wiring . . . the men of Hopewell loved to fix. On their days off they waited patiently for something to break down so they could fix it. It didn't matter what. They sat in armchairs patiently puffing on pipes till something gave out. This was often signaled by a cry from their wives . . . the water in the washing maching was backing up. Quick grab that tool chest and run to the cellar. Easy does it, darling, the cavalry is here.

It had been Gorm's experience to observe the neighboring men tear down the engine of a perfectly running automobile just to have something to tinker with. And if it ran more poorly after they put it back together, that was fine too. They then had an excuse to tear it down the next weekend.

And the next weekend, Gorm observed everyone on the block edge around the exposed engine to watch the pistons pump. They watched the pistons pump for five minutes . . . in absolute silence . . . up and down . . . down and up . . . relentless . . . uncanny the way it held their attention . . . like the way Basilman the Magician had cast a spell over Gorm and his friends at Tommy Bankowitz's fourth grade birthday party. Except a magic trick had a beginning and an end. The pistons pumped at one speed. The song they sang for Gorm was chug-a-lug, chug-a-lug. Then, Sunday dusk fell. The mill whistle or the whistle from Union Switch & Signal sounded. Monday the rhythm in school ran to the tick-tock-tick of the metronome, a slower pace by one beat in between. Still, it was warm near the radiators and on clear days you could make shapes out of the spirals of smoke wafting upward from Bog & Bliss. In the late afternoon, the rhythm of the weekday slowed further to a soft tramp . . . tramp . . . tramp. These were the footsteps of the early shift Gorm watched from his bedroom window making their way out of the latticed mouth of The Union Switch & Signal. They listed slightly to their lunch-bucket side. Heads bent, eyes narrowed as if the cracks in the concrete sidewalk had replaced the imperfections they hounded in ball bearings. The world itself shrunk to the size of a ball bearing but erected to full size in domestic machines on week-ends.

On the morning Gorm woke to discover himself a hero, a flock of sparrows were lined up on a telephone wire singing directly into his window. They cheeped forty-six different notes, all of them high-pitched, the kind of delirium tossed skyward by shrieking children on a playground. The sun cautiously peeped down the long row of interconnecting brick backyards into his room. Gorm felt one arm, then the other, and laughed to himself. When he had felt most of his parts and concluded they were about the same texture as when he'd laid them beside himself the night before, he smiled to think that he was near Home.

Indeed, Gorm thought of his separate body parts as armor and armaments he had dragged through the bog to daylight and they were nearing a resting place. The tender chorus of car tires rumbling over the cobbled bricks in the distance, the bleating song by the sparrows, and the trickle of warmth from the sun on his exposed chest hairs no doubt proclaimed this. A proclamation was in order announcing his birth but Gorm felt so ripe laying where he was he thought the proclamation could wait a few minutes. Certainly, he did not have at his disposal a crowd large enough and exuberant enough to deserve a hero but it was only a matter of weeks until he could create one. Such was Gorm's sense of heroism.

All of life chattered to Gorm a joyous chorus to his destiny. Gorm answered this morning hallelujah by wiggling first his big toe then three other toes. He would have had his little toe beckon but some brute had stomped on it in the third grade and it had never recovered its flexibility. He repeated this movement with the toes on his other foot, then the fingers of each hand as if they were elaborate strings on a violin, each in turn celebrating itself, then forming the requisite pluck to blend with the upstart orchestra. He wiggled all things that were wigglable including his navel which had been born in exile in the cellar. With his mouth he formed the letter "O"; his nose formed inverted "U's." Such was his control over his body now, Gorm could make individual veins rise and fall like pulsing rivers on a world map. Only his gonads asleep in their sacs and his tiny, tremulous bud of a pecker resisted the general call to harmony.

With the exception of these latter rebels, all things under the sun praised Gorm and Gorm praised himself.

The crude conduits in the cellar had been replaced with scraps of refinement which Gorm came to see as only befitting. Mrs. Vidoni had covered the bare light bulb with a pink lampshade with tiger lilies imprinted on it. Over the single window she'd hung white curtains with blue birds. When Pumperdink returned to the cellar a second time, he brought Gorm a colored poster of a surfer riding the crest of a wave under blue skies. Lester Day donated his Homestead Grey baseball cap which hung now on a nail next to the poster.

As other visitors came, they in turn brought tribute. Albert Goolantz painted an entire wall baby blue. In the process he painted a dozen spider webs right into the blue wash. He did not stay. He said he had his Borough work to attend to. But others remained behind to form a cortege of ragged humanity gaining a final bloom with each thrust of Gorm's body as he drove a steel bar loaded with weights toward the heavens. A former foreman from Bog & Bliss named Gursky, healing from a rupture, brought an armchair with its broken springs corkscrewing from its cloth undercover.

A one-armed girl brought a coverlet for the chair. After each set, Gorm plopped there, magisterially gazing with shiny eyes over his flock of disciples who varied with each day but gradually formed a hard core of six people.

Gorm found they were capable of some jobs but not others. For example, Fritz Yankowitz, who had lost the middle three fingers on his right hand, had no feel for stacking or applying weights. Since the muscles in his palms had developed inordinately, Gorm used the former roller from Bethlehem Steel to knead his back muscles after each workout. Lester Day was too dumb to keep a strength chart, and not coordinated enough to take part in the after-workout massage so Gorm seized his voice. It was a slightly raucous tongue, charged with the inflated violence and melodrama of newspaper headlines, yet resonant enough to carry across hills, through car doors or coal-room doors.

On days when he felt tired, uninspired, he assigned the idiot newsman coal-room duty. He had him say, "Grow delts, grow." Or, "Blossom pecs, blossom." Often the other cripples would latch on to the refrain. Lester Day chanted an invisible solo much as Gorm's junk had urged him on in the old days, "Bulge bicepses, bulge." And the choir of broken bodies, as if picking up a signal from a priest intervening on behalf of a sacred deity, would sing, "Bulge bicepses, bulge." And Gorm now bathed in the glow from of the pink lamp shade over the laundry tub and the shadows of his followers, dipped his body into an S shape which snapped into a 1-2-3 rhythm till his back was arched like a bow and the barbells hovered above his head, silent. And the coal room was silent. Gorm's followers were silent, their eyes transformed into little jewels of light.

Not all of Gorm's workouts went without a hitch. Lester Day, after years of playing the town crier for tabloid murder and rape, couldn't contain himself within the official liturgy. Some afternoons, he would follow the chant to Gorm's pectorals with "Kick the shit out of that bitch." Or, "Stomp that coon's balls." The second time he did this, Gorm yanked him out of the coal room and made him shine Mrs. Vidoni's wart. The cleaning woman was not anxious to have her growth tampered with but since it was Gorm's command she tilted her head to the light while Day bent to it with Bud Blossom Oil and Gorm's father's shoe buffing rag. Gorm's followers did not know how to respond so they looked to Gorm for a signal. He sat on his throne with the springs poking out the bottom, implacable, blond hairs curling down his poitrine. They sat with fixed expressions while Mrs. Vidoni's viral growth took on the gleam of the hood ornament of a car.

What reinforced Gorm's heroic feeling most, however, was the notion that he was accepted in total everywhere he went. Where previously he had never dared to venture outside after dark unless his father sent him to Donofrio's grocery for a pack of Camels, he now found himself looking forward to a stroll in the evenings to watch the elements celebrate his return to earth. Since he had become a strongman, the sidewalks more graciously accepted his feet. The winds were more subtle. No longer did they assault him directly in the face and make his nose run. Now they graced his body like a molding hand. Where trees had formerly been obstacles he might back into and knock himself silly when he turned to keep an eye for pursuers, they waved now like saluting hands along the victory path of an emperor. Windows didn't make Gorm nervous anymore. Instead of being watched for a false step, he watched to see what manner of creature was observing him for his newfound bounty, growth and sveltness, the blossoming of his Gormness. It was pleasant to take a walk in Hopewell at night. "Feel good," Gorm said to the dappled air and he could have sworn he heard the dappled air say, "Me too."

In the days when Gorm had been Hopewell's whipping post, all objects animate and inanimate conspired to ask him, "What are you going to do with your life, little fella?" Such was his sense of remoteness from all things, that even the houses had seemed to lean to ask this question. Gorm knew if they tried such a stunt now, he would say, "Fuck you, houses, protect your weaklings from the next storm." But neither did the houses lean nor ask nosy questions because he was what he was. The same went with the steelworkers at the Yakety-Yak Bar and Grill. The derision and amusement were gone from their expressions. Now they offered him deferential nods of the gravest respect. Gorm returned their deference but without the gravity. It was as if the universe itself were aligned one way or another in a constant evaluation of all things that moved. To make oneself strong was little more than to get in line with some higher power. It did not matter what form the strength took. You could be an expert at crushing BBs with your little toe and you would be in sync with the general scheme of things, Gorm thought.

"Hallelujah," he said to the cobbled bricks, the dark store fronts, the general night air. When the mills clattered and boomed at night with their surreptitious discharge, "I make a boom too, granted a smaller boom but at least it's all mine," and he had such control even over his innards now, he farted at will.

The changing shapes of the Bog & Bliss billows and their disintegrating centers didn't fascinate Gorm anymore. What he admired was the smokestacks themselves. At night they were silhouetted like pagan shrines pushing the hillsides apart. They struck Gorm as magisterial, solemn, forgetful. They went about their business and remained as stolid as plumes on a drum major's hat. They boomed like a bass drum and all of Hopewell marched to their cadence. The humps in the hills were formed because the land highstepped it to this monolithic drummer. Behind the humps lines of people—steelworkers and their families—formed to march in step to the cadence of the 20th century. The smokestacks were history, untouchable and unmoved by anything human.

From the furnace guts connected to the stacks came the raw porridge that congealed into engine pistons, forks, bridges, the shells of cars. When the instrument of human convenience died, it did not die, it simply passed to a new stage of usefulness. The corpse was fed into the maw of the furnace a second time to be ingested and spewed back into life as a refrigerator with five different compartments including a freezer tray for ice cubes. Could Gorm say as much of a human life?

Lying in bed contemplating his heroism, Gorm understood he was strong because he'd gotten in step with history.

His power and acceptance in Hopewell fascinated Gorm to such an extent that he quit examining his bowel movements. He pooped without forethought, wiped, and flushed with only a sneaky glance backward at the cylindrical flashes of brown stuff which in their very solidity defied a name even as they'd eluded a label in the days when they were fragmented. At school, when someone farted, Gorm laughed with his classmates and held his nose and said "phew" in a chorus with a dozen other "phew's." He took to using Bloom deodorant, bathed once a day, scoured his teeth for signs of decay, and listened regularly to the hit song of that era "Smoke Gets in Your Eyes" by the Platters. He had not forgotten vast stores of coprolites concealed in the extinct coal furnace. He no longer stank so he assumed they would disintegrate as had so many other things in his short life.

On the morning Gorm woke to discover himself a hero, had contemplated the many signs of this new status, including the burgeoning row of sparrows on the power line who chirped with the rising sun and celebrated by shitting nonstop on his window sill, he delighted in the idea of cooking his father an egg.

He retrieved the seasoned wrought-iron skillet from the mulch in the coal room, scoured it free of rust with hot water and salt. He turned on the gas and patted a blob of oleomargarine at the black skillet's center. The blue claws of natural gas attacked the skillet and made it sizzle.

"Pop?" he yelled up the stairs, "How do you like your eggs?"

Gorm knew how his father liked his eggs, sunny-side up. He simply wanted to let his ol' man know he had power. And now that he had it, he was willing to share it. He was a hero now and he had energy to spare. He could afford to do things for other people because no matter how much he gave, there would still be his hulking, bulking trapezius, deltoids, pectorals, knotty spinalis and no one could take them away from him. Gorm sprinkled a little salt on his father's eggs.

"Don't do that for me," he heard a voice behind him.

"But Pop, it's your breakfast."

"It doesn't matter. You're the strong man. I mean you got all the gears meshing, the pistons pumping on all fours. Sit your ass down. I cook *your* egg.

Was there no way Gorm could be a hero except to be what he was—a specialist in strength? And no one wanted him to test this strength except in his cellar where his court let him exercise his power in a ritual fashion, complete with chants to various muscle groups and an atmosphere of complete reverence.

Neither would the community of Hopewell let Gorm do the thousand other tedious chores that usually fastened him to his waking life. That same day, a girl offered to carry his books between classes. Once, when he bent to tie his shoe, Caparella, the new kid in town, ran up, hovered over his feet like a shoe-shine boy and offered to tie it for him. When Gorm tried to thank him, the kid's ears reddened.

His tray was carried for him from the cafeteria line to his seat. The new hero of Hopewell tried to tip the girl whom he recognized as an alternate cheerleader for the Hopewell Tigers but she shook her head, smiled, and said, "You can take it out in trade after school, big boy." She was nowhere to be seen after school but for days Gorm wondered what she meant by that saucy remark.

Gorm tried to figure all this out logically but there was a mystery at the center of it. In the days when monotony, helplessness, despair had fed on his guts like a wolf burrowing from the inside out, he could not do enough for other people. And enough was never enough. When he was demoralized, his pants torn, his body exhausted from some torture inflicted by The Boys, his father had him scrub the bathroom floor, and wash the mirrors at the end of which he always came to the broken reflection of himself. Teachers gave him extra homework even though he hadn't handed in the regular assignment. Now that he had left-over energy, no one would let him lift a supple pinky, not even to help himself.

It was a strange world and Gorm's feeling of heroism lasted only one day before despair set in again because he could not see any logical foundation underlying his rise to power via Charles Atlas.

The only daily chore the community did not appropriate was wiping his ass. Since he'd vanquished all thoughts of the missing ball bearing, the daily wiping of his ass grew perfunctory, surreptitious, but the next day the thought flashed across Gorm's mind that soon someone would approach him with a roll of toilet paper in their hand and a shy smile across their cheeks. He wondered if General Ike had an official court ass wiper.

If a great shadow fell across Gorm's notion of his heroism, he still remained a budding hero for the community at large. Each day when school let out, he found one or two smaller boys waiting for him. They said they had been appointed to carry his books. Gorm said he had no books since he never did homework. He asked them who had appointed them. They shrugged and pointed back toward the school. It had been generally agreed upon, they said, and walked away, their eyes downcast.

Each day after that, someone showed up to help him with his books and each day Gorm stood baffled that a deity called "generally agreed upon" had sent him escorts. After one week he gave in. He appeared one afternoon with his entire collection of schoolbooks. Two new boys showed up. They smiled when they saw that where their predecessors had failed, they would be able to tote Gorm's possessions.

They never spoke to Gorm except to ask at his doormat what time they should come to carry his books back to school the next morning. And when Gorm peered out into the first grey sheet of light lifting the night over the hills that surrounded Hopewell, there, standing beneath the streetlight, pacing back and forth like detectives were his book carriers Claude and Paul . . . or was it Paul and Claude?

After school they walked behind Gorm like flag carriers in a parade. The personnel changed so often Gorm could never remember their names. He took to addressing them as "You" which didn't bother them. They wore the frozen, feverish gladness of religious converts.

Gorm walked the streets of Hopewell like a person who knew he was somebody. That is to say he looked straight ahead of himself at a point in the distance which was not too far away and not too close. A modest point! To carry one's power with a minimum of strain was everything. It was in fact the medallion of power. In a word it was style. But did not the casualness of the style hint at reserves of energy? It was just as important not to let one's eyes stray too far to the left or right from the magical point in space. This had the advantage for the bearer of never having to deviate from his chosen path. Thus he became an object of certainty for those who chose to view him. He did not behold; he was the beheld—a true citizen, a leader, purveyor of law and order, a morally upright individual. It was all in the stance.

And such a posture was the opposite of Gorm's earlier posture which could best be described as a rubberized corkscrew. This was in the days when he was either a scavenger or an object to be scavenged and dived into front yards either for a valuable piece of junk on top of a junk pile or simply to hide behind a hedge from his pursuers. His eyes shifted with the rapidity of a squirrel's in those days when any sort of crevice or tree which could hide the width of his body might be his salvation, for an hour anyway. Then his eyes danced a wild and unsyncopated rhythm.

As further evidence of his newfound power, Gorm learned to summon wide shoulders. This completed the vision his eyes fastened upon and was a reminder to his head to stay in one place. It had the secondary advantage of lending the entire body the appearance of sweeping aside all before it, leaving the world trailing in its wake like a magnet towing scraps through a junk yard. Gorm recalled that many teachers and administrators in Hopewell wore corduroy sports jackets with reinforced shoulders. The shoulders were a reminder that the body rode in place, up and down . . . up and down, and like the universally admired piston was a source of power as long as it did not veer from its appointed cylinder.

There were dozens of other habits of body that one had to be aware of if one were to be regarded as a manifestation of power, but if the eyes were positioned properly and the shoulders buttressed, then everything else fell into place. The hands could not swing too little or too far without disturbing the equilibrium of the eye's gaze, or the legs step in too jaunty a stride without throwing the brute shoulders into a subtle vacillation of their role; the protruding tummy bloated from starches and additives from canned foods might want to assume its natural droop but if it did so the eyes would wander horizontally into no man's fields and the shoulders bow, which if all Gorm surmised was correct, would not only lead to loss of power but if disaligned far enough would make a man a veritable fruitcake.

Men Gorm had formerly despised for their rigid, authoritarian stance were now indispensable as models. These included Heinie "Click" Clougherty, the junior high football coach who had been decorated for his services on Iwo Jima; Papa Daddy Cosnowski, head of the numbers racket in Hopewell; and Dickie Little, the senior class president.

When they entered a room, all murmuring stopped; doubt vanished. Thought itself was suspended. One waited only for their first utterance. If that utterance was merely a grunt, students and citizens took it for a sign whose import had to be ferreted out. When such people entered a room, Gorm's first thought was "What did I do wrong?" He knew by their bowed heads that dozens of other students were asking the same thing. These were men whose authority inspired fear and Gorm knew such an inspiration was closely aligned with power. Had not such a *modus operandi* been in force when he converted his first follower in *his* alley?

What amazed Gorm was their ability to walk into a room, and without varying their focus from that magical spot in space, zero in on something askance. It was not unusual for Dr. Gordon Pringle, the principal, to enter a classroom and without a moment's hesitation, without so much as a glance downward, advance to the chalk trough, pluck an offending piece of chalk from the floor, and leave without saying a single word. Unknown to Gorm, the chalk would be presented to the errant teacher two weeks later at a teachers' meeting.

It was their passion for order that bound these four men. This ability to spot the odd, the unwanted, the unruly, the no longer useful, and quickly dispense with it so that the gears of their particular machine couldn't be disturbed was what gave them their sense of impregnability.

A certain analytical thinking had fastened itself around Gorm's brain from the days when he was in the habit of probing his failures in his cellar. Though his new and powerful stance had the effect of making him forget not only himself but his career as a scapegoat, occasionally there were agonizing flickers of those days when he was at the mercy of the entire world. Such flashes were inevitably accompanied by the pungent odor of his own feces and often took place on the commode. Such were Gorm's reductive powers he traced his beatings to smoke. If he had never imagined them as having forms that did not exist, he would have paid attention to the immediate world around him. Did the president of the United States make cows and cooking pots out of clouds? Did the Hopewell police chief, Fat Ernie McLaughlin talk in raptures to Laverne Link? Of course not! Their power was based upon the supreme premise that there was only one voice— that with which they spoke to other people. Clouds rained rain, smoke was smoke. They banished the unfamiliar to the basement of their bodies. What was, *was*! If a clock couldn't be fixed you got rid of it. The world was not so difficult. The basement of a body was its asshole. Precisely. And the indigestible parts of the world funneled their way out that cunning little contrivance. It would have been ideal if a system had been devised whereby the asshole could be plugged up and everything that went into the mouth incorporated in some fashion. As that was impossible the best thing to do was to wipe quickly and turn your back on your shit, shat, stools, feces, dung, turds, no. 2's, do-dos, dadas, and ka-kas before they sang their song of the unknowable.

Gorm was girdered on the "throne" when he worked out this equation. Such were its consequences he bolted without flushing, a streamer of toilet paper flying like a pennant from his scabrous bumgut.

"Pop!" he cried at his father sitting in his room, "Get down to the kitchen and fix me two eggs, over easy."

That afternoon when Gorm's court assembled for his daily workout, he sent Mrs. Vidoni into the alley, his, Gorm's Alley, for two medium sized stones. He specified they should not be too big or too small but the size of an average man's big toe. Furthermore, he quietly asked that one of the stones be colored two shades of the same color while the other hold to one color through and through. Finally, he asked the cleaning woman to make sure her stones clacked.

Throughout these instructions, the court—Lester Day, Pumperdink, Clara the one-armed girl, Traynor a forty-year-old art student specializing in coat-hanger mobiles, Gursky, the ruptured steel worker who'd taken up model railroading while he awaited the outcome of his insurance claim, and Yankowitz, whose fingers unfurled to a perpetually vulgar sign—nodded appreciatively as if stones were just the thing that were needed for that day's workout. Mrs. Vidoni studied Gorm's eyes for signs of hokum only to find them as stony as the gifts he demanded.

A few minutes later she returned with stones that met Gorm's requirements. Indeed they clacked. Gorm held them over his head and clacked them, nodding and clacking while the court nodded and smiled to his tempo. He advanced around the cellar, held the stones close to the ear of each member of his coterie, clacked them ever so gently, the first traces of a smile on his lips, a smile of small triumphs, as if he'd just captured a bloodworm though Hopewell was not a fishing area. First Yankowitz, then Lester Day wagged their heads with appreciative smiles at the flat music the stones played.

When the circle was completed, Gorm threw the stones into the lower mouth of the coal furnace where his coprolites were stored and commenced his continental dead lifts. At the conclusion, as the loaded bar made its habitual splat on the layered plastic mat, Gorm said, "It's spring. What are we doing in this dark, damp cellar?" No one answered him. "Yesterday the temperature was 62 degrees. The sun shone brightly on the two budding trees on Orchard Alley. Our loyal town cannon was all aglitter."

"The body is always developed in dark, quiet places," Mrs.

Vidoni announced. "The weightlifters at the Y lifted in the darkest room I ever saw."

"But I'm not a weightlifter," Gorm said, "I'm a body builder What if I were to lift my weights in front of the town cannon? Don't I deserve as much light and air as the town cannon?"

Lester Day, in a rare burst of eloquence, said Gorm could do that. First he would need a public performer's license. This would have to be renewed every month but it was simply a matter of lining up the right people.

Gursky suggested Frick Park, one mile away, where there was as much light and air as any person could want. A permit would be needed there, too, but since it wasn't so public as the town cannon it would be easier to renew.

"What about the barbells? We'd have to drag them over Shit Creek and through the woods."

"Better not leave here," said Mrs. Vidoni.

Pumperdink concurred. He said they were safe where they were at. Mumurs overlapped murmurs. Gorm stood alone under the shaded lightbulb staring at his strange crew. They were fearful at what he would order next.

"Why is it freaks and garbagemen seldom see light and are seldom seen?"

"Priests work in dark places," Clara advised Gorm.

"Steelworkers, too," Gursky chipped in.

"The man with two heads at the CIO carnival only used one candle," said Pumperdink.

Lester Day, with his vast experience at reading front pages of the Evening Herald, said his astrological chart revealed he'd been conceived in a dark house with only a street light separating his mommy from his daddy.

"Given the results," said Gorm, "it might have been better if someone had shone a spotlight on your parents and separated them completely."

Pumperdink advised Gorm he faced the sun first thing in the morning and did his toe-touching exercises.

"A lot of good that will do," Gorm told him. "Your stomach's half rotted and every day you stuff it with canned spaghetti."

"My mother never cooks me anything."

"The hell with your mother. Find out what's easiest on the stomach and cook for yourself, freak."

"We're not freaks," said Mrs. Vidoni.

Gorm smiled and tapped the zinc side of the laundry tub.

"If you're not a freak, what are you doing with me every afternoon? I'm 17 years old and you must be fifty-five. I've never

been out of Hopewell. I don't know how to do a single thing
that's really useful to other people. Up until five months ago, I
was the town loser. So I whipped my trapezius into shape. I
firmed up my deltoids. I said 'abrakadabra' and my bicepses
swelled into golf balls. I played the cellar air heavy and became a
heavy but I couldn't cure my asshole."

"You own an alley," protested Mrs. Vidoni.

"That was just hysteria. If anybody but you had come along,
I'd be squeezing cell bars now instead of barbells."

"Take what you can get and quit bitching," Gursky told him.

"You got muscles. They're useful," said Clara.

"For what?" Gorm asked.

The one-armed girl smiled, smiled as coyly as all the two-
armed girls Gorm had observed on the TV.

"The muscle you're thinking of is underdeveloped. The others
are just show. My aunts were right. What good. . . ."

"It's fun to be around a muscle builder."

"Muscles are cute."

"Muscles make the man."

They were all shouting now, a current of anger firming up their
giddiness.

"Make me a muscle pie."

"Out of the sky," continued Pumperdink.

"I eat muscles with my Wheaties."

"I rustle with the muscle of my gustle."

"A muscle, a tussle, who's got the pussel?"

"All Herald Gorm the Strong!" Gorm screamed at them.

Instantly they lapsed into obedience.

"All Herald Gorm the Strong," they repeated.

"Say it again louder, All Herald Gorm the Strong."

"All Herald Gorm the Strong," they chanted in unison so loud
a five pound weight made a deft clink against its neighbor, a ten
pounder.

"Dismissed!" Gorm cried.

"Forever?" someone asked.

"As you like," Gorm told them.

They filed out as if they'd been punished for an unknown
crime.

"Air . . . sweet air's out there," Gorm cried after them.

But they didn't want air, they wanted Gorm and glanced back
sorrowfully at him near naked in his white Charles Atlas gym
shorts.

The idea of flexing his muscles in public took such a hold on Gorm, he did what men seeking power have always done in the twentieth century—he put on a suit. To this he added a pink shirt with whipped-cream ruffles, a tartan cummerbund and a black bow tie. He slipped into his oxblood loafers, placed a penny in the slot of each shoe, and buffed them with his father's shoe-shine rag, the same rag that had once been the recipient of his desire for Laverne Link.

In this getup he resembled the barkers for traveling carnivals which camped each summer on the cinder field across from the Union Switch & Signal. Were not their sport coats always buttoned in a final, elusive effort at appearing civilized? They moved like shepherds around the fringes of the fairway gathering the stray lambs to introduce them to a world of spinning wheels and bright lights and freak lambs with six cloven hooves so the weary steelworker could say to his wife afterward, "Thank God, Mary, we were born normal." And like the barkers', Gorm's suit fit him like an afterthought.

His arms were bound like broken appendages in plaster-of-Paris casts. He knew if he tried to breathe the buttons would pop. After he'd strutted around for two hours with his shirt buttoned and bow tie clipped, Gorm was certain he'd be discovered in an alley strangled by his own effort to become civilized.

He was 17 and he did not know how to tie a tie. He had only been inside a church one time. He had never learned the Boy Scout motto, "Be Prepared"; he had never officially passed his minnow test. His lone effort at joining a group other than The Boys was Little League Baseball where his three-week tenure was accompanied by inferences from his coaches to overhanging cliffs, a watchman's shed, dense copses where he might go in case of an attack of diarrhea. He had never collected pop bottles for spending money, shoveled the walks of the elderly, or stood dutifully in front of Hopewell Bank & Trust with a tin can to raise money for polio victims. He had never sold magazine subscriptions to raise money for the Hopewell Tiger scoreboard.

On Christmas, New Year's, and Easter, Gorm's father took advantage of double-time pay to work while Gorm went to a double feature at the movies and treated himself, upon returning home, to an entire can of Chicken of the Sea tuna in white chunks which he ate standing at the kitchen window.

He had never actively provoked trouble. For this his father had rewarded him since he was seven years old with an allowance each week. He might as well have handed the boy an elephant tusk. Gorm had the habit of placing the coins in his hand and walking with them. First he would walk from the dining room to the living room and back. When he had completed this route, he would make the journey to his bedroom. There he could be observed each Saturday walking from a bookcase stacked with horror comics to the window where as a child he had first glimpsed the voluminous billowings of Bog & Bliss. His right hand would fill with sweat till the coins of his week's worth threatened to slip from his palm at which point he would place it in his left hand. He was not a person who was used to gripping or grasping. This meant he could make a return trip of three rooms at most around the house before the right hand beckoned where his left had failed. And if this relief hand had dried sufficiently from its previous sweating, Gorm would find himself in the exhilarating position of being able to go all the way to the cellar, gazing like a stranger at the asbestos furnace pipes, the coal-room door balanced on its one hinge like a broken tabernacle, the spider webs splaying out from the one window like strands of gauze across the retina of an eyeball before the responsibility of converting the money to some small item he might enjoy so overwhelmed him that he jammed the coins in his pocket and raced his own ghost across town to the Hopewell business district.

For ten minutes Gorm stood in front of the Hopewell Bank & Trust waiting for someone to recognize him. He hummed "When Johnny Comes Marching Home" off-key and smiled at each passerby as if he or she were an old friend. Most people averted their gaze as soon as his eyes met theirs. One young couple released their hand holding to make the sign of the nut after they'd passed him. The only persons to show any sign of recognition were two old Polish women. They were lugging groceries and smiled shyly back at him. Gorm winked and switched in midmelody to a new tune, "Yes, We Have No Bananas."

The first person to recognize the new Gorm was Lieutenant Choppy Doyle. He was casually flicking his billy stick, smacking it into his palm, and every fourth stride turning the handle of a parking meter.

"How's it going big boy?" Choppy gave the billy stick a baton-like twirl.

"There's nothing more miraculous than the human body," Gorm told him.

"And it takes a young fella like you to remind us. You're a lesson to all those punks who hang out in front of Ma Goo's. You set yourself a goal and you went out and got it."

The lieutenant gave no sign he recognized Gorm's preposterous outfit.

"What lesson, Choppy?"

"Whattaya mean what lesson? You made yourself strong."

Gorm stared at his arms, first one arm then the other, with an amazed look. He stared at the cop.

"I eat rusty nails for breakfast."

"Whatever it takes to cross the finish line," said Choppy. "Self-improvement's something we could all use. Take me . . . I started out as a coffee boy for the Fire Department. That was '39. Then the war came. Took my civil service test, worked my way up...."

"Hard-nosed," Gorm advised him.

"That's it," said Choppy, "I was hard-nosed. You got to be to get anywhere these days."

"The nose is mostly cartilage, Choppy. Elephants have trunks, hippos a flattened piece of bone that's welded to their skull. The giraffe's nose is out of reach. A bird's beak is harder than bone. Only the human nose is expendable, Choppy."

"Whatever it takes, don't let anybody stop you."

The policeman slapped his weapon against his thigh and meandered down Frick Street toward his next appointment with a parking meter.

A block away a trolley screeched around the corner secure in its steel tracks. Its overhead electrical wire sparked briefly. Gorm waited till it passed and sauntered across the street to Woolworth's Five & Ten.

A blinking Christ in cardboard with his eyes wired proclaimed there were only nine more shopping days till Easter. At the rear of the store, at a counter behind the stuffed chocolate bunnies, a man stood above a crowd of women. He spoke in rapturous tones to a microphone while gesticulating to a near-naked woman with a frozen expression at his side. As Gorm neared the crowd, he saw the numb-looking woman was a manikin with a baby-blue brassiere over her plaster-of-Paris pectorals and a girdle the color of her skin. A bright name tag over the man's heart proclaimed him to be DILKES ASSISTANT MANAGER. He was enthusiastic and bore a generous spread of acne around his chin. It was the girdle he addressed.

"Look," he said to the women, "I yank on it. . . ." He pulled the girdle so hard the manikin swayed his way. "Careful with that lady," someone yelled. ". . . and it keeps its shape," he said.

"Guaranteed for thirty days. No stretch, no sag. You'll be the pride of your husband. Half-price, do I have any takers?"

"What happens if I start to look so good I get raped in an alley?" a pasty-faced woman with a protruding stomach asked. The women laughed. The assistant manager blushed.

"This is strictly a one-day sale. You may never get another chance," he yelled into the microphone. No one was impressed. They drifted toward the counter loaded with edible bunnies.

Gorm leaped onto the platform and pushed the man aside.

"The man's right," he cried shrilly. "You may never get another chance. The Angel of Death is waiting for you. . . . The Great Scrapyard in Heaven . . . bring your corsets, girdles, false teeth . . . let me introduce myself. . . ."

He halted their retreat in midflight. A couple of women returned to the edge of the platform. Others looked up from mid-aisle, baffled, malignant at the mention of death. They clutched plastic-wrapped, hollow bunnies in anticipation of the resurrection of the Son of God.

"You may have heard of me," Gorm said. "I'm Gorm."

There were some groans.

"A long time ago I was called 'The Little Trash Collector.' Later a number of nicknames were attached to me which referred to my number twos." There were muffled snickers. Everyone crowded around. Gorm noticed they were uniformly stout. Land of the macaroni and fried sausage. Tummies galore with jowls to match. He was eager to flex, to show them the body's miraculous potential for recovery. He felt like an interlocutor about to introduce the boys in blackface who would sing, "When the red, red robin comes bob-bob-bobbin' along." It was the best he could offer.

"Give me your huddled masses yearning to be free and I will offer them cut-rate girdles," he cried.

The ladies stared up at him stone-faced.

"I'm Gorm," Gorm said uncertainly. But who and how and what should that mean? Exactly what was a Gorm? Gorm snapped the girdle at thigh level of the manikin.

"Six months ago my problem was the opposite of yours. Put a two inch screw into my navel and you would have hit backbone. Now look at me." Gorm firmed his abs. "In those days I had to avoid crowds. There was always the danger of getting pinched between two heavies. I avoided ball games, crowded department stores, the junior prom. I hid out. I was everyone's shadow.

"Frankly, I think you people have overdone it. But me . . . I am my own girdle. Watch!"

Gorm placed his hands on his hips. After he braced his shoulders, he inhaled deeply and held it for a five-second count. Two buttons on his suit coat popped, sailed, landed at the feet of ladies in the front row.

The congregation smiled. They applauded politely.

"Don't underestimate the power of the tum," Gorm told them. "It digests food, hides babies, ferments juices sweeter than wine. When you're happy it gurgles softly. And when you're sad, it rifts and bubbles over, wilder than volcanoes, more odors than all the foods in the world, more pungent than smokestacks . . . one thousand and eight gases at last count. No, stop please. Don't giggle. There are secrets in that tum."

Several women held their stomachs while they laughed.

"Listen, Gorm loves your bellies. He would return if he could . . . burrow there for a while . . . then when the Dow Jones averages peak and our great land celebrates the growth of plastic, Gorm would stretch your girths inside out, bumgut to bowel, esophagus to anaconda fallopian tube, the great tabernacle of the void in your holy wombs to let the world see your magic. . . ."

A snippet of voice from the front of the store diverted the ladies' attention.

"If you don't get off that platform, I'll call the police."

"You could do that," Gorm called at the assistant manager, "but the police wouldn't help you sell girdles."

"You sell nonsense," the assistant manager said.

Gorm braced his entire body for a charge down the buttons of his pink shirt. Delts, pecs, abs, sternum, knotty spinalis . . . a shower of buttons sprayed over the ladies gathered at foot level. A woman with a pheasant feather in her hat caught one on the fly. Gorm congratulated her. She smiled graciously. Above them all, Gorm stood precariously, half undressed, a tuft of blond navel hair protruding above his belt buckle. He resembled a derelict who's wandered into a rummage sale.

"I sell what's available," Gorm yelled at the assistant manager. "In this case it's casing to firm up the belly. I can't return there. I'm stuck with what I see. You're stuck with me. Gorm loves surfaces. The sleeker, the better. In the great city that spawned us, Stillwell, just three miles away, there are figures, sleek and gleaming, without any belly at all. All those who love the Aluminum Company of America Building raise their hands."

All hands remained at their sides.

"It's impressive but I can't say I love it," a woman in a wool coat and babushka ventured.

"All right . . . strike love from the record. Just for one day . . .

one day only . . . who would trade places with the high-rise ALCOA Building?"

"Would the building have to wash dishes, dress the kids, and sew buttons?" a lady in the front row wanted to know.

"Do the truly grand ever have to do anything?" Gorm asked. "You'd be looked up to. You wouldn't have to do anything but appear mysterious. Armies would volunteer to help you for duty's sake. That's what the powerless are for."

"OK," she said, "I'll be a building for a day."

There was good-natured chuckling. A chorus of jabbering had the ALCOA Building enlisting neighboring buildings to scrub porches, climb ladders, pull weeds from between the bricks on the brick backyards. Gorm observed the assistant manager move closer. Another woman raised her hand.

"The ALCOA Building can see everything," she announced. "Would it have to look in the windows of the hotel across the street and watch people taking their toilets?"

"A figure as sleek and tall and proud as you would be doesn't turn away from anything."

"I don't wanna be a building above window level."

"You could look at the heavens when you got tired, study cloud drifts, the tops of mountains. You wouldn't have to look at toilets all the time."

"All right, I'll be a building but just for a day."

"That's wonderful," Gorm announced in his brightest voice, "who else will be a building for a day? Who else would like to tower over the pygmies on the street, sniff rain in the clouds, maybe sight an archangel or two?"

"Why not!" said a woman whose generously rouged face made her resemble a sad clown.

"Yes, why not!" cried a half dozen others.

"Excellent," said Gorm, "but you've got to firm up those tummies."

From the edge of the counter, a chorus of groans welled out, from high contralto to fierce bass. Gorm guessed the latter dwelt in the full throes of menopause. He sighted lips for signs of moustaches.

"Does the Empire State Building bulge and sag at its 19th floor? Do its innards gurgle and sigh and make embarrassing noises? Gorm loves your protruding tums the way painters of old loved them. But listen! These are modern times. We can replace your rotten teeth. When the heart gives out, we stick a plastic one into that romantic little cavity. Break your back and our wonderful surgeons can weld you back together with steel. Blow your leg off and we got wood, aluminum, the material to match your pocket-book. And it holds up. Our soldiers get blown up defending us against the Red and Yellow Menace. They find the body in six sections over the length of a football field. No problem! No problem at all . . . not as long as there's a little tick somewhere. We stitch it together with nylon . . . replace a few inoperative parts with metal, plastic, a skullplate in the skull, a dainty silver knee-cap where the knee used to be. But . . . we can't replace a stomach. Garden hose for the intestines but when the stomach sags, rots, disintegrates, forget it, my lovelies."

Gorm discerned eyes that no longer wished to be recalled to the vision of junk or the singer of junk. The ladies had shifted their gaze from Gorm to the manikin at his side.

"What's under the sleek, slim frame of the Aluminum Company of America Building?" he asked the women. They looked puzzled.

"I'll tell you, dirt. The foundation's dirt. Dirt's soft eventually. Dirt sinks, eventually. That aluminum you see is just a girth, outer rainment, like a saddle or a chastity belt. Peel it away and you get people. People bent over accounting sheets, memos, people bent over people, people bent over dictaphones, teeny erasers, paper clips. People bent.

"Without the grand girdle of aluminum these people are exposed to wind, hail, sleet and the Mail Pouch hockers of paraplegics begging, blind men begging, beggars begging. Exposed I tell you. 'Oh it's just a job in another building,' you say. If that's true, picture yourself helping your husband harvest corn in open fields, your ankles sinking in the muck. In ALCOA nothing gets in, nothing gets out.

"ALCOA eats celery and drinks prune juice. It grows straight and tall. It smells heaven and is rewarded with protection from Finkerton. You . . . you too can be part of the bargain as long as you opt for UP. UP exposure, UP the falling waistline, UP death. Listen . . . Gorm offers you protection."

Letting his wild, egoistic gaze penetrate first one, then a dozen, smiling ladies, he said, "Who would like to be my assistant?"

Gorm gave them his best smile. They answered with smiles, great gooey silly smiles. He was their *performer*. He had authority, mystery. If they waited long enough, he might even have a miracle for them.

Gorm searched for one who was shapely. It was like looking for a gourd in a warehouse of cantaloupes. Finally he spotted a woman on the fringes of the chocolate bunnies whose moustache wouldn't manifest for several more years.

"You!" he cried, triggering a forefinger over the crowd at her, "Wanna be a strong man's helper?"

The woman blushed. Her eyes were blue with dashes of light in the corners where the last traces of adventure waited. The song "Easter Parade" floated down the aisles courtesy of the Woolworth sound system.

"What's your name, lady?"

"Mary Jane Mazoupa."

"Ahh," Gorm sighed, "an American name after my own heart. Fragrance of goulash and steamed noodles."

This was more the Woolworth ladies' fare. They chuckled heartily and poked one another.

"She who would cast the first stone at Mazoupa let them come forth and try on a Woolworth's girdle."

Gorm had them ha-haaing now, belly laughs they hadn't used in years.

"Ask that lady her name," said a woman in the front row, pointing behind her.

"This is not Ellis Island. This is s serious business." Gorm did not like multisyllabic Italian and Balkan names stealing his thunder.

"What do I have to do?" Mazoupa stood below him looking coy as if Gorm had just talked her out of a dance hall and into a parked car. Gorm stared down at her comparatively demure bearing. No jowls, aquiline nose, forthright chin. Pearl earrings wavering delicately from her lobes. A newcomer from a more affluent milltown who'd fallen on hard days, Gorm decided.

"You have to hit me with a lethal weapon," he told her.

The Woolworth ladies cheered.

Mazoupa got a knowing gleam in her eyes.

"You'll be the sixth man I've decked in 16 years," she said.

She vaulted to the girdle counter like the heavy in a ladies tag-team match. The other ladies wedged tight around the counter, chattering like eager squirrels.

Mazoupa was told to take off her coat and bare her right biceps. Gorm slid his hands over her arm ever so gently, first along the hard bulge of the biceps then under the taut triceps.

"Oh boy, am I in trouble now. I picked the wrong lady," he crooned loudly.

The Woolworth ladies shouldered closer to the platform.

"Where's my weapon?" said Mazoupa.

Gorm rolled his eyes the way he did when he went "Gormmm" after weightlifting exercises.

"Quit stalling!" someone yelled.

Gorm looked down to see twenty pairs of eyes alive with vindictiveness. He spun and twisted at the arm of the manikin. Around and around. He knew it was hollow but he told Mazoupa through clenched teeth, "If you hit me any place but the stomach, I'll break your ankles later in the alley."

"I led the office softball team in slugging percentage," she replied.

Gorm held the plaster-of-Paris arm high over his head.

"Mrs. Mazoupa will hit me in the stomach with this," he told the ladies. "It has the power of a baseball bat and my loyal assistant here informs me she led her softball team in hitting."

"Slugging percentage," Mazoupa corrected.

"Thank you. Now who would like to verify the lethal force of this manikin's arm?"

Gorm offered the arm along the front row, maintaining his hand over the shoulder end. He let members of the audience weigh it to gauge its heft but he made sure the thick end faced him.

Gorm had always admired magicians, the air of anticipation they could hang like an impending guillotine over the most tepid audience. He pulled himself out of his sport coat and shirt. When he flexed the wave of ripples in his abdomen, the crowd oohed and aahed. He let his guts buckle and surge, the months of labored knots sliding in unison up and down the white V of his torso. Off to one side Mazoupa warmed up with vicious, level swings at the air. The air whistled.

"Mrs. Mazoupa," Gorm cried, "Are we ready?"

"I'm ready any time you are." She smiled like a woman who has a mean secret.

Gorm held his arms over his head and flexed his abs. "Proceed," he cried.

Mazoupa lined up his navel as if she were anticipating a fastball down the heart of the plate.

She took a wide stance, reached back with the bat, and then drove her shoulder forward, bringing the bat behind it in a wide arc. The flesh-colored arm, hatched in a mold and lean as that of a New York model, made a surreptitious whistle.

For years Gorm had taken punishment, never quite knowing where it would come from or from whom. For eleven years he had been a minor and tedious spectacle. The difference now compared with his former life as a scapegoat was that he had a sense of choice. You picked your time and place and audience. The lines, the gestures could be imagined ahead of time without the coercion of insults and fists. All you had to do was give the audience the illusion you existed for their benefit.

The flesh-colored, dismembered arm made a dull thunk against his abs and recoiled. Mazoupa found herself in her original batter's pose and would have swung again if the ladies hadn't immediately applauded Gorm's abdomen. A band of red blazed across his stomach and he smiled shyly at his admirers.

"That's not fair," cried a woman wearing an Easter bonnet. "You're a young man." "And a weightlifter at that," yelled her partner.

"Listen," said Gorm, "Gorm was once an orphan. He was worse than an orphan; he was a half orphan. A real orphan learns quickly the heart's pulpiness. A half orphan is in awe of everything. He forgets to harden; he doesn't know how to look for protection. But if a throwaway like me can blossom from nothing to something, maybe Gorm has a secret for you. If Ben Franklin began with some metal and a prayer for lightning . . . if Abe Lincoln hatched from a log cabin, what's to say Gorm can't make girders where only girth existed, steel suspension cables where that bulwark of flab wobbles at your sides. Gorm wants to firm you up, girls."

"Ha!" a stout woman cried. "I'm fifty years old. Born fat and I'll die fat."

"Gorm offers you protection. Do you want your grandchildren to make fun of a fat corpse?"

"How?" several voices cried at once.

"Before there were silicon treatments there were gay deceivers. The crudest beginnings of protection always begin in deception. You pretend what you want to be . . . then you become it."

"Beauty and protection, they're one," he shrieked. "Does Miss America ever get mugged? Sleekness makes the vicious marauder keep his distance. Do the svelte wives and girlfriends of the Bog & Bliss owners worry about sneakthieves, rapists? Gorm offers you protection, ladies."

A group of women by the white bunny rabbits turned to leave. "Now take Mazoupa here," he cried. The exiters stopped. "Mazoupa has no defense against your average thug."

"Try me," she said. There was real scorn in her voice.

Gorm recalled passing a counter full of crucifixes on his way in. "Take those crucifixes," he cried pointing over the ladies' heads. They turned and as they did so, Gorm delivered a swift right hand to his assistant's stomach. "Follow my directions," he whispered in her ear as she doubled over, tears filling her eyes.

"Hey!" several women yelled at him. "What's going on up

there?" Dilkes hollered. The women who'd been about to leave filtered back.

"We've got a thug right in front of us," a hefty woman near the back yelled at him.

Gorm gave her his most tortured smile. He reached down to the manikin and in one motion raised her from the floor and yanked the girdle from her thin hips.

Some women gasped. Others averted their eyes.

"Mazoupa has a body that won't quit," Gorm said, proffering the girdle daintily from an extended forefinger.

He jiggled the girdle at them. "If no one wants Gorm's head, perhaps you'll take his advice. Consider your vulnerable tums and wombs. They digest your food, make it possible for babies to hatch in the only serenity they'll ever know. Your love juices gurgle there. Your wombs and tums deserve protection which Mazoupa, my loyal assistant will now demonstrate."

Gorm jumped from the counter, guided his assistant to the floor, and led her back to the dressing room. He handed her the girdle and gave her further instructions.

When he returned to his audience, he said, "Look out the window . . . out there . . . there are lessons to be learned out there." He babbled for several minutes about how everything was protected but human beings. "Even the chocolate bunnies have iron gates, glass, and burglar alarms to protect them during the night," he cried.

"I'm ready," he heard a voice at his side say and with all the pathos he could muster, he said, "And what does my lovely assistant Mazoupa have to protect her glands.

"She has a glide-on girdle made in Zelienople."

The women guffawed. There was massive tittering around the jelly bean counter. The ladies around the light-up crucifix merely smiled.

After he'd offered the ladies a chance to certify Mazoupa's protection, which they refused, he had her plant her legs wide and hold her arms above her head.

"This is the way she would stand if a robber held her up. Think of the good-for-nothing making off with your husband's hard earned money."

Gorm watched their faces turn peevish and sorrowful.

The first time Gorm swung the manikin's arm at Mazoupa's girdle-protected innards, the ladies clasped their hands and held their breaths. Mazoupa winced but remained intact.

Gorm swung again. The dull "thunk" echoed along the Woolworth air vents. The willing assistant was knocked two steps backward but she remained upright, forcing a smile out of the dull, nauseous void Gorm remembered from his own blows to the stomach only six months ago.

"All Herald Mazoupa," he cried.

The ladies applauded generously.

Gorm snatched another girdle from its box.

"Who will buy a girdle from me?"

Gorm felt beside himself with understanding.

"If you won't protect your tender innards, think of that little tadpole who could be the next President of the United States. There are bullies who would crush him, drunks who would mangle him with their steel cars. Protect Junior Luzowski," Gorm cried a little too shrilly.

He spotted a black woman making her way to the cosmetic aisle.

"If not the President then George Washington Carver," he said.

"That man was a fink," the black woman told him.

"Okay, how about Godfrey Cambridge."

"Now you're talking," she said.

"You've convinced me but I've got to charge it," she said.

Dilkes bolted through the crowd with a charge stamper.

"This lady understands the value of protection. Who's next?"

A box-shaped woman stepped forward.

"I'll need an extra large," she told him.

"Extra large? Do we got extra large?" Gorm cried with mock-concern. "Bring me your huddled hippos yearning to squat. Who's next?"

Mazoupa stepped from the counter and played the role of cashier. Dilkes handled the charge cards. Eleven women bought, roughly one-fourth. What amazed Gorm was the women who didn't buy. Some hung about the cash register listening to the deft, little pings. Others gossiped with women they had never seen before today. Others studied Gorm and smiled at him when they caught his eye. He had created a carnival for them and they didn't want it to end. "No truth but in hocus-pocus," he mumbled to himself.

After the last woman bought, Gorm followed Dilkes back to his office. He figured the assistant manager was seven years older than himself. One glance at his narrow probity and Gorm knew he was the type who would always keep his life insurance paid up.

"Fifty percent of the take," Gorm told him.

"Get out of here you bum before I call the police."

"There's nine shopping days until Easter," Gorm advised. "I'll call up every priest and minister in town and tell them about your blinking cardboard Christ in the window. That ought to make a nice sermon on the modern corruption of resurrection."

"Fifty per cent would put me in the hole. I'll give you thirty. You cracked the arm on that manikin. Besides, your assistant disappeared with a shower mat."

"I had to protect her Dilkes. She could have sued. Fifty percent."

Gorm had put his undersized suit coat back on and now he slowly removed it along with his shirt.

"The cops aren't going to buy your innocence after you let me stand on one of your counters and blabber for a half hour."

The assistant manager took a small deposit box from a shelf behind him and opened it. He counted the money and threw it across the desk at Gorm.

"Don't ever let me see you in here again."

"That's no way to treat someone who's just earned you money. You deal in junk at highly inflated prices. You want lessons in merchandising, you come to Gorm, you hear. I know all about junk. It's been nice doing business with you."

"You fucking nut," Dilkes yelled after him.

Mazoupa was waiting for him outside the store.

"I want my cut; I took a lot of punishment," she told him.

Gorm smiled a slash across his face.

"Why is it, Mazoupa, nobody trusts a teenager? We're not allowed to drink. You adults try to convince us we'll catch a combination of beriberi and the Grand Itch if we screw. You let us be taught by the most bored adults in town. And those schoolrooms are more like interrogation rooms. Then if more than two of us assemble on any street corner, the cops show, winging their billy sticks as if our bodies were weeds."

"I'm just a housewife," said Mazoupa, "I don't know nothin' about that."

Gorm flicked her stomach with his fingers. She flinched.

"You hide behind that housewifeyness," he said. He told Mazoupa not to move. He was going next door to Shard's Dairy Store to get change for her cut.

Shard's, no matter what season, gave the odor of stale milk and air conditioning. Scoop after scoop of ice cream in plaster-of-Paris molds sat in metal cones along the counter. Pensioners sat silent, each to his own table, at the back of the dairy store staring out the window into an alley.

After Gorm made his phone call, he waited inside the door, till he spotted the Hopewell police cruiser turning the corner toward Woolworth's, its beacon lit and spinning like a terrified mammary.

Gorm went to meet it.

Lieutenant Choppy Doyle leaped from the cruiser, his eyes bloated with adrenalin.

"Is this the shoplifter?" he said, pointing to Mazoupa.

"Feel her stomach, Choppy."

"This is absurd," said Mazoupa.

"It's true, it's true," Gorm agreed.

He had been searched so many times by Choppy, it gave him a thrill bordering on ecstasy to be responsible for someone else's frisking.

"The matron will do that at the station. Not that I wouldn't mind." The fat Irishman gave Gorm's assistant his best leer. Then he winked at Gorm.

In full view of Hopewell's Easter shoppers, Mazoupa, her face grown livid as a radish, hiked up her coat . . . pleated skirt . . . pink slip. Gorm and the lieutenant casually pondered her chubby but serviceable thighs. Shoppers pretended not to notice. One old man walking his terrier, smiled, and winked at the air in front of him. With a great bluster, the garments fell back into place. A shower mat plopped at the lieutenant's feet. Gorm stared innocently at a nearby fire hydrant.

"He made me wear it for protection."

"Sure," said the lieutenant, "Gorm goes around town fitting ladies with shower mats. He's got an investment in a company full of them. Next thing you know he'll be shoving golf balls into brassieres. For protection, I might add. Get in the car, lady."

The following day Gorm appeared on top of a ten-foot stack of Firestone retreads in a Sunoco station during the rush hour. With the aid of safety pins for buttons, he wore the same carnival barker's getup. Across the street, the early shift of the Union Switch & Signal was emptying and Gorm greeted their bent, fatigued faces with:

"Oh give me your huddled masses yearning for a softer ride." He seesawed on the tires like a man adrift on a life raft.

"What makes us float through the night?"

Gorm pointed to what he was standing on. He asked the handful who'd wandered up to the base of the stack what got them from Hopewell to Biloxi, Hopewell to Albany, Hopewell to Sacramento?

"Money," someone mumbled.

"Money's something to make your palms sweat. When the rubber trees are gone, all the money in Hopewell won't get you to Stillwell."

He noticed a group of men lingering at the entrance to the Green Door Saloon, watching him.

"Traitors," he cried at them.

They moved en masse towards him, a slow, mean force welded together by a single word.

"You think you've got yourself a freak, or better yet a Commie. You're ready to pounce. A freak or a Commie's a throwaway. But what about these tires? Are you going to desert them?"

Gorm rattled on so quickly that the hostility dissipated into stares of incredulity.

He advised the twenty men gathered in a crescent at the foot of the retreads that deserting their tires because they'd gone bald was like betraying an old friend because he'd lost his hair. He labored at some length on the loyalty of the tire, the lightness and smoothness it brought to their lives, the distances it had carried them without complaint, its endurance given the unpredictability of Hopewell's roads. Here he cited potholes, glass, rusty nails, and the cobbled brick roads which threw them out of alignment and because of their owner's neglect wore them smooth far sooner than they should have. Did not the lonely tire exposed to all the hardness and ruthless cutting edge of the world deserve a better fate than to be scrapped at the first sign of baldness?

At that moment Gorm's expression took on considerable pain and bitterness. He became the tire carrying the dead weight of Hopewell, its bloated carcass stuffed with macaroni and bulbous sausages and noodles groaning with the effort of the journey through the large intestine and the eyes of the intestine's owner fixed and hard as ball bearings in the horribly strained eye sockets. His own hands and feet felt chafed and raw from the tire's trip. If he gave out, he would not merely be tossed on the junk heap he was standing on and manipulating now, but the entire world of crawling breathing creatures would die with him. A sharp pain rose up from his esophagus and made his Adam's apple wobble.

To hide this pain, Gorm disappeared down the center of the stack of tires. A moment later he reappeared, smiling, a retread saddled around his shoulders. He rocked then from side to side and got the castoff tire whirling around his hips with a copulatory rhythm.

"If I don't desert my tire, it won't desert me," he cried.

He disappeared again, this time rising from the heap with two tires, one moving around his shoulder, the other weaving with the gyrations of his hips.

There was modest applause.

The two tires slipped down from his body like discarded garments. Gorm felt the entire pile to be an extension of his body.

"If your arm burned, you wouldn't ditch it. You'd let a doctor graft skin. Who will buy one of Gorm's retreads?"

Three men stepped forward to rub the tires.

The next week Gorm helped a basket case sell pencils, the Elks' Ladies Auxiliary with their annual tag sale, the Hopewell Post Office auction a rebuilt Special Delivery Jeep—"This machine still has the urgency of those letters saying 'I forgive you, Maude.' " He helped three six-year-olds selling lemonade across from the fire station on Blunt Street. He sold directly to the firemen playing poker behind an antiquated hook n' ladder.

"Only you men know the sweat you lose at a fire. Don't give me those fishy looks. I can tell by your eyes you've been hitting the hard stuff. You're dehydrated. If the alarm went off right now you couldn't save my grandmother's paisley shawl. Fuel up, firemen, protect the community at large, drink lemonade."

The three children set their pots on the ground to applaud Gorm. The firemen looked at him as if he were tetched. But they bought, first one glassful, then another when Gorm stared malignantly at them.

He sold two defective irons at a Saint Vincent de Paul store. Here he developed a craving for a waffle iron to sell. He was reminded of the odor of waffles browning in the cast iron waffle presser in the days before his mother had run off with the sporting goods salesman. But the manager of the second-hand store told him waffle irons had been out of style for years since the frozen food companies started packaging them. Gorm had one in his coal cellar but he wasn't about to surrender it.

On his way to school, after school, Saturdays and Sundays, and on hooky days, every spare moment of his waking day, Gorm stalked Hopewell, searching for waste to resuscitate. The more absurd the waste, the faster his adrenalin pumped. Because he had never fared well in other people's games, except as a scapegoat, it was easy for him to invent his own games. He took such relish in his efforts to convince people to buy the unusable, the bleak, the forlorn, the unfashionable and the needlessly deserted that he practiced rhetorical speeches for junk he hadn't even seen yet as he walked along the winding streets and alleys of Hopewell.

Though the sleep-inducing picture box had by now been installed in every house, Gorm's rhetoric took its inflection from radio in the days before the TV squatted in his house. The voice he served up to Hopewell's workers and their wives echoed the plight of *The Fat Man, The Great Guildersleeve, The Shadow*—"What evil lurks in the hearts of men?"—the emphatic pauses of Harry Truman, Kefauver Committee testimony, and the staccato of Lucky Strike and Philip Morris pitchmen.

He was Gorm; his reputation had traveled before him. His movements like his voice were abrupt and angular in the tradition of men who coveted power. The enemy was doubt; the worst thing Gorm could do was display hesitation. He won the small crowds over with his sureness: the wiser wisecrack to answer the heckler, the spurious optimism to salve the doubter, the novel absurdity to get the attention of their withdrawn, passive eyes and ears.

"I am the enemy of all those who would throw away your pasts," he'd announce and then summon a brass curtain rod from a pile of that day's junk.

Like the retreads he sold, he saw the crowd as an extension of his body, the pulsing femoral artery in his thighs, and the bony fingers that beckoned them. They formed in tight crescent knots around him—a cummerbund to his guts and whatever doubt might have lodged itself therein. The crowd was both a receptacle and a shield, a bottle into which he fired salvos of rejuvenation and heard that splurge of hope echoed back at him, a thick membrane of a girdle which kept the shadow of doubt from his entrails. Gorm lived for his crowds.

He no longer saw his well-being as a personal matter but something for the community to participate in. Therefore, the idea of "personal improvement" in a dark, damp room alone, or accompanied by a handful of silent cripples was repulsive. Gorm wanted the heft and boisterous applause of the crowd. It was not believers he wanted but the giddy thrill of making new converts, the unimpeded expansion of his bicepses, tricepses, latissimus dorsi, his svelte, compact and alert body revived from the alleys of Hopewell and spread over all of Hopewell till Hopewell was little more than an extension of himself.

One night he was standing before the mirror, admiring the bulge in his pronator, while a diarrhea of syllables tumbled from his mouth about the efficacy of rusty cotter pins, waterstained

lamp shades, wide neckties, and metal drinking cups, when his
father called up the stairs, "Son, telephone!"

"You don't know me," a low, edgy voice began, "but you
manhandled my wife."

A heckler at the edge of the fairway, someone who could inter-
fere with the girth of his girdle, the flair of his cummerbund, a fly
in the ointment of resuscitation.

"Your wife is a kleptomaniac."

"Do you know who you're talking to?"

"Mr. Mazoupa! Your wife climbed a girdle counter to show off
her sweet bod."

"My wife's had three kids. She has a pot. She would never do
that."

"Ahh haa," Gorm cried, "you don't love your wife because her
tum sags."

"I didn't say that."

"But you believe it. You know she's getting close to menopause. Washed up. You study secretaries' knees on your lunch
hour."

"Hey you! That's not the point. You hurt her and you're trying
to dodge the issue."

"Say something nice about Mazoupa," Gorm advised him.

"Listen," snapped the husband, "You made my wife's insides
hemorrhage. The doctor bill's over a hundred bucks. When are
you going to pay up?"

"Say something nice about Mazoupa? Say she's still useful."

"You're talking about the mother of my children."

"Children are gluttons, worse than vultures; they'll eat anything and never say 'thank you.' "

There was a long pause. Gorm waited.

"What do you want me to say?" Mr. Mazoupa asked.

"Say what you feel."

"I love my wife. What are you trying to make me do?"

"You love her because she's provided you with three kids."

"When she's in the mood, she's a marvelous cook," the husband confessed. "She keeps a neat house, is dependable. . . ."

"Is she as pretty as the new Buicks with Dynaflow?"

There was another pause.

"You crazy punk," the man said.

"Is Mazoupa as sleek and tall and powerful as the ALCOA
building?"

"That's my wife you're making fun of," the man said in a
solemn voice.

"Don't kid me," Gorm yelled into the mouthpiece, "You treat

my noble assistant like an iron skillet. Any day, you're liable to trade her in for an aluminum one. You listen to me hubby. She won't be a reject. I'll teach her to firm up, gallop like a sleek filly. No easy trade-ins on Gorm's products, you hear me. . . ."

But the husband of Gorm's assistant had hung up long ago.

The next night more complainers called. One of Gorm's irons had short-circuited the house wiring. Fuses had blown, a babushka was singed; when sparks first flew and the lights went out, Gorm's Goodwill buyer had pissed herself. It was the husband who gave the boy this information. Why did the victims never call themselves?

"Resurrect!" Gorm barked at the embittered husband.

"Whattaya talkin' about?"

Gorm identified the caller by his lingo from the East End. In the days when the Mellon, Scaife, and Frick empires were being founded, the near-wealthy camped there vying with each other with chandeliers in every room and when the bowling craze rattled Eastern cities, a bowling room in their cellars. Gorm recalled this from the fifth grade when an inspired substitute teacher had given him a week's respite from the metronomes in the cloakroom. Now the East End's large brick houses with gabled roofs and ornate cornices were considered the marginal part of Stillwell. A few thousand down-at-the-mouth transients hunched over single burners in rooming houses like quarantined mice. They were white, a final inner city buffer zone against encroaching blacks whose proximity they saw as the last circle of hell in their tumbling existence.

"The coons are getting closer every day," Gorm told the caller. "Fight falling property values. Skip the petty shit. Paint the front porch. Buy a new lock for the front door. Protect yourself, engulfed one."

"Hey! You're dodging me. What about wife's babushka? She paid five bucks for that iron."

"Strip the skin, slash old worn muscles, pull the good ones as tight as they'll go, find new connection points. It's a good iron. Don't give up."

Finally a buyer called him directly. A gruff voice told Gorm he had had a blowout on a retread the boy had recommended.

"Which side?"

"Front passenger."

"Was your wife in the car?"

"Yeh, but what's. . . ?"

"She's overweight, isn't she?"

"I'll say but what's. . . ."

"Waste on top of a recent salvage job is bad luck," Gorm said. "You can't have a lousy fuel pump connected to a rebuilt carburetor."

"She's a human being. She doesn't make the car go."

"Everything's connected, good sir. Your wife was sending her defeatist attitude through the seat and down the shocks. Shitty vibrations. Is it any accident India has more malnutrition and more decrepit cars than any country in the world? Have your wife skip the potatoes and the chocolate pie. Celery, man, celery. Make her jog, do Yoga exercises, take meditation, buck up her karma. The load a tire carries is seldom its own. Strip down your existence, rebuild, celebrate the good life."

"I'm poor," the man pleaded.

"Then rehabilitate poor man. Take inventory. Don't throw anything out. Rebuild from scratch. Roust the blubber and bad vibes from your belongings. Kiss the reborn wife and tell her you'll be hers forever." "I'll do what I can," the man said with unfeigned weariness.

Every time Gorm returned home it was to discover the defective had become dangerous, waste malignant, each hour of inspired rhetoric a fart on the wind.

"Don't give up," he whispered to himself each time the phone rang. He borrowed energy from his deltoids and pecs. His mind was grateful and sang appropriately to each complainer, "Cope, Cope." They came to Gorm full of spite and ended in a personal limbo ringed with awe for his accuracy. And still the calls came.

Gorm was beginning to understand that if you began from point zero you had the freedom to experiment, to try almost anything. Afterall, what did he owe the world?

It was exhausting being a hero. No sooner had he pumped a little air into old things or tired people than they went flat on him. The complainers became fewer because Gorm placed emphasis on his own rhetoric and not the junk he was selling. The bits of junk served as props to rally his crowds but even then he could not keep a few people from inspecting them afterwards and making him an offer.

Even without the telephone complainers, Gorm sensed everywhere he went that people waited for him to say the right word, make the appropriate gesture that would momentarily free them. In the morning there were still his book carriers waiting for an order; at school clusters of students would quit talking when he passed, turn and watch him as if expecting something out of the ordinary; when he returned home in the late afternoon there was his court surrounding the cellar steps in casual positions as if they'd been waiting for days. Everywhere he went there was this sense of suspension. Even Gorm's father walked more softly these days, his ears attentive to any request his son might make.

When Gorm crawled into bed at night and stared at the ceiling, he felt as if someone was sitting on his chest. When he turned on his side, the weight crawled up to his head and sat on it. When he tried to ignore it—close his eyes and pretend it was only a bad waking dream, he saw a dump truck dumping all manner of junk and half-alive bodies on top of him. Some were people he knew and after they'd burrowed through the debris and he could feel their fetid breath on his face, he opened his eyes to see them smiling at him.

These apparitions between wake and sleep so disturbed Gorm one night that he hopped out of bed and ran to the bathroom mirror to study his body and remind himself he was still a hero. As in the old days, in the cellar when the mere mention aloud of his name along with the grand swell of his deltoids, sternomastoid, and pectorals was enough to assure Gorm he was making progress, he posed first with his hands on his hips, then sideways letting his tricepses persuade him he was no longer helpless, the blue arteries and ripcords of his shoulder muscles advising him no one could sit on his face with impunity.

The first hint of consternation came because Gorm was no longer content to judge himself on the reflection of a part or even several parts. He wanted to see all of himself, top and bottom, frontside and backside, sternomastoid to gluteus maximus, preferably in one grand sweep. By quick glances, he was sometimes able to get a hint of the total Gorm in his three mirrors in the cellar. But that place reminded him of isolation and self-doubt, particularly at night.

Thus far the bathroom mirror had only revealed his upper half and that only from the front side. His neck muscles had become so thick it was difficult for him to crane his neck to gauge the sleekness and heft of his backside. He had become dependent on reflections of reflections in the three mirrors in the cellar to get a bead on his whole self.

The first problem Gorm had to solve was sighting his bottom half. He did this by climbing on top of the commode (its seat habitually closed now because Gorm shared the view with the rest of society that there was something innately repugnant about toilet water). There was the additional problem of ascertaining the full 360 degrees of his bottom self while offering to his view the posed ripples and bulges of his muscular development. He braced one hand over a wrist while holding his right arm in a state of flex, firmed up his abs, and poised one foot to get the maximum surge of his thigh and calf muscles. This was the side view. But Gorm did not hold it. He quickly spun to a back view, that is the backs of his legs, ass, and hips. Without holding that pose either, he spun to a frontal view.

It was a difficult choreography and made more difficult by Gorm's sense of a brazen imperfection which he did not stop to pinpoint but eluded by turning faster and faster on top of the commode seat as if his body, or the bottom half of it, would attain a measure of success as soon as he converted it into a kaleidoscope.

The imperfection which he only sensed, such was his desire for an emblem of his personal worth, grew so aggravating in his mind that he leaped from the commode onto the floor and began rapid spins and poses to hook the power and beauty of his top half to what he remembered of the definition and bulk of his bottom half, but his consternation was such that his memory of that recently reflected bottom half was weak indeed so that he no sooner completed several spins of the bulwark of his lats, delts, etc. than he had to leap back on the commode seat to revive the spectacle of biceps femoris, gastrocnemius, obliquus muscle, vastus externus, and gluteus medius and maximus. No angle blended with any other angle. Rather than reviving a sense of his wholeness, of his integral Gormness, Gorm had a sense of his arms, legs, chin, nose, delts, lats—all of his parts—flying away from him, only to return within a new pose to their first position, then exploding from his body, clattering off the bathroom walls till they resumed their original position in still another pose. He became so dizzy trying to keep up with this centrifigal force grown beyond his will, he had to clutch the towel bar over the bathtub to keep his balance. Even this near fall did not dissuade him from searching out his wholeness.

In his latest spins before he'd grabbed the towel bar, Gorm had spotted one muscle that had neither bulk nor definition. Compared with the grandeur of the rest of him, this "pecker," "prong," "stinger," "rod," "dick," and "lance corporal" as The Boys referred to it, was so tiny as to scarcely deserve a name at all. It neither blended with his other parts nor had the potential for rising in stature in Gorm's eyes. It was such a feeble-looking spout that Gorm viewed it as little more than an appendage to his better self, which like his tonsils and appendix, might be lopped off at the slightest ache and inconvenience. In Gorm's manic state, all this was lightning reflection; what he did, before and after grabbing onto the towel bar, was to hold his legs close together and squeeze the embryo of his manhood out of sight while he concentrated on the svelte power of the rest of himself.

Because of its timid length, it was not necessary to do this on the back poses, and he might have continued squeezing it between his legs on the frontal ones if he hadn't felt a constriction in both his guts and the style of his posing.

The alternative was simple: he would tape it out of sight.

Gorm was halfway down the stairs when he heard his father cry out from his room, "What's wrong, son?"

Gorm's mind was in a state of vertigo so that he did not pause to consider who was asking the question but cried out, "I'm going to get tape to hold me together."

Mr. Gorm was stricken to his adrenalin by this response. He thought the boy must have cut himself. He leaped out of bed and followed his son down the stairs.

Gorm did not want anybody, especially his manly father to see him in his present state so he ducked into the clothes closet and hid under a pile of coats. He heard his father mumbling "Where are you, son?" throughout the darkened house. "Get out here and tell your old man what the problem is." Gorm had no intention of letting anyone see him naked. Not now when the body he'd worked so hard to perfect felt like it was flying from his bones to the ends of the earth. One of his hands lay on a piece of soft cloth which he recognized as his father's shoeshine rag, the same one he'd used to wipe his sperm so many months ago when he'd had a self-orgy with Laverne Link. This reminded him of the terror his tiny bud of a pecker inspired in him and he grabbed it the way one would a newborn bird when one wants to strangle innocence. It was like a small child's and Gorm wondered what he had done to make so much of himself appear manlike and yet leave this one minute part of his body so hopelessly out of touch with the rest of him as to split his brain up the middle. "Idiot," he whispered at it and gave it a good bang against his thigh. At this moment his father opened the door and spying the prominent bulge at his feet, yelled "Cut the nonsense and get out here and tell your father what's going on."

Gorm leaped to his feet with a coat in his hand, threw it around himself, and hustled up the stairs. "Nightmare!" he cried as his father stared after him.

The next morning in despair, Gorm wrote his old mentor Charles Atlas.

"I know you get thousands of letters each week but maybe you remember me. I was the guy with the fouled bunghole," the letter began. He did not feel it was appropriate to tell the great one about a tiny pecker so he explained about the man who had sat on his chest, then his head. He felt himself shrewd in not telling Atlas about his search for wholeness because he figured Flex Enterprises would try to dump some more mirrors on him. He explained how he had conquered so many of his body parts and the people of Hopewell as well. The problem was that so many things he had revived eventually collapsed. The man sitting on his chest at night, he said, gave him doubts about his ability to perfect his whole body and he underlined whole, hoping Charles Atlas would get the hint about his pecker. He ended by saying, "It all seems like moving a rock ten paces and moving it back to the first spot like they used to make convicts do. I don't want to be a convict.

Yours respectfully,
Gorm the Improved"

A week later, Gorm got a reply.

"Dear Mr. Gorm,

I do indeed remember your early afflictions, most notably your chronic diarrhea. And speaking for the entire staff here at Flex Enterprizes, we have noted with great pride your progress in building your muscle fibers. Coal dust or sand, it gives me great pleasure to know the bullies won't kick earth's elements into your face anymore.

As for your latest affliction (and this is not so uncommon), you need to have someone apply firm, soothing hands to your muscles between workouts. This someone should offer you trusting smiles in the evening, expressions of awe and wonder when you thrust your muscles into the air and extend the barbells which we offered you at bargain rate. Because a body builder is constantly tearing down old, tired muscle groups to rebuild them into dynamos, he is often vulnerable. We suggest a partner therefore who will not overwhelm you with their own demands, someone who will value your sigh as their commitment.

Many of our members prefer the female gender as a partner in muscle growth and while this is a majority, it is by no

means 100 percent. Regardless of your choice of muscle relaxer, let me recommend our soothant and disinfectant for
acne—Clean Cream. Our maxi jar offers enough applications
to scourge those facial volcanos for one year. It is also effective in concealing unsightly pocks and craters. Don't be a
pimple puss. An order form for Clean Cream is enclosed.

Any further problems with the head or the body, feel free
to consult me. And don't forget Clean Cream.

> Yours For Fastidious Habits,
> C.W. Atlas"

Gorm wrote back to Charles Atlas immediately:

"I think you misunderstood me. My suffering is internal,
probably in the head. I think nothing is worthwhile doing as
if the earth itself were a beachball toppling through space.
"Anyway, I already have a muscle relaxer. . . ."

And Gorm went on to explain about Mrs. Vidoni, whom he
readily identified as an ex-babysitter and listed her many affirmi-
ties. He noted how she helped organize his workouts and gave
his bench presses focus by centering her wart over his upward
vision. She helped relax him as much as any person possibly
could, he told America's premier bodybuilding authority.

A few days later Gorm got this reply from Charles Atlas:
"You need a piece of ass, fool."

Such shenanigans struck him as a vastly overrated proposi-
tion, especially from an adviser as heralded as Charles Atlas. In
17 years his one foray with the milder sex had been with the
Firechief's daughter, the homely but beguiling Dorothea Millikan, in junior high school. This brief courtship, provoked in
memory by the flailing tails of coprolites, proved that even the
most unassuming of girls could prove capricious, revengeful,
stealthy, and altogether ego shattering. Sitting under the laundry
tub bulb with Atlas's letter in his hands, Gorm recalled the
numbness he'd felt in the days following the discovery by a wiser
suitor of the Sisyphus-like cargo in young Dorothea's bookbags.

The same feelings overtook him now—hopeless lassitude and
an unalterable feeling of doom—as had clenched his gut so many
years ago as he curled on his bed, the April sun looming in
spiraling dust shafts, the individual motes spinning loose but
always returning to the vortex. Gorm hadn't been stricken with
love, only with familiar loss. Dorothea Millikan would never be
accessible to him. She had outwitted him. Even if they met on
totally different terms ten years from now and he thought her the

most desirable woman he had ever known, he knew he would stand little chance of wooing her, not as lover, friend, or occasional accomplice, simply because he had failed to guess there were bricks in the bookbag she made him tote up steep hills.

Worse, it pronounced a verdict on all future dealings with women. If Gorm acted as dumb as he felt with them, as passively eager for acceptance as he had with the fire chief's daughter, he knew they would eventually name a room in a mental asylum after him, not an alley.

It was not an arena he was eager to enter.

Yet, the alterconscience of Charles Atlas hovered over him saying, "A devout lass is the cure for your ache. A devout lass is the cure for your ache."

Gorm liked the idea of a "devout lass" stroking his forehead and playing with his bicepses. Yet the mechanics of procuring one amounted to the same problem which weighed him down— Gorm arousing one more human from their soddenness only to have them go limp when he left them and join forces with the man who sat on his chest at night.

Finding a "devout lass" involved flirting, wooing, and conquering; above all it meant using words at a nose-to-nose level. This phenomenon bewildered Gorm because he had had so little experience with it. The whole process seemed to demand an energy and know-how that overwhelmed Gorm just thinking about it.

He didn't believe for a second that he would ever be able to see the complete Gorm without fortifying the tremulous bud between his legs but even this involved a contradiction. For the bud to gain entrance to a woman's opening and remain there, it would have to increase notably in both length and girth. He had never actually seen or felt a slot but there were numerous stories and jokes from The Boys and their "jo-jo" books about the prodigious size of a cunt. Such was Gorm's ignorance of female anatomy, which the American education system, with its desire to fashion every young man into a mean jock or a factory eunuch, had done little to dispel, that he imagined himself launching his head into that slick cave and wiggling his ears in lieu of having a large enough pecker.

Worse: largeness of coital tools struck him not only as a worthy ideal but in the natural order of Hopewell. Was not everything else valued for its size? Bemoth linebackers who starred at Notre Dame? Pneumatic jackhammers that could rip a hole the size of an elephant in a city street? Buildings that were squatter and taller than their next door neighbor? Had not Gorm's aunts always appraised his progress with the comment, "My, how big you're getting?"

A man's tool was not only meant to imitate the size of the structures around him but their hardness and durability as well. It was in fact a "tool" for grinding, for shaping, for penetrating, for coaxing shrieks of joyous resignation.

His source for this information was actual printed matter, the "jo-jo" books The Boys studied like math equations on rainy nights at Ma Goolantz's Confectionery. Daddy Warbucks' member was the size of a club as he pursued Little Orphan Annie across the kitchen. The Boys, including Gorm, didn't think these crudely printed drawings on mimeograph paper were ludicrous or even worth a chuckle. Little Orphan Annie had to be put in her place. Her first problem was that she wasn't thankful to Daddy Warbucks for all he had done for her; she resisted his advances. "You ungrateful slut!" Daddy cried as Annie backed away from his throbbing club. Yet when Daddy Warbucks did peel her panties down, Annie's sluice proved so enormous Daddy Warbucks' head disappeared inside for a few minutes before he popped out and pronounced, "This bitch is endless." Only a club of a tool could keep Daddy Warbucks from being swallowed up. Only an aggressiveness bordering on savagery could combat the stealth of women according to street corner mythology.

Gorm thus imagined a woman's rift as just as deep as a chasm, as unpredictable and chaotic as life itself, as terrible and wild as nature, the woman, herself, as sneaky as a Comanche Indian, who as every boy knew, was the enemy of civilization and progress. Above all, she had to be tamed.

It was easy enough for Gorm to fathom the enormity of the task before him but when he felt the utterly resigned bud between his legs, the situation seemed hopeless. The next day he wrote again to Charles Atlas but in the style of an Irish bard he'd observed on the TV.

"Methinks my tool isn't big enough for the pot I have to stir. It is truly a wee thing and I think some sort of contraption is in order such as the head strap which allowed me to develop my sternomastoid."

The answer from Charles Atlas was no help at all:

"There is no rehearsal for the muscle to which you refer. You must simply plunge and take your chances. Practice makes perfectly for a wilier and stronger tool. However, for Flex members only, I can offer you an ointment for fast penetration called Ripple. It comes in three flavors. . . ."

Gorm did not read further.

Though he had no desire to venture out to lose his cherry, the notion of an inferior muscle goaded Gorm to rejuvenate and buttress that drooping spout. Late afternoons, before his father returned home from work, before Mrs. Vidoni and the rest of his court showed to supervise and cheer his workouts, Gorm took to sliming his underdeveloped proboscis with anything that was viscous and in immediate range of the medicine cabinet. Such lubricants included Vicks Vapo, Dr. Sloan's Miracle Linament, his father's Gilette Aerodynamic Foamy (because Gorm did not shave yet), Camay soap, sometimes together and sometimes separately, the frothy porridge of such a concoction producing such a foam as to conceal both instrument and Gorm's five fingers and slopping onto the bathroom floor so that at the first scuff of his father's work shoes on the rubber welcome mat, Gorm was forced to leave his heaving tool to pounce on the mess with wad after wad of toilet paper, often using up a half roll in order to conceal the latest effort to blossom the underdeveloped portion of his anatomy.

When the result of all this left his bird more withered and enfeebled-looking than ever, along with dried rings of soap that made him gouge and scratch his genital area so that thighs, foreskin, and balls became so chafed it seemed some unknown scourge, related to the pox, had affected Gorm, he began assaulting Laverne Link. Since despair about the nature of power had usurped all lust and he himself with his home remedies seemed to be stewing an airy broth, Gorm turned the channel to "2" and flapped his dong at the persistently smiling mug of Laverne. At first this was done with Bud Blossom Oil to lend a proper truncheon length and effect. When that ran out, he borrowed mucilage and putty from his father's tool chest and flapped his doodle at the unaware heroine, who continued smiling and making googoo eyes through a week of unseemly assaults.

When such desperate lubricants dried and encrusted an already purple foreskin and he had to spend hours peeling the head of his dong free so he could pee, Gorm momentarily relinquished muscle lubricants and "I Love Laverne."

The rest of his muscles had been buoyed up without their having to perform a practical function. Why did his penis have to be entrusted to the hidden, hairy holes of strangers to gain normal size, a sense of its own power? Gorm suspected it was also the one muscle that even while offered in plunging coitus might be extracted from the pit smaller than it entered if the female in question chose to belittle his performance while he was in the saddle. If not that, she might writhe so convulsively that his meager offering might slip into the dirt, cinders, whatever provided the bedding for his first tumble. Though Gorm had no experience of such pitfalls, jokes were plentiful enough among The Boys about such happenings. Usually such jokes referred to coons who, depending on reduction or exaggeration of the joke, disemboweled their victims with one stroke of a stupendous tool or suffered humiliation when their manhood slipped into the mud or was mistaken for a finger or twig by a lady in volcanic heat.

Even the Encyclopedia of Sexual Knowledge belittled his developing manhood. Its closeup diagram of the penis divided into 31 components reminded Gorm of the map of Italy, teeming with dark ungovernable fluids and so many principalities fighting for control, that Gorm wondered whether his own failure wasn't caused by an unruly urinary tract.

Gorm returned to his habitual way of analyzing things, much as he had when searching for the ball bearing, and came to the conclusion he should seek out advice on this matter. The Boys were out. Anything remotely concerned with a sexual or anatomical nature drove them to frenzied parody. Once when Mrs. Tomlinson, a high school math teacher, was rumored to have had a bout with hemorrhoids, they discussed the matter for two hours, working themselves into hoarse hyperbole and finally agreeing that doctors would have to enlarge the passage in her right ear to spare her pain and allow the larger turds to escape by that route into an oversized balloon lapping her lobe which would fill with hot air as the feces began its escape. Apply the same unusual proctology to the other ear, they said, and you had the beginnings of a new Walt Disney character: Shitmouse.

No, The Boys would not be the best source for advice.

Gorm approached his father hesitantly. His old man was standing by the stove stirring Mother's Oats in a saucepan. Gorm braced one hand against the refrigerator. The odor of the breakfast food he associated with his mother on cool mornings rose in moist quiffs to his nostrils.

"Hungry, Pop?"

"A little, Son. Shouldn't you be getting ready for school?"

Gorm could never remember approaching his father for ad-

vice. The man moved stolidly, his whole weight and being concentrated in each step forward, no matter how small the chore.
Now he concentrated on the oatmeal as if it were a chemical
formula for advanced research he had been working on for a long
time. He was more a presence than a father in Gorm's life. They
had fought only once and that over some trivial matter both had
forgotten. Since his mother's departure they had been like convicted accomplices determined to make the best of things.

Gorm shifted his weight to his other hand against the clothes-
chute door. How do you ask your father the proper procedure for
making your dick bigger?

"It's about my muscles. . . ."

"You're coming along fine, son. You seem much stronger and
assured since the barbells arrived. Landini mentioned you at the
plant the other day."

"It's about one of my muscles, Pop."

"I'm sure you can handle it. The whole neighborhood's impressed with the way you've matured."

Gorm's father stared at the oatmeal and stirred as he talked.
He stirred and stirred. Cars rattled over the humped-back bricks.
In the alley, Gorm's Alley, other cars coughed and wheezed and
gunned into existence. From across the hollow where Skeetersville lay shrouded in river fog and blast furnace smoke, an open
hearth boomed its discharge. And Gorm's father stirred and
stirred. The smoking oats went round and round. And Gorm's
father stirred.

Gorm had never before asked guidance from anyone in his life.
Not a teacher, coach, minister, mayor, pharmacist, neighbor or
parent. He shifted his weight back to the refrigerator. His fingers
did a little dance on the white, porcelain finish. The depression-
model Stuart-Warner motor rumbled under his palm when he let
himself be balanced by it.

"It's about women." Gorm heard his voice go ragged, scratching from some other world.

His father spun with the smoking pot in his hand. His eyes
were wild with the effort to focus.

"Got a chippie knocked up did ya?"

"No!" Gorm cried.

"Caught the clap, hmmm? Weiner starting to fester?"

"No," Gorm cried.

His father breathed heavily into the smoking oats.

"Whew, you shook me for a second son."

"I don't even have a girl," Gorm began, "but. . . ."

Mr. Gorm spun on his son with a broad smile.

"But you need money for one. Why didn't you say so?"

Gorm stared stupefied as his father set the pot down, fished out his wallet, and proffered a five-dollar bill. Gorm watched it flap in midair. His father slapped it down on a table the other side of the stove.

"Don't blow it all in one night," he advised his son. Then he scooped the mounds of oats into a bowl. He poured milk on it. He sprinkled sugar deftly around the circumference of the bowl. His back was to Gorm now.

"Ahh, there's nothing like a bowl of hot cereal to get a man going."

He swallowed great, steaming mouthfuls.

Gorm did not go to school. After his father left, he stripped and wandered around the house as if looking for something. He made a tumultuous shit and forgot to wipe himself. Instead, he scooted downstairs to the kitchen and wiped with the five dollar bill. He held it above his head and pranced about the house, singing, "I'm just a little boy in heaven."

The rest of the day he spent in a reverie whose spirals were more the shape of his mind like those first clouds whose shifting shapes imitated his state of being. He did not answer the knocks of his court later that afternoon, and when dusk settled over Hopewell with its easeful limbo, Gorm wandered to his bedroom window, placed one finger in his nose, and mistook Venus for an eager star. While he worked old crusts around his septum, he saw Hopewell and the city of Stillwell beyond as a dreamer's landscape, unpredictable as those first visions released of his early torments by the junk in the coal room, the pulsing lights from the hillsides like those of a sprawling Ferris wheel, the larger guidelights of the bridges to the west ringed like dancing pearls on an old whore's necklace. The silhouetted smokestacks piping their ubiquitous streamers seemed more like salutes to a topheavy fantasy land than the grim daylight producers of impenetrable metal. It was just above the streetlights of East Bessemer, a hill town to the east, that Gorm first spotted the paternal grin of Hopalong Cassidy.

Hoppy wore the same faintly smiling, fatherly expression he had in the days of double features when he guided his white horse Topper from town to town securing justice for sheep ranchers. After these double features, it was the child Gorm's habit to race the back alleys, not imitating the virile cowboy he had just viewed, but the gait of the horse. To get the proper rhythm, Gorm found it necessary to stiffen one leg for a "hop-a-long" effect. Viewed from a distance, Gorm might have been mistaken for a cripple; at close range for a lad suffering from dementia praecox, such was the gleam in his eye of his own heroism. As with junk, the alleys of Hopewell alone offered a breeding place for acting out greatness.

When Gorm arrived home, it was his habit to take a nap. Curled under covers, he often pictured Hopalong—the man—scooting from boulder to boulder, firing with his six-shooter as he did so and picking off bad men. Sometime before he drifted off to sleep, Gorm piled his pillows high and changed places with the man in the white hat. Inevitably he was nicked by a bullet—just a scratch wound but sufficient to bring Nadine Radakovich, the prettiest girl in the sixth grade, hovering over his outstretched body. Nadine brought him water and placed a hand on his forehead to check his temperature. For a long time they stared into each other's eyes while gunfire raged all around them under the Western sun.

When Gorm awoke from such naps, Nadine had disappeared; so had Hoppy. Only the white horse Topper remained and its slavering tongue worked on his face with rhythmic swashes. After the penumbra of dream had been absorbed by the sun shafting into his room, Gorm found himself lying in spittle from his own mouth. He had been chewing on the bedsheet.

It was a clear night now. From his bedroom window he could see an occasional delicate tongue of flame savor the night air then dip back into the mouth of a furnace in the valley. After Nadine Radakovich disappeared, Myrna Tedesco came out from behind a boulder to minister to his wounds. A dozen doe-eyed cuties tiptoed onto the western range during Gorm's childhood and early teenage years. Each one was succeeded by a horse.

In that limbo between dream and wakefulness, he had become companion to the Lone Ranger's Silver, Roy Rogers's Trigger, Gene Autry's golden palomino, the Cisco Kid's white horse, Wild Bill Hickock's chestnut mare, and at least twenty other horses of assorted colors belonging to both hero and villain. They had all licked his face. Gorm, in turn, as he'd entered still another limbo—this one between the Hippodrome Theatre and the real world, the labyrinth of alleys where Hopewell's citizens dumped their waste or could be seen scouring their waste—had returned their adoration. He had imitated their gallops, canters, head tossing and whinnies as he ran home from the movie, the thrill of being a simple horse sometimes resulting from a scent of the hiding enemy or simply from his own high-falutin equestrian spirits.

As Gorm stood by the window, so many years of hoofbeats resounding in his head, it seemed there was a considerable gap between man and horse. In the blinking of stars in the black pit beyond earth, he reflected like a boy who has been kicked in the head for imitating horses instead of heroes. Was not his favorite, The Lone Ranger, the essense of virtue? Did he not expose injustice and then eradicate it? The deep masculine register of his voice suggested that no matter what the difficulty, he could make everything better. If the Lone Ranger signified all that was good and manly, Gorm asked why a white horse bent over him when he awoke and not the masked man of virtue?

Though Gorm had never thought of himself as having the power to perform acts of virtue, he never doubted the value of men like the Lone Ranger, the Cisco Kid, and Wyatt Earp who rooted out the truth and acted upon it. The truth, to Gorm, was all well and good if you thought of yourself as a man, but what if you were nearly a man and would become a man when you found the secret to developing one small part of your body which until now had resisted development. This did not answer the question why horses and not heroes stood over him at the end of his dreams but it did raise more questions.

For example, how did the Lone Ranger develop his pecker to match the heroism of the rest of him? It was easy to imagine how the rawness of life on the prairie developed a young man's shoulders and arms and legs. Horseback riding gave him a strong but resilient back. Gorm had enough experience with danger to understand how the lawlessness of frontier days gave The Lone Ranger a detective's scent. Had not Gorm himself done some detective work, albeit unfruitful work, on the missing ball bearing? Gorm, too, like his heroes had often wanted to protect the weak against the cruelty of the strong. But if wholeness, by which Gorm understood his manhood, was to be achieved what could he learn from these heroes?

The boy understood for reasons of taste that the various stages in the development of their peckers, or their pectorals for that matter, could not be broadcast or shown on a screen. Gorm himself had offended the tastes of refined ladies when he'd posed for aunts Lydia and Alvena. Yet, none of Gorm's childhood heroes ever mentioned their body parts unless they'd been shot or horsewhipped. For that matter they never talked about their development, not the Lone Ranger, Hopalong Cassidy, Batman, Superman, Tarzan, Buck Rogers, Roy Rogers, Wyatt Earp, the Cisco Kid, or Wild Bill Hickock. Not Al Capone, or Joe Di-Maggio or Captain Video. The *how* of their arrival at fullblown heroism was never discussed. They simply *were*. They arrived: through clothes-line logic, they discovered; they conquered; they offered a tidy moral; they departed.

Doubt had not manipulated whole months or years of their lives. They did not lie awake at night thrashing over a sense of their weakness as Gorm knew he had. They slept comfortably on boulders; coyotes howled; Indians were all about; but they never admitted to so much as a bad dream.

If a large and wily pecker was so important to full develop-ment, to that arrival called manhood, why was it never even hinted at? Neither Davy Crocket nor Abe Lincoln nor Daniel Boone nor Ben Franklin had ever discussed the development of the weenie between their legs. As ignorant as Gorm was of sexual anatomy, he knew a dong was one-half responsible for the creation of a child.

Yet when children did show up on a radio or television show or in a movie, they were treated as momentary pests to be tolerated at best. Gorm could not conceive of himself sprouting little Gorms. But that was because he was busy figuring out and developing his own notion of what it meant to be a Gorm. Stand-ing by the window he stared at the blinking stars above Hopewell and Stillwell and decided he didn't want a lot of little Gorms fucking around in his alley, Gorm's Alley. Living by the law of waste had been too hard on him. He wanted his kids to walk upright on main avenues, not slink about in back alleys looking for old waste but good waste to revive. He did not want kids but surely if a man was a hero he would want to sire little heroes. A hero like The Lone Ranger would be confident of passing on to little rangers (would they be masked?) the lessons of truth and justice and freedom and heroism. If a hero like Matt Dillon had made Dodge City safe from outlaws, surely he would want to make some little Dillons to enjoy that peace, but all he did was sit in a bar ruminating over a glass of beer with a lame sidekick, an alcoholic doctor, and a cathouse madam.

"Where were all the pretty girls?" Gorm cried by the window. Then, aware that he was alone, he lapsed back into reverie.

Where indeed were they? It seemed silly of him to meander into questions of the hero's family when the hero didn't talk to women. There was little evidence of women unless they were pretty ladies who'd come to be betrothed to a wealthy rancher, or whores who bedded mainly with badmen. If the hero wasn't interested in women, who was he interested in? Whom did he talk to? Above all, practical man that the hero was, how did he get his bud to blossom to match the quickness and deadly fire of his mouth and gun? How did Gorm's favorite men become whole men?

Well, The Lone Ranger talked to a he-Indian named Tonto. Tonto said, "Where to now, Kingushubby?" and the masked man answered, "Where innocent people are victimized and there is no one to help them, Tonto." This was fine, thought Gorm, if he was concerned about injustice, but his own brief experience had taught him that no sooner did you cure it in one area than it broke out in another. People always had to have something to beat on, and if they found they could no longer do it to one person, they'd bang on someone else. It was not impossible that he could do with justice what he had done with junk—mosey about the town restoring its worth, but that would have meant devoting all of his self to a single enterprise when he didn't have a whole self. He had nearly a whole self, but thinking about The Lone Ranger was not giving him so much as a hint about how to fortify his pecker to attain this wholeness. It did not seem reasonable that a man who was not only all man but a hero to boot could travel through life accompanied only by a stone-faced Indian. Best not to think so long about The Lone Ranger, Gorm decided.

He decided to think about Wild Bill Hickock. Wild Bill combined wildness with a passion for order but his serialization during eight years on television gave no hint that any ladies had helped him with the development of his tool. He traveled with a naive, fat, jolly sidekick named Jingles. Gorm could not remember a single program in which woman had come between Wild Bill and Jingles.

Gorm realized he would never have felt the chills run up his spine as he entered the real world as a child and galloped like a berserk thoroughbred if the heroes of the West hadn't offered him freedom and justice combined with a shrewd practicality. They were men who lived out their ideals; they got the job done and the world was better off for it. But what went through their minds as they lay by the campfires next to their snoring sidekicks as a dark, liquid swelling surged from between their legs to their justice-filled brains? Surely there was a time when they had to jab their dongs into some sort of receptacle if only to exercise that drooping dismal appendage and give it the heft the rest of their muscles had.

Now, Gorm was aware that two of those champions of justice and freedom, Roy Rogers and Gene Autry, had gals back at the ranch. Though it was never explicitly stated, Gorm surmised Roy

Rogers maintained a prong as strong as a biceps via the frothy pudding of Dale Evans. Yet Gorm could never hope to woo a girl with perfect teeth and a wholesome smile loaded with good nutrition and expressions like "Gosh darn, Roy." Even Nadine Radakovich had a chipped tooth and was known in moments of pique to shout, "Tease me one more time, Hunky Joe, and I'll bust your balls."

If such a slick gal as Dale failed to offer Gorm a hint of his own potential sexual prowess, Roy Rogers, himself, raised even greater doubts. Without warning, on the way to fight bad men, he'd stop on the trail and sing a song about prairie dogs and sagebrush and the great blue skies. Gorm knew the knotlike tension that built in himself just before a fight so that the fight, itself, was often a relief. To stop and sing a song about dappled blue skies just prior to a fight struck Gorm as gooeyness approaching insanity. Roy Rogers had none of the rough edges to survive in a mean, lawless place like the West, or Hopewell for that matter. He was a dude rancher and Gorm suspected they stuck him on the TV to woo silly nannies like his Aunts Lydia and Alvena who needed charm in their heroes. But what if Roy Rogers hadn't always been that way? What if he'd been strong once and then Dale Evans had gotten hold of him and made him sing dewy love songs and hang around the kitchen?

Gorm was starting to suspect why so many heroes avoided women. They weakened a man so that he could not live up to his own notion of strength and invincibility. If Gorm's model of such invincibility was the piston in a car, he figured the cowboy had the clamor of horse's hooves for his model. The lightninglike clippety-clop from town to town—the sound that both warned him of danger and echoed in his dreams as the source of all freedom.

At this point in his reverie by the window, Gorm stuck his hand in his pants. He was astounded not only by the smallness and helplessness of his bud but by the fact that his convoluted line of reasoning and reverie hadn't made an iota of difference in his immediate situation—HOW TO MAKE HIS PECKER AS BIG AND STRONG AS THE REST OF HIS MUSCLES THUS GIVING HIM A SENSE OF BEING A WHOLE GORM?

Gorm felt fury and hopelessness tighten his neck and jaw muscles. He was beginning to sense that for the important tests in life there were no guides and no guidelines. He squeezed the two pods between his legs for an answer to why this should be so but they did not reply; they just ached. In rapid succession, he checked off the other heroes of his childhood for some clue as to whether they'd developed the one muscle that couldn't be strengthened except in a girl's yawning chasm.

The only hero who passed the test was Tarzan with his jungle lady Jane but that was in Africa where Gorm's father had advised him uncouth practices were common. Tarzan not only had a woman but a boy named Boy. It was never clear if the boy, Boy, had come from Tarzan's loins, or Jane's loins, or the two loins locked in fashioning Tarzan's tool but Gorm was certain Jane never showed up to sit on Tarzan's lap till Tarzan had swung around on some vines for two hours fighting jungle adversaries. Gorm knew if he had had to swing on some vines for two hours before he got to stir his tool, he would be too exhausted to sit upright on the commode.

Each time Gorm squeezed his bud, panic and bile rose simultaneously in his gullet. "You've been fooled, little man," a voice whispered, perhaps that of the man who sat on his chest at night. Gorm was prone to agree but this still did not explain why he'd had the sensation of a horse licking his face when he'd awakened as a child. Gorm was sure he had no feeling for horses, only for vigilant men. He was unsure how long he'd been standing by the window, looking out at the blinking night. Perhaps his entire life, such was his sense of bafflement at that moment, had been spent with a glass window separating him from the world. Junk and secret hideaways and the swelling of his own flesh had made him feel good but what if they were ruses like so many of the heroes he'd been offered as lessons for his development? After all, he did not really *know* The Lone Ranger. Where did that mask come from? Why did he wear it? And where did the masked man get his silver bullets?

Such questions struck him as futile as figuring out why the culminations of his dreams had been filled with horses' tongues. What did become evident as he wandered in his mind among this labyrinth of hero props was that he was going to have to venture in to Hopewell and perhaps adjoining towns without any help at all in trying to find a female opening that would bring his pecker up to snuff.

"Goddammit masked man, you asshole," he cried and at that instant, it all fell into place. It was not for nothing that the Lone Ranger had a servile Indian accompanying him or that so many heroes had beside them chubby sidekicks on the lonely range at night. When The Boys indicated they wanted to harass someone, they said, "Let's get so-and-so's ass." The word "ass" was paramount. It signaled a servile creature who needed the protection of someone stronger. Indians and niggers naturally fell into that state but the word could be applied to almost anyone who was weak. Gorm knew it had been applied to him numerous times.

Putting two and two together, Gorm found it easy to picture the Lone Ranger saying to Tonto late at night on the range: "It's about time me and you got behind a boulder, Tonto. It takes *all* of me to deal with this lawless West and one of my muscles needs tuning if we're going to deal with that Dalton gang tomorrow." Tonto would answer "Whatever you say, Kingushubby," and go behind a boulder and peel down his buckskin breeches.

Now cornholing between two men was not a regular topic with The Boys but when it was, usually as a putdown, there was no doubt in Gorm's mind that it was perverted. Intimacy between men, Gorm figured, had to be discouraged because it was important to look strong and intimacy always revealed a weakness that men would eventually take advantage of in one another. Gorm knew how foul his own bunghole was and the idea of dealing with another person's made him nauseous. Yet it was precisely another person's ass which made a hero a hero. For years, Gorm knew now, the Lone Ranger had remained strong by bending that dumb Indian over a boulder. He wore a mask because Tonto might someday get the upper hand, along with lots of other Indians who'd been cornholed, and try to get revenge, perhaps reversing their positions over the boulder. Fat men, Gorm knew, were more accepting of their lot than Indians, so it wasn't necessary for Wild Bill and Cisco to wear a mask, they had to just keep their sidekicks riding slovenly horses so they couldn't run off. It probably wasn't easy to replace a chubby ass once you'd broken it in. Gorm had had numerous problems with his own.

As for silver bullets, Gorm quickly figured that one out, too. Tonto's innards had been in a state of rebellion much like Gorm's when he'd lifted weights and firmed them up and his ass had responded with precipitous volleys of farts and finally hardened little nuggets that even in their fresh state resembled coprolites. Add to this, the Lone Ranger's heroic fusillade, quick fire, and purity of discharge, rivaled only by the purity of his love for justice, and you got Tonto shitting silver bullets clinkety-clink into a pail at night as the Lone Ranger stood by, observing, "Only a few more Tonto and we'll be able to chase that Dalton gang from the territory forever." Tonto replied, "Whatever you say, Kingushubby."

Gorm then understood why the horse would lick his face. The horse was the only natural creature in those movies. It copulated freely with other horses thereby having a dong which measured up to the rest of its stature and it didn't have to play hide-and-seek with this process. If it was natural to be natural, then Gorm no longer felt odd for imitating nature, that is to say the cantering, whinnying, snorting, and head tossing of the truly natural horse. Oh, Silver, oh, fierce and gentle Topper. No wonder he had felt freest and happiest just after the movies in back alleys and would have remained so if the doe-eyed girls like Nadine Radakovich hadn't crept into his dreams. Even here he was only replacing in dream and fantasy what was missing on the Frontier—women who soothed you in a time of need. But if one were to gauge the lack of manhood in a Roy Rogers (with or without that chubby rascal Gabby Hayes) or Gene Autry, their having to hang around the kitchen and sing romantic songs was just as perverted, given the dangers of the West, as bumfucking behind boulders. Grateful as Gorm was to himself for having figured out The Lone Ranger myth, he was back in limbo again, not impotent bud or flailing pecker, but the profound choice of Man or Woman, and he would have lain his head against the window and sobbed, he was so tired and confused, if he hadn't heard his father opening the door and yelling, "Son, pickup tomorrow, time to put the garbage out."

The paternal grin of Hopalong Cassidy still hovered over the blinking milltown of East Bessemer but it was like a surrogate father returning after an absence to watch the results of the bad joke he'd played on his son.

During the next week, Gorm paced the three stories of the house . . . first the cellar where he would open the door to the extinct coal furnace . . . stare at the stony coprolites as if he were seeing them for the first time . . . race to the top floor to his father's bedroom . . . open the dark-grained cedar chest to gape at the imitation furs his mother had left behind so many years ago with the eyes of dead animals staring up from the collars . . . then down to the ground floor where the yellow eye of an A&P egg watched Gorm from the aluminum skillet in which his father had cooked early that morning until the boy stabbed the yolk with a paring knife, pretending the yolk was the rump of Jingles, and Pancho, and Tonto.

Such was his rage that he should be saddled with a stable of heroes whose sexual preference was the flaccid bums of jovial sidekicks that Gorm developed odd mannerisms in addition to wandering aimlessly around the house. First he bit his fingernails below the flesh level. Sundry other items began to find their way into his mouth. The tips of pencil erasers were shredded; his father discovered his Camel butts had little incisor marks in them. When these were unavailable, Gorm gnarled a hole in one end of his handkerchief. At school, teachers and students observed him staring out the window while nibbling at one end of his wooden ruler. But such was his reputation for strength, one and all assumed this was another bodybuilding exercise, perhaps for strengthening the jaws, or gums, or both. In short, all things remotely edible found their way to his mouth and Gorm continued gnawing right through the habitual barbell exercises at which time he chawed away at toothpicks.

Gorm's court took this later infantile symptom of nervousness for still another insignia of their hero's strength and imitated him. Their friends copied them and so on till a good third of Hopewell was walking about within two weeks with toothpicks in their mouths. The A&P, ever responsive to the needs of the community, had to order toothpicks by the gross instead of the customary carton and even advertised these pine splinters on the weekly handbill next to the cabbages, Idaho potatoes, Brillo pads, and disinfectant for floors and toilets. Indeed, the accumulation of toothpicks in the town's gutters was so overwhelming that the bristles on the street sweeper were innundated with them and were no longer effective and Albert Goolantz was called forth from his crosswalk lines by the town council to precede that hissing gutter machine with shovel and bushel basket so far reaching was Gorm's nervous reaction to a decade of fag heroes in Hollywood.

Mrs. Vidoni alone saw in Gorm's penchant for toothpicks, a sign for distress. She remembered his rapacity as a child for lodging all things in his mouth. She had recognized the habit then, even in a child, as frustration.

One evening after the barbells had been stacked and the rest of the court had left, she said to him, "What ails you?"

Gorm tried to joke away her query.

"My right delt wants to marry my trapezius and my trapezius is holding out for a big wedding reception."

"I was your babysitter, Gorm. You can't kid me."

Gorm stood by the laundry sink washing the talc from his hands.

He remained with his back to her when he spoke and said in a euphemism because he knew that manners above else were important with a woman who was one's elder, "All of me wants to be strong, Mrs. Vidoni. There are some things, or I should say one thing barbells can't develop."

Mrs. Vidoni took this as confirming her earlier suspicions and asked, "What's your faith, Gorm? Your mother was a holier-than-thou Mick but that was before you got any instruction. I don't remember your father being anything."

Gorm knew then he'd been misunderstood and turned with annoyance on the cleaning woman.

"The Lone Ranger liked men, Mrs. Vidoni. And worse he picked on a poor Indian who'd deserted the reservation and had no place else to go."

His helper took this as a mockery of the Lone Ranger's aloneness, springing from Gorm's own loneliness, and made up her mind to get him spiritual help.

In lieu of knowing how to proceed with his full development, Gorm decided to do what he had done with his own body when it was but a frail twig that was bent every which way: He researched the female anatomy at the Central Library in Stillwell. There he discovered that what The Boys called the "twat" was a labyrinth shaped like a leaf and that the stem had a life of its own. It could open and close to accommodate anything from a pipe cleaner to a baby's head. Such possibilities reinforced his own notion that a terrible chasm lay in wait to swallow him. The endless dissection showing compartments leading into compartments and tunnels and hoses filtering in and out of those compartments made him see why the Lone Ranger had preferred the simpler receptacle of Tonto's bumgut. But he was determined not to give in to perversion and came out of the library mumbling, "Labia majora . . . labia minora," certain that naming a thing would help him overcome his fear of it.

When he got home he conducted further research in his mind, the way he had with the ball bearing, and decided he was about to embark on a "conquest." This is what *True Confessions* magazines had termed the wooing by the man of woman, and though they were never actually shown locked together, Gorm suspected that this "conquest" included penetration by the pecker for development of its girth and muscularity. Pumperdink the Pukeroo had stolen these *True Confessions* from an aunt, and he and Gorm had pored over them by the hour, looking for clues as to how they should proceed with the "conquest" of tender but devious girls.

Yet a problem arose when he pondered those days of investigating the mystery of Man and Woman in *True Confessions*. Once the conquest was completed the man had to "go steady" or marry the instrument which shored up his dependent appendage. Gorm did not want a partner whom he would have to clothe and feed and perhaps have her run off with a sporting goods salesman; he merely needed a receptacle till his pecker was as strong as his other parts. Again the street lore of The Boys came to the rescue: Gorm needed a "wench" to "conquer."

"Wench" struck just the right chord with Gorm because no "good girl" allowed so much as a "French kiss" unless she was your steady. Only wenches allowed this and there were three in Hopewell: Alexandra Babchek, Flo Vanderbunt, sometimes known as The Prune for the incipient dryness of labias majora and minora, and Mary Ann Bunch, sister of convicted burglar Emil Bunch. This last "wench" was known to take on as many as nine boys at a time without changing her expression of truculent boredom.

Gorm thought: "Why not line up an administrator to my tool in advance?" and the giddy wisdom of such planning made his pecker jiggle in his undershorts as he dialed the first wench on the list, Alexandra Babchek.

As soon as he heard a female voice, he said, "Alexandra, perhaps you've heard of me. I'm Gorm the Strong. Once I was weak but I've worked hard and now I am strong. But not all of me is strong. I have been advised by the strongest man in America, Charles Atlas, that I may need help with that part of me that isn't strong." And Gorm would have continued ad infinitum, he was so nervous about requesting aid from another human being, if the female voice at the other end hadn't cut him off.

"This is Alexandra's mother and I don't know what you're talking about. Alexandra's at a Christian Youth Fellowship meeting."

"What time will she be home?" Gorm asked.

"You sound so screwy I really don't know what difference it would make," and the woman hung up.

It deeply annoyed Gorm that the mother of one of the easiest three humps in Hopewell would be so arch with him. He was tempted to call the woman back and advise her of the conditions under which her daughter had lost her cherry, a story he knew from The Boys to have taken place in the back seat of Chubby Chuck's green Hudson. Instead he dialed Flo Vanderbunt's number next, wary that a dry labia would be insufficient to develop his tool, but concerned that he might not secure any labia at all.

After the first ring, a woman with a voice of corroded zinc answered and cried, "God help the pigshit Irish." Glass crashed in the background and a man's voice cried "Up yours!" whereupon the woman hung up.

At the next residence he dialed, the female voice that answered was a little more mellow.

"Is this Mary Ann Bunch?" Gorm queried hesitantly.

"Archie," cried the voice, "that no good Angelo was supposed to be here an hour ago. Where the hell is he?"

"I don't know anything about Archie or Angelo. This is Gorm."

"Who?"

"Gorm. We sat beside each other in math class in the seventh grade. You used my eraser and when my inkwell ran dry you let me use yours. . . ."

"Is this Beanhead Simko?"

"No, Gorm, G-O-R-M . . . some of the kids threw spitballs at me . . . but I'm stronger now. . . ."

"Chuckie Grimwald. . . ."

"No Gorm. Listen, they used to kick the shit out of me. . . ."

"Don't cuss!"

"I'm sorry but you must remember me. Just last week we passed each other in the hall. . . ."

"Do you have big blue eyes and a Tony Curtis?"

"No, my hair's parted but I have big muscles and roll up my sleeves to the biceps. I guess that's vain but I don't want sand kicked in my face anymore."

"I still can't place you. But look, call me some other time. I gotta run. I'm in the middle of my first true love affair and he's due here any minute."

"Wait you! I'm not that easy to forget."

But the third most reputed lay in Hopewell had hung up.

It was evident now Gorm had no choice but to venture into Hopewell and offer himself to the first wenchy-looking woman who came his way. To call maximum attention to himself, he would wear his barker's outfit that had enabled him to hypnotize the Woolworth ladies: jacket, pink shirt with the whipped-cream ruffles, bow tie, tartan cummerbund, and ox-blood loafers with pennies in the slots. The pearl buttons had popped on his shirt when he'd shown off his torso selling girdles but the urgency of his mission now could excuse such a breach of fashion. It was spring. He used safety pins and kept the jacket pulled close.

As always, the sight of himself in the mirror in his barker's uniform made Gorm feel cocky. He gave his image a sprightly wink and feinted a couple of left jabs. As a feeling of benignity crept up his legs and latissimus dorsi, Gorm pondered further the mechanics of this wooing of the opposite sex. Was it not the duty of the wooer to bring the wooee a present? Had Gorm had a sister or a mother, he might have borrowed a babushka or a pair of panties to give to his new lady. Having neither, he began to wander the house in search of some little trinket fit for a wench. He had no luck until he spotted a large soup pot on the stove. Granted he was after a wench but did not every woman who wanted to lasso a man prepare her bait by tossing little tidbits into a pot and stewing them into a heady aroma? The soup pot was a logical choice and Gorm was pleased with his foresight.

He was about to leave when it occurred to him that whoever the lucky lass was that got to stroke such a body as his, she might want to be treated to some sweets. This took money. Gorm did not have money nor had he had much interest in money because there was so little he wanted from the world. Now that he wanted a wench it did not seem like a bad idea to take some money along to appease the tart before or after she buttressed his feeble spout.

His father had left for work so he could not ask him. Then he recalled the fivespot he'd wiped himself with and flushed down the toilet. He bolted up the stairs certain that where there was money there was hope.

Having had so much trouble with his bowels early in his life, Gorm knew it was not unusual for his daily feces to be regurgitated. The adjacent row houses all piped into central plumbing so that if two or more houses flushed at the same time, the main pipe accepted only one, sending the other waste back to face its owner. Occasionally the main pipe got the waste confused, sending a nonsmoking and fastidious family the butts of cigars and Q-tips and cotton from nosebleeds while the offender got off clean and had the joy of watching his commode fill with clean water to great sighs and hisses. Gorm was familiar with all this and used to confronting his feces again and again with the obligatory five-minute wait, whereupon he flushed again, his success dependent on no one on his right or left hunching to poop or flicking a butt into the can.

Gorm was in luck. His father's gift floated serenely, the mournful visage of Abe Lincoln reminding the boy that whatever torturous route the money had taken only to be rejected, it was useful though waterlogged and slightly shit-stained around Abe's solemn eyes. By turning up the thermostat on the gas furnace and holding the bill before the living room vent, he was able to dry it out. Gorm was annoyed by its stench as he stood there waving it, and wondered if the bill hadn't been jostled by someone else's turds before it was returned to him.

With his gifts in tow—one in an envelope against his chest, the other in a shopping bag—Gorm embarked toward Hopewell's center to find himself a wench.

Gorm tried to woo his first wench by positioning himself at the bus stop across from Woolworth's. Yet when the first bus stopped and let off passengers, their eyes were so fixated with the thought of a meal, he could not tell the wenches from the coy virgins. As the red tailights of the bus receded in the distance, a wind wrapped his coat around him as if he were a sack of sardines.

Gorm was ready for the next bus. He placed the pot in front of him and when the passengers got off, he gave it a couple of kicks. Several people, including a black man with an eye patch, stopped and threw change in the pot, mistaking Gorm for the Salvation Army boy. Again, not a single woman gave Gorm more than a perfunctory glance.

He dumped the money into his pocket, picked up the pot and walked east toward the Monongahela River. The trouble with procuring a wench, he decided, was that there was only *one* to be sought when he was the kind of person who was used to addressing crowds when he bothered to speak at all. He thought he probably should have retained Mazoupa, but what with her insides hemorrhaging, she would be no good at all.

He left the Hopewell business district and passed along a treeless street that offered a lodge at succeeding corners: the VFW, The Honorable Knights of Columbus, The Shaggy Raccoons of Greater Hopewell, and The Lodge of Acorns, as if joining one of these was the entrance to the business district and the greater community beyond.

But Gorm was going the other way.

Increasingly the houses grew squatter as if they had made a pact to sink into themselves and show as little of their stature as possible. The few trees that existed rose like modern sculptors' memorials, shaking in the wind like twisted wrought-iron parodies of the living thing. Gorm heard a boom and clatter of a blast furnace releasing slag as he turned down a steep hill.

The feeblest aorta of a business district staggered before him. Sometime in its battered and remote history there had been an attempt at lighting but many of the streetlights had been shot out and the neon signs jutting over the sidewalks offering pleasure for the stomach and throat and brain and groin no longer blinked but hovered like tarnished medallions. There was activity though.

Clots of children broke before Gorm and exploded like confetti into alleys. Music like hot syrup oozed out of an open window and ran down his arms and legs. Gorm felt the dimmest of stirrings in his groin and knew he could be in only one place—Skeetersville. Some men in peg pants and conk jobs that made them look like glorious black roosters strutted out not 20 feet in front of him. They smacked their thighs and did spins to something funny one of them had said, then launched themselves into a yellow Hudson Hornet which rocked with their joyous entry. From inside an establishment labeled "RIBS," Gorm heard, "Tell that bitch to shut her mouth."

Gorm would not have been surprised to see or hear anything in Skeetersville though the thought of such freedom tightened his cummerbund and made the bow tie squeeze his larynx. This was the land where the impossible took place, not through kings draped in mail riding elephants over mountains but through one-eyed ogres waiting in alleyways to swallow little boys who ventured too far from their mommies' starched aprons. It was always dark in Skeetersville and the darkness itself could swallow a stranger. Gorm's mother had sung its diabolical mysteries everytime her child had strayed from her control.

"One of these days you're going to stray so far from Home, the Bogeyman in Skeetersville is going to get you."

"What will he do with me?"

"He'll do what he does with all little boys who disobey their parents."

"What's that, Mom?"

"He eats them up."

"Does he digest them?"

"No, he vomits them up but they're never the same afterward."

Now Gorm the child knew the story of Jonah and the Whale so he asked his mother if the Bogeyman's stomach was as big as the whale's.

"Bigger," she said.

"Is The Bogeyman bigger than The Whale?"

"Just when he sees little white boys who've wandered too far from home. He expands, you see. He gets as big as a whole town."

"Could he swallow Hopewell?"

"Hopewell is protected by the police."

"I thought you said The Bogeyman gets so big he could swallow a whole town."

"He could if the police didn't have guns."

"Then I'll get a gun and if The Bogeyman tries to swallow me I'll shoot him."

"No you won't. You'll quit arguing with *your mother.*"

"Does The Bogeyman eat little colored boys too?"

"No, they don't have mommies and daddies who care about them like you do."

"If you and Dad quit caring about me, will the Bogeyman eat me?"

"We'll *always* care about you. Now go play with your building blocks."

A few years later in his pursuit of junk, Gorm defied the law of The Bogeyman to scour the railroad tracks around Skeetersville for old junk but good junk, but at the first sign of dusk, he'd turned his wooden red wagon around and bolted back to Hopewell. His mother's hyperbole got refurbished in junior high school when The Boys pinned the gamut of lust on "coons" in Skeetersville. The Bogeyman then became not so much a singular monster but a lusty, capering physicality. Most of The Boys' sexual jokes dealt with coons in heat. Their tools were so large and able as to have the quality of truncheons and it was said that colored women sat on the front porches rocking in perpetual heat and sometimes mounted by as many as twenty coons in an evening, whereupon they went on welfare. Indeed, Skeetersville was a dark and enraged incubator of babies and knife scars. Despite The Boys' attempts to reduce the Bogeyman to a level they could fathom, he never entirely lost his hold on Gorm as some sort of punishment—a gorging and disgorging—for those who wandered too far from home.

Even now it made sense to Gorm that The Boys should have reduced colored folk to inflated genitals perpetually running with lubricous desire. He could never recall a single white person in Hopewell admitting he was in heat. Was not heat, as he'd observed it in numerous tomcats in his, Gorm's Alley, necessary for breeding babies? Had he, himself, not felt it when he'd been wooed by Laverne Link on "I Love Laverne"? If Charles Atlas was right, the only way to develop *all* of himself was to stir his tool in a girl's frothy pudding, did not such development call for HEAT if the tool had to be hard to enter such pudding? It was an odd question for Gorm and it made him wonder if desire was not related to other kinds of development as well.

He was growing tired, as much from his habitually convoluted way of trying to ferret a path to the truth, as from the walk. In a flash he made up his mind to plop himself down anywhere there might be modest pedestrian traffic and see what manner of help offered itself. At the next corner there was an establishment whose exact nature Gorm could not identify but it had a sign that worked and it said "The House of Gumbo." He sat to one side of its doorway and placed his pot in front of him.

He was staring into the distance at a police cruiser when a dapper little brown man stuck his face into Gorm's.

"What can I get you, big man? Ornery Ike at your service."

The man breathed like an acetylene torch into Gorm's face.

"There's an alley named after me," Gorm told him to make him keep his distance.

"That's nothin," the brown man said, "I got me a president of the U-nited States named after me, ha ha."

The man leaned toward Gorm, again perfuming him with whatever he'd drunk in The House of Gumbo.

"You look like a man who's in pain. For a small fee Ornery Ike can get you some pain killer. What's your preference Alley Man, Mogen David . . . Thunderbird?"

Gorm said it was not wine he needed but a wench to aid in the development of his tool.

Ornery Ike said he was the wrong man for "poontang" but if Gorm would slip him "a few coins" he would return with a "tool adviser pronto." Gorm clawed from his pocket the coins the bus exiters had tossed him and awaited the return of help for his drooping tool.

The man had only been gone a few seconds before Gorm heard a tremendous bang behind him followed by a succession of echoing clatters. He darted between The House of Gumbo and a shabby frame home and came to a hillside that opened on to the Monongahela River bank with its plumbing mills, warehouses, and railroad yards. A freight train being connected had made the noise that startled him.

Gorm had felt himself all his life to be living in the shadow of the mills yet now that he actually stood in physical proximity to them, he no longer felt awe, but a massive disorientation of his senses. The sulphur in their discharges made his eyes water and the odor was like inhaling the fumes of a bus. He was perhaps the length of a football field from the Monongahela shoreline but the decay of rancid carp made his nostrils quiver and his stomach dance under the tightening cummerbund.

Even though it was night, a spring night at that, antlike activity marshaled itself along the millfront. Forklifts darted between boxcars and warehouses like solemn insects whose pincers were ever alert for grasping and whose movement was dictated by a force beyond Gorm's sight or imagination. Freight trains shuttled back and forth to receive cargo. Everything moved with an amphibian stealth as if such business could be conducted only at night. Men with hard hats were carried with the greatest deliberation in and out of the loading by official-looking pickup trucks.

The trains did not seem to proceed toward a particular destination but slunk forward like Serengeti lions ready to devour an as yet unseen prey with the stately jaws of their engines. What the trains couldn't devour the barges would. They eased along the river front like sea monsters from another era, their stern and bow blue lights accentuating their ponderous amphibian tendency of waiting, waiting. All these machines told Gorm they were wily creatures of the night. He, himself, was a hungry, willful creature who pounced on things for his Gormlike expansion and yet of recent weeks he had felt himself to be shrinking with each manful effort to assert himself.

He staggered backward and fell to brooding beside his pot. There was still no sign of this helper for his tool and without thinking he stuck his hand in his pants. His tool was solemn as ever and to Gorm's acute sense of growth and dimunition, it had shrunk while he stared at the riverbank. If there was actually a demon called the Bogeyman in Skeetersville, Gorm was certain he'd made a pact with Bog & Bliss Steel. The two of them had made a contract to swallow little boys who strayed too far from home. The air was a miasma, an umbrella of all that was putrid and it swallowed everything in its midst—people, tricycles, houses, neon signs. All that was called civilization was swept up in its smoky paws, pulled into its jaws, digested in the maw of its progress, and shat out in smoky, curling claws to complete gestation: victim and victimizer were finally one, the victim joining with his accuser to stroke and pull fresh initiates into the furnace of hope, Hopewell and Stillwell and Skeetersville progress. Gorm felt all of himself subside into the bud that cried out for the porridge of development.

"Quit playing with yourself. It breeds discontent and hinders the development of the finer things of life."

Not the erudite swing of the words, but the tone was instantly familiar to Gorm and he took his hand from between his legs and looked up to see a lanky brown man with a patch over one eye and a demeanor of great dignity.

"I was just checking my development," Gorm told him.

"Development is everything a man in search of his essence could wish for in the truest sense of totality. Unless a man cherishes that part of himself that is most unique, ushers it toward grace and well-being, what does he have to offer his fellowman? You tell me."

Gorm stared with considerable bafflement at the origin of this diarrhea of words. He had never heard a colored man talk with such aplomb but he chalked this up to his limited experience in Skeetersville. It reminded him of his own soup of words that frothed out of him before crowds. But he had had a definite purpose, whereas he had no idea what this one-eyed man meant to do with so much gobbledygook. He felt a keen sense of competition with the man. He also understood it was the same one-eyed man he'd seen get off the bus across from Woolworth's. He had not tossed money into Gorm's cooking pot.

"Say 'Waydown . . . hoedown . . . traaashh,' " Gorm advised him.

"You want development or you want junk?" the man asked him.

"You gave me a lot of trouble as a child," Gorm said.

"How was that? I ain't been pimpin' but four years."

"I used to like skillets . . . big, round skillets. Heavy ones that were black and tempered and made of iron. Alarm clocks too. I liked the old-fashioned kind with real glass fronts and metal bottoms and. . . ."

"Sliding curtain rods of pure brass that went for 14 cents a pound," said Black Jack.

"Yeah, and lead and iron soldiers. Enough to make a whole platoon. . . ."

"And fancy lamps with all kinds of grooves in the shaft. . . . I could sell those outright for a good price. Yessir," said Black Jack, "there were all kinds of good things that people threw out in those days."

"For you, maybe," said Gorm, "most families wouldn't give me anything until you had first pick."

"Trash is always meant for niggers."

Gorm said he had gotten plenty of good trash.

"Maybe you was a nigger and didn't know it."

Gorm replied that whatever he was, he'd outgrown it, all except for one muscle.

"That's right, you're interested in development."

Black Jack again launched into a rhetorical flow. He said all things under God's skies needed developing and he wiggled his smallest pinky in midair to emphasize the point. It moved only at the hand joint. It was a stunned, useless appendage. He repeated this maneuver with great pride with two fingers on his other hand.

"Even a nigger needs to know where his humanity lies. Bog & Bliss unknowingly supplied me the chance to rise above my humble beginnings. They broke one finger, then two, then three."

"They forced you to make your fingers stronger than ever," said Gorm, with great certainty and ignoring the evidence before his eyes.

"No," snapped Black Jack, "some things can never be mended."

Gorm shuddered that his pecker might droop permanently.

It became obvious to Gorm that this residue of his childhood liked to talk almost as much as he did. With an expressive raising and lowering of his arms, Black Jack spoke as if addressing a tumultuous throng. He said the vast energy which had once transformed ingots into sheet metal went straight to his brain. After his fingers had been broken in a series of accidents at Bog & Bliss, he'd taken the workmen's compensation and signed up for the St. Fillmore School of Great Books and never been sorry.

"Paid for me to sit and read the musings of Montaigne. I've always felt a debt to Bog & Bliss for breaking my fingers."

Gorm was tempted to ask why one part of the body had to be broken for another to be utilized but he was anxious to get down to the business he'd come for. Black Jack ignored his impatience, and gestured wildly at the cloudless sky overhead.

"Plato, Marcus Aurelius, Gibbons, Shakespeare . . . they all taught me the glory of the mind's musings. Why, if Bog & Bliss had cracked my legs, snatched my arms from their shoulder sockets, I wouldn't hold a thing against them."

To illustrate his premise, the black man fell to his haunches, held his arms behind him, and rolled against the peeling frame wall on the side of The House of Gumbo. In this semblance of a basket case, the one-eyed man cried, "I'd still have my mind. Only God can look inside my brain and even then only with my permission.

"The unexamined life ain't worth livin', " he cried at Gorm.

Gorm was perfectly willing to admit that. For the moment, though, he had more pressing problems. The longer the man had talked, the smaller Gorm's dick had felt so that he was anxious to get on with the business of securing a wench to get the final aspect of his development over with once and for all.

Still hunched against the wall in an imitation of a paraplegic, the one-eyed man cried, "To be or not to be."

Gorm kicked the cooking pot.

The colored man abruptly stood at attention.

"What you got there, my good man?" he said genially.

Gorm explained that he'd brought the pot as a gift for that special woman who could aid in developing that one part of his body that needed developing.

Black Jack stared at the pot. In his four years of pimping he had heard dozens of euphemisms for an hour of pleasure, but this "development" business took first prize.

The ex-junk man had already decided Gorm was a freak who was a waste of time. Teenagers often came to him for their "official breaking in" but they wore the clothes of their own race, not a nigger getup like this character did. The young man reminded Black Jack of the old days when white folk performed minstrels in black face. Besides, who had ever heard of a white person, even a child, competing with a black one for Hopewell's trash? But it would not be easy to get rid of him.

"History was made on this street," he cried, hoping this husky virgin would get weary of his rambling and drift away of his own accord. "All the adaptations from Bessemer to the open hearth, the development of the rolling mill, the systematic shift from iron makers to steel processors. . . ."

Black Jack first pointed his finger one way down the street, then another way, then gestured at a peeling frame house directly across from The House of Gumbo.

Gorm was incensed with all this babbling. He said, "I'm more interested in my own development than this broken-down town."

"Ahhhh, but it all began here," said the one-eyed man. "Once Stillwell was the most productive city that had ever existed on the face of the earth. Now you take the combined tonnage in 1944. . . ."

"I need a wench!" Gorm screeched.

The one-eyed man smiled and said, "Even wenches took pride in production in those days. Only they were chauffeur driven and they came to that house right over there."

Gorm looked with interest to where Black Jack pointed. It was the peeling frame house directly across from them. Its bare yard was filled with the carcass of an automobile and assorted children's toys. The back wheel of a bicycle was propped against a tall watering can; a deflated beach ball sat sunken in its crown like a pre-made bird's nest. A baby doll lay spread eagled staring at the sky. A rusted metal Chinese checker board kept her company. Marbles and bubble gum cards of black baseball heroes completed the deserted toyland.

Gorm felt a surge of interest in so much junk but he told Black Jack he didn't understand why any limousine would pull up in front of such a house.

"The nephew of H. Clay Frick, the Coke king, lived there. Where yesterday's brains resided is today's asshole."

When the one-eyed man saw his client hesitate, he added, "History's always a bitch with a wagonful of junk."

History, unless it was his own, had always bored Gorm in school but the sight of all that junk in a single front yard made his adrenalin flow.

"The only answer," said the one-eyed pimp, "is to rise above it. One morning I awoke and heard the clarion call of Thomas Aquinas . . . Spinoza . . . Machiavelli. . . ."

"What did you do with all that junk?"

"What junk?"

"The junk you got and I didn't."

"Sold some, kept some. I figured you could never tell when junk would make a comeback."

"Where at? Where do you keep it?"

Black Jack tried to talk Gorm out of visiting his "apartment" to see junk but the boy was adamant. The idea of a reunion with his childhood friends—metal, rubber, and wood—sent chills up his spine. He completely forgot about his diminished pecker and chattered and skipped by turns, leaving the saturnine ex junk man puzzled.

To reach the "apartment" they had to take a steep wooded trail toward the Monongahela River. Sounds and smells grew more distinct as if by leaving the world the signs of its life became more pronounced. A train engine hooted and a rhythmic clang signaled a man pounding on metal. Then the wind picked up the fumes of smoldering garbage from the Skeetersville dump. The acrid waves made Gorm dig in his nostrils as he walked.

The "apartment" turned out to be a large tin warehouse. There were no windows. The padlock that protected it was as long as a tire iron. Black Jack stuck a skeleton key into it and turned to Gorm.

"You can look at the junk if you want but I ain't got time to waste on you. I can get you your nooky, signed, sealed, and delivered, but I need the bread up front."

Gorm explained that he was not interested in "nooky." He merely needed that last spindly portion of his anatomy developed so the queasy feeling in his heart and stomach would go away.

Gorm went on at such length, burying what Black Jack thought was his natural lust in a bevy of euphemisms that the trash collector slammed the flat of his hand against the tin siding. From inside Gorm heard scurrying; pigeons flew up from the roof with great commotion to a nearby tree.

Black Jack said he didn't have time for "fool talk."

Now, coming down the wooded trail, Gorm had felt such a lifting of his spirit at the thought of seeing the collections of a master junk collector that he did not want to irritate the old man more than he already had. He pointed toward the shopping bag.

"Take that," he said.

"Where I come from, that pot's not worth pissing in."

"My mother cooked lentil soup in it," Gorm advised Black Jack.

"And where is she now?"

"I don't know."

"Ha!"

The one-eyed man slapped his thigh with vindication.

When he'd settled down, he asked Gorm what else he had to offer besides the cooking pot. Gorm then proffered the five-dollar bill. The colored man said he didn't like the smell but money was money and snatched it from the boy's hand. "Poontang in these parts normally goes for ten and fifteen. But I'll put out the good word for you and see if I can get you a quick sniff."

He opened the door to let Gorm inside and said he would return before the boy could say, "Jack Robinson." Gorm stepped into the pimp's home and heard the lock click behind him.

Gorm's first reaction was that he'd metamorphosed into Hansel. Everywhere he looked lay the candy of his childhood—junk. It was piled in corners, stacked to the ceiling; it was never-ending chaos that wrapped about itself, a porridge of the discarded that begged for resuscitation. Heaps grew into mountains and mountains spilled over on one another. And there was another room.

Gorm crawled over a ruptured Chippendale couch, two bushel baskets of lightbulbs, an Easy Boy chair with its leg rest dangling like a crippled wing, to get to this second room where a light shone. He wanted to take in this reincarnation in a single gulp.

But the second room immediately disappointed him. He frowned into the stark light of what was clearly new goods, serviceable ticky-tack from Hong Kong and Tokyo. Television sets with their price tags still dangling from the volume knob were stacked in one corner. Next to them, their cheap chrome flashing all that was fashionable, sat varying sizes of transistor radios. There were hubcaps too, not the veritable knights' shields of Buick Dynaflows, but tinsely jobs for modern economy cars, hubcaps that would never clang and rattle when they fell from the wheel but make the most feeble ping, that would buckle in a child's fierce swordfight. Hot! All of it hot.

In the middle of this "debris" sat Black Jack's bed. It was an army cot covered with a blanket with suns and moons on it. This condescension to living was surrounded by stacks of mohair sweaters, Fruit of the Loom underwear, and boxes which were labeled "Automatic Cordless Playing Card Shuffler." Junk! Gorm wasn't disturbed that his childhood competitor and hero of sorts was a fence. Only that he would deal with the blatantly synthetic, the obviously fashionable, that he would turn traitor to what Gorm assumed was their mutual visions: Old Stuff but Good Stuff.

"Shit!" cried Gorm and his cry disturbed the equilibrium of the transistors. One slid down from its narrow ledge. "Shit" it said and came to rest face up, its volume knob jostled to "On" whence a hot pop number blasted into the room, "It's so easy to fall in love . . . it's so easy to fall. . . ."

"Shit," said Gorm.

In still another room, Gorm discovered objects that had real weight and resonance. Stacks of Mason jars reminded him of lightning bugs. He ran shrieking with children at twilight up summer alleys. With hands outstretched, they groped and skittered after pinpoints of neon flashing that would later become caution signals at street corners. Some of the lids on Black Jack's jars had air holes punctured in them and Gorm remembered how difficult it was to keep the little bugs alive in an enclosed area even with ample oxygen. This front room was lit by another naked bulb from a far corner. Still there was enough light for Gorm to hold his right palm face up to his eye to study the snail-like scar running the length. He smiled to think he carried a whole way of life on his body—giddiness, folly, misapprehension as well as delirious excitement at chasing down light, capturing it, feeding it greens and air, wondering the next morning, with a great stillness embracing his arms, how something that was so darting and effulgent as a lightning bug could become utterly dead after capture, unmoved and unmoving, identifiable by its mere generic—INSECT—a speck in the dried, overnight grass. Gorm clenched and opened his fist. The scar shrunk and grew like a streak of lightning.

Everywhere Gorm wandered under the tin roof, he discovered weight and resonance. A wooden darning egg made his heel quiver with the remembrance of the tautness of a newly darned sock like a membrane which he converted to a softer glide in his stride. Hanging from three number-10 nails were coal stokers. Their handles were curved and Gorm held one for a long time, poking and ushering the air in new waves in imitation of January mornings when he had shoveled coal into the mute furnace and stoked and stirred as if he were the Man of the House. Now as then, the cold, tempered steel felt as if it had been born for his palm, his light grip. They were perfectly balanced, these archaic tools. Gorm let the middle of one ride his palm like a seesaw and it did not tip.

In the right-hand corner of the warehouse, Gorm stumbled on Black Jack's desk. It was a rolltop with a separate slot for everything: pens, inkwell (from a time when elegant penmanship mattered), trays for carbon paper and letterhead paper. A lower door opened to a cavernous space for a typewriter but six dead soldiers of Thunderbird were stored here.

Gorm took his place at the desk and pushed up the sleeves of his tux jacket. On top was a black ledger marked "Accounts." Gorm opened it. It was blank. He flipped through the ledger's pages of red columns and blue horizontal lines and felt a great importance pass through him. His guts gurgled the way they always did when a solemn issue took hold of him. In the top desk drawer, among dozens of Bic and Playmate pens he found what he was looking for: an ink bottle marked "Black Permanent" and a Sheaffer fountain pen. Its barrel was speckled like the coat of a wild cat.

When Gorm unscrewed the cap and held the tip to the light, wind rushed under the tin siding and sang, "Round your O's Little Gorm, round your O's."

Gorm would have preferred the wooden pens of Miss Diefenbacher's penmanship class with its stem tapered to fit the hand and workmanlike scratch of its split nib resistant enough to force him to labor to achieve elegance. A fountain pen was better than a ballpoint pen. The latter's smoothness was predetermined; a fountain's had to be earned with the proper grip and roll of the wrist. Thought could never outrun reflex. A ballpoint rolled across the page in a rounded flow no matter the style of the writer. A fountain pen had an edge; it must be fit to the style of the message.

And still the wind blew under the tin siding, saying, "Round your O's' Little Gorm, round your O's."

Gorm sat in Miss Dieffenbacher's penmanship class, his head bent in earnest, his eyes fixated on the space between the lines. He must never go outside them. He must roll and execute and stay within the lines. Gorm bent in earnest.

"Oh Gorm you did it again. Oh what a mess. Zigs and zags and little wigglies. And you've got ink all over your fingers. Class, I think Gorm would rather fingerpaint than write. First, he'll decorate his nose, then. . . ."

The class of wiggling worms eager to please laughed and laughed. Oh that Gorm . . . when would he ever learn.

"Take a book and go to the cloakroom, Gorm."

Again the metronomes sang with their nervous tick-tock.

In the shadow of Black Jack's, Gorm bent earnest to the lines. He swung the evasive O's in perfect balance to one another. Then in the Accounts Ledger he wrote, "Gorm: one penis serviced with the aid of local wenches. Payment: five dollars and one stewing pot."

All the letters moved ovally and gracefully along the lines; none of them strayed unless it was a "g" or an "f" in which case Gorm dangled his loops deftly.

He'd just screwed the cap to the barrel when the lock clicked and the door squealed open with Black Jack followed by not one, but two, giggling black girls—the hired liberators of Gorm's one weak muscle.

Black Jack bowed. He stepped to one side and presented the two black girls with a thrust of his upturned palm. "This is Beatrice Jackson," he said. "Beatrice is a young lady of indefatigable charm. If Dante were alive today, he would be struck by the sight of her to write deft terza rimas."

Gorm had no idea who Dante was and didn't care. As for the girl's charm, he had his doubts. Her face was moon-shaped and at the mention of Dante her forehead wrinkled as if clouds were scudding across the surface. She quickly resumed her smile and Gorm noted a considerable gap between her front teeth. She bowed from the waist, aiming a copse of braided tufts at Gorm as if she meant to gore him.

Imogene Humphrey was taller than Beatrice and didn't have any front teeth. She, too, bowed when Black Jack introduced her and offered Gorm her gap. While Black Jack discoursed on the efficacy of youth—their stamina and versatility—the girls shuffled and giggled. They reminded Gorm of the silly girls at the Hopewell Junior High sock hop who squirmed and peered from the corner of the gym. Gorm began to have doubts that this was the right type of girl to develop his remaining feeble muscle.

He motioned Black Jack with a beckoning forefinger to the corner.

"They weren't what I had in mind at all," he told the graduate of The St. Filmore School of Great Books.

"Is it not Montaigne who advises us to stay within our means. What kind of girl did you have in mind?"

"A wench," Gorm advised him.

"They're wenches all right."

"They seem awfully young for the chore that has to be performed. I would imagine it'll take knowhow to stir my tool. It's mighty small."

"They'll stir your tool . . . been doin' it since they were ten years old."

"I'd hoped they'd be prettier."

The mention of "prettier" coupled with "wench" made Black Jack's head slump a notch. He stared off toward a basket of rusty hinges.

"What you need is Mary Magdalene in pigtails."

"I need my tool developed, not crucified," said Gorm.

Black Jack scratched some of the gray hairs at his temple.

"I've been studying the desires and motives of the homo sapiens now for six years. I'm damned if I can figure what you're talkin' about.

Gorm told him he was no "homo."

"Maybe not," said the black man, "but you better tell the girls exactly what you want. They're getting restless."

"I began from nothing and now I'm well on the way to something," Gorm began in a speech to the girls. The clouds scudded across Beatrice's brow again.

When he noted Abe Lincoln's humble beginnings in a log cabin and Ben Franklin's early poverty in Philadelphia, Black Jack said, "Now you're talkin'. Humble beginnings . . . there's hope for all of us."

And Black Jack concurred again when Gorm said his rise to power had been inspired by junk. But Gorm saw puzzlement on the girls' faces and felt the need to explain.

"It was something like a religious vision," he told them. He explained how the broken alarm clock and waffle iron and other collections from his childhood had cried, "Grow delts, grow,"

and how this had inspired him to add weight to the bar and lift all
the harder.

The girls looked at one another and their eyes made big "O's"
but Gorm did not notice. The retelling of his rise to power imbued him with confidence. Adrenalin flooded his saliva glands
and he waxed at great length over the naming of his alley, the
conversion of Mrs. Vidoni, his salesmanship of girdles, lemonade, and used tires, and finally his exchange of letters with
Charles Atlas. He did not feel it necessary to tell them about his
vision of Hopalong Cassidy and other Western heroes. He assumed they had little interest in shooting and justice because
they were girls.

When it came time to describe his immediate need to the girls,
Gorm struggled for the proper phraseology. He smiled at the
girls and said, "I am here tonight because there is this portion of
me that hasn't developed with the rest. This portion is hidden
but without its proper execution, I am told by Mr. Atlas, no man
can discover his destiny. Mr. Atlas advises me that the restlessness I always feel inside of me is due to the failure to develop this
particular muscle."

"You wouldn't be speakin' of yore brain," said Imogene. She
flashed Gorm her purple gums.

"No," said Black Jack, "I think the ancients called it a penile
infantile longing for erectus."

The girls were equally baffled by this. The pimp's remark gave
Gorm a chance to further elucidate.

"It seems that when I've had the most power, I've *felt* least
powerful. I came to know great stirrings in my stomach. My head
felt crazy. I took to chewing toothpicks. I was largely imitated
which leads me to believe my affliction —if you can call it that—is
everywhere. Now the strongest man in America—Charles Atlas—has advised me I need help developing this one muscle. Not
that this is the end. Mr. Atlas says what I really need is a relaxer, a
woman to massage my pectorals between workouts. To get one I
have to develop the width and length of the retarded part of my
body."

Beatrice and Imogene were truly baffled now. They turned to
Black Jack who turned to glance over some junk. Weariness
showed on his face as if he understood he'd made a mistake in
ever hooking up with a creature like this Gorm.

He called a huddle and asked Gorm to return to the far corner.
The boy watched them turn and gesture at him as if he were an
object in a show window they were considering purchasing.
They jabbered considerably among themselves, firing a spate of

thumbs and forefingers over their shoulders at Gorm. Then the girls motioned Black Jack away and draped their arms about one another's shoulders and bent at the waist till their noses almost touched. They reminded Gorm of Indians at a war dance. They bobbed up and down with shrill cries, shook with anticipation, and seemed to run in place, they were so excited. Gorm became wary of placing his penis in their hands for nurturing.

Beatrice and Imogene called for Black Jack and whispered in his ear. The pimp, fence, junk collector, and connoisseur of great books threaded his way to Gorm and advised him of the negotiations. The girls, he said, had been advised that it was not lust that possessed their client. He was not like other "johns"; he was a bodybuilder and, Black Jack felt, a perfectionist. He'd told the girls that Gorm merely wanted his member stretched and widened so it would be as powerful as the rest of him.

All this seemed so obvious to Gorm, he impatiently tapped his foot.

"Remember," said Black Jack, "the men who usually come to these girls want love, affection, to feel important. The girls aren't used to dealing with a young man who already has an alley named after him."

"So they want more money," said Gorm.

"You misunderstand," said the pimp. "They are shy girls at heart. At least they feel shy about your watching them merely stretch your member."

Gorm said that was no problem; he would close his eyes.

"They don't want to take any chances," said Black Jack. "If they were to catch you peeking, it would interrupt the flow."

"What do they want?"

"We'd all be happy if you'd wear the pot," said Black Jack.

By the time Gorm had stripped, placed himself on a chair, and lowered the cooking pot over his head, the girls cried they were almost ready for him. He knew that one went outside because he heard the tin door slam. A short time later, she returned and he could hear them puttering in the sink behind the partition where Black Jack led his personal life. They clattered pans and chattered in low voices, punctuated with peals of hysterical laughter. Gorm never imagined the burgeoning of his penis could be so funny. He sat patiently, letting slow, heavy breaths ease out his nostrils into the circumference of the pot.

Black Jack sat beside Gorm and advised him to think of his pot not as a cooking receptacle but a crown. After all, did he not have an alley named after him?

Gorm answered with fierce mumbling from under the pot.

"What's the name of the alley?"

Black Jack could not hear exactly what Gorm had named his alley but this did not stop him from talking to his young "john."

"Fine! Think of yourself as king and rightful ruler of your alley. Call yourself King Gorm," and the pimp let out a hoarse laugh.

The idea of King Gorm had more appeal for Gorm. He knew coons worshiped odd deities on the Dark Continent and he wouldn't have been surprised to see (if he removed the pot) Imogene and Beatrice fall, babbling hosannas on his toes. Already he could feel his bicepses swelling and his deltoids riding herd like shifting glacial drift. He had no doubt this blossoming of power would extend to his penis and end his miseries. Gorm smiled under the pot, breathing heavily for there was little air in that region.

At last he heard the girls pittering about his feet, getting ready to minister to his ailment. They had dug up their own cooking pot, albeit a rusty basin into which they poured hot water. They set it by Gorm's feet. Around him they spread other instruments necessary for exorcising the demons from his dick and giving it realm to blossom. These included a trowel, mustard plaster spread on a 1940 copy of The Police Gazette (the year of Gorm's birth and showing a picture of Adolph Hitler playing ball with a puppy dog), a pair of novelty store wind-up dentures, a fistful of poison ivy, a bottle of rubbing alcohol with a crust around the rim, a wooden spoon, soap, and pieces of balsa wood and a sling.

Imogene took the wooden spoon and tapped a one-heavy, three-light rhythm on the pot, which reminded Gorm of Indians preparing for war in innumerable John Wayne movies. Beatrice stripped and danced all around him. Gorm received her undulant movements as shadows bellying up from the floor.

Soon Beatrice took up a pair of pie pans and clattered them as she wove around the subject. She chanted, "Hail the Conquering Peepee."

Gorm heard Imogene chortle briefly then she, too, took up the chant: "Hail the Conquering Peepee."

This sounded to Gorm like mockery of his privates. He started to remove the pot to give them advice on a new chant but one of them slammed it back down on his head and the familiar redskin thumping resounded at him in the darkness.

From under the pot he shouted at them to get a new song.

The pounding on his head left off; his two initiators conferred. The new chant went: "Fly Stinger, fly."

Though Gorm thought of himself as having considerably more

heft than a little bee, this new exhortation was more applicable than the old one. But no sooner had he crossed his arms and settled back to await the burgeoning of his one slack muscle, than he felt a crusty palm wrap around his dick. It was given a brief tug, then left to dangle. He heard a slopping sound. Seconds later Beatrice applied warm water and soap and kneaded him like bread dough while Imogene resumed the beat on the pot.

For the first time in months, Gorm recalled his mother. He felt like an infant being given a sponge bath and having his diaper changed. The daily wiping of his piss and shit forgave everything and warm ablutions between his legs made his eyes swim in a dark, warm, undersea world. His fat, baby hands clapped together in applause for himself and the world. His pores opened as if a layer of dead skin, useless as week-old adhesive tape, was being peeled from his body. Administered to like this, his infantile cock groping toward the one naked lightbulb in Black Jack's, Gorm felt ready to love the world, coons included.

"Oh my, looky there!" said Imogene, leaving off her beat momentarily.

"Yessir," said Black Jack in the background, "That's one healthy stinger."

"Just needs a little heat," said Imogene.

"Yessir," said Black Jack, "lil' heat never hurt anyone."

"Heat it is," cried Beatrice, "but where's my drum beat."

"One drum beat coming up," said Imogene and a fierce thumping began on and in Gorm's head simultaneous with a prick grown fiery as Beatrice applied the rubbing alcohol.

When the heat got too much for Gorm, he cried, "Ow!"

Beatrice dipped him back in the basin of water and said, "I baptize you . . . what's your name?"

"Gorm."

"I baptize you, Gorm, in the name of Beatrice, Imogene, and Black Jack."

"Leave me out of this," said the ex-junk collector.

"Judas," snapped Beatrice, and went back to work with the rubbing alcohol.

When Gorm's underdeveloped muscle stood at attention and was sufficiently inflamed, Beatrice again applied warm soap and water. This balm made Gorm smile blissfully under the pot.

"Now, what did you want us to do for you?" asked Beatrice.

"What you're doing's fine."

"I mean the coomlative effects . . . what you wanted us to do when we first walked in here."

"Well . . . at that time . . . I was looking for proportion . . . you know, all muscles more or less the same."

"And you're not interested in anything else?"

Gorm said he supposed he was normal like any other man. He told Beatrice whatever she wanted to do to him was just fine with him. Gorm let his potted head loll till the cool metal lay against his eyes.

Imogene resumed drumming on the side of the pot, lightly with the wooden spoon.

Beatrice said, "I don't suppose you'd be wantin' a little nooky tonight?"

Gorm had known it would come to that eventually; he didn't want to let on he had never done it before or was afraid. He said whatever the girls wanted to do to help his muscle grow was okay. He didn't want to lose the present soothing action.

"But I would appreciate a new chant," he told the girls.

"What sort of chant?" asked Imogene.

Gorm said he didn't want to fly so much as surge. The right chant made all the difference in muscle development. He said he didn't expect them to believe this but since he was the one paying, he wanted them to chant: "Surge, penis, surge."

Gorm thought he heard some chuckling at this request. Beatrice said, "You's a big spender all right. Whatever you say, boss."

Imogene dropped her wooden spoon. She and Beatrice lightly lashed Gorm's genitalia with the poison ivy.

They chanted: "Surge, penis, surge."

At first the stinging was almost pleasant.

Gorm had long been accustomed to the idea that to learn anything required suffering on at least a modest level. You did not learn a lesson so much as it was imprinted on your body and soul. The more obstinate had swollen fingers, welts on their asses or the gaunt and haunted features of the chronically isolated. Isolation could happen in a school or by silent agreement of the Hopewell community. There was never any doubt that the punished would be better persons for their isolation.

The lessons of punishment operated at a more finite level in Hopewell. A bad hop from a ground ball that left you with a chipped tooth was a lesson in your failure to keep your eye on the ball. A black eye in a fight was a sign that you should avoid fighting. The more boredom attached to a given school lesson the better chance there was something worthwhile in that lesson, because everyone knew pain suffered in silence was a sign of something learned. Whatever the pain, the solitude, the ennui, you had only yourself to blame.

Lightheartedness day after day in Hopewell was a sign you were becoming a slacker, indulging yourself while other people bent to their tasks with dutiful, humorless expressions as the wisdom of life eased by osmosis into their pores. Or so Gorm had been taught. Had not George Washington, rich boy that he was, suffered in the cold, snow, and muck at Valley Forge before he crossed the Delaware in a flimsy boat to beat off the enemy and found the Great Republic Gorm now developed within? Honest Abe had chopped wood and read by candlelight. Franklin had wandered penniless about Philadelphia for a time, probably the time he was gathering wisdom . . . or having it gather him. Even Gorm's former cowboy heroes, buggerers that they were, had fought through thirst, Indians, windstorms, and horses with badly shod feet to arrive at a philosophy where nothing hurt. They were stoics. They endured everything life had to offer man and did it without complaining. They sang in the saddle, though probably saddlesore, and offered wry jokes as a testament to their toughness. They were men. Men's men.

What was a little lashing compared with what the heroes of his country had endured? Though Gorm had little evidence they had developed "all" of themselves, they had certainly developed "part" of themselves. Did this not involve a minimum of suffering? He made up his mind for the sake of his growth to endure the girls' lashing which had grown considerable by this time.

"Surge, penis, surge!" they cried in giddy fashion. Beatrice switched with Imogene drumming the pot with the spoon so the latter could get in her share of licks. Even Black Jack, who liked to claim he had seen "'bout everything there is to see" couldn't help joining in on the refrain which urged Gorm's one underdeveloped muscle to grow quickly.

In turn, both girls did a kind of war dance while meting out lashes. They bobbed and hopped, threw their shoulders back while offering the chant "Surge, penis, surge," chuckled briefly, swung the poison ivy at his cock—hovering in the air like a raspberry tuning fork—did a little soft shoe reminiscent of American minstrel music and began the whole procedure over again.

Tears filled Gorm's eyes under the pot.

His tool had begun to itch and he asked the girls if he might scratch it. No, they told him, it would spoil the spell to make his dick grow. Should his itch become unbearable, they said he should tell them and they would scratch for him. Gorm said it was unbearable.

Beatrice wound the novelty-store false teeth and set them at the head of his cock. They chattered and hopped smartly to the middle of his hardon leaving little toothmarks all the way. Then they hopped backward the way they had come leaving more little toothmarks.

For years now Gorm had only heard about blow jobs and he smiled to think he was getting his first one. He wished one of The Boys here here to witness this triumph. When the dentures ran up and down his shank again, he flinched and asked Beatrice if he couldn't have a little tongue action to soften the bite.

"Tongue action comin' up," she cried. She laid the mustard plaster on the trowel and applied it in deft pats to the raw, afflicted area.

Gorm's itch was somewhat relieved but a new heat, a deeper inner heat originating in his seminal vesicle made him crave for release.

"Surge, penis, surge," the girls cried.

And Gorm's tool did surge, wobbling under the moist pats of the trowel till even Gorm took up the chant under his domestic helmet: "Surge, penis, surge." And his penis, exhorted on for the first time since the days of "I Love Laverne," did surge, firing its juice with perverse accuracy directly on the trowel.

Gorm heard loud applause and smiled to think he had finally lost his cherry though that had not been his primary objective. He raised his hands to lift the suffocating pot from his head but someone banged it and said, "Not done get."

Imogene and Beatrice bound his cock in a splint and sling. They used the balsa-hood wings from a P-39 model fighter plane, fastening them to his shank with the rubber bands that had once lofted the 89 cent toy from the hands of a small boy. Strips of bedsheet from Black Jack's junk pile were bound around the splint three times, then wrapped around Gorm's waist and tied at his navel.

Black Jack said "Amen." The girls said "Amen." Gorm asked if now could he remove the pot. He was answered with a series of heavy blows to his "king's crown" and saw the hand of an alarm clock fly across his vision and felt his neck tighten like a tourniquet had been applied.

When he came to and peeked from under the pot it was as if another pot had been deftly slipped over the entire room. He yelled "Black Jack" once then leaned back in the chair and tried to restore his breathing. Neither the desertion nor the darkness surprised him.

One did not seem complete without the other. He smiled to think this had been his natural state most of his life. He had wriggled out of his mother's womb looking, he supposed, for light and air but one of his few memories of the time between birth and school deposited him in a deserted icebox where he'd swallowed a deserted ball bearing. After his mother left with the sporting goods salesman, he'd wandered Hopewell's alleys at dusk looking for deserted but salvagable goods. He'd spent much of his early school days in a dark cloakroom listening to the relentless beating of metronomes. He'd graduated to alleys and the nooks and large crevices between garages and undersides of houses and when they weren't available the space under cars where he came to understand the hardness of axles and the relentlessness of bearings. The cellar where he'd undertaken the development of his body had been only a small improvement. It was dark and airless as was the coal cellar where he reviewed the junk from his childhood. Even his careful analytical review of America's Western heroes had a pot lowered over it. The umbrella of sulphuric smoke over Hopewell made fewer than 50 days of sunshine possible a year. The owners of the mills lived in the country, took summer vacations in Scotland or the Caribbean. Desertion . . . darkness. Gorm smiled at the consistency of his destiny.

Though Gorm was experienced at making his way through piles of junk set in darkness, he had not accounted on having his cock in a sling. Owing to the lavishness with which the girls had applied mustard plaster, his one inferior muscle now felt on a parity with his other muscles, so much so that it bumped into a vise on the table, then a broom which fell against a stack of plates. Two plates crashed at Gorm's feet. His new dick bumped into walls, got its sling caught on a coat hanger. The coat hanger remained hanging, jangling each time Gorm bumped into more junk. When Gorm steered into another table, a vegetable grater hooked onto the coat hanger. It was as if Gorm's cock had been converted into a poorly trained seeing eye dog. Like the dogs whose tails wagged in his head, it had no sense of smell, no intuition at all. It was at the mercy of made *things* and those *things* took revenge on it at every turn.

It drove head on into another table. A sock hanging over the edge fell into the sling. A lamp's shade was jostled. An ironing board lowered itself at a nudge from Gorm's guide and might have been dragged away by the sling, such was the fury of Gorm's newest muscle, if he hadn't detached it. His soaring prick hit a television head on, upset a row of Jack's hot radios, and waltzed into the space bar of the ancient Royal typewriter, which Gorm, only an hour earlier, had lifted over his head. The space bar humped two spaces and the margin bell sang as if

"Dick Development Class" was finally dismissed for recess. A few seconds later Gorm found the ancient tin door and entered into the night.

He saw then the predicament of his one inferior member. Bolts, cotter pins, and a dozen other discards both metal and cloth had fallen in the sling and been carried aloft by his reconditioned member. And more: a tow chain had hooked itself on to the potato grater, which was connected to the coat hanger. As proud as he was of his dick's newfound strength, a profound itch had begun and it was necessary in the dark for Gorm to strip away everything—metal, cloth sling, balsa wood—and scratch away the fried remnants of mustard plaster before such itch was momentarily appeased. But all the way home it surged and flopped and demanded Gorm veer into dark alleys to pay heed to its inflamed, witless head.

When Gorm awoke the next morning he'd scratched his cock and thighs and genital area to a bloody mess. The poison ivy had blossomed in those areas to a solid, chafed blotch. When Gorm spotted some of the raspberry-colored swellings, he quickly decided he was dying of syphilis. If he didn't die, he knew he would go insane and spend the rest of his life in a place where no mirrors were allowed and the inmates amused themselves by shrieking. Because junk had deserted him, he talked to God for a while, promising Him he would never get near another woman, certainly not a coon.

If he could die now, it would be okay, he thought. It was the slowness of the disease's ravaging that scared him. Before his mother had left with the sporting goods salesman, he remembered finding pamphlets between the mattress and the springs in his parent's bedroom. They were all entitled "More Wild Oats." The pamphlets, in story and photos, detailed the horrors of promiscuity. Gorm recalled one man who'd caught the disease and taken four years to die. A hasty sketch had outlined which parts of his body were attacked first and which parts later. Gorm recalled that a rash on the chest and face, similar to the one he had now on his thighs, was the next to last stage. In the final stage your brain rotted. He could have tolerated his penis falling off. He had little use for it and he supposed a hose could be fitted there for him to pee. The rest of him was another matter. He grew nauseated when he thought of his bulging pectorals succumbing to the disease, his hulking delts and wing-like lats wobbling on his frame like a turkey's throat.

When his father came to roust him for school, he said he had a fever and a sore throat. His father laid a palm on his forehead. If he wasn't better by evening, his father said Dr. Pound would have to be called. Gorm groaned at the mention of that venerated quack.

All day Gorm stared hopelessly out the window at the wisps of smoke threading along the horizon from Bog & Bliss Steel Company. He thought if only he had the knowledge that he would not live out the day, he could relax. He tried to speed death by quietly imagining the deterioration of first his limbs, then his bowels. He pictured little malignant spirochetes poking holes in his brain till he was trucked to a nursing home where he babbled all day in a corner and tried to lift the nurses' skirts when they spoon-fed him.

He worked at this a long time, his only awareness of the outside world the maddeningly slow ticking of the plastic Bendix on his dresser and the wallpaper lofting a cataclysm of bleached violets all about the room. Just when he felt his brain drifting with the disease into that netherland where mindlessness is balm and the gates on his heart and urinal tract were about to close, the telephone rang.

Gorm stumbled out of bed certain the party at the other line would be The Contagious Disease Clinic advising him that it was known he'd had congress with two black girls loose in Skeetersville and what he should report to be examined and have the date of his impending death fixed.

"Hello," he said in his weakest voice.

"What's wrong with you, Gorm?"

The voice was sharp as a razor blade. Gorm was surprised at the lucidity of his brain and the quickness with which he recognized Miss Tarp, the Hopewell School District truant officer.

"Sick," he whispered.

"Ha!" the voice cried.

Miss Tarp had been known to march unannounced into a student's home, waving a thermometer and crying, "Let's check this fever once and for all."

"What!" she cried, "Gorm the weightlifter, the one with all the muscles out for the count. I won't believe it till I see it."

Gorm knew if she got into the house there would be no getting rid of her. After she'd asked about his habits, she'd want to know his father's—what kind of hours he kept, what kind of women his father brought home, all the times his father had spanked him. She had the reputation of announcing herself as a rehabilitation psychologist who could set any young person on the right track if they'd only tell her what was on their mind. The woman was insatiable.

"I came down with this here fever," he said in an apologetic voice.

"I thought strong men took lots of vitamins."

"I'm not supposed to be out of bed."

"Are you sure that heat you're feeling isn't *spring* fever? Lots of young men let girls turn their hot water faucet on and then they boil over."

"I don't know any girls," he told her.

Miss Tarp said it was very strange that a powerful, healthy young man like Gorm wouldn't know *any* girls.

"Look, I'm not very well at all. I have to go back to bed. My father's arranged for Dr. Pound to visit at 4:00," he lied to get rid of the old snoop.

Two people knew he was sick now, perhaps more with Miss Tarp's penchant for blabbering. He felt his fever must waste him entirely or he would lose face. Gorm stretched himself prostrate on his bed, waiting for the inevitable. He could sense the mattress slowly sucking him into its fibers. In a few hours he would become one with the metal whorls of the bedsprings. A hard, coiled inanimate slab of metal. Gorm had heard death produced an erection and this gave him some consolation. No doubt the undertaker would fasten it down before he was stretched for viewing. It would only be justice if the one muscle he'd been unable to control in life should spring up like a jack-in-the-box just as some girls from Hopewell High peeped into the casket.

He saw his proboscis popping up so dramatically that women seated all around the viewing room shrieked. He saw it burgeoning big as a baseball bat, then growing rubbery, supple, swatting the carnations into confetti. His pompous, money-stricken aunts would try to run from the room. They wouldn't make it. His Doom and his Lifeline, his Soul, his Cock would swish along the thick carpet and clip them at the ankles. No one would get out of viewing Gorm at last in his perfection.

The undertaker, old man Need, would try to grab his Bone-Soul and stuff it back inside the gray viewing suit. Unresponsive in life, his cock would defend him through all eternity. It would snap at the funeral director like a snake.

Drifting deeper and deeper into dream, Gorm had a glimpse of his Hell. It was himself, his Soul, his Avenger, his Cock. No sooner had it tamed everyone in the viewing room, seated them at a respectable distance, than it began to itch. In real life it would have taken both of Gorm's hands scratching full time, 24 hours a day, to appease the irritation. Now in death, he had no hands. They lay inert at his sides still in the coffin while his prodigious erection wagged in broad circles, crying out mutely for help. The viewers—friends and relatives he hadn't seen in years—observed it redden, saw its fine slit of a mouth wrench back to make a plea. The skin on Gorm's cock peeled, first one layer, then another. With each shedding, the mammoth dong wagged more feverishly for someone to come and scratch it. The funeral viewers thought such wagging was further testament to the cock's wiliness. The men smiled, the ladies applauded. Though Gorm was the victim of his dream, he was also one of its viewers. His friends, relatives, neighbors, Hopewell's professional funeral watchers were enamored of his power. No one saw his rise and exhibitionism for what it was—a cry to be scratched or lose himself to eternal irritation.

A veiled woman rose from her seat and came toward the casket. Speaking directly to his cock, she said, "You were absent from the most important class. You'll be held for detention. I don't know what all else."

Gorm's tool wagged back and forth. No sound at all. He knew an interpreter was needed. He turned to the viewers, hoping to catch someone's eye who might intercede on behalf of his cock. No one looked at the other Gorm, Gorm the viewer.

The woman was still addressing him and he knew he was the only one who could speak for himself, on behalf of his most recently developed muscle which was out of control. To expose *it* alone and naked in detention hall would risk defamation of character. The Boys would reserve their hardest spitballs for it. No matter its size, it would be laughed at. Oddity of any kind brought the giddy wrath of The Boys.

"Couldn't it paint the boiler room?" Gorm heard himself mumble. Pumperdink had once incurred that punishment for drawing a sparrow with a prodigious tool on the school wall by the principal's office.

"Who paint what? In your condition, you couldn't paint your fingernails."

Even in dream the voice was so familiar that Gorm pushed hard with his hands and feet to reach the surface of consciousness. "I'm comin'," he yelled, "I'm comin'."

"Take your time, Gorm, I'm not going anywhere."

Gorm rolled on his back. He blinked twice into a thin smudge of carrot-colored face. He sat upright. The old fears made him tremble. How to get out of the harsh light? How to make himself accountable?

"I'm not going to school," he whispered at Miss Tarp.

"With that itch in your privates, I would think not."

Gorm stared at his crotch where the covers were bunched like rolled mountains of papier-mâché.

"Was it a cathouse or some street trollop?"

"Colored Indians," Gorm told her.

Miss Tarp rolled her eyes back in her head.

"In your present discomfort I wouldn't think you would be so cute."

"I'm going to Hell," Gorm said to no one in particular.

Miss Tarp moved with the abruptness of a woman who knows she is needed at once. She plopped on the edge of the bed and took one of Gorm's hands in her own.

"Discipline," she said, "Anything can be overcome with discipline."

Gorm did not resist her embrace.

"Where I'm going, all I need is my bones."

"Listen," she said, "I'm here to help you. Nobody's going to punish you. Venereal disease is not a crime. You simply need to be rehabilitated in the right hands."

Gorm's eyes focused on the long freckled hand holding his own. He remembered then that his fingers had once gripped barbells, waved like batons in a five-and-dime store, held the shovel that scooped his shit into the coal furnace.

"Take your hands off of me," he said.

"Think of your condition, Gorm. The world's not such a lonely place."

"If you don't remove your hand, I'm going to break it off and use it for a spatula."

Miss Tarp tilted her face to the faded violets on the ceiling.

"Think of a life of peace, Gorm. Calmness . . . the end of frustration . . . a ship in a storm unbuffeted by the waves of lust. . . ."

Gorm looked up to where the truant officer looked. The violets blanched into one another, a washed, dull field of indecisive pastels. They'd been up there as long as he could remember.

"All Herald Gorm the Strong, Miss Tarp."

". . . a life where you're not at the mercy of disease . . . where the community. . . ."

Gorm snatched the freckled hand from his own.

"Get off my throne," he cried at her.

The truant officer stood upright as if she'd received an electric shock.

"No one can help you. That's what I'm going to say in my official report. You have a contagious disease and shouldn't be around other children."

"All Herald Gorm the Strong, Miss Tarp."

"Whattaya use to stir you up. . . ?"

The inspired woman fell to her knees and poked under Gorm's bed.

"*Nugget, Gent, Modern Romance* . . . huh?"

Gorm could see only her shapeless butt poised like an ironing board followed by oak-colored stockinged ankles, equally shapeless, then the obligatory brown oxfords that all female school personnel wore.

"Your friend Pumperdink gets off on the brassiere ads in Cosmopolitan."

The woman was a fountain of information. How she knew such intimacies puzzled Gorm.

The springs under his ass squeaked with her search.

Gorm took the pillow from behind his head and belted her exposed rear.

"I get off on 'I Love Laverne,' " he told her. "Why don't you take the TV set."

Miss Tarp crawled out from under the bed. She braced herself upright, brushing spiderwebs and dusters from her shoulders.

"I wouldn't be surprised," she said, "No, I wouldn't be surprised if you weren't the origin of your own disease."

She snatched a black briefcase from an armchair and stalked from the room.

"All Herald Gorm the Strong," Gorm cried after her.

The effect of Miss Tarp was to leave Gorm with a semihardon. He was enraged and embarrassed as though the woman had denied him a terrible but necessary adventure and offered him instead a child's toy to play with. He dipped his rubbery tool under the cold water faucet. Ten minutes later it was half arched again. It hovered over the rest of him like a stalk of bruised berries. Some of the poison ivy welts were red. Others he'd scratched to wounds the color of blueberries. He lay back in his bed, certain the disease would resume its ravaging now that he was left alone with it.

No sooner had Gorm closed his eyes and heard some trumpets against a background of sheep, than he felt a hand on his forehead..

"Feverish," his father said.

Gorm knew Miss Tarp's visit had inflamed him but he also understood the final stages of venereal disease could be accompanied by fever. He could feel a burning inside his cock now that wormed itself back to his asshole. His father said it was time for Dr. Pound.

"That old quack will hand me two aspirin and charge you fifteen bucks."

"He's been our family doctor for thirteen years."

Gorm groaned and said, "No wonder families fall apart."

Between the time Mr. Gorm called the doctor and his arrival, a vigil formed at Gorm's bedside. His court arrived as a group to see what ailed him. Everyone came except Mrs. Vidoni, whom they said didn't feel well either.

Gorm kept his hand between his legs. He moved it as stealthily as possible and kept his eyes on their eyes so their glances wouldn't stray to his crotch. He made his speech as formal as possible using such terms as "in the unforeseen future," "heretofore," and "in point of fact."

Gorm's court nodded restlessly at all this till Gursky asked Gorm why he was in bed.

"A grave disease," he told them. "It started a long time ago, I think. Now it could be quite out of hand."

Gursky, Clara, Pumperdink, and Lester Day lowered their heads at this news.

The group revived when Clara said, "You look perfect."

"You look fit to bench press 250," said Lester.

"Make that 270," said Pumperdink.

Gorm brought his scratching hand from under the covers and drove a forefinger into the air.

"I am not in any condition to lift anything."

"You wouldn't know it by your complexion," said Clara.

"And there seems to be a little mouse under the covers," Gursky winked.

Gorm bolted upright against the backboard.

"This is a serious matter. I have to be honest with you. I may not make it." And he slid back under the covers as if an invisible hand pushed him.

They were outcasts, all of them. Gorm pictured 50-year-old orphans combing their hair before hotel mirrors on holidays with nowhere to go. He remembered the futility of stones and the futility of barbells as being equal. He was about to raise himself and cry for his father to show them the door when his father entered with Dr. Pound.

As his court shuffled from the room, Pumperdink turned and said, "You look fit enough to do bent-over rows."

"And don't forget continental dead lifts," said Gursky.

"Not to mention squats," said Lester Day.

"There will be no workout today or ever again," Gorm shrieked at them.

"Now now," said Dr. Pound, adjusting a stethoscope into sides of his chubby pink face, "ever and never are two words we in the medical profession never use."

The sight of Dr. Pound's bald head and baby face in which the eyes were so small they looked as if they'd been stuck there as an afterthought galled Gorm. As long as he could remember Dr. Pound had given him his yearly school-district test for rupture. As an assembly line of giggling genitals trotted past the doctor's nose, he drove two fingers into the prostate gland and mumbled, "cough."

He was the doctor for the athletic teams as well. For any injury he was rumored to have one cure—aspirin. At Hopewell football games when he moseyed toward an injured player The Boys would cry from the stands, "Give'm an aspirin doc, give'm an aspirin." He placed the fat end of his black tubing on Gorm's chest while his neutral porcine expression swam up the walls toward the faded violets on the ceiling.

"For what I have there is no cure," Gorm advised him.

Dr. Pound grunted and removed the tubes from his ears. He told Gorm to stick out his tongue. He shone a tiny flashlight into the boy's throat, and jammed a wooden depressor on his tongue.

"Go aaahhh," he said.

Gorm thought this more of the old quack's nonsense but he went "aaaahhh" anyway, letting the final "h's" expire with ample futility.

"Eating regularly? Passing urine? Bowel movements regular?" the doctor asked in rapid succession.

Gorm made some movement in his throat.

Dr. Pound waved it away and said, "Strip."

"Look here," Gorm protested, "What I have is in its final stages. There's no use you fooling with me."

But already he had his pajama tops off.

"Final stages of what?" snapped Dr. Pound, "egotism? A young man with a body like yours complaining . . . you ought to be ashamed of yourself. The bottoms, too."

"What for? You gonna check me for rupture again?"

"I'm going to report to your father you're a smart ass who needs spanked. Turn around."

Gorm held his breath while the doctor thumped in the hollows of his back.

"Have you recently received a blow to the head, vomited dinner, or swallowed any foreign objects?"

"Many years ago I swallowed a ball bearing. As far as I know it's still down there."

"Don't talk nonsense. The body gets rid of what it doesn't need."

Gorm wanted to ask the Aspirin Man how he knew this body didn't need ball bearings. How did he know some bodies didn't feed on metal? Or scrap metal? Wood and glass?

But Dr. Pound pushed him down and stuck a thermometer in his mouth. Gorm thought he could have eaten the glass right there to prove his thesis if he hadn't needed confirmation of his impending death.

The doctor pulled out the thermometer, glanced at it, and mumbled some indistinguishable sounds down his chest front.

Gorm slid under the covers. The itch had him again. He tried to operate as stealthily as possible but the irritation was at the crown. After he scratched, he slid his hand up to his stomach, smiled weakly at the doctor, slid his hand on tiptoe . . . inch by inch downward . . . dug one fingernail into the head . . . dug around till the itch quit and he felt pain . . . worked his hand mouselike back to the resting position on his stomach . . . glanced up . . . smiled guiltily at Dr. Pound.

The doctor grumbled something in his throat which Gorm couldn't hear. After which he said, "Take your bottoms off, Gorm."

"Since when do you have to check my lower half to complete an examination?"

"Since I watched your hand mauling your testicles for the last 10 minutes."

"Penis," Gorm corrected him.

He removed his pajama bottoms.

Dr. Pound took one glance at the boy's ravaged prick and fished in his black bag for a rubber glove. From the bag he also removed a black optical glass that reminded Gorm of a gumball-machine telescope and a metal prong that resembled a tuning fork. He held Gorm's inflicted bird with the rubber-gloved hand while leaning forward and peering at it, holding the black glass to his eye. He went "h'mmm" then "h'mmm" and removed the glass eye.

"I suppose the bacilli are getting close to my brain. How much longer do I have, doc?"

"About 50 years," said the doctor.

"In this state?" Gorm cried.

Dr. Pound did not answer but took Gorm's penis in his gloved hand again. Despite Gorm's assumptions about his own disease and his dick's motley state, Dr. Pound's clinical handling of it had aroused it to a semihardon and it wagged about like a rubber hose.

Dr. Pound raised the prong and said, "Tell me if this hurts."

"What are you going to do?" cried Gorm, trying to pull away, but the doctor had him by the cock.

He brought the metal prong down snappily on the purple-red, swollen head.

"Ow!" said Gorm.

The doctor hastily shoved his paraphernalia into his black bag. As he was leaving, Gorm studied his face for some sign of his fate.

"Well, what's the verdict?" he yelled after the doctor.

Without turning, Dr. Pound said, "In the future if you want to whack off, I suggest you use something more soothing than mustard plaster. And do it at home where there isn't so much poison ivy."

"I have not been naked in the woods," Gorm cried after him but already the portly physician was thundering down the stairs.

A few minutes later Gorm's court filed back into his room.

"I thought you people left," Gorm cried.

"We did," said Pumperdink, "But we saw the doctor pull up and decided to come back for the verdict."

"What verdict? What is this, a trial?"

"We wanted to be with you in your *time* of trial is what he meant," said Clara.

A moment later, Pound filled up the doorway, the slightest smile spreading triumphantly over his baby pink face. Gorm's father stood behind him.

"I checked with another doctor, just to make sure, Gormmm. He confirmed my findings."

Gorm's court watched the doctor . . . their breaths held to a communal vigilance . . . their eyes fixed like glass beads along a prayer string.

"Poison ivy of the gonads, Gormmm. Spread calamine lotion on your privates ever four hours and take two of these."

Dr. Pound took a plastic bottle of aspirin from his pocket and set them on Gorm's bedside table.

Gorm's court filed out behind Dr. Pound.

"Poison Ivy of the gonads. That's a very strange disease for a weightlifter to have," one of them muttered.

Alone with his "disease" and calamine lotion, Gorm watched his dick shrivel to a small bud, his balls to harmless pods.

III

Here was the very heart of industrial America, the center of its most lucrative and characteristic activity, the boast and pride of the richest and grandest nation ever seen on earth—and here was a scene so dreadfully hideous, so intolerably bleak and forlorn that it reduced the whole aspiration of man to a macabre and depressing joke. Here was wealth beyond computation, almost beyond imagination—and here were human habitations so abominable that they would have disgraced a race of alley cats.

—H. L. Mencken on Pittsburgh,
from essay "Libido for the Ugly."

T hrough the window he saw the first light make a slash over the chimney nearest Gorm's Alley. At first he did not understand if it was dawn or dusk. The air hung matted waiting for something, a blue-gray beyond all quiet. A single bird twittered and sank abruptly into silence. A car rumbled over the humped, brick streets. Then, that too was silent.

"Gorm's a Gorm's a Gorm," Gorm said to the limbo but it meant little more to him than groping syllables, a rub on the wind.

Gorm wiggled his thumb. He mumbled, "Wiggle thumb, wiggle," just to see if words and movement matched up. His words were like ants trying to crawl up the thumb's shaft.

Dibbs, the biology teacher, had said the opposable thumb separated man from the dumb and belligerent ape. Gorm felt neither apelike nor human, just there. He was reminded of the retreads he'd resuscitated from their dumb pile. But who would resuscitate him?

He felt if he could reach bottom everything would be all right. But reaching bottom was as hard as climbing to the top. He had never really arrived at strength. There had always been the dogs' flapping tails to deal with and later his growing awareness of a world stacked like retreads waiting for someone to come along and give them life. There were his limp dick and his desire for air and light. There was his desire to have the community see all of him.

"Betwixt and between," he mumbled but that had no more meaning for him than "Gorm's Gorm" or "opposable thumb."

The calamitous itch did not bother him on his privates now; it had moved inside so that he wanted to scratch himself from the inside out, first his gall bladder, then his colon. He wiggled slightly and this wiggling kept him from relapsing into his previous stupor.

In a modest way, then, he was prepared when his father walked into his room, and observing his wiggling at the hips, advised him to spend another day in bed.

"Wouldn't want you walking around scratching. Town will talk . . . liable to think you got the crabs. They'd think you got them off my toilet."

Gorm was struck by the possessive adjective. Money conferred ownership. Ownership was reinforced with respectability. Crush them crabs. Gorm the syllable infested with parasites.

"Write me an excuse," he told his father.

"Promise not to scratch?"

"Scout's honor."

As Gorm approached Hopewell High, he felt like a minor commodity going to check The Big Board to see whether he had risen or fallen on the stock exchange. The measurable commodities at the end of a newscast had always infatuated him precisely because they were measurable. Like the shroud that hung over Hopewell, every other item on the news was bathed in uncertainty. What made the Eagle Scout kill his sister's babysitter? The plane crash into a doughnut factory? The whale give birth in captivity? The outcome of causes, guilt, injuries, and zoo adjustment might linger on for months, years, but the stock-market averages were final. Your investment either lost or gained, no mystery but how to deal with defeat or victory. Gorm sought to ascertain whether his reputation had fallen or risen on the faces of the occupants of Hopewell High. Their acknowledgment of him would be his Big Board just as his tape measure and three mirrors had been the Dow Jones of his lats, delts, and bicepses.

From his own body Gorm knew how the nuggets of estimation filtered from the lower middle—the approximate position of his ass—so he decided to first study the face of the school secretary for some sign of his advance or decline. She would catch it from both ends—the administration and students—much as his ass caught the flow from his torso and legs. From the past, Gorm knew her expression and voice contained a dozen gradations from a bursting smile for Dickie Little the class president to a stern wrinkle of the forehead for Pumperdink the Pukeroo.

Yet as she came toward him she said, "Good morning," with casual efficiency, her eyes meeting Gorm's in the briefest of exchanges. She took his father's scribbled excuse, initialed the bottom, handed the blue re-entry pass to Gorm, and turned to a girl holding her jaw in her hands.

"Relax Mary," said the secretary, "We'll get you in to see Dr. Heilbronner."

Gorm glared at the girl with the toothache as if she'd committed a crime by being ill.

"The name's Gorm," he cried, "G-O-R-M."

The secretary looked up at him with the same cool efficiency she'd offered him earlier.

"Didn't I sign your re-entry pass, Gorm?"

He looked down in bewilderment. The mention of his name appeased him momentarily.

"Why yes you did," he said.

He could detect no sign the secretary knew two black girls had inflamed his pecker and gonads with a mustard plaster and poison ivy. Then again he could not detect a sign that she didn't know and was merely concealing this knowledge for the sake of propriety.

When his name was called during roll, he listened for a twist in the inflection of his name that signaled the jig was up. Yet the name Gorm sounded like a chip of mortar between Gallagher and Gunther so that Gorm couldn't fathom a fraction of his reputation on "The Big Board." During his first class he watched to see who would watch him but there was no sign of interest at all in him except when he stared too long at a potential watcher and that watcher turned his eyes on Gorm in bafflement. All of the students were busy reciting passé composé and watching the clock. The bell rang and shot the students through the doorway as through a funnel. Gorm studied the deferential nodders of the past, the spitball marksmen and scribes of yore, the kidders, rib pokers, the secretive graffiti boys, the shy girls who listened to everything and said nothing, the boisterous girls eager for a fall guy, those baffled by school. He watched them all and found no one watching him. Some made way for him and some didn't. Some nodded deferentially but most of the students were busy being students which meant filing along, not fastening their attention on much of anything. Twice when Gorm thought he spotted students who had given him unusual expressions, he turned to see them swallowed up by other students heading for the next class. It was all ebb and flow, a gelatinous mass of ebb and flow.

After lunch Gorm returned to school, where he walked a network hoping for hope conferred; a social test score fixed on seven months of muscular self-improvement. He saw the incessant movement now as a gesture of parts, a silent movie conducted without a narrative. Students, teachers were all moving to an appointed place.

Their routes were as charted as a commercial airliner's. There wasn't enough individual or collective consciousness for Gorm to feel out his score on the personal stock exchange.

Everything echoed him without hinting of judgment.

Gorm stared at his desktop the rest of the afternoon. It was April but the radiators still clanked and sizzled. He watched the clock move like a sinister toy toward the end of another toy day. He flexed a biceps but it felt like a dull reflex to dullness.

On the way home from school he made one final attempt to discover what esteem the world held for him. He placed his ear against a telephone pole. Previously, in the days when he had been a scapegoat and a newcomer to Flex Enterprises, had not the dull skillet, the one-armed clock, the sinking coal told him

more about his condition than his own thinking or any pronouncement from a human being? He held his head against the
pole long enough to hear a dull hum which repeated itself end-
lessly so that he couldn't tell if it was an extension of himself or
Hopewell's communications network which he was condemned
to join.

"You're losing faith again, Gorm."

Once again Gorm was sitting on his bench-press bench clad in
only his Charles Atlas gym shorts. He had returned to the cellar
from habit to find Mrs. Vidoni talcing the weight bar. She'd
always been thin but now she appeared to Gorm as emaciated.
There were dark circles under her eyes and she breathed in sharp
rasps.

"You don't look so well, yourself," he said.

"I'm just getting over the flu. But that has nothing to do with
heart. You look like somebody kicked you in the stomach and
you're still looking for your wind."

"You think you've been doing what's best for you; then one
morning you take a look around you and feel like you've been on
a conveyor belt all your life."

"That's because you're drifting alone."

"What should I do, knock up Mary Alice Woiczesheski and go
to work for Bog & Bliss?"

"That wouldn't help you. Faith's always a miracle."

"Are you telling me to hang out at Lourdes?"

"No, but you ought to believe in your body. It will be your
ticket out of this town."

"You mean I should hang around this dark, damp cellar for
another year getting strong for a purpose I don't even know?"

"You could build up for the Mr. Stillwell Contest in two
months. That would be a purpose."

The idea of posing before a mob struck Gorm as futile as trying
to sell them girdles.

"What for?"

"You'd be the best, stupid. People would look up to you."

Gorm said people had looked up to him once before. Then
he'd gotten the itch and had had to sit out a day and had been
forgotten that quickly.

"Oh, you ain't forgotten. People are just bein' busy. Only the
other day old man Donofrio was telling me how much better you
looked since I been supervising your workouts."

When Gorm hesitated, Mrs. Vidoni told him he couldn't give up being strong. It was all he had. What he needed, she said, was inspiration. She suggested Gorm come with her to see Joe Majarac.

Gorm faintly recalled the Polack from an elementary school text as a blocklike superhero, a white man's John Henry.

"What do you mean, see him? He was never alive. He was just something people made up."

"Oh, he's alive. He's everywhere you see steel, and steel built this city."

Gorm couldn't think of anywhere he didn't see steel or some residue of it.

"So where are you going to take me, to knock on bridge girders for luck?"

Mrs. Vidoni said Joe Majarac was on a museum wall near the university in Stillwell. He was up there in color, she said.

"Chances are he'll remain there since they got him painted right into the plaster."

"You mean a mural."

"Yeh," said the cleaning woman, "rich folks get paintings. Us poor people get murals which are bigger since there are more of us."

Gorm watched some color return to his helper's face.

"When I used to hang out with The Boys," he told her, "we took the strings from a kid's cello and made suspenders out of them."

"This ain't no artsy fartsy, Gorm. This is a Polack bigger than any man on Channel Eleven Studio Wrestling. He's bending steel and he takes up three walls."

Gorm then and there wanted to tell her how junk had inspired him. He wanted to tell her how he had never had a hero or inspiration that wasn't inspired by throwaways of some sort. He wanted to tell her the official heroes—the Washingtons and the Lincolns and the Christs and the Paul Bunyans and now even his childhood cowboy heroes—had meant little to him because one way or another they were always offered in the guise of making him a "good boy." But he didn't tell her any of these things. She was loyal to him and she was tired and he knew he'd break her heart if he didn't go to see Joe Majarac with her.

It was a torturous trip to the Carnegie Museum with the old cleaning woman. It was hot and muggy for April and a bank of cumulus clouds conspired with the plumes of smoke from the open hearths to seal the city like a casserole in an oven. Sweat ran from under the hat brim of the streetcar conductor who pulled a cord to allow their money to fall down a metal chute. His white shirt was gray around the sleeves and collar, and when the sweat emerged there, it ran through his collar as if gray ink seeped from his veins. When Gorm and Mrs. Vidoni sat down, the streetcar rocked them like bloated carp down an assembly line. The streetcar whined on its rails like a nail being wrenched from a board. Gorm sat upright and stiff; he had to because Mrs. Vidoni slumped against him gathering breath as if each intake were a sliver of burnt rope.

They had to switch streetcars two miles later and again Mrs. Vidoni leaned against him for support. Gorm felt the dull weight of her as if someone had driven a bolt through his shoulder-bones. He made up his mind that on the way home he would buttress her against one of the support poles.

When Mrs. Vidoni caught her breath, she talked about Joe Majarac with the reverence she'd once reserved for FDR and Garibaldi. She said his father had been a piece of iron ore and that the lad had been conceived in the Allegheny mountains. When the mountains were scooped for iron ore, Joe was transferred to a furnace where he spent much of his childhood. "It was the roar that made him strong. He fed on flames," she said.

"What else?" Gorm asked without enthusiasm. He'd been watching people moving across the Cheat River Bridge. They moved as if they had iron ore festering in their knees and hip sockets. So what was new? They imitated the hard and the up-right—smokestacks, furnace doors, Polack linebackers, bridge abutments. The exception was a cluster of blacks Gorm spotted moseying along. They were a testament to corkscrews—rubber ones. Maybe if you couldn't get a job your body was free to make its own shape.

"What else?" he asked to humor her.

"Joe didn't let anything get to him," she snapped. His hands were like buckets, his shoulders as wide as furnace doors. If a crane operator showed up skunked, mighty Joe just picked up the crane and whirled it around the plant until the crane operator got his bearings.

At every turn the streetcar swung like a cantilever jostling the old woman on to his lap. It rattled them toward the learning center of the city as Mrs. Vidoni gathered momentum for the murals of the Prince of Bog & Bliss. It was familiar territory to Gorm—bulk and force. It was a coach's dream, a production manager's ideal time study, a carnival impresario's sure-sell exhibit. It was the Song of Gargantua played at a Polish street fair. Impervious . . . incontestable. . . . Joe stirs the boiling steel with his fingers. Dip and stir . . . dip and stir . . . he licks his fingers . . . so much for excess ketchup.

So much for thought, thought Gorm. Mrs. Vidoni droned on.

"It was nothing for him to make eight rails between his fingers," said Mrs. Vidoni.

Gorm listened to Joe Majarac treat the steel plant like a dollhouse. During the obligatory ten-minute break, he walked on the furnace rims. Ten steps and he was halfway across the plant. He broke half-ton dollies when they didn't get the work done as fast as he could. Time to eat—hot steel soup, cold ingots for sandwich meat. And everywhere he went there was the mob of workmen. Cheering him on through all three shifts was the mob, exulting in their own togetherness; the weak felt the same strength as the strong; Joe Majarac was their glue and instant porridge.

Mrs. Vidoni was talking in lilting singsong now. Songs lied. Gorm preferred chants. Magicians and priests chanted. Chants evoked, songs lulled. He began to doze, sung to sleep by Mrs. Vidoni's melodic prattlings and the rhythmic rattle of the streetcar. Even its high-speed screech over the rails, its ting-a-lings signaling stops were part of the melody. A large crowd followed Joe Majarac to the Monongahela to watch him rescue an overloaded barge. Water was not a hero's element, Gorm thought. Water had its own laws which had nothing to do with bulk and strength. Through the exhaust fumes at a traffic light . . . the dull humidity in the streetcar . . . the ghostlike pall from the mills banked like snowdrifts. . . . Gorm heard Joe Majarac plop with as little noise as a bolt hitting the water and sinking. Gorm waved from his dream. Watch out for water but already the mob on the shore had grown sullen and was murmuring its discontent and did not hear Gorm's warning.

Someone was shaking him. Gorm opened one blinder to see two stone lions roaring at him through the window. Mrs. Vidoni was holding him by the shirt collar and yanking him. The conductor stared back at them.

Now it was Mrs. Vidoni who did the leading. She took him by the arm and led him down the streetcar steps. Still groggy, Gorm backed down. Honking horns, brakes screeching, the clatter of a firetruck, the hiss of streetcar brakes, a wailing siren, a boom from the mills all poured from the mouths of the stone lions.

"You're still asleep, idiot." Mrs. Vidoni tapped on his skull with her knuckles.

Promptly the two lions let their mouths relax to gray, lolling tongues. As Gorm passed them he watched their paws for an abrupt movement.

Inside, at the entrance to the mezzanine, Joe Majarac took up his stance like a comic-book hero. He wore the obligatory black, steel-toed work shoes and heavy blue-jean bib overalls. The straps outlined his pectorals, which Gorm said needed some work on their definition. Heading up the steps, Gorm saw he was aimed precisely between the Polack's legs and had he been a boy to walk through walls he would have had to deal with a mythic crotch. He and Mrs. Vidoni leaned against the railing to study the steeltown myth.

The colors were ochre—red, brown, flesh—tones and odors of stolid mountains, excavated seams, mohogany forests. Gorm had never seen a raw mountain closeup. Mohogany was a chest of drawers for the rich. He saw the powerful Polack as a hero for other planets. From Mrs. Vidoni he knew Majarac had been around a long time but he felt him as an instant concoction like Spider Man or The Mauler who would disappear the following season in tied bundles for the Rag Man. Joe Majarac tilted a vat of molten pig iron above his head into a mold. To Gorm he seemed dolefully familiar.

Just then a middle-aged black in gray overalls wheeled a mop plunged in a pail out of a side entrance.

"My own father worked thirty-one years at J&L. Never missed a day," said Mrs. Vidoni.

Gorm nodded and turned to look at the mural on his left. Here Joe was pounding ingots into shape with an enormous mallet. Sparks flew in perfect arcs. The background was equally dazzling. Ingots blazed in the furnaces. There was molten blue and white light everywhere. Cable lines ran overhead along with catwalks where foremen gazed with awe. Crane ladles dipped. Everyone bent to their appointed tasks.

"Kids now don't want to work, Gorm. In the old days the spirit of Joe was right next to the men. They worked twelve-hour shifts. And if orders were heavy, they went right back for another 12 hours after they got a little sleep. Not like today."

Gorm watched the motes circle each other in a dust shaft. His first museum reminded him of the library. Everything was so easily threatened. There was no room to cry "All Herald Gorm the Strong."

In every frame Joe was flexed. Even in the act of mundane work, his muscles had the alertness of eyes while his real eyes pursued a dutiful oblivion. In this pose, Majarac stood like a poor man's vision of the scales of justice. Two vats filled with hot slag hung from a steel beam Joe braced across his shoulders. It was a profile shot but even the Polack's jaw muscles were tensed for an admirer behind the rolling mill. He was On . . . eternally On. Every day was a peep show with him as the center of attraction.

Gorm was reminded of a bodybuilder he'd once observed at a Kresge lunch counter. In the act of lifting a paper cone in a metal container full of some soft drink, he posed. The man was chronically on the alert for biceps viewers.

Gorm was reminded of Gorm. Of how Gorm had been On for the past six months. Every movement from lifting a teaspoon to wiping his ass had been measured as if a pair of eyes were watching his progress, saying, "Yes, Gorm, you truly lift your spoon like a man who's poised for the world. Develop, Gorm, develop."

He'd branched out, it was true. He'd converted chain stores, public-service centers, a gas station to his personal stage. He was a boy who watched to be watched. The uniformed museum mopper poked at his heels with a wet mop.

"Watch your feet. The reg'lar man went south last night."

Gorm stood back.

A slick even path glided through Gorm's old footsteps.

The janitor turned, and poking a thumb at Joe Majarac, said, "The Polacks gave that man to the Irish when they found out his name meant 'Jackass.' The Irish tried to palm him off on the niggers but we weren't having any of it. You think you'd like him, Big Boy?"

Before Gorm could form an answer, the janitor said, "Ha ha," and pushed away with his mop.

Gorm turned to look for Mrs. Vidoni. She was leaning against a railing, staring at her feet as if she were deep in thought.

He returned across the room to her side.

"Hey," he said, poking her in the arm, "only a jackass would heave weight around all day for a steel company."

Not only did Mrs. Vidoni not seem to hear these words but she started to slide along the railing and would have conked her head on a pillar if Gorm hadn't reached out and snatched her. He propped her upright. He said, "Get your wind, I just found out Majarac means 'jackass' in Polish."

No sooner had he said that than the old woman fell his way. Gorm reached out with one hand and kept her from slamming into him. He held her at arm's length for some time, thankful that his weightlifting experience was finally coming in handy in a practical way.

"If you're not feeling well, I'll take you home," he told her. It seemed to him that she sighed but he could not be sure.

He propped her upright again. Her chin lay against her chest and her wart seemed to gleam as it never had before. Gorm had little experience with fainters. Sickness was tantamount to "gold-bricking" in Hopewell. Once when Gorm had told his father he looked ill, his father had said, "I'll lay down as soon as I fix this gas jet." The gas heater in the living room was plugged. But when he rose from his knees, after unplugging the jet, he said to Gorm, "Naw, I'd better not lay down now. The stove has to be cleaned and the car washed." Gorm had grown up with the philosophy that work healed whatever ailed you. It was poor tact to even mention that someone looked sick since that presumed they were unfit for work.

"These pictures are like comic-book covers."

Again his bodybuilding helper slid toward him.

After he'd propped her upright, Gorm decided she might be ill in a way he did not understand and she was reluctant to talk about. He should go get help in the museum. The trouble was he couldn't get her to stay upright. Every time he positioned her and started to back away, Mrs. Vidoni slid sideways, still stiff as a mop handle.

This problem, however, was quickly solved when Gorm spotted the cleaning equipment of the colored man, who'd advised him of the derivation of Majarac, standing unattended on the other side of the pillar. He worked his way around Mrs. Vidoni while maintaining her upright with his free hand till he reached around the pillar and snatched the mop from its bucket. Gorm jammed the dripping slop end against the base of the pillar while adroitly nudging the handle tip into the cleaning woman's ear. He tilted her at an angle so the mop formed a buttress. He was satisfied with his work. Aside from his barbells, it wasn't often Gorm could manipulate simple mechanics to his advantage. Given the average Stillweller's fear of sickness or weakness of any kind, he hoped the casual museum visitor would view her as a woman who'd had a spell but did not want to get too far away from her work. He went then in search of help.

At the information counter he was directed down a long hall-way full of glass cases with flint stone and teeth in them but he made a wrong turn and entered the Mesozoic room where work-men in overalls gathered on scaffolds at the spinal column of Tyrannosaurus Rex. Gorm stared for a time at the great beast but he wasn't impressed. Rex struck him as mawkish. He knew such behemoths had existed but this one looked more like a prop for a Halloween float.

"Hey," he yelled at the workmen, "I've got a woman resting near the Majarac pictures. I need some first aid for her."

"Not here. Try over in Cenozoic," the man cried.

In Cenozoic, a workman said there had been a man there who knew first aid but he'd been fired for trying to steal a Smilodon's tusk. They joked then about the use a man with a frigid wife in Beltzhoover would make of a saber-toothed tiger's tusk. They said Gorm should try Paleozoic. A great chorus of laughter wafted after him into the hallway.

He glanced into other rooms and saw that he was in a bone factory. Each set of bones was alloted its space on a platform much like grim-featured generals on rearing horses in the park. Each commemorated the purposeful pose. In this they ressembled the Hero of Tireless Industry, Majarac. All of them were preposterous fusilages celebrating defiance. But defiance against what? Even the Cro-Magnon fellow in the glass case bent like a tired blacksmith signaled little more than aloneness. They might have been jewels or trading stamps or shards of pottery restored. Where was the testimony that the Cro-Magnon man had woken one morning, like Gorm, and decided he was a hero? Had the trees spoken to him? Had he been terrified of not developing his pecker? This boneyard of history struck Gorm as little more than a collection of freaks.

When he arrived at the First Aid door, a crayoned sign said, "I am out to dinner."

Upon his return to the landing below Joe Majarac, he discovered the cleaning equipment was still there—the pail of dirty water on one side of the pillar, the mop upright on the other side. In place of Mrs. Vidoni a note was taped to the mop handle.

"Your lady friend did not look well and museum policy does not allow viewing areas to be used for naps. I have put her in the custodial storage closet, second door to your right on the mezzanine.
                                        Gaston Bitwiler,
                                        Chief Custodian

Mrs. Vidoni was sitting upright, or rather had been propped on a barrel of disinfectant. Her eyes had taken to bulging in the chlorine darkness.

"You rested yet?" he said to Mrs. Vidoni. There was a quietness about the room that made him think that whatever institutional forces resided there wanted to claim his bodybuilding helper for their collection of bones. The silence within the silence of the room made him reach for her. At the same instant the old woman fell forward into his arms. Gorm caught her and for a moment was mindful only of her tremendous weight. The woman's wart pressed into his neck and he received the kind of mental shock that can only be delivered in great stillness—this was the first time in his life he could recall ever holding another person. If his mother had hugged him and he'd hugged her in return, he had no memory of it.

"This is strictly for friendship," he said to his helper.

Hearing no reply from her, he cried, "Bitwiler!"

He got no reply to this, either.

And still she lay in his arms.

Gorm quickly made up his mind that he could get no help from people in a building whose main purpose was assembling bones. His only hope was to carry her back to Hopewell where Mrs. Vidoni had friends and someone would have the time to stop and identify her illness.

The brilliant red streetcar shuttled into view far up Mellon Avenue.

"Time to move, Mrs. Vidoni." Gorm lowered his shoulder into the lifeless belly and hefted her upward.

Gorm was about to drop two full fares into the glass cylinder when the conductor scowled at the head hanging over the boy's shoulder.

"The dead go half-fare," he said.

Gorm knew there was no way his helper could die on him so suddenly.

"Just overworked," he said to the conductor. But he deposited the unexpected savings in his pocket and started for a seat, jostled from one steel hand rail to another with his unwieldy cargo by the streetcar's lurch.

Since it was rush hour, every seat was filled with a sweating body; most of the vertical handrails were gripped by some tired worker. Yet a space instantly cleared for Gorm and his cargo as if by the wave of a magic wand. His eyes had grown very quiet in his head. He was pleased that his power was reviving and that people sensed as much to make space for him the way they had after he'd named an alley after himself when he still had the belief he could perfect all of his muscles. He said as much to Mrs.

Vidoni sprawled across his shoulders.

The cleaning woman felt as limp as a sack of potatoes on his back. One of her arms was flung over his chest. The hand of that arm clutched her purse. At each stop and start of the streetcar the arm flopped like a rag doll's, the purse alone seeming to have authority as it banged against Gorm's stomach. It occurred to Gorm that he might stop and get them some food and revive the woman on his back.

A stillness beyond the usual workers' fatigue rose like a miasma of yellow fog. Each passenger looked strapped into his seat as if they all rode a rocket hurdling through space instead of a trolley car shuttling along at 20 miles per hour. Each passenger offered a line of concentration as pure and unswerving as the blunt nose of the streetcar.

None of this struck Gorm as unusual. Humans had always appeared to him as wearing blinders. Gorm had adopted a narrower line of vision as he'd progressed under the guidelines of Charles Atlas's Flex Enterprises. Yet in the days when he'd collected junk and before he'd become a scapegoat, he had felt as if his head was attached to a 360-degree swivel such was his desire to scan Hopewell for throwaways which he might revive. The second and third-hand had made him hopeful.

Gorm smiled down at a woman he was standing beside. She was sixty and her henna-red hair glistened like copper coils.

"We could use some rain," he said to her.

Her mouth parted to answer him but nothing escaped.

Gorm's remark thickened the silence of the already silent cargo.

"This is a city where you need rain often." He did not address anyone in particular. "Things pile up . . . dirt, soot . . . day after day . . . the air seems to hang. . . . Now, you take me. . . ."

But the woman's stop had come and she rose from her seat unsteadily, eased under Gorm's arm fastened to the handrail, and bolted for the door. The passengers in one motion rocked back in their seats; those standing did a sway and a shuffle to keep their balance. The streetcar was underway again.

It careened and shuttled as if it had a life of its own past row after row of soot-frayed red brick houses joined with one another, then a business district offering cherry Cokes and corn plasters from makeshift signs. The latter looked as begrimed and lifeless as the living quarters on the fringes of Stillwell, and though the scene was nearly identical to what he had grown up with in Hopewell, its inertia weighed him considerably. He felt a terrible need to talk to someone but he couldn't catch anyone's eye except the conductor whom he saw eyeing him severely out of the mirror on the visor.

As more and more people came to their destinations, Gorm noted the seats around him remained empty. This angered him because the temporary lifelessness of Mrs. Vidoni did not seem an iota worse than what he saw in the seats. Something terrible was happening and Gorm meant to have a talk with his body-building helper as soon as he revived her.

"Blossom life, blossom," he mumbled without conviction.

The next stop was Squirrel Hill where Gorm and Mrs. Vidoni were to change cars for Hopewell. As Gorm stepped forward with his cargo, the arm clutching the purse swung like a metronome across his chest. After he'd stepped down, he happened to glance back and saw every window filled with faces gawking at him.

He sat his helper on a stone bench in front of a stone bank that had a sign in the window offering a drinking mug with your initials on it if you invested your savings with its "dependable" officers. Mrs. Vidoni's arms were outflung and her head lolled on top of the backrest. The purse dangled against a sandstone pillar.

Squirrel Hill neither had squirrels nor hills. Many years before, when the commercial area expanded, the squirrels had left for the river bank around Skeetersville and the hills had been bull-dozed and leveled off to make room for the interstate and its numerous access roads, entrances, and exits in 1955. It did have a number of veterans of Auschwitz and Buchenwald and they were quick to question the fixed gaze of Gorm's helper.

An elderly woman with a fierce intelligence in her scowl set her shopping bag at Gorm's feet and said, "Your friend's not so well. You take her home. So what's so good about home? She'll rest more comfortable there. You fix her some hot tea when she wakes up. And give her this," and the well-meaning resident dipped into her bag and laid a cheese blintz wrapped in tissue paper on Gorm's lap.

"We just came from a place that's all bones and comic strips to make you forget the bones," Gorm told her:

The woman picked up her bag and held it tight to her chest.

"You kids don't know anything about bones. I come from a place that was bones on top of bones. Nothing but bones. There wasn't any comic strips to make us forget either."

The woman marched off as if she'd been insulted.

"But you and I appreciate muscles," Gorm said to his helper. "We know how beautiful a good body can be. The trick is to find something for it to do. I could go down to the river and work in one of the mills like your friend Donkey Ass. But what would be the point? My father comes home tired; he goes to work tired. No one cares about his muscles."

Gorm was aware people were staring at his helper in a fearful and suspicious way. Way down the boulevard he spotted a blind man pushing pencils. With considerable force he pried Mrs. Vidoni's fingers from the purse and took her last five dollars. In a minute he returned with the blind man's sunglasses and put them over his helper's eyes.

"We don't need to be stared at," he said.

He pulled one of her arms down to the bench and held her hand.

"I wish you wouldn't bum out on me now," he said. "You're right; there's not much faith around. Just a lot of people being moved from this spot to that spot to another spot."

He would have continued chattering to the dead cleaning woman but a numbing dread had seized his guts. It wasn't about death. He had as little familiarity with death as he did with birth. It was a process going on around him that flashed before his eyes like a switchblade. The inert led the living.

Clots of traffic heaved back and forth, the eyes of the drivers as lifeless as the manikin he'd dismembered in Woolworth's. They did not seem to drive so much as to be pulled along by the magnetism of their bumpers and ornate chrome grills, each car front pulled along by the one in front of it. Drivers did not park; the curb ushered them in. And they did not get out of their cars so much as they were pulled into another flow. First, though, they did not place coins in slots. Parking meters—metal and glass—with arrogant arms reached into the drivers' pockets and silently, shamelessly took what was needed to keep the glass faces of the metal bodies from becoming red and screaming VIO-LATION. The "drivers" then with eyes averted entered a pedes-trian flow which was pulled along by the gleam and sparkle of shop windows. Bright labels pulled the pedestrian into the larger stores where he didn't even have to grip a doorknob. Doors opened *for* him and more labels lifted his hands smartly to chest level, spread his palms into a receiving position for the cans and jars and smartly packaged frozen foods that had been prepared by machines weeks and months before. Aluminum carts did the job after that. Around and around the bright, air-conditioned confines, no pair of eyes addressing any other pair but sticking to its appointed task until a smaller, squatter bandit took the "pe-destrian's" receipts for his previous day's or week's work, and showed him what was being taken from him in another glass window as it rang ting-a-ling, ting-a-ling. Now instead of being merely a "driver" or "pedestrian," our man was a CONSUMER. Consuming as he did, he was able to enter the smart, smooth line of other consumers entering the combined flow of driver-pedestrian-consumer into the open air of the avenue where once again he proved he was ALIVE and HE BELONGED.

Not to drive or pedés or consume was to step out of the flow, to isolate oneself.

The world he knew was divided into compartments. There were avenues and alleys, houses, churches, schools, factories, athletic fields, parks, shops, banks, repair shops. The problem as Gorm understood it from his own experience, which was mainly limited to a 30-block area of Hopewell, was how to feel at home in one of those compartments. Each compartment offered protection. IF YOU BELONGED THERE. HOW DID YOU BELONG THERE? Well you became a driver, a pedestrian, a consumer. Now, this presupposed money to buy the car to drive, the shoes to walk, the decent clothes to enter shops since they would not admit you naked. To find a compartment and feel comfortable in it, you had to have money. It was his father's money which had allowed Gorm a compartment within a compartment—the cellar—to develop his frail and battered body. He, himself, had little interest in money since he did not want very much unless it was the brilliant, Technicolor images of heroes on the Hippodrome screen. Recently he'd understood just what went on with a hero and his sidekick—the incestuousness of all frontiersmen—which left him with the hero's horse to admire so that now there was nothing that money could buy Gorm except a little food to sustain his energy for developing his latissimus dorsi, deltoids, and knotty spinalis. However, this was but a pretext for getting his ass in shape so he could shit like normal people, which is to say drivers, pedestrians, consumers. Yet the more clear it all became, his ass was only a pretext for discovering the ball bearing which he'd swallowed as a child and had doomed him to being a scapegoat. Pretext built upon pretext, compartment upon compartment. Gorm squeezed the dead woman's hand and felt himself exhausted.

But he couldn't stop now. Lugging the inert body of his bodybuilding helper across town was helping him to understand a few things about this world he was to enter as a free soul upon his high school graduation in two months.

The value of compartments seemed unimpeachable. He had his experience with The Boys to prove that. When they had money, they were allowed to hang out in Ma Goo's. They nibbled Twinkies and played the pinball machine until they ran out of money. Then they had to go somewhere. Where? Another compartment. The Street! The street was the last resort when you didn't have money. Understanding this, you huddled closer together. He did that with The Boys. There was a false protection in this because twice he and The Boys had been carted to another compartment—jail. His father had had to pay a fine for LOITERING.

It was very strange. Some compartments you had to pay to get into but if you could afford no compartments you got taken to one where you had to pay to get out. In other words you were penalized money and put in a compartment because you did not have money to enter a compartment. It was a very strange world this world he was about to enter as an adult. Everywhere there was a man with a badge and a gun and, a severe judicial expression to protect the compartments. All the compartments except one—the body. Where was the policeman who would protect Gorm's asshole? At least until he got his shit worked out, surging in clean streams and hardened like a normal human's—which is to say a driver-pedestrian-consumer's. Gorm had no desire to join this latter flow but what other flow was there?

He couldn't depend on his father's alloting him a compartment in the cellar after his graduation. Anyway, he understood now the vague malaise which had made him queasy while lifting weights was the dank claustrophobia inflicted by the cellar. His court had told him he needed a permit to lift in the park; only the mayor knew what other permits he would need to enter other compartments in the outside world.

Gorm didn't talk with his schoolmates but he'd overheard enough conversations to know what they planned to do when they graduated and had to take up new compartments. Get a job, save money, become a driver, save some more money, drive to rent their first compartment—an apartment, introduce a girl to it, play her some soft music, linger around her eating compartment with their tongues, crawl in her lower compartment—the same type compartment they'd emerged from so many years before, put a tadpole in it, marry her before the tadpole got too big and crawled out, then find a bigger compartment to work in and a bigger compartment to raise the tadpole in, all the while driving and walking among shops and consuming in the general flow of things, watch the tadpole grow into a smart-mouthed frog who croaked at the dinner table, watch the joy of their loins—the frog—make other tadpoles, whence there would be a reunion with all the frogs and all the tadpoles gabbing and gobbling and snorting in the park every three years before they went home to their respective compartments to complain about all the greedy frogs on earth. Then they were pulled out of the general flow of driving, pedestrian perusal among shops, and active consuming by the final compartment—the one Gorm had only heard about. The one that was just big enough for your body and got lowered into the ground unprotected, like the formerly live body. The Great Feast for The Termites.

Though his helper's eyes were shielded, her head lay at such a distorted angle that pedestrians and consumers were still staring at her.

"Don't mind other folks," Gorm advised Mrs. Vidoni, "There's nothing they can do to help us."

"The trouble is," he continued, "we don't fit in anywhere. If you hadn't been my helper, what would you have done? Nobody wants an old cleaning woman who lives alone."

His helper did not reply but Gorm was getting used to a world that did not reply.

"The closest I came to fitting in anywhere was Woolworth's where I made a speech in the girdle department. I suppose I could have stayed if I'd kept on talking. Slept beside the manikin at night. Now I have to figure out where I'm going to go in two months. It's not enough to grow some good muscles and hang around inside your body for a while."

He still had the old woman's hand but he didn't squeeze it so hard now.

"What scares me is I feel like I'm being towed somewhere, to a place I don't know anything about. I can sit here with you and think about it but I'm still being towed. I could think all my life . . . the best thoughts a person could think and I'd still be towed without my consent. If I resist, every part of me gets scraped raw on the road but hell . . . in the days when I didn't resist I got banged up all the time anyway. There doesn't seem any way a person can win in this life."

There did not seem much else to say. Gorm had talked himself into a temporary calm. Around him the waves of people were carried over the hard, sleek surfaces toward their appointments with who knew what. It was a vast world of things that Gorm knew, had he remained a junk collector, would eventually end up in his cellar. Each thing exerted its pull on something else: tar with tires, tires with gearshift knobs, copper-alloyed doorknobs with hands, hands with shaped wood that led the hardening limb across the early evening to appointed darkness.

Layer on layer, the inert metal and wood remembered its glorious time at the hilt of volcanic eruptions, its company of gold, labyrinth crystals, mounds of spoors in that eon when it had first emerged from water and the dawn offered crawlies for company. So the hickory walking stick walked the old woman back toward the forest. The twelve-carat watch led a fashionable arm toward a mountain range in South Africa. The eyes crying perpetual tears did not long for relief, only to rejoin the ocean where its eyeducts had been formed. If a human did not have potassium in his system he got to gorge in the dirt where he could lunch on potassium till eternity. At the bottoms of oceans there was plenty of calcium for rotted teeth, lubricating oil for the joints, coagulant for the leaking heart.

At a nearby red light Gorm watched drivers hitch up their resolution for one last assault on the cobbled bricks and the winding arteries of the city before the good missus brought them a beer in an easy chair. But Gorm knew better . . . knew the fierce horizontal glare of their cars was all deception. He knew that men like his father had become bolts on assembly lines whose magnetism was towed by the iron in crankshafts, axles, cotter pins, and ball bearings toward a reunion with the mountain where the ore had first been mined. Though movies and school had taught Gorm the frontier had been "conquered," nature harnessed at the will of millions of Americans who had thrown a lasso around it, Gorm knew better. Nature had simply been transformed into a million manmade items through which it exacted its revenge. Only a compartment like "home" staved off the final appointment in the mountain, the sea, the sky for a few hours. Then the relentless tug won out, was even part of the "home." Each day in the assured safety of their homes, people were sucked down with the inert whose ghosts ached and spiraled in the whorls of bannister arms, the gleam of toasters, the matted wool of their rugs. They became one with the things they owned. They became things in themselves. The feeble registers of humanness were a charade: the voice that repeated itself year after year; the gestures that imitated gestures from a previous day, which in turn had imitated the hardness of possessions out of fear of being vulnerable. Things absorbed the gestures of humans and fed them in the angular, protective edges of their nature. Gorm had offered the Woolworth ladies the protection of things; he had extended his resuscitation of the dead and near-dead to the community. People were either alive or they were dead. As much as he could tell, most of the people he'd observed in Stillwell and Hopewell were dead. He had one on his hands now, and with considerable anger, he took off her sunglasses, placed them in his pocket, threw her over his shoulder and stumbled out to meet the No. 68 streetcar with HOPEWELL marked on its front.

For all of Gorm's trust in Hopewell, he did not know what to do with the body of his helper once he got her there. The streetcar dropped them a block from Ma Goo's confectionery. It was dusk. Because The Boys were moseying back and forth in front of Ma's, he and Mrs. Vidoni curled behind some bushes in a United Presbyterian Church yard while he tried to figure his next step.

It was a drastic situation for the young man to be saddled with something that was not considered usable that he did not have a compartment for. The extinct coal cellar stored throwaways from his childhood; the extinct furnace held his own coprolites from recent months; like a visitor to a cheap hotel, his mother was registered and dissipating in the memory box in his head. Gorm thought briefly of taking Mrs. Vidoni home and stowing her with the alarm clock, the waffle iron, the compressor, the patched inner tube, and the curtain rods but already the dead woman had shit herself and this smell made up Gorm's mind not to pollute his own house and to find another resting spot for the old woman.

Hopewell did not have a hospital and Gorm realized he should have remained on the streetcar and gone to the next town where there was one. Mrs. Vidoni's failure to stir at all in the past three hours was slowly convincing him he would never resuscitate her. In a rage of confusion his mind flashed with possibilities of releasing himself from her and her wearisome inertia: one of the large Dempster dumpsters outside Saint Humiliata of Our Lady of the Feast grade school, the back seat of a parked car. He peeked over the hedge and down the street to where The Boys were. They were still milling about Ma's, shuffling in abortive circles, poking one another, staring about with not much expectancy at the night's promise.

Gorm felt the old tug toward their soporific circle where at least he knew what was expected of him. When he was their thing, he did not have a queasy feeling in his stomach. Everything remained in its place; it did not confer its terrifying tug on all other things. All he had to do then was accept a few slaps about the head, resign himself to a position as low man in the pecking order. Most of his beatings had come from those outside the circle of The Boys who knew about his lowly position.

He could not return to The Boys, not with the body he possessed. He was alone with his body and he had to make the best of it.

He picked her up, adjusted her on his shoulders, and started down an alley that circled behind the church and eventually landed him against the backs of a row of businesses. He rested his cargo against the wall of a bowling alley.

Three hours of ferrying the dead woman, the rapid convolutions of his mind as it analyzed and reconstructed the inertia of Stillwell, and the dazed sense that everything about him did not so much as live as drift by him in slow motion left Gorm with vertigo. He knew roughly where he was at but he had a difficult time relating sounds and sights to their source, the accepted reality they embodied. When he first heard the solemn, gradual rumble through a wall of a bowling ball proceeding toward ten-pins, he imagined a locomotive bearing down on him and buried his head in his arms until he heard the dull clack of splattering pins and the residual silence which followed. When the ominous rumble began again, he draped the dead cleaning woman on his shoulders and got out of there.

He staggered along the alley with his body until a spotlight shining on a parking lot caught his attention. A black hearse sat alone, mute and expectant, its grill revealed like the mouth of a barracuda. He dimly understood he was at Need's Funeral Home. Almost as quickly he knew this would be the appropriate place to leave the dead cleaning woman. He pondered whether to put her in the hearse or lay her on the back steps of the funeral home. The smallest smile raised his lips. Finally he would be free of one small body of inertia that was trying to drag him down to its level.

In that instant Gorm heard a rumble similar to the one at the bowling alley. But this rumble had a regular cadence to it. It was almost as familiar as his earliest memories of his own existence. Unlike the bowling ball's trip down a neat, narrow pathway, this rumble hinted of space won in noble battles, horizons simple and clearly in view. He surged with his body toward the source of the noise. Shots rang out and Gorm dropped to his knees with his burden. He heard the heavy plop he knew unmistakably from years of watching Westerns as a man falling from his horse. The horses' hooves resumed their cadence and Gorm felt he and Mrs. Vidoni were caught in the middle of a stampede. With his free hand he groped about the cinder alley trying to locate the dead woman yet hunching to protect himself. He was certain a force which issued from this stampede had blown her from his shoulders. Someone in an ambush; someone connected with the funeral home next door.

This would have decided everything: made his helper's end dramatic, solved his own confusion, and made death palpable. There would have been a finality to it all.

Gorm's groping hand came up with a pop bottle and the tongue of a shoe. As he turned in the darkness to greet the next rush of horses' hooves, Mrs. Vidoni's purse thumped against his back. He reached out and felt the aluminum leg warmed by the sun that afternoon. The sounds of the Old West were coming from a heavy iron door which Gorm reached out and touched. He understood then he was next to the exit door of the Hippodrome Theatre, the one that had ushered him into the night from its Technicolor fantasies most of his life in Hopewell.

He held his ear against the door and heard more horses' hooves and gunshots. He cursed softly. He understood nothing so melodramatic as an ambush was going to relieve him of the dead woman. The movie sounds offered him the same ruse as Joe Majarac, as the bones and burlap and plaster in the Pleistocene room, as the matchcover ad for Charles Atlas's Flex Enterprises had offered him, as the rhetroic to promote girdles he'd offered the Woolworth ladies. False protection.

Everyone seemed involved in an unknowing conspiracy to promote inertia. Majarac kept the workers resigned and law-abiding in their little compartment of the world. Charles Atlas assured that the skinny alien Gorms would stay at home in their little compartments. The museum boys took the image of extinct giants, rebuilt them as Gorm had rebuilt his body, and offered them to the public as examples of the incredibly resurrected. He saw the Woolworth ladies locked forever in their hip compartments, hunkering toward an oblivion like Mrs. Vidoni. He trembled when he rose up.

He was certain of one thing: He wanted to be rid of this body on his back; he wanted to begin life anew.

He rose up with his cargo and ran from the shadows of the Hippodrome onto a bridge over a railroad. A freight train rumbled underneath and hooted. Gorm's feet trembled and he grabbed one of the steel girders to keep his balance. Vibrations ran up the steel girders. Gorm's legs jiggled like those of the soft-shoe man in a minstrel team. The corpse on his back vibrated too as if suddenly imbued with new life. Mrs. Vidoni's aluminum leg swung out and clattered against the girder. As if in a final effort to convince Gorm that she still carried vitality, her arm flew over his shoulder and the purse she'd clutched since her death banged against his chest just as the caboose passed under the bridge.

The young man staggered down a sloping walkway with his

burden. His own body now screamed for release as if the burden of its own bones was too heavy. He felt his bones, tendons, blood were about to fly skyward and his soul blow back toward the bridge girder like a duster wafted along the floor of the earth on cleaning day and take up eternal residence in that block of forged matter. A street light still animated from the passing train, whispered "drop her." Gorm passed a pastry shop and the bride on a wedding cake with her long, bashful lashes said, "Enough is enough."

"Enough is enough," Gorm cried aloud to the empty street. Even as he staggered toward a resting spot, his memory was failing him. He tried to recall himself as a child, when a person was supposed to have felt free, but it seemed the weighted ghost of the cleaning woman had straddled his back even then, like a woman on a child-horse crying "Giddyup, Giddgup," urging him faster, and that with each passing year he had gnarled at his bit while the weighted rider had urged him on with more rapidity the more he tried to unravel his bloated condition—the hopeless limbo of each grinding day behind a desk at school, the solitude of his room where he tried to forgive himself for his hopelessness, for the money he never knew how to spend because he enjoyed so few manmade things; the fists and the bruises and the eyes of every Hopewell grownup sizing him up with pity and amusement and condescension for what he was: barely alive though the weighted corpse had mounted him and laid the whip to him on both flanks.

He had shat himself and a soft, scabrous turd clung to his pants. He widened his stride so that it might fall without scraping his thighs but it adhered to him with all the adhesiveness of his corpse. Recalling his childhood, Gorm remembered it as infested with shit, the rapacious unpredictability of it. To get rid of this corpse, to find new life, to rediscover for the rest of his body, the energy implicit in his asshole and its terrible history, that was Gorm's goal.

He dropped his corpse in the doorway of a jewelry shop. Behind a grilled gate dozens of watches ticked: sapphires and diamonds resplendent of all that endured waited for doe-eyed lovers and their hope of calm days and an enduring pattern.

In Mrs. Vidoni's purse, Gorm found a pen and scratch paper. The latter had the museum hours for viewing Joe Majarac. He wrote on the back: "THIS LADY WAS A STRANGER WHO BELIEVED IN STRONGMEN." He took a safety pin from her purse and pinned the epitaph over her heart.

He had taken a few steps down the street when he remembered he had forgotten something. He returned to the jewelry shop doorway and smiled down at the wart on the dead cleaning woman's forehead. "If I ever become Mr. Stillwell, it will be for you." He meant the wart. Then he dipped at the knees and waist and kissed it.

Though Gorm was aware in an abstract way that the dead must be laid out for viewing, respected with solemnity and conservative dress, he had never actually visited a funeral home. He wanted to see the corpse of Mrs. Vidoni in his hernia belt and Charles Atlas gym shorts. When he explained this desire to his father, with the added blasphemy that she might want him to flex so she could relish a final glimpse of his burgeoning pectorals before she rose into the heavens, his father's face bloated and the veins in his forehead swelled.

"You crazy?" he screeched. "This is the dead you're talkin' about."

Gorm had felt pleasantly lightened since he'd deposited his corpse. It was as if several quarts of excess fluid had been drained from his brain and he were seeing the world clearly for the first time. He felt himself to be a cloud, alternately rolling itself into a ball, assuming a thousand shapes as it drifted over the spectral earth, sometimes enveloping and disgorging its own lining as he met with strong winds, a brief dance in passing.

So he felt no need to war with his father. He submitted to the tailor's fastidious measurements for the woolen charcoal suit that would serve not only his first view of death but his high school graduation in two months. A white shirt and a yellow tie with a blue parrot and a new pair of ox-bloods completed his costume. He resembled any young man out to make his mark in the city.

At the entrance to Need's funeral home, the suit was accorded passage by a dozen deferential glances and nodding heads down the long shade of the garden-hose-green canopy. If the deft knot his father had tied for him executed a solemn hush in his larynx, Need's carpet swallowed his footsteps. The tongues of humans struck Gorm as extraordinarily long like expensive carpets being unrolled for a visiting dignitary as each phrase was laboriously extended and perfected till it merged into every other phrase looming off the palate like an expensive lozenge till no sound of the mouth could be distinguished from any other sound. The room itself was an ornate show of neutrality, expensive and decorative but meant to blend with every other thing, to go unnoticed. The fleurs-de-lis on the ceiling did not suggest flowers but quiet order. They saluted the beige couch with its thick cushions and large, shady plants on each side and slender coffee table in front. Men and women advanced with neither languor nor hurry. Their dress harmonized with their deferential movements to produce a barely perceptible rustle like the first fallen leaves that decorate a lawn. It was a world in which no one was fat or thin, homely or beautiful, good or evil, austere or sensual, parsimonious or expansive, sad or happy. It was, in a word, modest.

A man, who appeared the aperture of this modesty, advanced on Gorm with a great, good, welcoming smile, a smile so benign that Gorm thought it might run down his pants leg at any moment. He was one of the director's sons and was responsible for "grief counseling," a new phenomenon to Hopewell but one which was advertised above a flickering candle in the *Evening Herald*. He tried to take Gorm by the elbow but the young man slid it out of his touch. This did not deter him. Through various pats on the back and sliding motions he led Gorm to a "Guest Register" which was as padded as everything else.

After he'd signed in, the "Grief Counselor" pointed him toward "The Slumber Room" where he said Mrs. Vidoni's body "lay in state."

As Gorm started forward to view his first body, the Grief Counselor trailed a half step behind him. Gorm paused to study the man—his effulgent good will, his clean lines.

"We did the best we could," said the man, "she didn't arrive here in the best shape, you know. We had to bring in an outside cosmetologist."

"To do what?" asked Gorm.

"To make her look good."

"But she was an old woman."

"Every person has the right to *look* good at their funeral."

"She's dead. What rights do the dead have?"

"The dead have the same right to look as good as you and me," and the Grief Counselor stalked off, piqued that the cosmetic job on the dead woman wouldn't be more appreciated.

There was a large crowd around the inert cleaning woman. This surprised Gorm because he'd always thought of Mrs. Vidoni as having spent her life essentially alone. Several old women in black babushkas knelt by the casket, offering a low litany over rosary beads. In every corner there were clustered modestly prosperous groups, the men quietly conversing with the men, the women adhering to their age group, offering the deferential nod Gorm had become accustomed to since his various muscle groups had gained contour and heft. As with the people he'd first observed in the greeting room, every application of voice, gesture, clothing, complemented the quiet of the rugs, the probity of the ceiling, the careful arrangement of the carnations surrounding the casket, the token ritual of the candles burning in red translucent holders below the mass cards.

Gorm glanced at the coffin, fearfully and expectantly, and was assured that the woman, who'd acted as the catalyst for his modest voyage into the world, fitted in with these circumspect surroundings. The once fierce and sinewy texture of her face and neck was now as mellow and handsome as a baby doll's in a crib. Like some of the women present, a trace of purple mascara gave her a faintly exotic look. Her once lean, ashen cheeks had been propped and emboldened with rouge. Her stringy hair had been curled; curls fringed her forehead like the edges of a lace doily.

The longer Gorm stared at the inflated body, the more he was aware of an obscenity he could not name. It was not the lacquered baby-dollness; he'd known homely women who'd spread it thick when they went to church bazaars. Gorm's eyes roved up and down the folds and ruffles of the long pink dress, from the cleaning woman's forehead to her feet, and could not make up his mind what disturbed him.

He was aware that many sights and sounds had fooled him during the last six months so he dipped his hand into the casket and let it stroll across the dead woman's forehead. Some pink powder came off on his fingertips but it was the unadulterated smoothness of her forehead which sent panic flailing to his hands and the arches of his feet. They'd taken Mrs. Vidoni's wart.

Just then a young woman in a pearl necklace gasped and a moment later a fat man moved beside Gorm to tell him it was inappropriate to touch the deceased.

Gorm paid him no attention but continued to stare at his old helper's smooth forehead. There wasn't even a mark where they'd cut away the wart. It was a sight to make him cry out for help. But he merely stared and the fat man, assuming the transgressor was afflicted with inordinate grief, returned to his group in the corner.

"What'd they do to her?" Gorm asked no one in particular.

"Shhh, pray for her soul," a woman hissed at him.

That was the problem; the wart signified for Gorm the soul of Mrs. Vidoni. The moonlight playing off her wart had first announced Mrs. Vidoni's presence in the alley. The wart positioned like a brown pole above the bench press bench had centered the resuscitation of his muscles, had lent gravity to her loyality.

He had taken too many blows in his life to understand what she meant by the word "faith"; he did not share her propensity for aping strongmen simply because they were strong. The idea though that she, a lonely old woman, should dutifully supervise his weightlifting workouts was manifested in the wart. Now she looked like any old woman trying not to look old, as if being old were like metal curtain rods, unfashionable and to be scrapped.

He felt he was suffocating in his new charcoal suit.

He turned on the assembled mourners, letting his eyes hover and bore on each separate group with a menacing stare. Had he the power here that he possessed in "Gorm's Alley," he would have made them strip. He would have held them hostage until they examined each other's bodies. Every time they found a wart, pimple, mole, odd protuberance of belly button, birthmark, burn scar, distortion of nipple, kneecap, or hair in an unwanted place, he would make them sing "Hallelujah" cheek to cheek in chorus. He would make them sing the praises of germs.

Gorm's glare had made everyone stop talking. He studied them with rising vitriol. They sensed something gone wrong and malignant. The very spell of decorum and reverence he was dissipating made several of the men slowly return his belligerence.

Gorm said to them: "Where's our wart?"

The tension of the room exploded in laughter.

Gorm was infuriated. He slammed the coffin lid on Mrs. Vidoni and climbed on top of it. A woman ran to get the funeral director. Several of the men started forward, crying, "Hey!" Gorm jerked himself free of the suitcoat and threw it into a stand of carnations. He flexed and cried, "All Herald Gorm the Strong."

The mourners stopped, baffled. "Get off the coffin lid and we'll talk," a clean-cut young man told Gorm.

"You don't own this body," said Gorm, "It's scrap. It's useless. Someone laid it out for the garbage man or Black Jack the trash man. You said, 'It's dead. Get rid of it.' It belongs to the first one who claims it. For now, I, Gorm, claim it."

"The police are coming," a woman yelled in a hysterical voice. Other women were running among chairs, sobbing and moaning as they collected their purses and ran from the room.

"Let the police come," Gorm told them, "Someone committed a theft here and maybe they can solve it. The dead woman I stand on had her wart taken from her. I think whoever did it, did it to make her more like you people—rich looking and not too bothered. It's impossible for her soul to survive without the wart. It grew out of her and was her best-known feature."

"Get off my aunt's casket before I come up there and put you in your own casket." The threat belonged to a well-built boy with a baby face who glanced about him for a reaction when he spoke.

"You're not going to come up here, baby face. You're afraid of death like everyone else here. You're so afraid of it you dress it up to look like everything else you know. You grew up afraid, babyface. You'll always be afraid."

As with the Woolworth ladies he'd touched a nerve. He could have gone on talking for another half-hour. The smiling grief counselor rushed into the room no longer smiling. His head pivoted in a half dozen directions before someone pointed him toward Gorm.

"I think we can handle your wart. I've placed a call downstairs and they're looking for it."

Several women broke out in renewed sobs at this news. The men stared malignantly at Gorm as the grief counselor led him from the Slumber Room and into an office just off the main entrance.

"I've had requests for every part of the body but never a wart," the grief counselor told Gorm when they'd sat down. "Most people bottle their memento. What do you plan to do with yours?"

"Hang it over my bench press bench."

"It's a growth caused by a virus, you know, not really a part of the body, just an accident extending from it."

Gorm told him most of the good things in life were accidents. He recalled the match cover advertising Charles Atlas's Flex Enterprises blowing within his grasp from a rooftop.

"Are you sure you wouldn't prefer a finger or a toe? Between the time the coffin's closed and actual burial I can relieve the body of almost anything including fillings. Better a toe, I say, than a public disturbance which could cost me future burials."

"I'm not interested in toes. I need a wart," Gorm advised him.

The grief counselor pushed a button on an intercom system and leaned toward it. "Any luck, Ronnie?" A garbled voice said something about a "clog in the drain."

A minute later the owner of the voice, a lanky boy with a nervous Adam's apple and eyes so protruding they seemed attached to mechanical springs, bobbed into the room waving a napkin and crying, "Salvation! Salvation found in the drain screen."

The grief counselor gave the napkin containing Mrs. Vidoni's severed wart to Gorm.

The knobby viral growth was hung from a basement rafter on the frailest of stitching threads Gorm took from his father's sewing kit, the one his departed mother had left him. This anchored Gorm's bench presses as he trained for the Mr. Stillwell contest. The dismembered wart hung at exactly the level it would have had Mrs. Vidoni been alive and centering his bench presses in person. It blew with each draft that filtered under the cellar door; a sudden vibration from his father's movement on the floor above would make it tremble as if it possessed a life of its own.

As Gorm lay on his back, his feet pressed against the floor, driving the stacked bar upward, he was able to relieve the piston-like tedium, the inertia posing as self-improvement by recreating the cleaning woman's face. During that split second in which his chest heaved upward, his face strained like a parody of a sneezer, and the elbows locked 240 pounds over his torso, Gorm smiled at Mrs. Vidoni's efficient, concerned eyes. The wart, perhaps responding to some minor creak in the house, nodded in acknowledgment of his brief triumph. The cleaning woman's eyes said, "Go Gorm. Power is wherever you find it." In that moment, the cellar so pregnant with its own stored presences resulting from the desertion of all that was unfashionable—coal furnaces, hand wringers on the washing machine, junk waiting for its tinker redeemer, the sad resignation of the marriage bed on which everything else rested—would offer the intimacy of the dead woman's face like an Egyptian goddess to whom he could raise unbearable weights in offering. Her nostril hairs surged like underwater villi in harmony with the spiders who'd taken up residence in the gaunt rafters while Gorm attended to the dead woman's funeral rites and spun webs directly over his head. When his mouth pursed with tension, hers did too. Her hair hung straight and unadorned like an afterthought from her head. This like all her other uncomely features struck the young man as beautiful because they were distinctly hers.

Above all, her wart reminded Gorm that like his shit, the most unacknowledged of growths could prove the center of a fruitful existence. The eyes, nose, lips, cheekbone, chin—all that he had been taught to consider normal, particularly if they harmonized toward some meager handsomeness—was now subsidiary to the wart. Its existence in the advertised scheme of things was as unacclaimed as death or sensuality or shit. It was all right to love someone for their "beauty mark" but Gorm had never heard of cherishing anyone for their wart. Well, he cherished Mrs. Vidoni for hers. In this world where there was so little direction, especially for a young man about to advance into it, it did not seem unreasonable to take one's sign and affirmation from a half-inch of dead viral growth. It alone centered her features, relieved the commonplace, emphasized her loyalty, concentrated her courage. Above all, the dead cleaning woman had believed in him, in his power to rise from the ghost of himself. Who else had said, "All Herald Gorm the Strong" with such regularity?

Delighted by what Gorm felt was the inventiveness of the wart, he hoisted and curled the weights with a sense of purpose for the next week. He loved his muscles for their own sake and relished palming his pronator, addressing his revived poitrine in one of the three mirrors as if it were an old friend who'd returned to the cellar to embrace him. Between exercises he enjoyed especially those transitions in the body: the cup where the forearm muscles quietly enjoined the biceps ones; the junction of the lats and tricepses; the no man's land between his abs and lower poitrine.

He saw his body as a map making its own journey, crossing and criss-crossing itself in the search for its center. One day it was a spear sailing above the jungle of its own chest hairs; the next week it was a chalice hoarding balm for the monk's retreat of its gonads. His toes extended and curled trying to guess the wishes of his heart. The nose held an endless dialogue with his fingers trying to fathom what in this world was worth grasping; what should be let go at an instant upon signal from his eye that often quarreled with his hand. He rose on his toes to heighten his calf muscles, their dialogue with his eye in the mirror urging him to extend them to their limit.

Gorm knew his body was the one friend he had ever had. It spoke to him the way his junk had when he believed there was hope for junk. His entrails made a soft gurgling sound when his body was content with the way he'd treated it. It joked with him when it farted and teased him with its presumptuous belches. He'd coerced it into emitting full-bodied stools and it had rewarded him with unlabored breathing. He treated it well and it taught him to walk on the balls of his feet and not on his heels. His body had even carried death for an afternoon and now that death in the grandeur of its surviving wart inspired his body to bulge and surge, each muscle group stretched stripling over his bones and capillaries toward a reunification with all the other muscle groups into one potent, silken body.

Gorm was so elated with the energy transmitted from the wart that he bellowed at his reflection in a mirror, "I got me a poitrine out of a dream."

The mirror seemed to agree. For when he lathered himself with Bud Blossom Oil and flexed in the three compulsory positions the Flex Manual advised him, it was like the good ole days. He beheld himself sleek and unburdened. He was Gorm the Strong without Gorm the Doubtful or Gorm the Bloated or Gorm the Bewildered. His body existed of and for itself. A perfect instrument shining in the levity of the three mirrors. It did not matter what it could do, it was. It was an end in itself. Gorm did not even care if other people looked at it. He saw. What he saw was perfection. Or almost perfection. There was still the matter of his pecker. When he got done twisting and bracing and bulging and showing his torso ricocheting with bulges, he sat down on the bench and dropped his shorts and examined that wee thing that had always defied him. It was still wee, and if his memory had failed him, there were scars where the poison ivy had caused him to break out and he'd ravaged the pink itch with his fingers. Scars up and down his scrotum and a long, thin one like the fossil of a snail over the crown of his pecker.

Gorm wasn't about to spoil a perfect session. He yanked up his shorts and flexed with fury in front of the three Flex Enterprise mirrors.

The next day Gorm did not hear the call over the school intercom for all those interested in the Mr. Hopewell contest to pick up a sign-up sheet in the office. He was staring out the window at dark stratocumulus clouds piled over Hopewell like the beehive hairdo's that were the new fashion. It was a retreat from all group activity going on around him that had been intensified since Mrs. Vidoni's death. He wasn't aware that anything important had happened until by stages he saw the entire room of students turned in their seats and staring at him. He then became conscious that his body must perform for other people.

The Mr. Hopewell Contest was a listless affair. Twenty or so people slouched in the junior high school auditorium and applauded perfunctorily when Gorm was handed a brass cup painted gold. Only contests that pitted Hopewell against outsiders elicited any interest, and Gorm was told that there would be a large crowd for the Mr. Stillwell contest. Here he would be displayed against the winners from 20 to 25 boroughs around Stillwell. The site revolved and this year it would be at the Hopewell High auditorium. "You'll have lots of rooters, 'cause Hopewell citizens don't like to see everything going to the niggers and Hunkies," Gorm was assured by the referee who checked his body for too much Bud Blossom.

Gorm learned a number of lessons at his first contest. He knew he'd been rewarded as much for his flair and slight unorthodoxy as for the bulges of his muscles. Yet he knew what the judges and other body builders didn't: he loved his body. They would have been shocked at his unmanly conversations with his abs or poitrine, the wart as a source of inspiration. Had they known he was a virgin, he felt they wouldn't have let him enter.

For the first time Gorm saw that these novices and intermediates had as little sense of proportion as he had sensed anywhere else in the world. They put all their effort into *power* so that their shoulders and arms looked monstrous. The body per se did not interest them except as an instrument. Befitting any Hopeweller raised in the shadow and smoke of steel mills poised like solemn artillery, the bodybuilders Gorm competed against had little sense of working an audience. The body was a raw product to be refined by others. They had not so much as posed as they had assumed positions the way a recently poured ingot might be viewed from a number of angles to ascertain its potential before it was shaved into sheet metal. It was heft they loved, not suppleness.

The Final Swelling began below his abdomen in that region for which there is no name, in that No-Man's Land where empires fight for sovereignty, and individuals like Gorm, desperate for well-being, can never decide if healthful nutrients are being purged from their most recent intake of food or waste is trying to work its way out their asshole. Gorm first felt this condition behind his eyes and he thought his brain had betrayed him as he lay on the bench press bench. For when he glanced sideways after completing some bench presses in the final stages of preparation for Mr. Stillwell, he saw for the first time his three selves, by pure coincidence resulting from the placement of the mirrors, blended into each other and overlapped, so that he could not tell his pronator from his lats from his deltoids. It was if a pair of thumbs inside his skull was pressing against his eyeballs. Over these odd proceedings hung the wart from the dead cleaning woman.

It was as if he now saw himself as a many-headed person with his own limbs spreading and engulfing him like snakes, Gorm competing for himself, Gorm gorging on himself. He saw the very essence of Gorm being overwhelmed by dozens of auxiliary Gorms. But where had all these minor and competing Gorms originated? If he . . . sitting here now on this bench . . . was the result of hundreds of thousands of little wiggly spermatozoa hitting the bull's eye of his Ma's pod, where did all these other creatures come from who called themselves Gorm and could not be distinguished from the original Gorm? Had they burst from inside him or been conferred from on High by assorted school principals, Little League coaches, gossipy neighbors, paperboy managers, the leader of the corner boys, in short all the dozens of authorities who had infested most moments of his waking life (could clouds be considered one? or simply a reaction to other dictums?) and yanked asunder an expedient Gorm from a readily available pile of Gorms lying in a trash pile?

He was reminded of the days when there were dogs' tails in his head competing for his attention. Gorm could not help wondering if the dozens of Gorms reflected in the mirror were those dog tails, resembling the flailing tails of his spermatozoa, frustrated by his pecker's failure to grow and then connect with a willing receptacle, grown in upon themselves like the families of royalty who fucked only first cousins, thus creating dozens of Laocoön Gorms, fullgrown and hard as pistons, all dependent on and competing for a central Gorm. It was surely a maze, one which he would never have gotten into if he hadn't rejected the idea he was a piece of shit for other people's amusement.

Such was the oddness of his body reflected from one mirror into another, then back to the third and the third mirror not merely reflecting the first two images imposed on one another but its own interpretation on its own image added to the first two, that when Gorm felt the hardening in the No-Man's Land of his lower abdomen, one hand was reflected where it indeed was—on the No-Man's Land of his hard and hardening lower abdomen. But in quick succession one other hand was reflected caressing the hand that caressed his bloating innards while the other hand appeared to slither between the first two. And more:

the images quickly multiplied in threes so that what was formerly three images became nine then 27 then 81 and so on till
Gorm came near to vomiting and bolted from the bench to the
laundry tub where he came up against his most recent triumph,
the gold-painted brass of his Mr. Hopewell 1958 trophy. It sat
there because there was nowhere else to set it. Gorm kept it in
the cellar for inspiration.

It was a cup, an empty cup, that was all. It sat on a hard gold
base and it said "Mr. Hopewell, 1958." Gorm had finally flexed in
public, shown that meager audience the fruit of lifting dead
weight every day for eight months, such effort itself inspired
from all manner of memory and aloneness and desire for wholeness, and now he had a gold cup to commemorate this period.
He ran his fingers around the rim, then down the innards of the
bowl. It was both very smooth and hard, smoother and harder
than any of the junk he'd caressed as a child. It was the emblem
both of his "success" and his relationship to Mrs. Vidoni; yet it
had none of her oddness—neither her wart nor her loyalty. It best
reflected Gorm's biceps when it was covered with Bud Blossom
Oil.

His hardness had yearned for the hardness of metal. He understood it now to be his proper reward. His trophy was hollow—
like he felt. It was a compartment.

Had he been able to perfect his pecker, he knew, the identifica-
tion with metal would have been complete. But he hadn't and
now the whole problem was compounded with the bloating in
his gut and behind his eyes, with the resulting appearance of
eighty-one elusive Gorms.

His life in the cellar had taught him to assume nothing, so he
felt up the Mr. Hopewell trophy, letting his fingers glide to the
sleek underbelly of the cup; it was smooth and hard with not an
iota of difference anywhere. Gorm dropped his Charles Atlas
gym shorts, then peeled off his athletic supporter. He ran his
hand over his abdomen and lower into his pubic hairs. These
areas, which he thought of as his No-Man's Land, sent a tingling
into his fingertips. Compared with metal, it was pure pleasure to
touch himself there. Like the rest of him, his lower abdomen
(beyond the muscles of his abs) was hard but just to the side,
above the pelvic girdle, he found small areas that had evaded the
development of the rest of him or the inexplicable hardening in
his lower abdomen. They were like little velvet gloves of possibility. While Gorm knew that unlike his abs they could not resist a
wicked blow, they could harbor little Gorms. As he continued to
touch these minute areas of delectable softness, he heard a gur-

gling like a deep, under-pavement sewer trying to clear itself before it accepted more waste water. The idea of valleys and troughs and waterways inside him was a source of immense joy because it signified that there might somehow be enough room for the eighty-one Gorms and that his bloated condition might eventually be transported till the impacted condition behind his eyes was relieved and he was free to view the world clearly.

He would have continued touching himself for the pure pleasure it afforded if he hadn't tried to extend his palm to those silken areas. His palm simply refused to flatten to the necessary length to fit his skin. His hands were curved like claws from so many months of grasping that he could not open them fully. He had hungered for strength and now his hands were tools whose only function was to promote that strength. In that instant he stared with embarrassment at his cupped claws. It was if they were metallic scoops; turned the other way they became clasping mechanisms to swing from tree branches.

Gorm pounded his chest, made hooting sounds, and fell despondent. For eight months now he had goaded his will toward all manner of personal development and he was rewarded with hands fit for grasping a club to ward off the enemy or swinging from tree to tree to escape.

Where was his jungle that allowed him to grasp and swing? If there was an immediate enemy who needed to be fended off, where were they?

In quick succession, a volley of farts answered him. He remembered that the jungle, as he'd first known it, was in his intestines. In a darkness as moist and secretive as the first diminutive splat he'd made in his ma's womb, lay the grasping, clawing, fleeing jungle. By law or will or circumstance he'd blundered from one womb to another. He stared about the cellar and was not surprised at its moist, dazed wombiness, only how he should emerge from it.

In the succeeding days he studied his Mr. Hopewell trophy often, each day more amazed, more baffled. He no londer bothered to wear his jockstrap or Charles Atlas gym shorts and meandered about the cellar with his bud of a pecker bobbing like a cork on a stagnant lagoon. His bloated condition had grown worse to the extent that it sometimes made objects rise from their landings and float across his vision till he studied one at some length, whereupon it made up its mind to sit serene for his probing.

The trophy was one such object and Gorm wondered if they would have given it to him if he'd been constipated at the time and insisted on talking about his condition. Or if he'd insisted on

talking about anything for that matter. For it seemed to him he'd
been rewarded with a brass cup painted gold for avoiding words.
Like most objects, be they a well-functioning piston, the hulking
open hearth that created it, or simply his shit, he was respected
for imitating their silence, the smoothness and solidity of their
precise functioning. The trophy differed only in that it had no
usefulness save reflecting the glory that was the hardness and
sleekness of Gorm. But neither it nor the award committee nor
the public at large knew about Gorm's little deltas of transition.
There was his lower abdomen and he assumed others. He meant
to deal with them as soon as he figured out what to do with the
trophy.

His first instinct, after he'd analyzed its fetish-like stillness that
echoed so little of him, was to squash it. But he still believed
there was no such thing as a totally useless thing. Was he not
Gorm? And had not Gorm, despite the hardening process he'd
overlaid on his body, learned to love Gorm, even now as he
relished the pits and crevices that had somehow resisted hardening? No, he could not desert his useless trophy any more than he
could desert his stools which at least had identified the condition
of his health on a day to day basis. But he must take it out of his
view till he had figured a use for it. It must go to its own compartment and relive its embryo state till it learned to speak as his junk
had done. Only then would it have true worth. It was a momen-
tous decision. Dizzy from his bloated condition, so much profound thinking, and giddy with this decision, Gorm took the Mr.
Hopewell cup from its resting place on the thin ledge of the
laundry tub and tossed it in the extinct coal furnace with his
coprolites. His fossilized turds greeted their new neighbor with
stunned silence, but then Gorm had not expected more.

After that it was much easier for Gorm to roam about the cellar
naked. Though the sight of his bobbing bud sent tremors of fear
into his bloated gut at the reminder of so much failure connected
with it, it also struck him as comical when compared with all the
power and definition of his torso. When he walked (at the same
time glancing at himself out of habit in one of the three Charles
Atlas mirrors), his bud bobbed to its own rhythm, sometimes
left, sometimes right, sometimes two rights and one left, or the
reverse. The whole area from the No-Man's Land of his lower
abdomen through the little forest of his pubic hairs to the two
pods of his gonads swinging with presumptuous authority
struck Gorm as curiously frail. That area endeared itself to him.

Like his little "O's" that could never stay within the lines in
penmanship class, this area was unpredictable. It had defied the

example of pistons, was immune to the rewards of metal the way the wily "O's" defied the metallic-looking little gold stars that were pasted on the forehead as a reminder to the world of excellence. Gorm spent many hours wandering back and forth among the three Flex mirrors and was always amazed at the innocence of that part of his body. He was certain after such strutting that it needed both more attention and more protection than he'd offered it but he was unsure how to accomplish this. It was not simply a matter of jockstraps, or protective cups, or hernia belts but a kind of protection he had not imagined.

Gorm was suspicious of innocence but there was no other word for his genitalia and surrounding territory. If his pecker had been longer he knew it might have moods the way his face did but it could not have distinctive emotions without a nose which centered all the other features. This in turn corresponded to the wart which centered all the shadings of moods in the cellar. For now, though, his pecker resembled little more than a plug in a drain. This in turn led him to believe that it had grown inward, was only posing as innocence, and when its time came would surge into the world with considerable fury the way his pronator, deltoids, and latissimus dorsi had done after they'd had a proper period of hibernation.

But how was this magical blossoming of his pecker to happen? With the aid of Charles Atlas, he had trotted out a massive willpower first to burgeon and harness his muscles, secondly to address the condition of waste in his community, thirdly to sanction his pecker toward an imitation of his torso, and he'd observed all of it sink back toward the inertia he was trying to escape from. Gorm began to think that too much emphasis was put on willpower. He had yearned for inner strength and wholeness only to discover the harder he worked toward that end the more his ends were mistaken for corruption and he himself tottered toward the same abysmal sludge in which his junk had sunk in the defunct coal room.

He remembered then what had released both a desire to improve himself and the knowledge of where his shit had gone foul, coming up shat. Both had come about by accidents, the first a wind-blown speck of paper with a message on it, the second also a message which he received standing on his head, informing him he must go inward. He had been very still that second time and though the results were not all positive—i.e., the original ball bearing was still missing—his shit had become more solidified and at various stages he had overcome his fear and had broken out of the womb of his cellar. "Ha ha ha" Gorm laughed

to Gorm, and though he still saw the eighty-one Gorms competing for his one Gormness, he ignored them; he decided to pur-
sue stillness. He untied Mrs. Vidoni's wart hanging over the
bench press bench and rehung it from a beam over an empty
patch of concrete in front of the extinct coal furnace. He spread
some newspapers on that spot and, still naked, curled there in a
fetal position to contemplate his life.

In that position he immediately saw there was little to contemplate that he hadn't already thought about. His bloating gradually grew worse but he was able to soothe it by sending his
fingertips coarsing through his abdomen's No-Man's Land. He
soon discovered other No-Man's Lands. The first was in his left
arm pit. It was as if a miniature hydraulic scoop had scooped out
a section between his lats and his pectoral muscles. It was quiet
in there. And soft. A place to nestle in and be absorbed . . . to
linger . . . grow sleepy. Gorm hummed a song of an uncertain
melody . . . closer to a drone . . . a refrain of "uurrmmm" . . . a
"Gorrmmm" whispered once or twice, softly . . . his fingers
were cautious reflexes, unsheathed toes exploring the ice. When
he came to pithair, he thought of jungle . . . of Stanley and
Livingstone . . . of small creatures swinging from those hairs,
invisible germs microscopic as Gorm in the scheme of all healing
among myriad things. Or still tiptoeing he came to western
grasslands . . . he was an Indian, a Nez Percé dressed in a coyote
skin . . . in hiding . . . waiting for the moon . . . around and
around—the soft white mooniness of his pit . . . waiting for
prey. . . .

Gorm awoke watching Gorm waiting. Now was always Tomorrow. Tomorrow began somewhere in the head's memory. Gorm
waited watching himself wait and wondered why he had never
felt part of anything. Even as he peered out at the world as a
fledgling coyote waiting for dinner, he watched Gorm waiting for
a crowd to assemble to in turn wait to watch him flex.

Life was never NOW. It was just ahead . . . out beyond the neat
circumference of the Bog & Bliss billows. Once a day, then once a
week . . . Gorm knew families who waited for life to begin at
Christmas. For years as a child he had sat by his bedroom window staring out at the columns of smoke from Bog & Bliss waiting for relatives to come, certain they would bring a new dimension into the tedium of his life. When they did not come, he
studied the humped hills with their houses clustered like toys
propped upright under the Christmas tree. His father snoozed in
the large chair by the fireplace that was no longer used as a
fireplace. The Christmas tree lights on the artificial Christmas

tree blinked. Gorm had decided to wait no longer for relatives; school was only another year away. Surely the monotony would be broken when he entered school.

There were plenty of windows at the school to look out of. He was thankful for that. Twelve years later he was still looking out of them, watching for a break in the clouds. The sight of an airplane had always sent a chill up his spine, a breakthrough. In the early fall and late spring the drone of a lawnmower framed his boredom. Like the extinct coal furnace, he sat and waited for someone to come along and breathe fresh fire into his veins. He set the metronomes going and waited and waited. He waited with The Boys in front of Ma Goolantz's Confectionery. Something was about to happen; something would break the song of the metronomes "tick-tock, tick-tock" in his head.

Time waited like the wrought-iron skillet in the extinct coal cellar waiting for a use. Time now reminded Gorm of a crowd huddled in an auditorium waiting for him to appear, to show them the glory of development. If he was able to flash an armpit and show them the secrets in there and have them applaud it, he thought there might be hope for them all. His armpit was that transition place where everyone could meet. He was not certain they would see it that way. Their center was work; it was like the nose; it spread a uniform pallor over all their features and all the features of those around them. Gorm's center was a wart. Between wart and work he would have to meet the world. What better place than his armpit?

Or the soft cup behind his kneecap. It was all hub and rub and tender protectiveness as he crept toward dozing on the cellar floor. His awareness of his dreamy tiptoeing toward sleep, itself a No-Man's Land but always sliding forward or slipping backward as if a secret fluid were being secreted to make him nimble, was accompanied with what part of his hand he could lodge in the harbor behind his knee. The soft whiteness, the curious stealthiness of those hidden parts. Gorm dozed on the newspaper on the floor beside the coal furnace relishing his Gormness.

He did what he could and that was feel and probe, as much as his claw-like hands would allow, in those previously undiscovered areas of voluptuous softness. He probed and played in his nape, rolling his neck from side to side while fingers tiptoed like little animals looking for a spot to nestle. He played in the wedge of flesh between his delts and collarbone and he played in the line between his nose and cheekbone. He discovered little areas that defied development everywhere but unlike his defiant pecker, they were indentations, grooves, minute fissures, hints of vast secrets, playgrounds defying bulk and definition. Gorm hummed as he poked a finger in one, then another. Some days if he was curled tightly enough, he let his fingers wallow between his toes, imagining himself a heady frog looking for fissures at the bottom of a pond.

The effect of his sleepy fetal probings was to make Gorm walk more softly. He swung his arms slightly, walked on the front part of his feet, bobbing slightly. His head, as if of its own accord, developed a slight swivel so that his peripheral vision increased. A new quiet took hold of him. He was able to sense objects or people coming up on his rear. Most important, he took an interest in everything independent of its reflection of his power. He stopped to poke at a tree that had a long white fissure running up its trunk. There were only eight trees on his route to school but he spotted little oddities on each and paused to poke in them.

His love of minutiae was unquenchable. He knew all the places where the sidewalk buckled, which storefronts were yellow brick and which were red brick, the texture of their window displays, the flash of recognition of their owners' eyes. He knew which houses had hedges (few), and which had a patch of grass in their tiny patch of front yard. He studied car fronts, not for the grandeur their grills' reflections could afford his bicepses, but for the designs of the bumpers themselves.

Much of what he looked at did not hold his interest. It was hard, all hard.

The slick glimmer or stolid bulk reminded him of his trophy reminded him of his body reminded him of Hopewell's frantic efforts to imitate metal.

It was softness he hungered for and with his newfound swivel which left him a gaze that took in everything, he found himself becoming more and more curious about people. Were they aware their armpits, nape, the transition between lower abdomen and hip contained secrets? Did they take any joy in curling fetus-like and touching their bodies and listening to their bodies retire to a distant land to the hum of lullabies? Above all he was curious if they had avoided imitating metal?

On his route between home and school he watched each passerby for signs. Except for young children, there was little to see. People kept their eyes to themselves. They stolidly eyed some point in front of them on the pavement. Most were slightly bowed. But they were fully armored despite their appearance of fatigue. Gorm found this out when they responded to his stares. They threw him looks of indignation as if he'd violated their privacy. A few looked back after him looking back at them.

There was nothing subtle about Gorm's curiosity. He stared, this staring magnified twenty times by the bloated condition which was expanding from his gut and taking hold of every part of his body. He reminded people of an impudent frog. They gave him their fiercest glare and moved on.

Only when eating did people lose their protective covering. Gorm observed this in Bard's dairystore. He watched their eyes swell with each mouthful, little O's trying to stay in the space of their sockets. Round and round went their mouths. Their features did not so much grow soft as limpid. The whole body became a thin, membranal sack for digestion, the mind and its accompanying armor slipping away as if in a bog. Here, too, his curiosity was so boggle-eyed, diners quickly resumed their armor and threw malignant stares at him.

At school there was no hint of the soft interstices Gorm had grown to love. A few students nodded off; most humped along to the tick-tock-tick of the metronome they had all marched to since first grade.

Disdainfully, he returned home to further celebrate his own body. He curled on the newspaper by the defunct furnace and would have nodded off to the melody of that land between his ribs and hips known as the "love handle" if his father, searching the house for a screwdriver, hadn't spotted him there. Gorm was curled into such a tight ball, his father thought at first he had discovered a dog. He was about to give it a kick when he heard the low humming that Gorm used to accompany himself to the land under the pond where he explored secrets. Mr. Gorm then saw a hand tiptoeing down the ribcage.

Mr. Gorm was proud of his son and he thought this strange position of Gorm's but one more preparation in the assault on Mr. Stillwell. Yet the utter queerness of it reminded him he had meant to have a talk with the boy. He nudged his steel-toed Majarac work shoe into Gorm's ass and said, "I want to have a talk with you upstairs."

"Talkie walkie boom boom," Gorm replied.

Mr. Gorm heard the later as "How soon?"

"Immediately," he said.

"Heatedly worth praying," came the unwanted reply.

The father heard this as "without saying" and saw it as a final affirmation. He went upstairs to wait for his son.

Gorm in the distant land of half-sleep let his hand luxuriate in the long crevice between his gonads and thigh. When he let his hand graze upward it was if he were scaling a mountain, striding at his leisure through a pine forest where the scent cleared his head and made him more sprightly with each step. In such a land, where everything seemed promised and his body obeyed at an instant his command, it was terrible to feel an instrument cold and hard suddenly trying to force its way into his ass. His first instinct, as it had always been when so many other things tried to force their way into one of his orifices, was to climb the mountain faster, to outrun the goad at his ass. Yet in this distant No-Man's Land of soft pine needles, inspired by the soft tissue to one side of his scrotum, Gorm chose to make his stand. He turned and sat down and faced his pursuer.

When Gorm opened his eyes, it was not his father he saw but the Majarac work shoes with their enormous steel toes, poised not merely as a protective shield against falling beams but as a weapon that was self-willed. They stood there under the naked lightbulb, under the shadow of the wart on its frail string like a judge's gavel, a reminder of all Gorm had escaped. The shoes shifted slightly then he heard them speak: "I need to talk with you. Now!" they cried.

One has little control over a policeman banging on one's door in the middle of the night. Gorm had little choice but to follow it. They sat at the kitchen table, Gorm and the shoes. He was still naked and he noticed by peeking under the table that this made the shoes nervous. They tapped and shuffled. Then he heard what he knew was his father's voice but he could not disassociate it from the shoe.

"Son, in a few weeks you'll finish school."

"Sure enough," replied Gorm and peeked under the table to see what the shoe was doing. It seemed serene enough.

"Is there something wrong with my feet?" asked Gorm senior.

"They're powerful," Gorm said.

Mr. Gorm dropped his head to have a look for himself.

A moment later it bobbed to the surface, silent, but satisfied that indeed a certain power did reside in its lowest extremities, work-shoe encased.

Gorm could feel the bloating in his lower gut expanding like it never had before. As yet he did not feel sick but his outlook was changing rapidly. First the salt and pepper shakers wobbled and rose from the table then set themselves down with great aplomb. The tea kettle shifted on one of the gas burners ever so slightly. Then the sink, which stood behind his father, tilted and water shot from the faucet. Finally, everything righted itself.

"Would you find something to cover yourself. What I have to say is important."

A potholder lay on the stove. Gorm could reach it without

rising from the chair. He placed it over his genitals.

"Don't be a smartass," and Gorm's father rose and stomped briskly from the kitchen, the leaden thump of the steel-toed workshoes repeating his command to cover nakedness.

His father returned and threw a pair of his son's pants across the boy's lap. Gorm made no move to put them on.

This was not rebellion on his part. It was simply that as the bloating inside him made him stiller and stiller, the objects in the room were granted an odd freedom and took full advantage of it. They had no reliable place to sit. That morning's tea saucer swayed and danced in the sink as though trying to free itself of the cup which sat on it. The way Gorm saw it, it too had been meant to imitate metal but now it was resisting human designs, taking advantage of Gorm's sluggish circulation to escape from the house. Home was not truly "home" unless the beleaguered saucer continued to serve its narrow function. It has its dreams, too, Gorm thought.

"It will soon be time for you to work."

He raised his boggle eyes to his father. They had taken on the look of a baffled stare for all things outside him.

Irritated, the father said, "Look, my father worked. So did my grandfather and as far as we know his father, the Prussian cobbler Gorm worked hard at his specialty—inner soles and heels."

A saucepan of canned ravioli had been sitting on the stove. Gorm's father rose and turned on the gas jet under it. Gorm watched the blue claws grab it and make it sizzle. Mr. Gorm turned the gas to low.

"What for?" said Gorm.

"What for? What for? This, dum-dum." Gorm's father pointed to the can of precooked ravioli in the saucepan.

Gorm smiled weakly out of his condition.

This was taken for assent.

Mr Gorm grew thoughtful.

"It's not just food," he said, "Soon you're gonna want the good things in life."

Again Gorm looked at him with his baffled myopic stare. Beyond the soft, sleek transition areas of his body, and the soft sounds that nursed him to sleep by the coal furnace, he could not imagine the "good" in Hopewell.

"You'll want yourself a house, enough loose change to pay the electric bill, have a beer with your friends on Saturday night, fool a little with the girlies . . ." (Here Mr. Gorm grew coy and turned his head to one side, smiling to himself as if an old joke had just occurred to him.) ". . . single one out, marry her, have some little ones of your own, protect your family with a little insurance, keep your chin clean, take the family to a movie on Saturday night. . . . What I'm saying is all this takes money and money takes work. They won't pay you for playing with yourself in the cellar."

Gorm's father took the steaming ravioli from the stove and put some on his plate. He was staring at it, thinking of what else he could say to goad his son toward some sense of urgency when Gorm said, "Pop, I'm having trouble shitting."

For the first time in many years Mr. Gorm felt a sense of amazement. It was if his son had never developed at all. It was as if the scabrous bumgut he and his wife had wiped when Gorm was but an infant had defied all their lessons. Their son became Mr. Hopewell then complained about his ass.

Mr. Gorm thought for some time.

While he was thinking, Gorm took the opportunity to peek under the table to see what the massive work shoes were up to. It was not an inspiring sight for a boy like Gorm newly in love with the soft transitions of his body. In the last few minutes it seemed they had grown to a dimension so prodigious they created their own solemnity without losing their poise. They had a sureness and readiness at all times. They were independent of his father's life and could exert a force far beyond what his father could.

"Son," said Mr. Gorm, "when you work hard you take your place alongside other men."

Gorm's head felt swollen and heavy and he propped it between his hands in order to consider his father's proposal. After a time he said, "I still might not be able to shit."

"Prunes!" his father screamed.

Gorm saw the Majarac work shoes with their rounded steel toes rising to usher him into a line of young men advancing into the mouth of the furnace.

He farted.

"And you'll have to learn to control those too. They will never stand you in good company."

Gorm watched his father remove the steaming ravioli from the stove and spoon some on his plate.

"Where should I begin?" he asked.

His father put some food in his mouth and as he chewed looked thoughtful. First his expression grew consternated; then slowly a thaw crept across it like a sheet of ice cracking and heaving in a succession of slivers.

"Why, begin at the beginning," he cried. "Where else would you begin?"

Gorm excused himself to go to the cellar. His last view of his father was of him masticating the canned pasta up and down and around like a relentless piston.

In the cellar Gorm delighted in having no barrier between himself and his body. As in former days, he curled for long stretches of time by the coal furnace, dabbling in his various No-Man's Lands and humming lullabies to himself. But now just as he was about to fall into a sustained sleep, he aroused himself and, to a tune only he knew, pranced about the cellar.

Some afternoons he would pretend he was a deer and that the overhanging pipes and surrounding brick walls were trees lining a path to somewhere important. In this way he did not feel surrounded by hopeless barriers, and such was his desire to escape the cellar, he saw patches of sunlight between the trees and they looked like puddles of gold to Gorm. He threw his head this way and that, testing the heft of his new antlers, then spotting the sewer drain which did not strain waste water but was a salt lick where Gorm lingered waiting for other deer to come along.

There were afternoons when Gorm did not imagine anything but simply broke into an odd combination of prancing and dancing. He whirled about the concrete, stopped abruptly and balanced on one foot and raised his arms to invisible gods. He made a slow arc of them as if paying homage and then he would take his two index fingers and gently run them down between his nose and cheekbones. This was followed one day by a series of spins, the next day by shuffles at the end of which he touched his toes.

Thus the problem of what Gorm should do with his life was solved. He would do what felt good at the moment. He would follow his nose and do what it told him to do next. Some days this meant massaging his calf muscles; other days he did nothing at all but stare at the furnace door and shut out all thought. He was dimly aware he was Gorm but to be Gorm the Strong did not mean anything to him since it meant working his muscles like his father's mastication. It meant forming his hands like claws and procuring steel to eat like Joe Majarac and that seemed as futile as eating merely to shit merely to work so one would have enough to eat and hence shit the next day. Better to curl up by the extinct furnace and dream his little thoughts.

In this way Gorm learned to relish movement when he needed

it and stillness when he desired it. He invented little songs or snatches of old songs which he reinvented to accompany each stage. For example, instead of singing "Throw Mama From the Train" he sang "Throw the Train from the Tracks." Quietly Gorm reasoned the train never gave the right of way to the deer and the deer had been there first. The train had gained the right of way because it was harder than the deer therefore likely to do more damage. Gorm had only seen deer on the roof racks of cars so if he saw them running it was only by imagination. But in such a world as Hopewell many things had to be imagined for even the hope of their possibility to exist. "Oh throw the train from the tracks," sang Gorm, and the wind whistled through his imaginary forest.

Gorm might have gone on indefinitely with his willynilly, catch-as-catch-can existence, mindless of the outside world and rejoicing in whatever his bloated body and mind concocted, if someone hadn't set a bottle of milk of magnesia on his doorstep one morning. That afternoon he returned from school to find a box of prunes.

What had happened was that his father, in fear that his son was feeling the stress from too much weightlifting and and not only would not enter the Mr. Stillwell contest but prove an embarrassment by remaining in front of the coal furnace playing with himself when he should have been out in the Hopewell work force, telephoned Dr. Pound and told him about Gorm's constipation. Upon hearing that it was none other than Mr. Hopewell who had trouble shitting, Pound had snorted and, remembering Gorm's claim of a fatal disease the time he'd treated him for poison ivy of the penis, said, "I take it your son has decided to join the living."

Mr. Gorm said he didn't think his son was about to join anything. "He parades around the cellar all afternoon naked," he told the venerable physician.

"Needs a head doctor, not an ass doctor," Pound said and hung up.

His next patient, however, was none other than Mrs. McKivitz who complained of "internal troubles."

"Mr. Hopewell's constipated, what'll we do now?" he said with great mirth and told Mrs. McKivitz to take off her clothes.

Word of Gorm's most recent ailment thus had no trouble leaking out of the doctor's office. It moved with all the stealth and certainty of a silent gas across the railroad trestle bridge to the center of Hopewell where it made a brief stop at the A & P, then moved on tiptoe to Need's funeral home where interest in Gorm had remained high since the burial of Mrs. Vidoni. It made the rounds of the Yakety-Yak Bar & Grill and, still only slightly altered, found its way to Ma Goolantz's Confectionery where it fed the fumes of Albert Goolantz's fire hydrant paint. Some said Dr. Pound was administering enemas to prepare Gorm for the Mr. Stillwell contest. This was quickly rejected by others who said Mr. Hopewell had such dignity he would never allow such a violation of his body. The rumor of Gorm's ass problems roved among the housing projects to the north and the circular, smooth streets of Hopewell's first suburb to the west. One evening inside a wooden shack on the banks of the Monongahela, one black teenage hooker said to the other, "Poor Gorm, his ass has closed shut."

"Poor Gorm, he does have his problems," said the other.

But such condescension was rare.

More often the conversation took the tone of kindly concern. He was not the Gorm of beatings and pranks but the modernized Gorm of self-improvement and constant development who represented Hopewell in a bodybuilding contest. His constipation was viewed as a minor setback which he would correct in time to honor the community with a Mr. Stillwell title.

Wanting to share in Gorm's anticipated success, people began to leave all sorts of remedies on his doorstep. After the prunes and Milk of Magnesia came three other laxative bottles, a bag of apples, and a pound of hot sausage.

Rather than rejoicing in such community support, Gorm was outraged. Where had they been when he was but a specter with a runny ass and in desperate need of some kind of support? Their motives were so clear they shone before him like an X-ray of all Hopewell. They were paying homage, not to the Gorm of impulsive movement and gentle armpits, who saw the hope of sunlight where none existed, but to the Gorm of the easily discernible success. They relished the obvious—lats and delts and the bicepses which any idiot could develop.

Though Gorm would have liked to spend all his time in the cellar, which struck him now as a last refuge, it was still necessary to walk to school and run errands for his father, usually for another can of ravioli for dinner. Thus he felt growing pressure from everyone to prove that Hopewell was not an inferior town compared with other towns. It began to match the pressure from inside him, and though he was not entirely sure what produced this inner pressure, the outward cant was unmistakable in its clarity and produced such a rage in him that Gorm became silent and smiling before each person who wished him well.

Mrs. McKivitz and her circle of A & P ladies were positively doting. They cooed over him as they might have over their canaries, his smile being mistaken for sweet song. In addition there was always advice. "Prunes and water," cried Mrs. McKivitz, "Flush and come out of your corner fighting. We're all proud of you, Gorm."

Instead of posing, Gorm had the feeling he represented Hopewell in some wrestling match to the death. It was not so much his contest but their aspirations that were at stake. The pure quantity of hope he inspired threatened to overwhelm him. He was pointed to and stared at. Everyone who had shared in any way in his past came forward to wish him well and Gorm understood that it was his very rise from the scrap heap that fascinated them. They had predictions.

"Keep at it," said Cott, who worked alongside his father at Union Switch & Signal, "We all think you're a lad who's going somewhere. Don't let a few bowel movements stop you."

He stared at Cott's steel-toes work shoes. Cott thought he was abashed.

Gorm saw not so much a crowd of rooters waiting for him as a mob terrified of the ultimate chaos—their bowels gone amuck. In this small steel valley of hackers and wheezers, spewers of phlegm clots, arthritic knot-fingered fumblers, begrimed laborers, ex-linebackers now stooped, women round as barrels with child-bearing, children old at fifteen but carrying the urchin's brow into adulthood, Gorm was accomplishment defined. In his very bulk and definition and grace in posing he redeemed whatever it was they had hoped for, mostly conveyed in the word "winning." To be a "winner" was to be carefully defined: to have all one's muscles intact and on display without a hint of sag or drift anywhere. He was so near success they could smell it. And everybody wanted a whiff.

Gorm could smell their smell. After so many failures to resuscitate junk, waistlines, his own sense of buoyancy, he represented their resuscitation. But what of his own? In fantasies of deer and frog, old songs converted to his own measure, lullabies to lull him to sleepybye and the exploration of those parts of his body that had defied development, he smelled the beginning of beginnings. Still he was as bloated as a waterlogged warthog and as much as he strained on the commode nothing came out.

His bloating grew so distorting that two days before the Mr. Stillwell Contest, he pressed on his stomach and immediately his head separated from his body and floated beyond him. It was necessary then in a desperate lunge to grab it and stuff it back on.

Again he pressed on his gut, stared dismally at the hanging wart, listened to inner reverberations, heard some listless sputtering in his rectum, and watched his head depart from his torso again, this time making for the rafters. Gorm reached out and caught it and fitted it neatly back into the hole between his shoulders. It was a pleasant enough game but it gave him no hint as to how he could relieve his ass.

He paced about the cellar for almost an hour. He was about to go up to his room when in a fit of petulance, he flung open the coal furnace door. Cautiously he peeked in. Five months of coprolites lay against one another, historical nuggets which Gorm saw as further evidence of his failure to make himself truly strong. He smiled that so many turds should stay so well preserved. Many had been disassembled in his search for the ball bearing. They lay in neat slices like Pompeii carrots being readied for a salad. He smiled too, remembering the turds' tails that danced, that had so much life when most of what he observed around him was dead though it passed for life. He poked one with a fingernail. It remained intact.

He would have poked another one but it flashed the face of Dorothea Millikan and instantly he felt the sting of having made a fool of himself for someone for whom he felt nothing. He blinked but there was another dried turd with the face of Lester Day on it. Each coprolite offered him a face from the past and each face was a reminder of one more sting he carried within himself.

In quick succession he saw a dozen faces, no face repeated twice, as if he were reviewing his life inside a kaleidoscope. Each face brought home the measure of his own timidity, each face suggested a wave of insults, fists, sticks, and spitballs. Then he saw his father's face and his father was crying "Time's running out, Gorm. Time's running out." This admonition was the most piquing of all, more damaging than all the blows and insults because Gorm understood his father represented everyone he'd ever encountered. Had not Dorothea Millikan, the fire chief's daughter, cried, "Hurry up, Gorm." Had not his elementary teachers tried to spur him on year after year with the metronomes? Even when he kept his little "O's" within the lines he never went fast enough. And in the playground he was always staring at something in the distance or daydreaming inside his skull so that teachers felt forced to prod him with a poke in the shoulders, "Move it Gorm. Get in line with the rest." Inside the somnambulant shell of Hopewell everyone had tried to make him keep a beat which was not his own heart's. The closer Gorm had gotten to stillness, the closer he'd come to happiness. His mind quickened as his body came to rest. But now all the little coprolites, the chorus of the community, were singing cheek to cheek, "Hurry, little Gorm, hurry."

But where was he to go?

For whom should he accelerate?

Hopewell was the home of machines and hence progress, but it seemed to Gorm that his father and his father's friends who made these machines got more tired and more stupid each week. The gullet of the machine swallowed only what was immediately useful; the rest was spat in a great heap just under the Earth. Each person left his legacy in turds, in boogers, wrecked cars, tin cans, plastic bottles, and poorly formed children who repeated the lessons of their parents by discarding anything that didn't appear immediately useful—that is, speeded up the jaws of the machine. Bones mingled with bedsprings, faces of the kindly were obliterated alongside the belligerent features of punks. It all flowed together, that was the thing. Layer after layer, year after year, it piled on top of one another, till the restless movement of the discarded produced a terrible hum, then broke into song in the underworld. It was the Song of Waste stumbling through the wreckage of its deformed larynx in wails and moans.

It was the underside of The Earth taking its revenge by trying to suck each person into the Great Bog. Even as Gorm stood by his makeshift tabernacle, feeling his guts sinking at so much memory waiting to ambush him, he saw why the workers of Hopewell were like old, battered books—dogeared and thumbed to exhaustion, their titles abraded, spines cracked, innards gone yellow, pages ripped out when they weren't immediately useful. These men around him were like walking stories with great blanks between their eyes, ponderous silences propelling them from time clock to lathe to bed, all the while a metronome beating furiously inside them. The discarded, like his coprolites, sang their song to them each day and it was this collection of voices— conscience without a drain plug—that tugged their bowels toward the underworld. Casings.

Gorm had no doubt these were the same voices that had originally spoken to him and made him deal with his past. Most people heard them too, he felt, but chose to ignore them. But that did not change their effect, their whirlpool-like suction on each Hopewellite. He knew enough of history to feel certain only the shock of an explosion would clean their bowels and heads . . . if it didn't kill them. Men eagerly marched into the line of gunfire to get rid of the feeling of a terrible gravity on their bowels. If they survived, they returned to life with a feeling they were the first people on earth.

It was as if the singing coprolites had set up a mock battleground for Gorm. When he could stand no more, he slammed the furnace door shut. He sat under the wart of Mrs. Vidoni and knew immediately his head had as many layers of waste and abandonment as the Earth contained right under his feet. He saw his head composed of dustpans and skillets, garage corridors coated with spiderwebs, rust on the undersides of cars, scars of his own tissue, as well as bucket after bucket of advice telling him to speed up and stay within the lines. His bloating was such that what he really wanted to do was burst from his body but even to do this was merely to ascend into the smog which covered Hopewell on most days. Sometimes river mist from the Monongahela met this smog and the air was so dense that men suddenly appeared in front of him as out of dreams. They had only to take a few steps and they disappeared out of Gorm's life forever. He heard their voices receding like marbles cracking along the pavement until there was nothing.

People then became presences, more sensed than seen. Gorm felt himself disembodied on such days and sometimes spoke loudly to make sure he existed. Then it was as if his voice was a fierce tugboat on a miasma of sulphur and hydrocarbons, its blue light blinking and his horn sounding out of all proportion to his body in announcing his existence and simultaneously the existence of the dumb curtain around them all.

Standing under the wart, he remembered "Grow delts grow" from the coal room and knew it was the voice of trash he would remember, not the growth of his bicepses or the quantity he lifted on a given day. In terms of his power he would remember his voice as it presided over his first disciple, Mrs. Vidoni, that evening so long ago on his, Gorm's Alley.

As for these eight months in the cellar, Gorm knew it was a strong inner voice that had been aroused to the surface that was important and not the blossoming of his lats, delts, and abs. His voice was more supple than any part of his body. The community could go apeshit over the potential of his body winning a contest against another community and thereby shedding glory on its own body. But that was pure illusion. Gorm had observed their bodies being sucked by their own waste toward an underground scrapyard.

With this analysis a sudden light burst in his head: he knew what he should do with the mob that would come to see him in two nights. Had not his father said, "Begin at the beginning." He ran to the coal-room door, yanked it open, and snapped on the light. All the debris of his childhood lay against a dark stain that was all that was left of the coal pile it had rested against eight months ago. His wooden red wagon sat to one side. Its rims were rubberless now so that when Gorm towed it across the cellar floor it made a deafening rumble that soon had the neighbors beating on the wall from both sides. Gorm let it rest in the middle of the cellar over the drain and sat on his bench press bench smiling at it.

Two days later, with less than an hour before the start of the Mr. Stillwell Contest, the rubberless rims of the red wagon began their reverberation across Hopewell. The wagon was filled with all of Gorm's childhood toys so that the rumbling bore a solidity that had been missing even in his days as a junk collector. There was a soft mist that dropped over the Monongahela Valley and made Gorm, clad in only his Charles Atlas Gym Shorts, appear like an apparition from a romantic novel. He was still bloated and still very much under the influence of the coprolites so the world looked as insubstantial to him as he looked ghostly to it.

The wagon raised such a racket that people poured to their windows thinking that a water line had broken and their streets were being drilled. But when they saw who it was, they said, "It's only Gorm" and fell back in their couches to finish watching "The Price Is Right," a game show in which contestants were questioned on their knowledge of current trivia.

Their children had a different view. They raced from their porches thinking Gorm had something sweet to sell but he told them they would have to wait till after the Strongman's Contest. Hearing that he was part of such a contest, they insisted on tagging along behind the wagon. "All Herald Gorm the Transient," he cried at them and within two blocks of Hopewell High, he had fifty kids crying, "All Herald Gorm the Transient." Many of the kids, upon hearing that "old stuff but good stuff" would eventually be sold, ran back to their parents for money.

When they came within sight of the high school, Gorm broke into song: "When the red, red robin comes bob, bob, bobbin' along," and the children joined in. It was like a knight leading the devout during the Children's Crusade, except that this battalion had no moral code to fight for, only the hope of the unexpected to stave off another day of boredom. "When the red red robin comes . . ." they sang right up to the back door of Hopewell High. Gorm told the auxiliary cop guarding the door he had a couple of helpers and when the old-timer named McGonigle peered out to check the situation, all fifty kids thundered past him and into the auditorium.

The unearthly appearance of things continued inside the building. The corridors and lockers Gorm had known for four years rocked and swayed in their battleship gray uniforms as if they too were filled with longing to escape. The last corridor to the stage was dimly lit and reminded the boy of prisoners walking the last block to their execution. But he had a wagon filled with toys, and its rumbling filled the walls with new energy so that they rumbled too.

He pulled up behind the inner stage curtain and promptly curled up next to his wagon for a last snooze before his final pose in Hopewell. Already he felt the town receding from his mind, even within his dream, as if he had physically lowered a trapdoor and Hopewell had slipped into a bog, forever beyond the reach of recorded history. In some distant burrow he was mildly curious what lay beyond the town and in this half sleep he had so many questions that they threatened to swarm over his head like a blanket and smother him. He wondered if his body would be seen as a mere instrument? If all his unaccounted fissures and clefts would have some meaning for someone? And would there be a place where one could imitate deer without being thought a fool?

Yet because Gorm had already made a leap forward in time, having ferried his past to a point just beyond which it could prick his nerve endings, he woke to perceive the last remnants of Hopewell with a clarity he had not known since the day he'd carried the dead body of Mrs. Vidoni on his back from Stillwell to Hopewell. His first view was the contestants shuffling behind the stage making their final preparations for their compulsory poses before the mob. They first struck Gorm as pieces of himself which had broken loose as on the day when he'd observed eighty-one Gorms in the Atlas Flex Mirrors. Here a magnificent pair of deltoids, there a pair of surging lats, so expansive they seemed about to spread into wings and offer flight, and over there next to some wooden horses a single biceps flexing and unflexing in the imitation of a piston.

The only light was that which seeped from the auditorium under the curtains and it had the effect of offering Gorm an assembly line of body parts, interchangeable and removed from any passion which facial expressions might have shown on them. Indeed, when Gorm did get a glance at a pair of eyes they were as steeled as their body parts. Sight was a minor accident which they would shed as they perfected their muscles. Most of the contestants gripped dumbbells which they whipped in furious repetitions to seed the passage of blood into the seats of power—their bicepses and tricepses. "Oh loyal pistons," Gorm announced to no one in particular, and no one in particular paid him any heed.

Just then a voice on the other side of the curtain echoed Gorm's sentiments in a style that parodied the fierce bunching of biceps muscles in a staccato nasal whine egging the Mr. Stillwell contest to a melodramatic frenzy. "We have before-us-tonight . . . the finest-muscles-shown . . . shown-outside-of-Bog & Bliss . . . honed in-lonely-garages . . . honed by the stark-light-of-quiet-gymnasiums-along-the-banks-of-the-Mo-non-ga-hela . . . honed my friends, HONED."

The crowd cheered lustily.

Gorm knew they cheered not just for the immediacy of his bizazz but for nostalgia's sake. In the days before picture boxes, Little Johnny had brought them radiothons for the March of Dimes, his passion for melodrama making metal braces jangle and iron lungs creak inside living rooms. Before boxing clubs had been discontinued he had emceed amateur boxing. The crowd remembered the days of auctions when his omnipresent voice had sold them couches and pedal sewing machines they didn't need. He had called out the dances beneath a spinning ball at the VFW and the Elks, and when the Knights of Columbus had their annual charity barbecue to buy rosary beads and pencils for the first graders at Saint Humiliata of Our Lady of the Feast, it was Little Johnny who told cornpone jokes that were now out of style but in memory made the crowd feel they had been nurtured in times when innocence and generosity were the rule. "Are we gonna have muscle or we gonna have muscle?" he cried. The simultaneous applause and roar of the mob answered him.

With Little Johnny before them, the crowd was assured things would run smoothly.

He said before the contest actually began, some introductions of celebrities were in order. With great splashes of emulation he gave them local heroes who had made good, as if they were part of a personal portfolio he carried with him. First there was Mr. Anthracite, Anthony Lupino. The next introduction brought people to their feet. It was none other than the dominant presence of Studio 11 Wrestling, The Crusher, formerly a laborer in the Tube and Sheet division of Bog & Bliss. He made some jokes about pretty girls. Then he became serious and said barbells had made him the man he was. As he stepped from the microphone, women shrieked and young boys cried, "The Crusher, The

Crusher."

He came backstage to wish everyone good luck, everyone except Gorm who curled next to his wagon and was mistaken for a stagehand.

The first of the actual Mr. Stillwell proceedings enabled Gorm to see his audience for the first time. All seventeen contestants were gathered onstage simultaneously for two optional poses, fifteen seconds each pose. The audience saw Gorm grin as he took his place third from the right along a piece of white tape that ran the width of the stage. They returned his smile, not knowing what had excited the burgeoning of his cheeks. Though he could not see the first ten rows because of the spotlights which bathed each bodybuilder in a pearl-like glow, the faces beyond that point arose for Gorm out of the body of a coprolite which was wagging its tail in a feverish fashion. He saw first Miss Purefoy, his first grade teacher, emerging out of a dried lump which had sat in his private tabernacle, grinning up at him as if to say "We knew you'd make good, Gorm."

The expressions of dozens of others who'd been part of his education said the same thing. Gorm tried to tell himself that these were people, flesh and bone and vital organs which actually moved and could not be reduced to dried turds. He closed his eyes to rid himself of what he thought was this hallucination. When he opened them, the oversized coprolites were still there, balanced like dachshund dogs against their chair backs. Gorm did not think he was losing his mind; reality had played tricks most often on him when it assumed the appearance of normalcy. What he had learned long ago was that it didn't matter what he thought. The faster he thought, the more confusing things became. What was important was to find the heart of stillness and wait quietly for appearances to give up their masquerade and reveal to him their true voice.

Therefore, when Little Johnny said, "We have one contestant who is stagestruck, folks," and the audience laughed heartily, Gorm heard instead, "Move faster, Gorm, and stay within the lines." To satisfy the demands of posing, and still be faithful to himself, he placed his index finger against his temple so as to listen to himself and understand what he must do. This pose shut out all sound but Gorm could observe all the coprolites with faces from the past rocking against their chair backs with open mouths and bulging cheeks. When they did this, Gorm saw their masticating teeth and he was not sure if he had amused them or they were preparing to eat him.

Around him, young men were offering the humanized coprolites back views of their knotty spinalises, profiles of their pumped up bicepses along with burgeoning pecs and power-girded thigh muscles. Gorm stood for what seemed a very long time in the stillness, one finger poised to his temple. This did not hinder him from observing so many faces from his past that he felt he was not in a bodybuilding contest but a race backwards through time in which all those responsible for his development took their appointed place. In addition to the witty Miss Purefoy, there was his interim babysitter (interim to Mrs. Vidoni) Mary Ellen Danline, who had once said he would wind up in Reform School before he was ten. There was Gorm's first gym coach, Heinie "Click" Clougherty, who'd mixed mild derision with snide asides while belittling Gorm's lack of aggressiveness in dodgeball. Aunt Lydia and Aunt Alvena sat with their hands folded primly on their laps. Jisum Jack Sodder and The Boys sat as a unit toward the back of the auditorium. Gorm could not see them but he could hear them snickering hoarsely. Albert Goolantz was there without Ma; Lieutenant Choppy Doyle was there in uniform, playing security guard and still smacking a billy stick against the flat of his palm. The fact that he was a coprolite did not hinder his authoritative manner. There were dozens of others including Gorm's father. Reduced to a coprolite, he struck Gorm as stiffer than ever. He did not smile at his son's search for stillness.

When Little Johnny told the contestants to assume their second optional pose, Gorm switched fingers. He put his left index finger to his left temple and resumed his thoughtful pose.

Again Gorm's coprolites shook with yellow and white bared teeth. The judges were not amused at all and focused their attention on the true heft and definition of the other contestants.

When this second pose was completed, the audience applauded politely and it was obvious Gorm's unintentional antics had taken some of the edge off the competition.

Backstage Gorm was handed a card which reminded him he was "No. 16." He rested his head against his wagon filled with his personal toys and tied down with bailing wire. He was still bloated but the calmness he'd first experienced when he'd curled up in front of the coal furnace had grown till he felt a lucidity he hadn't known before. With the assurance that at least for the time being he could see clearly, Gorm nodded off.

He never entirely fell asleep but in a dreamlike state he thought about his own body against the backdrop of other bodies being presented for viewing. Alternately his mind drifted to a cool pine forest where it was not so necessary to think all the time, then jolted from this fantasy land by the quips of Little Johnny ("Oh, get a load of them apples, folks") he found himself curling up inside his body and listening to it. His body had its own voice and he knew if he let himself listen to himself, he would not be fooled into seeing eighty-one Gorms anymore. Occasionally he heard an "ooh" and an "ahh" from the assembled mob and he knew the assembly line was proceeding as usual with its lineup of fleshy pistons and bulging valves. His hunger for growing lats and delts and accompanying applause for their growth now seemed to belong to one of the eighty-one Gorms which had clamored for the real Gorm that day in the three mirrors. He returned to the pine forest where he listened to the wind howl. No sooner had the wind calmed itself than a raucous cawing began over his head. Then someone was tapping him and he knew it was time to show the coprolites his index finger again.

Number 15 was posing and Gorm peeking out a side curtain could see immediately that he affected the judges. He was a tall Adonis, polished as a piece of blond mahogany and wore a brow as stern as an SS man, a man who courted nobility, at least as the judges understood it. He had the habit of tilting his chin upward as he slid into each new pose as if he were in the habit of conferring with a higher judge. Unlike most of the other contestants, he showed little strain. Power, Gorm saw, was what the judges were looking for, and this man gave the appearance of embracing it as easily as a flea collar did a housecat.

It was not just the grace with which he carried his inflated muscles, it was the keenness of his glance under his helmetlike brow. With each new posturing, he did not seem to be performing but issuing a command. Gorm's new sense of lucidity told him the audience and judges were not so much won over as enveloped; responsibility was lifted from them. Though there was no chore to immediately execute, this bodybuilder, as it were entertainer, by a mere gesture and flash of his glance told them authority was not necessary. He would bear authority for them, hence all need to make decisions. Gorm sensed relaxation easing into all the strands of the coprolites. There was a slightly perceptible give to the backs of chairs. Most startling to Gorm was that he'd seen it before . . . in himself . . . as he'd imitated it in Dr. Pringle, his principal . . . in Dickie Little, his class president. When the blond adonis completed his final optional pose, the

222 / William Joyce

coprolites beat their tails against one another's tails, not in a spontaneous burst, but in the clean, orderly pattern their commander had established for them.

Because Gorm represented Mr. Hopewell and was performing before the home audience, he should have been greeted with considerable enthusiasm but Little Johnny first stumbled on his name, pronouncing it "Goam" then "Gum," and when someone from the audience corrected him and he cried "Oh no, Gorm, yes Gorm," he interjected himself again into the mixture of applause and laughter by crying, "What? Only one name? Whatta we have here, some kinda genius like Michelangelo?" Because everyone who'd known Gorm thought of him as being on the stupid side, the mention of the word "genius" pitched the coprolites into gales of laughter. Gorm thus entered the stage to hundreds of open mouths which he immediately saw as masticating mouths. For just a split second he was again fearful of being eaten but then he remembered his wagonful of toys and realized if need be he could offer them junk in place of himself.

The boy had meant to have a talk with Hopewell about the education they'd offered him but seeing them still convulsed with his name which he had come to think of as his essential Gormness, he bent his head, dropped his shoulders, letting his right arm list slightly to one side, and walked in the fatigued manner of a Hopewell worker just getting out of work.

Such was Gorm's youth and muscularity, the crowd interpreted it as an ape and thought he was making fun of the event itself, which he saw as apes displaying themselves. Had it been anywhere else but Hopewell, he would have been chased off the stage but he was their Gorm. In this sort of competition with outsiders he was a member of the family. The only hint of annoyance in the audience came from the mob of kids who had followed Gorm across Hopewell. From the back of the auditorium, they cried, "Bring on the old stuff but good stuff." Gorm rose to his full stature and winked at them.

Little Johnny grabbed the microphone and squeezed hard on its neck. "May I remind the contestant, Hopewell's own, that he must stay behind one of the two lines." Here he pointed to two strips of tape equidistant from a table on which the Mr. Stillwell trophy sat. "May I also remind the contestant he is limited to 15 seconds on each of the three compulsory poses. He also has two optional poses, also 15 seconds. More than five seconds beyond his time limit, he will be penalized by the judges."

Gorm had no idea what he would do with so vast a mob, particularly one which had grown hard and cylindrical and had

the gall to imitate his coprolites, but for several days he had
assured himself this mob would be his . . . for a time. It was pure
reaction then for him to pick up the small vessel of Hopewell
nostaliga and shake him upside down till his keys and change fell
on the stage. The crowd laughed heartily; The Boys, from the
back of the auditorium, yelled his name; the judges tossed their
pencils aside, certain now this was the part of the program called
comic relief. Little Johnny, whom Gorm at last set back on his
feet, also thought this was a little surprise the program chairman
had sprung on him. When he had straightened his polka dot
bowtie, he cried into the mike, "A young fella who's putting his
development to genuine use. Maybe we should enlist him in the
army." The witty emcee got his laughter . . . and also the arm of
Gorm again. The young man picked him up again, this time with
one hand and set him behind the stage.

To someone used to listening to his coprolites, prancing about a
dark cellar and immersed in the delight of touching his body, the
idea that he should have all that he had learned during the past
eight and one-half months put to the use of the military, any
more than Bog & Bliss, struck him as the highest treason to his
essential Gormness. He advanced to the microphone.

"Perhaps some of you have heard of me," he began. "As a
child I had the runs. Lately I've discovered strength in strange
places. When you're a kid, you're sort of like a nigger. You get the
leftovers and make do with them. My name is Gorm; I'm making
do."

"Pose!" someone cried from the audience.

"Excuse me, but I just did pose. That was the pose of the worn-
out laborer coming home from work. His body is a thing, used
up, ready for the scrap heap. Since I've been a wee thing all I've
seen is used-up men."

At this a number of the coprolites banged together and ushered
forth an undercurrent of boos. Most of Gorm's past stared up
with a sense of curious surprise. Gorm, himself, can observe that
the dominant attitude is one of amused tolerance. To them,
shaped and inert like his past, he is harmless. Above all he is
harmless.

"It's just Gorm," he says, "making a little noise. Nothing to get
excited about. I'll shut up. I'll do the required poses."

He observes the 400 or so coprolites visibly relax in their seats;
there is a brief burst of scattered applause; he will be the good
Gorm—he will play by the rules.

Like a dancer he bends to the hardwood surface of the stage
with bent knees and a long sweep of his hands. He rolls into a

curled position, knees tight against his chest, chin touching his sternum, hands clapped to his face. For emphasis Gorm puts a thumb in his mouth and makes some voracious sucking sounds.

He rises quickly but sees by their baffled expression they have not guessed his intentions.

"My father advised me to begin at the beginning in joining the community next week after my graduation on this very stage. That was beginning at the beginning."

Still his audience shows no recognition of Gorm's second pose.

"Next pose."

He takes two steps back from the microphone. He braces himself as stiff as he can make his body. His arms are welded to his sides, fists clenched. In this pose he is unaware of anything save the rigidity of his bearing. His feet are pressed against one another as in a military drill parade. His eyes assume the blankest expression possible. To make certain of this, he stares off at a spot on the horizon. In this instance it is the tip of the metal eagle rising from the flagpole at the rear of the entrance to the auditorium. One's vigilance in such a stance is strictly of a waiting kind, waiting to receive one's next order.

Gorm eases himself back to the mike.

"I don't know what that was," he cries. The coprolites burst into laughter.

"But it was something stiff and straight. A ramrod, no a bolt. Maybe a screwdriver, a piston, perhaps a telephone pole to carry your most intimate messages. Turn me sideways and I could be your car bumper; I could be your knife, your fork to raise meat to your mouth . . . but don't bite down too hard. Gorm does not truly know if he's edible. But he knows one thing: he went from the first pose—the beginning of beginnings to being stiff and hard without anything in between.

"I figure there *must* be something in between because I carried a dead woman on my back a few months ago and she got hard and stiff on me."

Almost talking to himself, he says, "Probably you're right. There was probably *something* in between but I have no memory of it. Probably my mother picked me up and there was a give to my knees, a give to my arms as I embraced her and she held me. But I have no memory of it."

Gorm's voice grows to the edge of hysteria when he says, "I'm sure there was something between curling up like a helpless ball, a pod, a beginning and then waking to find oneself a ramrod, a perfect tool for a use you're not sure of, but a use all the same."

He looks out and sees whom he is addressing and his voice relaxes.

"I'm sorry to make a speech. I won't talk much longer. It's just that you gave me some things in place of lessons that would have taught me how to straighten out without becoming hard as a ramrod, you gave me things, and now I want to give them back. No, wrong, sell them back to you. Something of me has gone into them and as you have taught me, everything has a price. Don't leave, Gorm will return."

The audience is immediately restless and a handful of them make for the aisles but stop at the ominous vibrations the wooden wagon on its rimless wheels sets off in crossing the stage. A cheer comes from the ragtag group of kids at the back.

"Gorm's education and his playthings," Gorm cries into the mike. He grabs at the first object on the top of the heap.

"Hickory dickory dock. I set my clock by your nursery rhymes. Who will give me two dollars for this clock? It's an old clock but a good clock."

"Talk . . . all talk. Why don't you represent Mr. Hopewell?" he hears one of his old teachers cry from the middle of the auditorium.

"What could be more representative of Mr. Hopewell than a broken clock?" Gorm fires back. "You live in the same smoke and debris and shabby houses and littered streets as you did fifteen years ago. You make the world's steel and have nothing to show for your lives. . . . Well, tonight you have me. Who will give me fifty cents for this unarmed clock?"

The footlights blind his view of the front rows but beyond that he can see people making the screwball sign. Gorm smiles. He has never felt saner.

One of the kids who traipsed along the street with him comes down the center aisle. When he reaches the stage he extends a hand. Gorm takes his money.

"The kids understand. They can still have fun with anything."

"What happened to the hands," the kid yells up at Gorm.

"I swallowed one. Just like you, I swallowed everything when I was a kid. Kids don't produce, kid, so they get the leftovers."

The coprolites grow increasingly restless. Several wiggle out of their seats and squirm up the aisles.

"Home to the boob tube and more throwaways," he yells after them.

"Pose," someone cries again. Only this time the cry is taken up by dozens of people. In the dark confines of the room where he has spent so many enforced "study halls," little coprolites are chanting. "Pose, Gorm, pose."

Gorm knows his time is running out. He knows he has played with their value system but that he cannot alter their time structure which ordains that all things should proceed in a regular and orderly fashion. To blow up their assembly line, which he cannot do, is to invite mass chaos.

"Gorm has poses left," he screams at them. "I promise poses. Where there's a Gorm, there's a pose. Just one favor . . . one favor and I promise to be your little strong man, the incarnation of Joe Majarac and a Polish mother at bingo. Help me get rid of this junk. It's all through my house. This may strike you as crazy but it's inside me clogging up my system. . . ." Snickers greet this remark. ". . . Ahh, you've heard of Gorm's bum troubles. As a child he was a blight on your playgrounds, an insult to progress. Now he's a strong man. Help Gorm become truly strong. Buy things . . . here, who will give me five dollars for these bedsprings?"

For the time being, there is a mood of resignation to go along with Gorm's little game. At the sight of bedsprings, many of the coprolites raise up in their seats and chuckle.

"These are historic bedsprings. Just about the time the chinka-boos were blowing up Pearl Harbor . . . and our loyal Bog & Bliss was making gunsights to make the world safe for freedom . . . the preparations for Gorm's entry were taking place on these very bedsprings. To the lucky one who buys this, he need only imagine three or four creaks in the wee hours, then quiet, then little toddler Gorm emerging fullblown as the most ferocious shitter in Hopewell history."

There is much laughter at this burst of rhetoric. A laborer still wearing his work overalls and steel-toed work shoes hunkers up to the stage. He presses on the springs, nods and pulls a wad of bills out of his pocket.

"This good man doesn't reject Gorm's memories, who's next? Who needs an old but good compressor . . . trusty lampshades . . . curtain rods from the days of real privacy. . . . You want hard things, Gorm's got 'em."

Gorm instructs Lester Day to collect the proceeds. A few of the coprolites rouse themselves to come forward to the base of the stage but there are no takers. As Gorm suspects, only the kids buy. They got what they have come for and drag the heavy junk in a noisy procession up the aisles and out the front entrance. There are only two items left now.

He raises the first, still attached to its string, to microphone level. Some of the coprolites strain to see; others wiggled out the main entrance, weary of Gorm's nonsense.

"This here belonged to a woman who served you well. She had one leg and was poor. She was poor all her life even though she worked twelve hours a day babysitting your brats, cleaning your school buildings and churches, and washing your smog-filled clothes. She's been dead for eight weeks. I didn't see anything in the newspaper about what a fine woman she was. I did see some bigshots from Bog & Bliss who never did anything for anybody but look like bigshots get their histories in the paper when they died. I mean somebody could have written a letter or something but I didn't see nothing. She helped me and helped lots of other people and lots of times she didn't ask a dime for her trouble. But now it's as if she never existed. Except for one thing—this here wart. With Mr. Need's embalmer's help she left us this." Gorm sways the string so everyone can see. "I know it isn't much. I would have liked to have offered you a nose or a toe but I thought this would help you remember her since everybody has a nose and a toe but only Mrs. Vidoni had such a large wart in Hopewell.

"I know it isn't much, a little thing like a wart . . . some would even say it's ugly but it's what I saw when I was on my back and had to center the bar to develop my pectorals. I don't want to be stiff as a ramrod or as hard as the bumper on the front of your car but until I'd met Mrs. Vidoni, or rather knocked her down in an alley, no one had ever hinted that I had any worth. Nobody did it for you either so you don't bother to do it for anyone else. We're all imitations of the things we make—things to be used until we show signs of wearing down and then we're thrown on the scrap heap. Well, that won't happen to Gorm. He's discovered his armpits and other soft places that resisted becoming a thing. He won't let you forget one of the few generous souls in this town either. Who will give me five dollars for a luck charm?"

A silence unlike any other he's ever heard, even with his long experience of silence in the cellar, drifts like a burst of fog over the auditorium. Gorm observes muted stirrings in their coprolite-ness, piques of embarrassment, a restlessness that cannot disguise that they are ill at ease with themselves. He suspects he will not get more out of them.

"Do I hear a bid for this lady's luck charm?"

"Shame on you," cries a middle-aged woman clutching a babushka. "blazapheeming the dead."

Coolly, Gorm says, "If this woman meant nothing how can I mock her?"

More silence thick as Mother's Oats spreads over Gorm's collection of coprolites.

"If the dead are *posing* as the living and the dead cry out from their scrap heaps, what are we to do?"

He feels the silence curdling.

"Go home, you freak."

By the unified lift of the coprolites' heads he can tell there is agreement on this. A pencil stub flying past his ear reinforces their discontentment. A burst of other debris lands to his right. Into the microphone Gorm sings, "When the red red robin comes bob-bob-bobbin' along." More objects land on the stage. He observes the ubiquitous force of his childhood, Lieutenant Choppy Doyle, making his way toward the stage. A hair curler with hair still on it lands at Gorm's feet.

"No buyers for the luck charm?" Gorm yells.

"A gift then," and the source of his Gormness for the past eight weeks makes a wide arc swinging from side to side over the audience. For the first time Gorm watches the coprolites come to life. They make desperate lunges to get out of the way of the dead woman's wart. In the main aisle there is a pile up. In a small section in the middle, people are draped over and around one another in an attempt to flee the contagion of the viral growth Gorm has tossed at them.

"One more gift," Gorm cries.

Choppy Doyle arrives at the base of the auditorium stage, his billy stick assuming its nervous arcs as if by a force separate from that conscientious policeman.

"No more gifts, Gorm. Time to get finished with the show."

"Just one more, Choppy. Then I'll leave, Scout's honor."

Without waiting for an answer, Gorm reaches into his wagon. With supplicating hands cupped and held before him, and the expression of a most tender sense of loss, he carries several coprolites straight to the Mr. Stillwell trophy. Like his own Mr. Hopewell trophy (already redeemed by the kids) it sits quietly, some might say modestly, in the form of a large cup. It receives Gorm's testament to his search for the ball bearing, swallowed in childhood, without complaint. Its burden is almost as hard as its own surface and though it would have liked the coprolites shinier to echo its own ceremonial function, it is not in the habit of complaining. One must make do.

"Pass this around!" he screeches. "It's my gift to you."

He leaps from the stage and hands the trophy with its contents to a girl in the front row before the cop can reach him. He feints Choppy one way and darts around him as the billy stick slices the air. He leaps back on stage.

Though a coprolite has no odor, the first of the curious audience makes an extravagant "Phew" and holds her nose till someone snatches the trophy from her and throws it into a corner.

"A normal shitter at last." Gorm cries into the mike.

The mention of the word reminds him of the weeks of bloating he's felt recently. His head is clear but he suddenly feels a bloating more terrible than anything he's ever known, accompanied by pain in his lower abdomen.

"I've got an optional pose left," he screeches.

A voice at his side tells him he doesn't have much of anything left. Gorm knows better. He knows he is healthier than he has ever felt before. Such belief allows him to push Lieutenant Choppy Doyle so violently from the stage that the policeman lands in the first row on top of a coprolite.

Though in truth there are only a dozen men approaching the stage, these about to be joined by the other Mr. Stillwell contestants emerging from the right wing, Gorm sees coprolites coming at him from all directions. He takes a few steps but the pain in his gut is such that he must stop.

Without much thought to the matter, he yanks down his Charles Atlas gym shorts and offers his pursuers his final No-Man's Land, his ass. It is enough to make the men of law and order halt momentarily. The audience on their tiptoes, straining to see what is going on at the rear of the stage, lets out a collective gasp. But Gorm has not offered them his ass out of rebellion.

First one, and then two little nuggets that appear as well formed fecal matter, plunk onto the stage. But they are so hard and well formed they begin to roll. Gorm groans and promptly another volley of waste matter, each nugget in the form of the first two, rolls from his feet down the slightly sloped stage. They all sound like ball bearings and he is not sure which has been the clog in his system for so long.

Yet even the ball bearings are not immune to the human competitive system which has shaped them. It is true, they do not have the voice of humans, yet emerging from Mr. Hopewell's extended asshole they compete with each other to see who can reach the taped line where the most developed of its citizens posed just a half hour ago.

And it's a good thing. For the pursuing coprolites, meat-faced with rage, fall down on this shit which refuses to crumble no matter who steps on it or which direction it rolls. They gather themselves up again but Gorm's innards are insatiable in emitting what they can no longer hold. He continues to shit, his rectum wide enough to remind our scholars of antiquity of the

Cyclops' eye in the dark cave, though the result of such a travesty on order and progress is that Gorm can open his hand flat, freeing it from its clawlike freeze. This enables him to seize the last bit of waste which has emerged halfway but like a dead child needs the doctor's supple hand to pull it to freedom. This one of the missing hands of the clock which Gorm swallowed as a child. It hardly makes a "ping" when it hits the stage floor.

William Joyce was born in Pittsburgh, Pennsylvania. His essays in *The American Book Review* and *New York Quarterly* have created controversy in the writing community. His is the author of a collection of short stories to be published by Watermark Press next year, and has published the poetry books *For Women Who Moan* and *Listen America, You Don't Even Own Your Name*. Mr. Joyce has lived in the West Indies and Mexico.

He is at work on a new novel, *This Life Is War*, about television news and the student riots in 1964 in Panama City, Panama. Mr. Joyce resides in Washington, D.C.